FLUENCY

Jennifer Foehner Wells

Blue Bedlam Books
Indiana

Blue Bedlam Books
www.jenniferfoehnerwells.com

Publisher's Note: This is a work of fiction. Names, characters, places, and incidents are a product of the author's imagination. Locales and public names are sometimes used for atmospheric purposes. Any resemblance to actual people, living or dead, or to businesses, companies, events, institutions, or locales is completely coincidental.

Book Layout ©2013 BookDesignTemplates.com

Fluency/ Jennifer Foehner Wells. -- 1st ed.
ISBN 978-0-9904798-1-9

*To Harry, Charlie, and Mitch.
You believed in me and gave
me the time I needed.*

*To Ray Bradbury,
my first introduction to the infinite
worlds of Science Fiction.*

"For me, it is far better to grasp the Universe as it really is than to persist in delusion, however satisfying and reassuring."

—CARL SAGAN

1

Jane strained against the harness as the capsule shuddered around her, craning her neck for a better view of the ship they were hurtling toward. The Target.

"It's massive," Tom Compton, the pilot, whispered.

Jane could hear the commander and the pilot flicking oversized switches, tapping consoles, communicating in terse bursts of NASA jargon. Every crew member's eyes converged on the screen that displayed their destination, enlarging rapidly before their eyes. Jane was stuck in the tier of seats below the cockpit, though, her view fragmented by the footrests of the four people on the level above. At this stage in the journey, she was the least important person aboard.

"I'll be damned...they just turned on the porch light for us, boys!" Walsh crowed. "Open up a channel to Houston," he ordered.

"What?" Bergen demanded from beside Jane. Then he muttered, "Son of a bitch."

Jane twisted, heedless of the straps digging into her flesh. She knew what the Target looked like. How could she not? It was the backdrop for every lecture in Houston. The blown-up pictures that Hubble and various Mars mission probes had taken of the city-sized ship over the last sixty-plus years papered the walls of many of the non-public rooms at Johnson Space Center in Houston. Seeing it now, though…well, no photograph could have prepared her for it. It *was* massive.

From a distance, it resembled a hammerhead shark—a blunt head with a large tapering torso ending in a subtle 'T' shape, hanging in space. Its muted-bronze hull was intricate with extruded shapes, casting shadows upon itself, some areas gleaming more brightly than others. It was a beautifully moving study in texture, darkness and light.

A single asteroid hung in her field of view, some great distance away. Small motes of space dust caught the light between them as they drew closer, as the bulk of the ship filled the screen and the thrusters burned, pushing them toward the portal on the underbelly of the beast.

And there were lights, ostensibly for them to take aim at. If they'd seen those before, they'd have mentioned that at Johnson, she was certain.

A welcoming beacon? Jane tried to swallow, but her mouth had gone dry. She'd been told all the evidence pointed toward the Target being derelict.

She adjusted mentally to this development. She'd play the role of translator, then, presumably learning an audible language, rather than deciphering symbols and text left behind. It was the scenario she'd hoped for. A cold thrill coursed through her in a wave.

"You're saying those just came on? Just now?" Bergen demanded. His brow was knit and he glared at the screen.

"Indeed, they did," Compton replied.

Bergen turned to her. "Looks like they're ready to meet you, Doc."

She forced a tight, tolerant smile. It was the best she could do. It didn't make sense that he called her "Doc," because they were all PhD's or MD's. But, she guessed it was better than "Indiana Jane," which is what he'd called her at first.

"Go ahead, Commander. Channel is open," Compton said.

Walsh's voice was even and cool. "Houston, this is Providence. We have eyes on the Target and they have lit up our proposed docking site to receive us. Docking procedure will initiate in T minus four minutes. Providence out."

Mission Control would get the transmission in 26 minutes. It was comforting to know that even at this kind of distance Houston was still listening, though it took almost an hour to hear back from them.

The capsule reverberated with the thunderous sounds of small bursts of booster firings as Walsh maneuvered it into position to dock with the other ship. Earth's greatest intellects engineered the capsule painstakingly around the alien dock. Somehow they'd extrapolated exact dimensions from photographs of the thing. It was mind-boggling and filled her with doubt. *How could they possibly have gotten it right? What if it isn't even a dock at all? What if they were about to connect to a waste-disposal chute?*

Her heart galloped in her chest. In minutes she'd be stepping up to do her thing with no idea whatsoever of precisely what or whom she'd be facing. Dr. Jane Holloway would be Earth's ambassador. Why her? Because some accident of birth, some odd mutant gene, some quirk of brain chemistry, gave her the ability to learn new languages as easily as she breathed. Did that mean *anything* once she'd left the safe embrace of planet Earth? She was about to find out.

She noticed the fingers of one hand trembling and gripped the armrests with determined ferocity. She'd maintained her dignity this long—she wasn't about to let go of it now.

The unending, stifling journey was over. The nightmare of sameness, of maddening confinement, of desperate loneliness and unrelenting, forced togetherness, done. They'd finally climb out of this fragile, aluminum/lithium-alloy sardine-can that had kept them safe from the vacuum of space for ten months. They'd actually made it there alive.

The capsule vibrated violently. Jane glanced at Bergen for reassurance. His hand hovered at the clip that would free him from his harness and he grinned wolfishly through his ragged, blond beard. He was the closest she could come to calling a friend on this journey—and that label seemed a bit of a stretch.

The crew thrummed with the tension of tightly controlled excitement. It was a far healthier kind of tension than what had often prevailed over the last ten months. There'd been many a heated argument over issues as immaterial as who was eating disproportionately more of the chocolate before it all suddenly disappeared.

Bergen's voice barked in Jane's ear, startling her from her distracted thoughts, his sharp features contorting, "Walsh! You're coming in too fast—lay off the thrust a little. We're gonna bounce off it and break wide open!"

Compton, the oldest, most experienced member of the crew, said softly, "Relax, Berg." Compton's voice sounded fairly convincing, but there was a tension there, too, that spoke volumes to Jane's finely-honed senses. He wanted Bergen to be quiet, but he also wanted Walsh to slow down, she felt sure.

"Shut up, Bergen," Walsh muttered. "I've done this thousands of times. I could do it in my sleep."

"Let's stay focused," Ajaya Varma, the flight surgeon, admonished softly, from above.

Bergen slammed his chest into his straps. "Yeah, in simulations, you nut job! What if they got it wrong? Slow the fuck down, already! We didn't come all this way to die on the approach!"

He looked a bit crazed. They all did. They all smelled terrible too. Microgravity did something to both olfaction and body odor that wasn't pleasant. She'd ceased to notice it long ago except when she got too close to one of them. She put a lot of effort into avoiding that, though it was difficult.

It was bad enough they had to put water to their lips knowing that by now the lion's share of it was recycled urine. There wasn't enough water to do more than sponge bathe and even that was sparing by necessity. The men could shave their beards, and their scalps, if they chose, with a built-in vacuum-assisted electric shaver, but they'd given up the pretense of civilized grooming months ago. They didn't look like they belonged in this 21st century, modern ship on its maiden voyage. They looked like some kind of Neanderthal thugs who'd hijacked it.

Jane licked dry lips and darted a glance at Bergen. "Dr. Bergen, we don't actually have any technology that can tell us how many are aboard that vessel, do we?"

He drug his eyes from the controls he monitored to send her a pitying, disdainful glance. "No, Doc. This isn't the Starship Enterprise. We don't have a life-signs detector."

She nodded, annoyed that she'd actually put a voice to the question, but maybe it'd distracted him from Walsh for the moment. "Right. That's what I thought."

He huffed, muttered to himself, and sent her some kind of brief, mournful look. That *might* have been an apology. Or further scorn. She couldn't tell and was too preoccupied to pay it much mind.

The capsule lurched. There was a metallic grating sound from the outer hull. Was the capsule supposed to make those sounds?

"Goddamn it, Walsh, try a little fucking finesse," Bergen grumbled under his breath.

They were jostled again. Walsh announced the docking procedure was underway. There was a coarse, clicking sound and then a couple of loud metallic thuds. Those sounds repeated themselves.

Bergen was nodding, features tense.

The clicking sounded again, and again, followed by a duller, more hollow thud. The ship moved slightly, boosters firing in second-long increments, accompanied by a scraping, warping-metal sound that had Bergen scowling. There was more clicking and another dull thud.

Walsh let out a string of florid curses. Bergen unlatched himself and pushed off toward the level above. He'd led the docking design committee, knew the system better than anyone on board.

Things apparently weren't lining up as they should. Jane gathered that one of the four docking clamps was skewed and wouldn't fully latch.

Bergen exclaimed, "Three of four is enough! The system was designed with redundancy in mind."

Walsh continued to sputter angrily. Jane was sure that Walsh knew Bergen was right. This conversation wasn't about docking the ship safely. It was about the opportunity to twist the knife, to highlight the failure in the design.

Bergen turned away, rolling his eyes and remarking, "I don't know what else to tell you. It's simple geometry. Three points of contact is enough to maintain a seal. Test it. This is far from the worst-case scenario. It's time to board the damn thing."

They tested it. Apparently, Bergen was right.

And that was it. It was time to suit up.

Jane's extremities tingled. She'd been preparing for this moment for almost two years—the others for many more. Now that the moment had finally arrived, it felt far removed from reality, dreamlike.

She released the harness and began to strip down, slipping out of the royal-blue nomex flight suit and the gravity-loading countermeasure skin-suit. That left her in panties. She'd given up on bras long before—they were meant to fight gravity, after all, which was pointless in space.

Modesty was long-since gone. They were six people stuck in a container no larger than a small RV. Even the vacuum-assisted toilet was only a cubby with a small curtain tethered at both ends of the entry.

Ajaya opened the locker containing Jane's LCVG. "I'll assist with yours, if you'll lend a hand with mine," she offered in her lilting, softly-accented voice.

The LCVG was essentially a union suit overlaid with a network of water-filled PVC tubes, worn for the opposite purpose. It kept an astronaut from sweating to death inside the space suit—literally.

She started to put a foot into the spandex leg of the LCVG.

"Jane, don't forget the MAG," Ajaya reminded her patiently as she shoved one toward Jane.

Jane caught the MAG out of the air and froze. "Oh, God, really? I thought these were just for launch and re-entry?"

"We have no idea how long you'll be in there. The suits can support us for 150 hours, Jane. How long can you wait?"

Jane stared at Ajaya. She wasn't joking. Of course she wasn't.

Jane's eyes wandered and there was Bergen, wearing nothing but a MAG, shoving a leg into his LCVG, his clothing floating around him. His eyes met hers and he looked amused. He'd heard the conversation, of course.

Then his eyes traveled down and his expression darkened. He clearly liked what he saw. He seemed to come to himself with a guilty start and turned away to busy himself with his gear.

Jane's lips twitched. She covered the almost-smile with a sigh, peeled off her panties and pulled on the MAG. The cooling suit slid right on, a testament to how much mass she'd lost en route. Next came the puffy suit. She eased into it from behind and shrugged into the arms. Ajaya zipped it at the back and settled the Portable Life Support System onto Jane's back, connecting the umbilicus to the suit itself.

Jane loosened her ponytail and pulled the white snoopy cap over her head, her arms swiveling smoothly in the disc-shaped shoulder joints of the suit. She felt every pair of eyes on her as she surged toward Walsh and Bergen at the hatch. They thoroughly checked the life support modules on every suit and depressurized the capsule.

She was up. It was time for her part of the show to begin.

Jane's breath echoed in the domed helmet, coming faster, shallower—the sound of her own anxiety haunting her. She reminded herself there had been men of some kind inside the ship that crashed in Roswell in 1947—not monsters—no scary fangs and claws. Everyone assumed that small ship originated with this larger one. She fervently hoped they were right.

Jane clumsily pressed her comm to activate it. She hesitated. She couldn't stand up any straighter, because she wasn't standing—not that anyone could perceive her posture through the marshmallow suit. That hardly mattered when it was herself she needed to convince. So, instead, she squared her shoulders and said, "Look, I know it's been drilled into everyone. We've gone over every scenario imaginable, countless times—"

It came out more timidly than she'd hoped for. She'd thrown herself off when she'd heard her own voice coming through the comm. Walsh gazed at her with a cool expression. Bergen was intense, as usual, with a hint of an impish smile.

She lifted her chin and forced herself to put resolve in her voice. These things had to be reiterated. "Once the hatch is open, follow my lead. They may look or act very strange and we have to be ok with that. Stay calm. Remember your training. No sudden movements, no loud sounds—no matter what happens. Hands open, at your sides. Do not react. I'll do the talking."

Walsh nodded once. "Compton, let's send another transmission to Houston."

Compton's voice came back steady over the speakers resting against her ears. "Channel is open to Houston, Commander."

"Houston. Providence. We've successfully docked with Target. Three of four ZTS-clamps are functional and holding. The fourth could not lock. We're about to open the hatch." Walsh paused and seemed, for a moment, to be struggling.

Jane felt a burst of sympathy for him. She was certain he was feeling pressure to say something profound. He'd had months to think of what to say, but maybe none of it sounded appropriate to him now that the moment was actually here.

"Compton, activate the hatch's video feed."

"Video feed transmitting, Commander."

Walsh grabbed a handhold and pivoted to look at the camera behind them. "We'll do our best to make humanity proud," he said firmly, then swung back around and smoothly unlocked the outer door. He braced himself against the footholds and handholds placed strategically for this purpose, and, with Bergen's help, swung open the hatch. Then, he and Bergen pushed back, assuming positions behind her with Ajaya and Gibbs. Compton alone remained in the cockpit.

The Target was mere inches away, its metallic surface pockmarked, each dimple dulled by the smoky sheen of space dust. Was it textured by design, as a result of its journey, or by battle?

Blood rushed in Jane's ears. She noticed a humming or buzzing in her head, barely perceptible at first. The pitch started as a soft, low clamor, climbed slowly, then crescendoed in a high-pitched, frenzied crash that would have knocked her down if she'd been holding herself upright against gravity. As it was, she just floated there, bewildered.

Was that panic, fear, or...what? She darted a glance back. Bergen wasn't smiling anymore. Walsh stared straight ahead and didn't meet her gaze.

Minutes went by. Nothing happened. Had they come all this way for nothing? Were they snubbed at the door? Still, they waited. No one spoke.

She felt drowsy. Thoughts burbled slowly through her brain, not quite reaching their logical conclusions. How long had they waited? Jane's eyes drifted shut and she jerked, sending herself spinning. She scrambled to make it look like it was intentional.

Bergen extended an arm toward her, his brow furrowed. "Steady, Doc."

She wrapped her fingers around his arm and squeezed. She knew he couldn't actually feel it, but that didn't seem to matter.

She heard a rumbling, metallic creak and righted herself quickly. What had appeared to be a solid wall, parted into seven or eight subdivided, swirling pieces, retracting before she could count them. Inky blackness extended before her, with no hint of anything visible, no sound.

"They have a flair for the dramatic, I'll give them that," Bergen muttered.

She should have shushed him, reminded him of his training, but she was held captive, breathlessly waiting for something to happen.

One tiny light flickered to life above her head, just inside, casting a pale, greenish glow. She watched, transfixed, as another one came on just beyond it, then another and another, slowly illuminating, one by one, beckoning down a long, wide corridor.

She gasped involuntarily. Space. She wanted to run through that space like she'd run over beaches and fields and forest floors as a child. That was her first thought. Fast upon it, came her second.

There was no one there.

2

Bergen arrived just as the class was breaking up, uncomfortably pulling on the tie he knew was too messy and shrugging in the jacket that didn't fit quite right. They'd sent him to Stanford to meet with a linguist named Jane Holloway, to talk her into coming to Texas for an interview.

He told them to send someone else, but they were vetting eight other linguists at the same time and the pencil-pushers were busy. He'd done his undergrad at Stanford, they reasoned. They had something in common. Based on her profile, they insisted she was the most promising candidate and would be the easiest one to sell on the mission. Well, they were wrong.

Two women stood behind the podium in the small lecture hall, engaged in a hushed but heated conversation. One, a well-upholstered blonde, was perfectly coifed and primly decked out like a librarian in a long, narrow navy skirt and matching tailored jacket. She had pearls at her throat and pumps on her feet. She broadcasted uptight law-student vibes. She was in the process of laying out an argument, though he couldn't tell what they were discussing. He imagined it was a dispute over grades. She was probably terrified to take home a B to daddy. It really was too bad she wasn't showing more leg.

The other woman appeared to be standing her ground, but seemed taken aback, uncertain. She was more of a granola type. She must have grit in there somewhere, though, based on her file. She was trim, athletic, looked good in tight jeans and hiking boots, that was for sure.

This could be an interesting afternoon.

It was an old-school name, Jane. It brought to mind all kinds of interesting word associations. He'd been wondering, the whole drive up from Pasadena, what kind of Jane she would turn out to be. Jane of the Jungle—that was for sure. He wouldn't mind playing Tarzan to that Jane, but that would be pretty unprofessional and could screw up his chance of going on the mission. Not worth it.

He cleared his throat to get her attention.

Jane Goodall. Hm. Maybe. She'd lived all over the world, in a lot of remote places.

She didn't look much like a Calamity Jane, just now.

Jane Fonda? Eh. Nope.

The other chick would be more of the voluptuous, Jayne Mansfield type, if she'd just loosen up a bit.

The throat clearing didn't phase them, so he moved forward, extending his hand to the taller, dark-haired woman. He might as well rescue her. "Dr. Holloway. We spoke on the phone. Dr. Alan Bergen."

She seemed taken aback and shook limply.

"People usually call me Berg," he said nonchalantly.

She shook her head and turned to the other woman for direction.

14

"You do remember our appointment?" His gaze flicked to the blonde.

The blonde beamed a bright, friendly smile at him, her lips coated in a dark raspberry shade that complemented her clear, rosy complexion and large, grey eyes. She stuck out her own hand and said cheerfully, "Pleasure to meet you, Dr. Bergen. I'm Jane Holloway. I'll be right with you." She ushered the young woman toward the nearest door. "Amy, let's talk about this again on Friday after class, once you've had some time to think through what I've said, ok?"

He shifted uneasily from foot to foot, feeling foolish for having made such a blunder. She was a professor—of course she dressed the part. Why had he expected her to look like she was about to set off on an expedition?

He didn't relish looking like a fool right off the bat when this interview was so important, but her expression didn't betray a hint of reproach and she didn't seem to be overly amused by the blunder, which was a relief. He made a mental note to berate whoever had neglected to put a photograph in her file.

Holloway turned abruptly, the brilliant smile returning. "Ok, Dr. Alan Bergen, what's this about? I assume you're here to try to convince me to go out in the field again," she said brusquely, gathering up a few things around the podium and heading for the door. He scrambled to join her as she called over her shoulder, "Are you with OTP, ELP, or one of the religious-affiliated organizations?"

"OTP?"

"Oral Traditions Project." She stopped on a dime. His momentum kept him going for a moment, out of sync with her completely. She scrutinized him skeptically. "You don't know what OTP is? Who are you? You're not a linguist, are you?"

He huffed. "No. I'm an engineer."

Her expression became troubled and she gazed at him like he'd sprouted a horn in the middle of his forehead. "An engineer?"

"Yes. Aeronautics. I did my undergrad here, actually. Only set foot in this building once, I believe, before today."

"What do you want with me?" She seemed perplexed, but resumed her forward bustle. He followed her down a few flights of stairs and she finally stopped moving once she reached a claustrophobically tiny office. The space was crowded with a desk, credenza, and three floor-to-ceiling bookshelves, jammed neatly with books. An enormous, but half-dead tropical plant was propped against the door, holding it open. The single, unoccupied chair in the room did not look like it afforded the kind of leg room he needed.

The situation set his teeth on edge. He was completely out of his element. His suspicion that NASA had set up this little side-mission as a clever way to test him, grew exponentially. "Well, it's not me, obviously. It's the government."

She moved a stack of books from the chair to a corner of her desk and gestured for him to have a seat. "Our government has no interest in nearly extinct languages. They barely have a grasp on the one they use."

A laugh burst from him. Was she trying to be funny? Her narrowed eyes refuted that hypothesis. "No, I guess they don't. This would be a unique opportunity—something no one's done before."

She settled herself behind the desk and finally shifted all her attention to him. "Ok. Let's hear it."

He had no desire to be shut up in that nanoscale room and couldn't see his way to smoothly shutting the door with that damn, monster plant in the way, anyway. The hallway outside was busy with loitering students who might overhear. This was the part he was uncomfortable with—how to get Holloway to Houston without exposing too much. Finesse was not something he excelled at.

He thumbed behind himself. "Why don't we go get some coffee? Talk about this someplace more private. You said on the phone that you had a couple of hours free."

She drew herself up, her palms flat on the desk, a quizzical look on her face. "Let me get this straight. You're an aeronautics engineer who wants to talk to me, alone, about a unique opportunity to work for the U.S. government?"

He folded his arms and leaned back against the door jam, shrugging. "Yep."

"Your I.D., sir?"

He hesitated.

She was expectant, cooler, more business-like. "You must have some kind of government I.D."

He pulled out his wallet and forked over the I.D.

"JPL? NASA?" She looked intrigued.

"Jet Propulsion Labs." He added, nodding enthusiastically, "It gets weirder."

That seemed to settle it for her. She tapped his I.D. on the edge of her desk a couple of times, eyeing him thoughtfully. Then she grabbed a purse, deftly pulled out a set of keys, and brushed past him, keeping his card just out of reach.

She crossed the hall and stuck her head into another office. "Sam? I'm off to have coffee with an enigmatic engineer. If I'm not back by four to reclaim his credentials, please use this to track down my killer."

She disappeared inside. Muffled laughter and whispers emanated from the room. He held back, completely off-balance.

She reappeared, without his card, and broadcast a warm smile. "I'll drive."

She had good taste in coffee. The shop was busy, so they got the coffee to go, got back in her car, and drove off. She drove away from campus and pulled over at the entrance to the Stanford Arboretum. Her instincts were good. There were no other cars.

"So how many languages do you speak?" he asked, an attempt at small talk as they strolled down a neglected, overgrown path.

"A lot more than most people. How many do you speak?" Her eyebrows were raised and her tone was teasing.

"Some people might argue that engineering terminology is a language all on its own," he countered, aiming for a joke. It fell short.

Her lips curved in amusement. "I wouldn't be one of those people."

"Just the one, then."

She nodded and sat down on the steps in front of an ancient mausoleum, taking a sip of her coffee. "I feel like I should apologize for not noticing your arrival sooner. I'd just been blindsided. My most promising student just announced her intention to take off across country to get married and have babies before finishing her degree."

"Oh," he said, frowning.

Concern deepened the creases around her eyes. "That might have been a make or break moment in her career."

"Maybe she doesn't have the drive."

She shook her head. "What she doesn't have is confidence in her own abilities—a problem afflicting a great deal of American women, unfortunately. It makes it too easy for them to make choices they'll regret later. How many women work with you at JPL? Is it split 50/50?"

He furrowed his brow under her questioning gaze. He'd heard colleagues talk about the difficulties in recruitment, but he'd never given the topic much thought.

"And the women you do work with—are they any less capable?"

He glanced at her and realized she didn't expect an answer.

"Ok, Dr. Bergen. There's no one for miles, as far as I can tell. I think we can drop the cloak and dagger act. Tell me why you're here to talk to me today."

He stood there, awkwardly, unsure of where to begin. "Well, you know a lot of this stuff is classified, so I'm going to have to ask you to sign a nondisclosure agreement before I leave."

She nodded. "All right."

He never got to talk about work outside of the JPL compound except in the broadest of terms, so this was going to be a rare treat. He decided to just launch straight into it. "In

1964, the first Mars probe, Mariner 4, captured something unexpected in a handful of its photographs. There was an unknown object in the Greater Asteroid Belt. That object turned out to be an alien spaceship."

He paused to see how she would react to that statement. She appeared to be taken aback for just a moment, then quickly brought herself under control.

His hand went reflexively to the back of his neck. The jacket pulled tight across his shoulders and through the arm. He was getting too warm, so he slipped it off and took a swig of coffee. "They weren't that surprised to find it, really. They'd seen one alien craft before. That's my job, actually. I head a team that analyzes the remains of a ship that crashed in the desert in 1947—at Roswell."

He probably shouldn't have told her that. "Since then, every Mars mission's real purpose is to get more images of that ship. Hell, that's why they built Hubble, just to keep an eye on it. We call it the Target. Oh, they analyzed soil samples on Mars, ran atmospheric studies, *et cetera*, but every probe, rover, and satellite packed the highest quality photographic equipment of its era, for surveillance purposes."

She nodded slowly, like she was digesting that information, and took a long pull from her coffee.

He rubbed his hands together. "There aren't too many people who know about it, but I'm sure you can imagine—everybody that does has got a theory about the ship and why it's there. Some think it's a relay station for some kind of communication network. Others think it's watching Earth from a safe distance—that kind of speculation kicks everyone's paranoia into high gear. Quite a few, myself included, think it's abandoned. Here's what we do know: in over 60 years of near-constant observation, the Target has never moved under its own power. It has maintained a stable orbit with no apparent outside interference. We haven't observed a single resupply."

She seemed expectant, curious, so he kept talking. He was pretty sure he was giving up more information than he should. "There've been long-term plans to send a mission to the Target for decades. They couldn't send anyone in 1964. We hadn't even walked on the moon yet—but let me tell you, that jumpstarted things. Forget the Cold War and the Russians. This has always been about the Target.

"They set small goals, in order to develop and master the technology that'd be needed. Each disaster was a huge set-back—Apollo 1, Challenger, Columbia. The Target wasn't going anywhere, so they kept pushing things back. Just to explain the scale we're talking about here, Dr. Holloway—Mars is anywhere from 30 to 50 million miles away depending on how the orbits line up. On a good day, the Target is 185 million miles away, minimum."

Her eyebrows shot up.

"Yeah. So, while any kind of mission into space is inherently dangerous, they didn't want this to be a guaranteed one-way trip. So, they waited. But we can't put it off anymore. We have to go now."

"Why now?"

He sighed and sat down on the step next to her. "A NASA astronomer recently discovered there's an asteroid on a collision course with the ship. The asteroid's got an unusual orbit, thrown off by Jupiter's gravitational pull. Earth's orbit and the Target's orbit only line up every 28 months, so we've got two shots, just two launch windows, before it's obliterated. NASA wants you for the first mission, the Alpha Mission, to assess what's there. If necessary, they'll send a second mission to tow the Target into one of the Lagrangian points for further study."

"Why not just let the asteroid call their bluff, if someone's there? Doesn't that eliminate the threat?"

"The threat's only a small part of this. It's the fucking holy grail of technology and knowledge about what else is out there in the universe. We need to bring this thing home and spend lifetimes studying it, reverse-engineering it." He shrugged. His enthusiasm was showing.

She smiled a half smile and scrutinized him with an inquisitive look, "Well, that is some incredible story. Tell me what this means to me, exactly. Why is NASA looking for linguists? Why me?"

"I would think the need for a linguist is obvious. We need someone who can attempt to communicate with whoever or whatever is there, if there is someone there. And if there isn't…well, there's still going to be the need to decipher and document a new language. The focus has been on finding a linguist who has actual field experience learning languages from scratch."

"It's called a monolingual field situation, a scenario where there's no common language to build from. It's pretty rare. On Earth, anyway," she shook her head and blinked, for the first time showing disbelief.

"You're one of the very few who's done this kind of thing before. Under some pretty difficult circumstances."

She took a deep breath and blew it out slowly. "Yes. I have." She rose and started walking again.

He followed. Something had changed. Her mood was different. The curious, teasing air had evaporated. Now she seemed serious, almost melancholy. She paused in front of a creepy, marble monument surrounded by rusted wrought iron and a sea of broken black and white tiles. It towered over the two of them. Probably seven feet tall, it depicted an angel, kneeling upon a funeral altar, shrouded by its wings, head buried in its arms, weeping. It made something prickle in the back of his brainpan, and he didn't want to turn his back on it when Holloway moved on.

"So, when should I tell them to arrange the flight for you?" he called after her.

She stopped and turned, an incredulous look on her face. "What?"

"To Houston—the Johnson Space Center—for the interviews. You're the top candidate. There won't be much competition. It sounds like it's yours, really." He shoved his hands in his pockets. He shouldn't have said that—but it was true—so, what the hell.

"I'd be glad to consult from here, but I'm not the right person for that job. I can give you a few referrals of people who would be better suited."

That wasn't the reaction he expected. "You're wrong. I had a chance to look over the other files. You're the only person for this job. You're the only one with the kind of stamina, talent, and sheer guts it will take to do this."

Her expression was skeptical. "I'm sure it looks like that on paper—"

He let his frustration bleed through. "Look, they've spent months looking at linguists—we've been working with plenty of linguists already, on another, similar project—and none of them can match your level of natural ability and experience. Come on! You're a goddamn living legend in your field—and you're what? 35? Do you know what we've been calling you at NASA? We call you Indiana Jane."

The smile snuck back, just for a second.

"Well, ok—I call you that—but it's fucking true."

She snorted softly and looked away.

He rolled his eyes. They'd warned him not to curse. "Sorry. You were right when you guessed I don't spend much time around women." He eyed her, and dropped the exasperation. But he couldn't stop sounding perplexed. "I don't understand—why wouldn't you want to do this? You've already seen most of this planet, why not go see part of the solar system and an alien space ship, too? I mean, I'd expect you to be salivating to get into that rocket!"

"You are." It was a flat statement, an observation.

"Yes!"

"Are you going?"

He rubbed the back of his neck thoughtfully. "That depends."

She shot him a shrewd, evaluating look. "On what?"

"There are five slots plus a linguist. They've got us narrowed down to twelve. That's out of an original 108 possible astronauts. They're still testing us, quizzing us, deciding. It's down to the psychs now. The final decision will be soon. Then the training starts. We have a little over a year to get ready."

He watched while a variety of expressions flickered over her momentarily unguarded features. Some, he couldn't name. Some, he recognized. Indecision, for one. Longing, for another. She hid it quickly, but he'd seen it. She wanted it. She wanted to go.

He smiled at her, a slow, rakish smile, in recognition of a kindred spirit.

Her face went blank and she pushed by him. "I'm sorry you came all this way, Dr. Bergen. I won't waste any more of your time. I'll drive you back to your car and let you get back to your work. It sounds important."

"What?" Damn it—he was chasing after her again and totally clueless about what was going on.

She didn't reply. She was marching, fast, back toward the parking lot.

"Wait a minute!"

Heels and that skinny skirt weren't made for the kind of flight she was trying to take on the gravelly path. She stumbled a bit and he caught her arm. She pulled herself upright and wouldn't meet his gaze.

"What's holding you back? You were born for this mission."

She laughed without humor. Her golden-blonde hair was starting to unravel from its tidy arrangement.

He still had a hold on her arm. He squeezed it. "That little trip you took to South America took balls."

She cocked an eyebrow at him.

He shrugged helplessly.

She shook her head and more hair came loose. "That wasn't supposed to be me."

She seemed steady now, so he dropped his hand away. "What? Your file doesn't say anything about that."

"I study endangered languages, yes, but mostly among the remnants of the native tribes of Canada. I wasn't the one slated to go to Brazil three years ago. It was one of my students. She was the perfect candidate—excellent language skills, fearless, always ready for a challenge. But she turned up pregnant two weeks before she was due to leave. The project was funded. It was important work. It is so rare to find a tribe so untouched by the modern world. We knew that the things that could be learned there could potentially rock the foundations of what we thought we knew about how language forms in the human brain. We hoped it would—and it did—overturn entrenched ideas about recursion...." She stopped herself, probably realizing he didn't have a clue what she was talking about.

Her lips were tight as she spoke, "She wanted to go anyway. She wanted to.... I couldn't let her! The only way to keep her here, to keep her safe, was to go myself. That's why I went. My hand was forced. So, I went. I—"

"You proved what you set out to prove."

She shuddered. "Yes, but at what cost? Was it worth the lives that were lost to prove some ancient, pedantic academic wrong?"

"That was a bad break."

Her expression was bleak, full of anguish. "A bad break? People died. They left families behind—people who needed them, relied on them. I couldn't prevent it. I couldn't protect them. I couldn't save them."

He frowned. "They were adults. They knew the risks when they signed up—just like you did."

She shook her head slowly, her lips pursed together in a thin, white line. "Look, I'm not some wild adventurer. I'm not who you think I am."

"Your childhood would suggest otherwise," he said sardonically.

"That was my parents. That wasn't me." She resumed a crisp stride back to her car.

He trailed behind her, bewildered. He was going to catch hell when he got back. They were going to assume he'd made some kind of off-color remark that put her off. They were going to think he'd fucked up a sure thing. He'd failed their test.

When he came out of the park, she was in the car and the motor was running. He got in and she took off, her driving no longer measured and controlled. She was going a little faster, taking a few more risks.

"Is it fear?" he asked quietly. "Because we all...I mean, it's normal...."

"No."

It was a forceful answer. She didn't say anything more. He had to take that at face value. She parked on campus and sat there, staring straight ahead.

"They're going to ask me why. What should I tell them?"

"When people take risks, they do it for selfish reasons, for their own personal indulgence. They don't consider how their actions will affect others."

"Who will you affect, Doc? We've done our research. There isn't a thing about you we haven't considered. You tick off every box. You're divorced, have no children. Your one surviving parent appears to be off the grid and the grandparents you spent your teens with are both deceased."

She looked down at her lap.

He fished in his wallet for a business card. She took it silently and he got out. The car was already getting hot in the sun and he didn't know what else to say to her. He was just about to slam the door when he thought of one last thing, "Are you going to be like this girl, this student of yours, with regrets? Or are you going to fulfill your potential and do something absolutely amazing that will benefit the human race?"

She didn't reply, only closed her eyes.

He retrieved his ID card from inside the building and remembered he needed her to sign the confidentiality agreement. As he headed for his own car, he noted that hers was gone. So, he'd screwed that up, too, dammit.

Partway back to Pasadena, his cell rang. It was Holloway.

Her voice sounded cold, formal, rehearsed. "Dr. Bergen? This is Dr. Holloway."

He checked his mirrors and decided not to change lanes just yet. "Yeah, this is Berg."

She cleared her throat. "Have your people contact me about the arrangements."

He sat up in his seat a little straighter. "Oh, you changed your mind?"

"I'll go to Houston. That's all I'll agree to, for now. And that's just to satisfy my curiosity."

3

Bergen cursed.

"Sorry, Doctor Holloway—but it looks like you're out of a job," Walsh said flatly.

Jane let out the breath she'd been holding. She told herself she should be relieved. "Don't be too quick to make assumptions," she found herself musing aloud. "This could be a social custom that we don't understand. Visitors may be expected to follow the lights to a designated location. It could be a welcoming gesture."

"Like walking the red carpet, or something," Gibbs suggested.

"Think there's any paparazzi?" Bergen said.

Walsh shook his head. "The docking lights, the airlock opening, the interior lights—are probably automated, triggered by proximity. I think we're looking at the 'vacant' scenario here."

A gut feeling insisted he was wrong. There was someone in there. Jane eased forward, reaching to pull herself through the opening.

Bergen was grimacing. "So, where does that put us on the flow chart of doom?"

Walsh grabbed Jane from behind before she could go further. "Wait. Compton—getting any response to the radio transmission?"

"Negative, Commander. No joy," Compton said evenly from the cockpit.

Jane spoke up, "They've welcomed us. They know we're here. I think, maybe, they expect us to—"

"Run like rats through a maze?" Bergen put in with an arched brow.

Jane swiveled to face him, scowling. "Don't judge them, Dr. Bergen. We don't know anything about them. You jeopardize the mission with comments like that. They could be monitoring us, even now."

"You think they speak English, Doc?" Bergen said dryly.

Had they forgotten all the training? Jane put some snap in her voice, "We've been through this. It's a mistake to assume anything. We have to remember their culture is completely foreign. They don't think like we do. Perhaps they fear their appearance will frighten us. They may be shy— eager to observe our behavior before they show themselves. There could be hundreds of reasons that I'm not equipped to imagine."

Walsh turned toward the base of the capsule. "I don't think there's any 'they' to be worried about, Holloway. It'll be our job to figure out why that is."

Jane grit her teeth.

Walsh pushed off for the cockpit. "We'll give this some time."

Bergen fiddled with an instrument. "It's pressurized. We're at about 12 psi now. I should go in there and take some air samples, at least."

Walsh said, "No. Stay put for now."

"But—" Jane started to argue, though she knew she was pushing it.

Walsh turned, an eloquent pirouette. "Under the protocol of this scenario, you're working for me, Dr. Holloway. We'll do this my way." He proceeded to send another transmission to Houston, detailing what had occurred so far.

An elaborate "If this, then that" chart had been hammered out in Houston. Depending upon the circumstances they met at the Target, either she or Walsh were in command at any given time. Walsh wasn't going to hand over the baton without proof that there was someone in there, which was fine. Jane had never wanted the command, but she did care about getting this right. First contact was a delicate thing, even back home, among humans. And this was far more precarious.

Walsh was following the protocols they'd hammered out in Houston. At some point, though, she'd developed doubts that human logic would mean anything out here.

Jane lingered with Bergen at the apex of the capsule. Bergen was peering into the ship, getting as close as he dared without incurring Walsh's irritation. He was getting twitchy, checking his instruments and reorienting them on his suit. Through her helmet, she could hear the muffled scritch of the velcro peeling apart repeatedly.

"Which way is up?" she asked Bergen.

31

He thwacked her helmet with his gloved knuckles. "Turn on your comm, Doc."

Damn. She'd hoped he could hear her speaking quietly. Must every word, every movement, be public? At least her thoughts were still her own. She turned the comm back on. "Which way is up?"

"Hm." He gazed at her thoughtfully. "I was just wondering the same thing. In microgravity, it doesn't matter. Yet, we still like to think of an up and a down orientation. They may as well."

She nodded, as much as the stiff suit would allow. "Well, you're the engineer. What do you think? Did they put the lights in the floor or the ceiling? There aren't any other cues, are there?"

"Hard to say, since the lights are flush with the surface. It could really go either way."

"Gibbs' comment about the red carpet, though—and the way they turned on—made me think floor. You?"

"Mm. I'd like to get in there and take some measurements, but...." He glanced back toward Walsh with frustration.

Walsh studiously ignored their conversation.

"Does it resemble the craft at Area 51 in any way?"

"That's minuscule by comparison. So far I don't have anything to compare."

Jane inspected the smooth material that lined the alien craft. It was a gloomy color, not quite beige, not quite green, and darker than she would expect for a vessel in deep space from a purely psychological point of view—it didn't reflect light. But the passageway itself was spacious.

"It seems to be roughly human in dimension, doesn't it? If we were to construct a vessel of this size, wouldn't our hallways resemble this in size and shape?"

Bergen's eyebrows shot up as he considered. "Not really. You're comparing it to structures on Earth with gravity—where people are standing upright. I'd expect something a bit smaller for us, to conserve space and air. That looks to be about two and a half to three meters from floor to ceiling. I'd design something closer to two, or even less for a hallway."

Jane stayed alert, hoping someone might still come forward. If the vessel were manned by a skeleton crew and the controls to open the hatch were far away, they could arrive any minute.

The bizarre sensation she'd felt before hadn't lingered. What had that been? Some physical manifestation of fear? She considered that until she looked up and saw that Bergen was studying her intently.

"What are you thinking about, Doc?" he asked softly.

"I...well, I was thinking about when we opened the hatch. I—I felt so strange there for a few minutes. Did you—"

A hiss of static came over the comm and they turned toward the others. It was a broadcast from Houston, the voice of the NASA Administrator, Gordon Bonham. "Providence. Houston. Acknowledged. Received audio transmission. Awaiting video transmission at this time. Our recommendation: proceed with caution. Operation: Delta Tango Uniform. Houston out."

Jane shook her head. The message was in code, telling them to explore the ship with weapons drawn—expecting hostiles. Walsh would follow this order to the letter, she was sure.

Jane and Bergen eyed each other, both openly skeptical, as they lined up. They all would go in except for Compton, who would stay behind to guard Providence.

Walsh made a show of handing Jane a weapon. She refused it, as he knew she would. She had always objected to any contingency that called for weapons use.

Jane blinked hard. The buzzing had returned, though it was softer this time—a little easier to ignore. Something about it niggled at her. She'd never felt anything like it before. Not when she was struggling to drag her colleagues to safety by canoe, deep in the Amazon River basin, flushed with fever and starving, forced to push on despite the death of their guide. Not when she'd encountered giant snakes or carnivorous insects that swarmed over a person's body while they slept, nor when she'd stumbled upon hostile tribesmen who would just as soon deliver a poison dart as a greeting. Even in those horrifying, desperate, exhausted moments she'd never felt a fear like this, that tapped into her ability to reason.

Walsh and Gibbs were poised near the meter-wide portal between the two vessels.

"What color would you call that, Jane? Split pea? Bilge green? Puce? Ugly as hell," Gibbs commented with a wink, gesturing toward the Target.

Jane nodded distractedly. She couldn't answer Gibbs' call for levity. He was too excited to look disappointed.

Walsh pushed off and half a second later, Gibbs did as well. She pulled herself closer.

A strangled cry and a yelp resounded in her ears as Walsh and Gibbs crashed into a heap on the surface that housed the greenish lights.

The floor, evidently.

"Shit," Bergen muttered, his blue eyes lighting up. "Artificial gravity. Wasn't expecting that."

"Really?" Jane asked. "I was sort of—"

Compton shoved his way in, pulling Ajaya to the opening as he repeated, "Walsh, Gibbs—report."

Ajaya's fine features were pressed into a mask of worry. "They've passed out. Clearly. They shouldn't be out long. I dearly hope they haven't broken bones."

Bergen huffed through tight lips. "We have no idea how many G's that is. Even if it's only one-G—they're wearing 230-pound suits. They're going to have a hell of a time getting up. If that's more than one-G, this could be a serious problem. We still don't know if that's breathable air in there."

They peered into the Target, helmets gently tapping.

"They're so close. Shouldn't we try to pull them out?" Jane asked the others.

Ajaya frowned. "We could try—but I suspect we would pass out before we could get a hold on them. Let's give it another moment."

Walsh moved his arm.

"Walsh, report," Compton barked.

"Fffthff," was all Walsh could manage. Then he groaned, "Dammit, Gibbs, get off me."

Gibbs didn't respond.

Ajaya leaned in. "Commander, are you hurt?"

"Just my pride. Bergen, were you keeping this as your special little secret for me, or what?" Walsh wheezed.

Bergen was miffed.

"He was just as surprised as you are, Dr. Walsh," Jane put in.

"Would it have killed you to throw something in here to test for it?" Walsh groused.

"What should I have thrown?" Bergen countered. "This million dollar instrument or that—"

Jane placed her gloved hand on the side of his face shield and he went quiet, visibly stewing.

"Oh, man—that was a rush!" Gibbs sprung up suddenly, his startled, dark-skinned face looming close to the opening before he fell back toward the floor and jounced around, out of control—at one point landing squarely on Walsh's abdomen.

Walsh let out an "Oof," and scrambled back. "Son-of-a— someone's playing around with the settings on this gravity-thing and it's not funny!"

Bergen pulled closer, clearly intrigued. "What's going on in there?"

"A bouncy-house comes to mind," Gibbs said, grinning. He righted himself and took unsteady, springy steps toward the hatch, his smiling face bobbing up and down in front of the opening. He gestured at Compton, "Ha! Come on in, Pops. Tell us how this compares to the moon."

Compton, always good-natured, snorted. He'd never been on a Lunar mission, but had been selected to the astronaut program late in that era.

"You ok, Ronald?" Ajaya asked.

"Oh, fine, fine." Gibbs chuckled softly and glanced back at Walsh, who was getting to his feet. "Walsh broke my fall. It felt like a lot more than one-G when we fell in. Now it feels like a lot less. It just changed on a dime." Gibbs would know about the transition to gravity. He'd been back and forth to the International Space Station three times in his career.

"Huh," Bergen uttered, his eyes roving back and forth, analyzing what that might mean about the technology, Jane supposed.

"They must be observing us." Jane whispered. She turned to Bergen. "They don't know what to expect from us any more than we know what to expect from them. They adjusted the gravity when they saw it distressed us—it was a friendly gesture."

Bergen looked unnerved. "Either that, or they're enjoying toying with us."

Gibbs' smile faded. "I like Jane's idea better."

"Me too," said Ajaya. She hovered on the lip of the hatch, ready to slide in to check on her charges. "Commander, do we move forward now, or regroup?"

Walsh's expression was grim. He turned away from the capsule. He raised his weapon. "Forward."

One by one they slipped inside, springing uncertainly, cautiously, like kids on their first trampoline, down the hall. Jane reveled in the feeling of gravity tugging on her again, even though the effect was small. She could feel the long muscles in her legs stretching in a way only gravity could replicate and wished she could get out of the suit so she could fully enjoy it.

She was a little unsteady, a little dizzy, had some trouble heading in a straight line, but that was expected after such a long exposure to microgravity. It wasn't as bad as it could be. She'd been told some astronauts had trouble walking, turning, focusing their gaze.

Gibbs paused in front of her, made an about-face, and sketched a salute at Compton. "Keep the motor runnin', the home fires burnin', and all that jazz, Pops."

Compton raised his left hand solemnly. His right hand held his weapon.

They reached the end of that section of corridor and it changed direction by 45 degrees, laterally. As Walsh reached that point, the lights came on in this new section, individually, one by one, revealing a passageway dotted with doors. Jane counted five doors over the next 30 yards. Each door was taller and wider than human scale and segmented into thick, horizontal bars.

"Anybody else feel like Hansel and Gretel?" Gibbs joked.

Bergen rolled his eyes. "Birds ate the trail they left."

"Didn't a witch try to eat Hansel and Gretel?" Ajaya asked. She seemed to realize her gaffe and sent Jane a pleading look. "I wasn't raised on those fairy tales, you know."

Walsh ignored the fairy-tale talk and motioned to Jane, pointing at the wall. "Dr. Holloway, you're up."

Next to the first door he'd come to, there were two complex geometric symbols at eye level. She moved forward to examine them closely and record an image with her digital camera. They were heavily stylized, embossed into the smooth surface of the wall. Something told her they were more than just labels.

"These were not among the symbols I was shown from the crashed ship in New Mexico. But, based on their location, I think I can deduce—" She pressed the top symbol with a light touch and the door slid virtually soundlessly into the ceiling.

Walsh moved past her in full military mode, weapon drawn. As he crossed the threshold, the room lit up. It was cavernous, subdivided from floor to ceiling by stacks of what appeared to be large plastic crates in meandering rows. It was a storage room of some kind.

Gibbs whistled softly, the sound resonating eerily over the comm. "Damn. Gives new meaning to the word payload, that's for sure."

Walsh took long, bounding strides down an aisle. The rest of them filed in. Walsh peered at a symbol stamped into the side of a crate and beckoned to Jane. She snapped a picture of it.

Bergen waved a small, noisy instrument around a crate. "It's not radioactive."

"The exterior of the container is not radioactive," Walsh corrected.

Bergen rolled his eyes.

Gibbs ambled down an aisle nearby, studiously examining the symbols on the crates. "Jane? Am I seeing this right? Are the symbols on all of these containers the same?"

Jane hopped over to Gibbs in a few short bursts. She gamboled with him down the aisle for a bit, examining the symbols. "Yes," she confirmed. "Every symbol on these containers is the same. I have no idea what it means, of course," she added, in case they were expecting some kind of miraculous insight from her. "Yet."

They turned back to join to the others. Walsh had gone deeper into the room. Bergen and Ajaya lingered near the room's entrance.

"Will you look at that," Bergen muttered. She turned more fully toward him in time to see him digging his fingers into a recess on the crate nearest the door and lifting up. The top of the container came off.

"Dr. Bergen!" Ajaya exclaimed.

Gibbs made a wry face. "Berg, dude—Walsh isn't gonna like that you did that."

Bergen ignored that and shined his flashlight inside the container. Then he waved the geiger counter around inside it.

"Walsh isn't going to like what?" Walsh's voice boomed over the comm. Jane turned to see Walsh moving quickly back toward them down the aisle.

Jane had to agree. These things didn't belong to them. They hadn't been invited to examine them. And yet, she shared Bergen's curiosity and went forward to inspect the contents herself.

Bergen lifted a corner of the crate experimentally. Dull, sandy-colored crystals shifted to one side.

Jane wrinkled her nose in bewilderment. Cat litter came to mind.

"Some kind of mineral ore? A mining operation?" Bergen murmured. He was already scooping up a sample in a small vial and bagging it.

Walsh stormed up. "Bergen, goddamnit!"

Bergen didn't even look up. "Relax. The seal on this one was already broken. We haven't been exposed to anything. We're all wearing suits. It's not radioactive."

"We have protocols for a reason. Disregard them again and you'll spend the rest of the mission guarding the capsule."

Bergen's lips pressed together and he glared at Walsh. "Noted."

They filed out silently at Walsh's gesture.

Jane moved back into the hall and turned to examine the symbols outside the door again. She pressed the top one, to see if a second touch would close the door. Nothing happened. She pressed the bottom symbol. The door shut with a whisper and barely perceptible thud.

She left her fingers resting next to the symbols for a moment, mentally making a connection between the images and the concepts of 'open' and 'close,' as well as probing within for hidden links to other languages, a practiced mental exercise.

Abruptly, she could see meaning within the pattern. Comprehension breathed life within her mind—open and close, unlocked from somewhere inside.

She stumbled back. Her boot caught. She fell on her rump at Gibbs' feet.

"Jane?"

Gibbs lifted her by the arm. She swayed in his grasp, gaping at the symbols that now meant far more.

She could see *into* them, like a hologram.

Open...vastness, yawning...fresh and exposed, loose, lifting up and out, unfurling...expanding, stars and light...communing...forever without end....

Her breath caught in her throat.

Her eyes drifted down. A new experience.

Close...barrier, block...tightly cover, conceal, seal and lock...stifle...dark...inaccessible...halting...murderous, fence, trap, end.... End?

She shuddered and tore her eyes away.

"Jane, what is it?" Bergen's helmet skittered over hers, pressing her back into Gibbs.

She closed her eyes. Her whole body trembled. Couldn't they see it too?

The hum was back and it was stronger. There was an unmistakable sensation of vibration and movement. Were there actual bees inside her head?

Her own thoughts were mired while something else— something that was not her—zipped with glee, probing, searching.... Her brain pulsed in response.

Her limbs were heavy. She wanted to lie down.

She felt drunk.

She recalled the first time she'd ever been tipsy with sudden clarity. The bees latched onto that, pushed her toward the memory.

Control spun away. She went along as an observer.

She'd been nine. They were living in Belize at that time. No tourists came in rumbling, rusty, buses that day to hike the trails. It was a rare free day.

Jane batted away a slow-flying insect and looked up from the tattered, yellowed paperback that a tall German woman had carelessly left behind the day before. It was a book by a guy named Sagan, about a girl who was smart and curious, just like her.

She was bored. The daily rain shower would begin soon and she'd be cooped up in the casita for the rest of the afternoon, reading or playing chess.

Where had her parents gone? They were probably giggling under some tree somewhere. She sighed heavily. She didn't like it when they left her alone, but they'd come if she yelled and then she'd get a lecture about crying wolf.

She sat down on the dusty, worn boards in the doorway, fingering the wide cracks, smoothed over by time. She thought she heard a quiet 'kyow,' the tell-tale sound of a quetzal in the neighborhood, and picked up her binoculars, scanning the canopy for signs of the bird, its red breast, and long, flicking green tail, then the undergrowth for signs of her wayward parents. She saw movement, but that was the cow.

They said they were trying to make her a baby brother or sister to keep her company, but they'd been saying that for a long time and it hadn't happened yet. She didn't see what the big deal was. Why did they need to be alone to do that? It's not like she hadn't watched them before when they thought she was sleeping. She'd teased them that they made some pretty funny sounds, compared to the monkeys she'd observed.

She eyed the bottle of clear guaro they kept up on the high shelf. Grown-up drinks, grown-up sex, grown-up stuff was just silly stuff they didn't want to share. She pulled a chair over to the single wall-mounted cabinet and captured the nearly full bottle. She'd show them. She sloshed it into her small, plastic cup and gave it a taste.

Ugh. Terrible stuff. But it was warm going down and that was nice. Interesting sensation, actually. She coughed a little and took a more cautious sip and then another. It was a little sweet. It was sharp. Not so different from spicy food and she liked that fine.

She decided she was mature enough to get it down and turned on the radio. Mom liked to dance to mariachi music when she drank this stuff. By the time her parents got back, arms around each other, smiling, she was smiling too and humming along.

Humming. Droning. Vibrating.

It wants something.

Voices battered against her ears, yanking her back to see Ajaya, Bergen, Walsh and Gibbs crowded around her.

She asked them, "Do you see the symbols too? Do you hear the bees? Can you feel them moving? What do they want?"

"She's delusional," Ajaya murmured. "The stress—"

"She saved the lives of two men in the goddamn Amazon when she had malaria—this isn't stress," Bergen bellowed.

"We all know her record, Berg," Walsh said, gruff as usual.

"She hasn't been sleeping well for a long time." That was Gibbs.

"None of us have—shut up!" Bergen lashed out.

"It's not me. It's something in the ship. I'm fighting...."

"Fighting what, Jane?"

She let out a strangled laugh. "Bees? I don't know. I'm...."

No. She would not say that.

What if she gave them what they wanted? Could she appease them? She gazed into the consternated faces of her colleagues, unsure.

This is completely insane. Am I dreaming?

There were no options. She closed her eyes and she was back there again, inhabiting her own child-mind with adult eyes.

Her parents' faces fell, simultaneously.

Her mother gathered her up. "Janey—what's going on?"

She snorted with laughter that turned into whooping belly laughs. She bounced around within Mama's grasp and captured her hands. She felt dizzy like she'd been spinning too long and happy, happy, happy. Couldn't they tell? "I'm dancing. Let's dance."

"Kevin, turn off the radio."

Uh-oh. Serious voices. She went still, staring. "Why are you mad at Daddy?"

"I'm not. Jane, did you drink this?" Mama was pointing at her cup and the bottle of guaro nearby. Daddy seemed sick. He picked up the bottle and sat down heavily in a chair.

45

"Ha-ha—you're just mad 'cause I tried your grown-up stuff! I like it. It's good. Next time we go to town, I want to buy some juice. I bet it'd be good to mix it up together!"

Her mother looked stricken. "Jane, this isn't good for children. You're going to feel sick soon."

But she didn't. She just kept feeling good until she felt warm and sleepy, curled up on Daddy's lap. They kept telling her it was bad, but she didn't believe them. She dozed off and woke later when she heard them talking, but she stayed quiet, listening drowsily.

"Dump it out, Hailey," Daddy said softly.

"Kev, it's ok," Mama soothed.

"She likes it," he choked out.

"She's nine. She likes every new experience. She'll forget about it."

"What if she doesn't? What if—?" He squeezed her tighter.

Mama's voice went very soft, barely above a whisper, but urgent, "She's not going to be like your mom, Kev. We won't let it happen."

"No. Pour it out. Not...no."

There was a sound of liquid splashing in the dust, just outside the door. Then Mama spoke again, "You know, I've been thinking. We should move on, find a place where there's a school, kids her age to play with. Those Swedes last week were talking about snorkeling in the coral reefs in Australia. We have some money saved. We were both lifeguards—we could do that. It's a tropical paradise, they said. Cost of living's not bad, they said."

"Jane wouldn't learn another language there."

"Not from the locals. Tourists love to talk to her, though."

He kissed the top of her head. "Yeah. They do."

She felt warm and safe in his embrace. She didn't want it to ever end.

She'd never remembered this part of it before, and none of it with such detail. It was a gift. But she wanted to squeeze him back, tell him things she hadn't known how to say as a child, warn him that Australia was not the right choice.

She wanted to change it. She ached to save him.

Her parents had gotten quiet, then, and she dozed off.

The memory faded away.

But she was still there.

What had that accomplished? There was no tranquility in this silence. Only pain and heartbreaking loneliness.

Into the roaring stillness of the tiny one-room shack, Jane cried, "Is this what you want? Are you trying to hurt me?"

"No," a low-pitched voice buzzed softly.

It didn't come from the room around her. It came from inside her head.

She jumped with dismay. Her mother and father were gone. She could never have them back again like that. The thought made her chest ache.

She stood in the middle of the room, in the orange EMU, the umbilicus trailing out the solitary door into the rain forest. She could hear the raucous chatter of howler monkeys reaching a climax outside. Something they didn't like was encroaching on their territory.

Jane felt the same way.

She cast around. It was the same faded turquoise walls made of thick planks, the same rough wooden table, the same mismatched, rickety chairs, sagging, straw bed and trundle. Even Rainbow Bright smiled back at her from the small plastic cup.

Tears stung her eyes. She refused to shed them, blinking them back. "Show yourself."

"I regret that I cannot, Dr. Jane Holloway."

She quailed. *It knows my name?*

The voice was rich and resonant—it conveyed the impression of male gender, though she knew it could be a mistake to make such assumptions. It created a vibrating sensation in her head when it spoke and that seemed odd.

Because she liked it, too.

"Why?" There was anguish in her voice. *Damn it.* She steeled herself and drew an angry breath. *Stay dispassionate, Jane.*

"It is a simple matter. My form would be incongruous in your perceived environment."

What? What's that supposed to mean?

She stood straight as an arrow and demanded, "What do you want from me?"

"We both want something. You want something from me."

"I—We—"

The sonorous voice interrupted, filling her head, all other thought drowned. "It will be an even exchange, Dr. Jane Holloway. You have nothing to fear. You may explore as you desire. The gaseous composition and gravitational forces have been adjusted, are now adequate for your species. These things do not affect me. There is plentiful foodstuff, as you have already discovered. There are horizontal platforms, like these, where you may take rest. Your journey has been long, arduous, primitive. It is over now. You are home."

"But, where's the crew? A ship of this size must have a crew!"

"They have...departed, long ago. There is only myself. And now, you."

She sensed it was slipping away. The hum was receding. She concentrated, willing it to stay. "What's happening? Why are you being so cryptic?"

"I will let you rest now. You are fatigued."

Desperation propelled her a step forward. "Wait a minute!"

"Yes? You require something more, Dr. Jane Holloway?"

She blinked and softened her tone, "What are you? Where are you? Who are you?"

"This conversation will be more optimally resumed when the required mental link has been more properly established. With time, and repetition, it will become easier and no longer cause you discomfort or distress. This is prudent, Dr. Jane Holloway. I only desired to relieve your anxiety, to inform you that you are safe. That is sufficient. I leave you now."

"No. Please! Don't go. I—I still have questions...."

She fell silent.

It...he?...was gone. The humming was gone. She was alone again.

She walked over to the cabinet and opened it. It was as she remembered, though she could reach it without the chair now. There was a bag of ground coffee, masa, rice, beans, lard, a small paper sack filled with root vegetables and several yellow-brown plantains. She backed up slowly and laid down on the bed, fingers spreading over the soft, worn quilt her mother had brought from Minnesota.

Was she small again? The suit was gone. She was drifting, dreaming.

She sat up abruptly, aghast at her manners.

She hadn't even asked his name.

4

"What are you fighting, Jane?" Bergen urged, shaking Jane's shoulder, but she just flopped. She was out cold.

"Ronald, get her feet up," Ajaya ordered.

Gibbs crouched, bent Jane's knees, and propped her legs on one of his shoulders.

Bergen checked the display on the front of her EMU. It seemed to be working properly. "I need to run a diagnostic on her hardware. She could be hypoxic. Give me the laptop."

Gibbs handed it over and Bergen quickly interfaced it with the PLSS module on Jane's EMU.

"She's not cyanotic, Alan," Ajaya said, turning Jane's helmet slightly and shining a light into it. "Respiration rate is normal now. Let's give her a minute. I think it's just a panic attack."

He strove to control his movements, to be patient with the thick gloves on the keyboard while a bright flash of red-hot anger flamed inside. "A panic attack? Why now? Why not at lift off? Why not on the approach or, or, when we opened the damn hatch? Why would she close that door and suddenly, out of the blue, have the first panic attack of her life?"

Ajaya frowned and glanced at Walsh. "We can't know that."

"What—you think she lied at Johnson or somehow fooled them? She didn't even want to be there. I—we—convinced her to do this. She wouldn't even begin to know how to lie, Ajaya. You should know that by now."

He looked up. Walsh and Ajaya were exchanging knowing glances.

"What? You agree with that bullshit?"

Walsh frowned. "Right now, all we know is she's passed out. Let Ajaya look at her."

"I need to run a diagnostic on her EMU controls," he muttered.

Walsh sent Gibbs to scout ahead to make sure they were still alone, and knelt down in Gibbs' place, his face impassive, watching Bergen and Ajaya work on her.

"Bergen."

Bergen ignored him and checked another subroutine, mentally cursing the useless gloves as they impeded his typing. He'd be done by now if he weren't wearing them or if they were better designed—if he'd been the one to design them. But he couldn't do everything.

"Berg."

"What?" he said, exasperated, finally looking up to meet Walsh's gaze.

The soldier's mask was gone, replaced with a look of grave understanding, though only briefly. "Check yourself," he said curtly and looked pointedly at Jane, Ajaya, and then down the hall where Gibbs had disappeared.

Bergen bit back a scathing retort and focused on the screen, struggling to school his features. So, Walsh knew. He'd been more transparent than he'd meant to be. In the panic, he'd forgotten his game face. Walsh knew he wouldn't have reacted this way if it'd been Compton or Gibbs or Ajaya on the floor. *Fuck.*

Well, what did it matter now? He'd managed it—he'd passed all their tests, proved he'd be an asset instead of a liability. He'd made it there and that wasn't going to change anytime soon.

But, if Walsh knew...the others might too. Gibbs had loose lips. And Ajaya might get all girly when the guys weren't around. They'd screw it all up. They'd tell her.

Dammit! He didn't want anything to change. Not yet. He wasn't ready. They had to finish this first and go home. That was years away and they had to actually survive. By then...she...he...maybe it could work.

"If this were a simple episode of syncope, she'd be awake by now," Ajaya said flatly. "She may be hypoglycemic, or severely dehydrated, or perhaps her electrolyte balance is off due to the fluid shift with gravity. I can't determine anything, I cannot do anything for her, unless we get her out of the suit."

"You've got enough air samples to analyze?" Walsh asked him.

"Yes."

Walsh slipped a hand under Jane's back and picked her up with a grunt. "Fall back."

In the modicum of time he had to himself during the selection exercises in Houston, he found himself reading Holloway's file over and over until he had it practically memorized. He kept tabs on her remotely, but he didn't have any access to her once she came to Johnson. They were convinced he'd nearly botched it, so they wouldn't let him anywhere near her.

He heard through the grapevine that the big guys were wining and dining her and that she was a hard sell. She was really making them work for it.

He couldn't get her out of his head. He didn't know why. She wasn't particularly beautiful or anything, although she had a great smile. She was something of a Plain Jane, he tried to convince himself, frowning. She wasn't his type at all. She was all prissy and round—savvy, smart.

He liked bouncy, athletic girls, who could keep up with his six a.m. running schedule, who'd be up for an impromptu hike or day of surfing, if a free day suddenly came up. Sure, none of them were rocket scientists, but he'd given up hope of finding a girl with a mind he could really admire, not that he'd really been looking too hard. Maybe he was getting too old to be hanging out in college bars, hooking up with girls who weren't looking for more than a good time.

He'd been in the middle of a think-tank planning session when he was pulled out. He thought it might be bad news. There were rumors they were about to announce the final five and he was nervous. He'd done everything he could to meet every qualification, pass every test, but he was afraid it wasn't enough. He'd attempted to minimize their perception of his more negative personality traits. He knew they were a problem, but he already had a reputation within the organization and nothing he could do now would change that.

The psychological tests were obnoxious and verging on ridiculous, at times. They wanted to be sure they wouldn't select someone who would crack under the pressure of boredom and confinement. He understood that and resolved to stay patient with the process.

He wasn't even surprised when they shoved him into an MRI and barraged him with graphic and disturbing images, probably as a method of determining level of libido and sexual appetites. They couldn't risk sending a lascivious, raping pervert on a two-year mission with five other people in a small, confined space.

That had been three days before. Now, they'd sent him to sit alone in a small conference room, suddenly, without warning or explanation. He came to the conclusion they were probably softening the blow by telling the losers in advance of the big announcement. He braced himself for that possibility, determined not to let anyone see his disappointment.

But it was Jane Holloway who came through the door with a shy smile. "Hi, there, Dr. Bergen," she said with a flutter of her fingers. She was more casually dressed this time, but still crisp and neat. Her hair was down, swinging in a trendy, flattering cut. "I heard they interrupted a meeting. I hope it wasn't too important. I'm about to see the capsule for the first time and I asked if you could come along to show it to me."

He smiled with relief. "So are the rumors true? You signed the paperwork?"

"I just did. Yes." She sounded resolute, but also looked uneasy about that, unsure.

"What was the clincher? What made you finally sign?"

A laugh bubbled up out of her. "They told me who their second choice was and I thought, 'Oh, no—that would be a disaster!' So, I signed."

He chuckled along with her. "So, the secret button was competition. I wish I'd known that in Stanford."

She shook her head ruefully. "No. Not competition. Concern. He might pass among the good old boy's club here, but he's not suitable for a first contact mission. He's lucky to be alive, actually, after some of the shenanigans he's pulled. I couldn't convince them they were wrong about him so I decided I'd better stick around."

He realized he was standing there, nodding at her like an idiot, and headed for the door. "So, why haven't you seen the capsule yet?"

She raised her eyebrows and took a deep breath. "I didn't want it to be a factor in my decision-making process. They've given me all the tests over the last few weeks, like you, I suppose. I must have passed. They seem to think I'll be able to handle it, so now I'm ready to see it, I guess."

He rubbed his hands together in anticipation. "Well, then. This should be good."

All the big wigs were waiting in the hall. He greeted them cordially and they walked together to the construction bays. The others stood aside, congratulating themselves, while he gestured at the capsule and explained a few technical things to her.

He didn't notice anything amiss, at first. She just followed along as he walked the perimeter, showing her the four rock-et-booster shells that were about to be mounted. Then he opened it up and she climbed the short service ladder to peek inside. She sat down suddenly on the ladder.

His eyebrows drew together. "Don't you want to go inside?"

"I—" she plucked at imaginary fuzz on her khaki pants. "Dr. Bergen...." She trailed off.

He shifted his weight from foot to foot uneasily as he watched her struggle, then took a step to stand between her and the men chatting nearby, barely aware of her now.

She lost her composure completely. She glanced over his shoulder. Her eyes were wide with disbelief.

She spoke just above a choking whisper, "They told me this was the most advanced...they said no expense had been spared...the best and the brightest—oh my God, this isn't a scale model, is it? This is it? It's...this small? It's not going to be any bigger than this for six people, for ten months, one-way? We'll all be...inside there?"

It hit him, then—how weird it must seem to someone outside the space program. Every candidate for this mission would gladly give up a leg to be one of the five going up in this capsule—but they all understood the logistics, the me-chanics behind why it had to be this way. For her, it would be a shock. Of course it would. He couldn't take offense at that, could he?

Her eyes didn't leave his face while he considered what to say.

"Yes, Doc. This is it," he said gently.

She bobbed her head once and a tear fled down her cheek. She dashed it away, murmuring to herself so soft he barely heard it, and stood up. She laughed. It was forced, but she was actively re-taking command of herself. "I have a bathroom that's bigger than this thing," she said in a thick, pinched voice.

He grinned at her. "Sure. But can your bathroom manage twenty-five-thousand miles per hour?"

She smiled and it lit up her face with such warmth. She stepped down and stuck out her hand. He returned the gesture.

She squeezed his hand and covered it with her other one. It was a simple action, but such a full moment. "I think I can always count on you to give it to me straight, Dr. Bergen."

She *saw* him. She *got* him.

That was it. That was when it really started. If he hadn't already been falling for her, that would have done it.

There were flashes going off, but he was barely aware of them as he stood there, absorbing that amazing smile. He wouldn't realize why the photos were taken until the next day when he got the news.

The average taxpayer would never see any of these photos. As far as the public was concerned, this would be the first five-man mission to Mars. Dr. Jane Holloway would be on an extended sabbatical in remote Tibet.

Nevertheless, it was an historic moment and would be documented for the classified NASA archives. One of the engineers that had designed the capsule bound for the Target, who was also selected for the team to man it, was showing it off to the newly recruited linguist-cum-astronaut for the mission.

A copy of one of those photographs was one of the few personal items he'd been permitted to bring. It was tucked inside a technical manual at the back of a storage locker. No one had seen it except the air-quality scientist who screened and approved all the personal items. The photo didn't create any off-gassing, so it was allowed.

They climbed back into the Providence, shut and locked the hatch. Walsh and Compton went to work re-pressurizing the capsule.

Bergen helped Ajaya pull Jane's limp form to the medical compartment to go over the EKG data. The electrodes were traditionally worn for space walks when the stress on the body was so great that an astronaut's vitals were monitored every minute. Ajaya didn't betray anything as she perused the data.

Bergen stared down at Jane's face, keeping his expression neutral. She just seemed to be asleep. "Ajaya—her eyes are moving. She isn't having a seizure, is she?"

"No. It looks like REM sleep to me. Her heart rate spiked a few minutes ago, but has returned to normal now. There's nothing of concern here."

"We have atmosphere," Walsh announced and took off his helmet and gloves. Everyone else followed his example.

Bergen unlatched the seal on Jane's helmet and began to remove her suit. Once Jane's torso was uncovered, Ajaya started taking vitals.

It was unnerving, undressing her like a doll. He'd imagined stripping her bare many times, but never like this. He kept his hands steady, his thoughts on the task at hand. It wouldn't do to betray anything else now.

He was peeling the cooling suit away from the waist down when Walsh issued orders.

"Bergen, get on those air samples. Gibbs, Varma could probably use some assistance."

Bergen bit his tongue. Compton was trained on the GC-MS and could run the air samples. Gibbs, too.

Bergen hated the thought of Gibbs touching her. Gibbs was always joking around with her. *He damn well better not be joking now,* he thought darkly and pushed himself toward the science station.

He'd just loaded the first sample and was preparing the second when he heard a commotion behind him. He turned to see Jane flailing. She was conscious, nearly naked. It looked like Gibbs and Ajaya had been trying to get a flight suit on her when she woke.

Gibbs went sailing in one direction, Jane in the other. She clutched the blue garment to her chest, her eyes wild and terrified.

"Jane," Ajaya soothed, in cool, clinical tones, holding out a placating hand. "You are ok. You are safe. We had to get you out of the EMU so I could examine you."

"I—I don't remember coming back here. I feel terrible. My head hurts."

Ajaya approached slowly. Jane flinched but didn't push her away. Bergen's heart was in his throat. He couldn't tear his gaze away as Ajaya finished dressing Jane, murmuring questions and reassurances to her. Jane's responses were monosyllabic and her movements jerky, though he couldn't be sure what they were saying to each other.

Behind him, the instrument beeped. Walsh and Compton were speaking softly to each other and Gibbs was looking conspicuously self-conscious. Finally, Gibbs came over, looking like he needed something to do and Bergen reluctantly turned back to the machine. The results for the first sample had just come up.

"Hey, these are—these are good!" Gibbs said.

Bergen squinted at the results, frowning. He hadn't been sure what to expect from them, but he found them unnerving for a couple of reasons. Gibbs' remark induced Walsh and Compton to come closer.

"The first sample has been analyzed. I need more time to run the rest of these," Bergen said.

"This is not only breathable—this is really, really close to Earth's atmosphere," Gibbs enthused to Walsh.

Walsh eyed Bergen. "Why aren't you more excited about this?"

"Because it's so damn close. I wouldn't expect that. Oxygen in near perfect proportions. Nitrogen, which I would expect to make up most, if not all, the balance. Trace amounts of CO_2 and methane, indicating there are living things aboard. And there's something else—there's xenon gas. Four percent xenon seems odd. It seems high."

Compton looked thoughtful. "We use it for ion propulsion. Perhaps they use it for something. Maybe there's a leak somewhere."

Gibbs said, "We've only got trace amounts of xenon in our atmosphere, but there are much higher percentages on Jupiter. It might be normal for their atmosphere."

Walsh tapped the top of the instrument. "What was the atmospheric pressure? Once we got a few hundred yards in?"

Bergen shook his head. "That's weird too. It was hovering around 14.7 psi. Less, here, near the capsule, due to the fact that we decompressed to open the hatch. But the farther we went in, the closer it got to ideal—sea level, Earth."

Walsh narrowed his eyes. "I don't like this. Someone's in there. They know where we're from. They're turning on the lights, changing the gravity. What's their angle? Why aren't they coming forward?"

Gibbs offered, "Jane said they might be shy. They might be watching us."

"Well, we just gave them one hell of a reality show," Walsh muttered, glancing back at Jane and Ajaya.

Ajaya was zipping Jane into the sleeping bag attached to her seat. Jane's eyes were closed.

Ajaya's mouth was set in a line as she approached the group. "I've given her something for pain. She has a terrible headache—perhaps a migraine, though she has no history of them, not even of tension headaches. That's all I can determine. I cannot find anything anomalous."

"What's she saying now?" Walsh prompted.

"Not much. I asked her what happened. She said she's trying to figure that out. She seems reluctant to say more. She needs to sleep. In fact, we're overdue for a sleep cycle, Commander."

"I agree. Let's get out of these suits, have a meal, get some rest. We'll get back to it in nine hours." Walsh rubbed a hand over his face. "Keep your weapons at hand."

Bergen pushed himself into his seat and zipped up the sleeping tube. He turned his head to observe Jane sleeping. Now that everyone else was settling down for rest, he could have an unguarded moment, knowing the others couldn't see him anymore.

Something had happened to her, but he didn't have a clue what that might be. She'd been sort of entranced by the symbols on the wall then just flipped out. That wasn't like her at all. The entire journey, she'd been a rock—affable, even-tempered, kind. She worked hard to keep the peace under incredibly difficult circumstances—and succeeded.

She'd only once shown any sign that the stress was getting to her. It was shortly after getting a data stream from Houston about a month before, filled with personal emails, meant to be a morale booster. Within minutes of the download completing she was silently crying and trying to hide it. It kept happening. Frequently. For days. No one else seemed to notice. He'd seen Ajaya talk to her once, but it hadn't helped. He started to get angry that everyone was ignoring her suffering, or couldn't see it, which seemed worse.

One day she had herself tucked into a little nook that she haunted, an electronic reader in hand. He was nearby, eating a meal, when something splashed on his face. He was sure it wasn't food because he hadn't opened anything wet yet. He looked up and realized it was a tear that had escaped her efforts of concealment.

He had three younger sisters. He'd observed his parents performing miracles with hugs when they were all small. He'd even stooped to it, himself, when desperate. So, it went against his better judgment, but he just couldn't watch her struggle anymore.

He didn't say anything. He didn't want to draw unwanted attention. He just pulled up close and wrapped his arms around her.

She stiffened at first, then melted into him, tucking her face into his chest, heaving soundless sobs. He waited until she pulled away, murmuring apologies, but he didn't reply or even meet her eyes. He didn't want to embarrass her. He just moved away. It seemed to be what she needed, because she didn't cry again after that.

5

Jane woke up groggy. She jerked involuntarily when she remembered that this wasn't just another artificially constructed day among the endless, monotonous hours of drifting through space. Something had finally happened. Everything had changed.

The others were going to want answers from her, but she didn't know what to say. She felt their eyes on her from time to time. She feigned sleep and listened to them making plans.

They were hashing out how to proceed, based on the information gathered so far. Under most circumstances, the crew had been encouraged to make decisions democratically, though the final decision would always be in the hands of the team leader—in this case, Walsh.

Walsh was arguing in favor of going back into the Target wearing EMUs. That pretty much guaranteed Bergen would argue the opposing position. Bergen contended that would waste resources and limit their mobility. When Ajaya, Tom and Ron chimed in with Bergen, Walsh backed down and they agreed to go in unsuited, taking precautions.

The haze of pain had subsided while she slept, leaving her with a dull ache and a fairly clear memory of a surreal exchange. Could that actually have been telepathic communication? Or was it a hallucination? Had the confinement finally pushed her over the edge into madness? They'd coached them in Houston to be prepared for anything, but nothing could prepare someone for this.

She cataloged what she knew. The voice had sounded analytical, cold. Had she been sucked into some kind of computer-simulated virtual environment? Something that tapped into the memory centers of the brain to pacify the user and get information?

She brooded over the memory the voice had conjured. It was always there, tugging at the corners of her mind, reminding her in quiet whispers how life should truly be. Now freshly and wholly manifested in a way she could never have imagined—the three of them, as they were before Australia, warm and loving, in a happy place. She'd never managed to fully recreate that feeling again.

She'd had something like it with Brian for a while, but career and work had come between them, driving it away. There was a time when Brian argued a baby would bring them closer, give them a common goal. It wasn't a healthy solution for their relationship, but some part of her had longed for that kind of deeper bond. Brian had minimized her concerns about how it could impact her career, promised they would share the load, but he was always too stressed with his caseload or vying for partner to realistically contemplate starting a family at any given time until it was clear it would never happen. That was probably for the best, but it left her adrift, cut off from the warmth she craved.

Why would the voice remind her of that, of her personal failure? Was that memory seething so close to the surface that she selected it herself? Had it been random, or had the voice chosen it, somehow knowing the effect it would have on her?

Layered over all of these questions was a sense of unease. There'd been a disquieting kind of pleasure in hearing the voice that made her feel guilty, like she was a child who'd been tricked into taking candy from a stranger. It inspired an ominous feeling—she sensed that the voice was leashed, held terrible power.

She had so many questions and no answers. She peeked through her lashes at the others. Had any of them been touched by that disembodied voice in the same way? If they had, they weren't fessing up. That actually seemed like a sound strategy. If it was real, it would try again. The voice had said as much.

With that thought, she set her teeth, released the harness and unzipped the sleeping bag. The movement drew their eyes, as she knew it would. They were gathering equipment. She'd have to hurry to catch up with their preparations.

"Good morning," she said solemnly.

Ajaya pushed closer. "How are you feeling, now, Jane?"

"Better," she hedged. "What's the plan for today?" She met Walsh's eye squarely.

"Exploration. We go further in." He watched her warily.

She nodded. "I'll be ready in moments. You should have woken me." She pushed off for the food-storage locker.

Walsh's next statement stopped her. "You and Varma are staying here."

She grabbed the nearest handhold and twisted around. "What? You need me. I'm—"

"Varma has her orders. These are yours—tell her what happened in there yesterday."

She stared at him in disbelief. "I'm fine!"

He held up a hand. "Save it. Gibbs will be taking pictures of any language or symbols we come across. They'll download to your laptop automatically and you'll be able to hear us over the two-way. Get your ducks in a row and you'll join us tomorrow." He turned away to check his gear. They wore oxygen monitors and carried harnesses with emergency air supply, as well as packs holding a day's worth of ready-to-eat rations, tools and instruments.

Walsh and the three other men slipped out shortly thereafter. She could hear their surprise as they dropped into the corridor below, discussing the fact that the gravity now approximated Earth's gravity. Was that confirmation that the alien was still working to optimize conditions for them?

Jane bit her lip indecisively. Should she stop them? Ajaya closed the hatch, and the opportunity to speak up was gone.

Ajaya held out a two-way radio. Jane took it from her and began to prepare breakfast out of habit. She hadn't expected to be left behind. She sipped lukewarm coffee from a pouch and waited for the scrambled eggs to rehydrate. If they didn't need her to be there, why did they drag her across half of the solar system? She opened her laptop and stifled the urge to slam it onto its velcro pad harder than necessary. She could have studied images on a laptop from the comfort of home.

Ajaya hovered nearby, clearly waiting for an opportunity to do an exam and ask a lot of questions. "Jane? We should talk about what happened yesterday," Ajaya finally ventured.

At that moment, the first image from the day before came up on the screen. Jane inhaled sharply. Ok—she hadn't imagined that. She could see the symbol for 'open,' even in this format, as having depth and meaning, though her reaction wasn't visceral this time, only simple comprehension. She swallowed thickly. Maybe she wasn't nuts.

Ajaya eased closer and peered at the screen. "What is it about these symbols, Jane? They seem to affect you."

"I—you don't see it?"

"See what?"

"When I look at this symbol, it expands like a hologram. It relays information."

"A hologram?" Ajaya indulged her by looking again, then shook her head. "So, at first you saw them as I do and then they changed?" Ajaya's voice sounded a little too sympathetic for Jane's comfort.

"I know my reaction must seem extreme."

"You are under a lot of stress."

Jane grit her teeth. "I'm fine."

Ajaya furrowed her brow. "Jane, you must know your guarded attitude is troubling. I would like to do a physical exam. Will you cooperate?"

Jane reluctantly closed the laptop. "Of course I will."

She waited quietly while Ajaya took her pulse, tested her reflexes and other neurological signs, then asked a series of questions that were meant to determine mental status. She'd been through this exam before, several times. They all had.

When she was done, Ajaya turned to Jane, her fingers tapping the side of her laptop. "Your assessment is the same as it's been for the last six months or more. You are mildly depressed, but show no other clinical signs of mental infirmity. Physically, you appear to be in good condition. I cannot explain what happened yesterday unless you divulge more."

Jane blurted out, "Didn't anyone else experience anything out of the ordinary? A buzzing sound inside their head?"

Ajaya was quizzical. "Buzzing? You spoke of bees yesterday. Why didn't you say anything?"

Jane considered what to say. "At first I thought it was just nerves. But, it got stronger, building over time. When I deciphered the symbols, it suddenly became unbearable."

Ajaya looked thoughtful. "And that is when you passed out. Have you experienced tinnitus before?"

"Tinnitus? No."

Ajaya retrieved her otoscope, examined Jane's ears at length, then pulled back. "It could be Meniere's. That's a disturbance in the inner ear. It can have sudden onset and lead to severe vertigo. Headaches are common with it, as well. It's very treatable. Do you hear the buzzing now? Are you feeling dizzy or perceiving any hearing loss?"

"No. I feel fine."

"It can be very intermittent. A year may pass between episodes or they can happen every day. Do you feel any pressure in either ear—now or yesterday?"

"None."

"I wish I could perform an audiometric exam on you, but I don't have the equipment. Stress is known to make tinnitus

worse, though it doesn't cause it." She seemed vexed and
stowed away the equipment as she continued, "Your passing
out in that moment may have been simple orthostatic hypo-
tension. More than 80 percent of long-flight astronauts experience it. I don't know, Jane. It doesn't fit well with one
diagnosis and that makes me uneasy. Let's cautiously watch
this. You will tell me if you have any of these or any new
symptoms, won't you?"

Jane's vision blurred. "Of course. Of course I will." Perhaps Ajaya could understand if she told her the rest. She
swallowed and blinked, then finally said, "I'm sorry. I'll be
more forthcoming in the future, I promise."

Jane scooped cold scrambled eggs out of a pouch, but
didn't taste them. She was itching to get back into that ship.
She didn't want to stay cooped up in the capsule for another
twenty-four hours, where she couldn't see anything
firsthand.

She resumed scrutinizing the symbols, concentrating on
the images taken from the exterior of the storage crates with
the granular contents. The cipher was elusive. She could almost see a hologram, but it was hovering just out of reach. It
didn't help that her mind kept wandering, going back to all
the things the voice had said to her the day before.

*"There is plentiful foodstuff, as you have already discov-
ered."*

She blinked, stifling a startled gasp as the hologram
sprang to life.

*Nourishment,   sustenance...palatable,   appetiz-
ing...satiety...healthful,   wholesome...aggregate,   composite,
blend.*

71

She wrinkled her nose. The crates were filled with some kind of nutritive food-base, a raw material used to manufacture food. The concept that formed in her mind was completely foreign. She was puzzling over that as she cleaned up the debris from breakfast, when the radio squawked. "Providence. Gibbs. Over."

Ajaya picked up her two-way. "This is Providence. Over."

"Just checking in. Did you get the pictures? Over."

Jane picked up her own radio. "Yes, Ron. I've got eight new images. I need a little more context to be able to decipher them. I'd like to join you. Dr. Varma has determined there's nothing seriously wrong with me. Over."

Gibbs' cheerful drawl came back, "Copy that, Jane. We'll get back to you. Over."

Moments later, the radio came back to life. "Providence, this is Walsh. We're splitting into two teams. Gibbs and Compton are going back to get some extra shots for context and Bergen and I are going forward. Walsh out."

"I could meet you—"

"Stay put, Holloway. Walsh out."

Jane ground her teeth. Hiding in the capsule couldn't protect her from what happened the day before, she was certain of that. Of course, they didn't know that.

While she waited, she prepared a pack of things she'd need when she did go back in there, all the while ignoring Ajaya's disapproving eyes on her. As she pulled an air canister out of its compartment, a delightfully dreamy drowsiness came over her. She blinked slowly, her limbs drifting around her, pleasantly thick and heavy.

Her heart started to pound.

She fought down panic and contemplated her options. She could try to resist. That hadn't been an effective strategy the day before. It had only served to wear her down, exhausting her. She'd gotten next to nothing out of that interaction—certainly nothing that anyone would believe.

The hum had already begun. It was happening again.

She reminded herself that this was an opportunity to get answers. She closed her eyes and concentrated on breathing deeply. The throbbing buzz grew stronger. Her thoughts slowed. She schooled herself to stop resisting, relax, stay in the moment....

She felt a surge of pleasure as awareness of a presence filled her mind.

She drowsily opened her eyes in the casita. "Hello?"

"Dr. Jane Holloway—you did not explain to the others about our arrangement."

Jane snapped to alert. The voice sounded...pissed. Could a computer sound pissed? She slowly turned in a circle and forced her expression to be neutral, though it felt wooden and uneasy. "Hello? You haven't told me your name—"

He interjected, sounding impatient, "I do not understand. This is vital information. You must make them aware."

She shook her head. "They won't believe me. They—I have no proof."

She thought about what she was doing—producing virtual words from a virtual mouth—because her body was actually inside the Providence, unconscious, floating around, probably bumping into things. She sank on the bed, suddenly unsure. "Maybe I am crazy."

"Dr. Jane Holloway, there is an urgent matter to which you must attend. This is no time to indulge in delusional fantasies."

She stood, wary. This bizarre interaction had a way of disarming her. She was forgetting how precarious their situation was, forgetting her normal caution, forgetting all the questions she needed to ask. "What?"

"I cannot protect them from peril. I have attempted containment and exclusion, but the controls are not responding as they should. The nature of the infestation disrupts the applicable neural-electric pathways. I am fixed, immutable. You are the only possible liaison. The others are not open to me. I cannot influence them. You and you alone must act." The voice resonated with a note of hysteria.

Jane tensed, suddenly filled with dread. "What are you talking about?"

"I presumed that your personage would accompany any exploratory efforts. I could guide you, dissuade you, if necessary. However, at present, there are four individuals occupying two discrete chambers and two of these are perilously close to endangering their very existences. I do not wish for their extinguishment." He sounded haughty, self-righteous.

Her hand reflexively clutched the back of a chair. "Extinguishment? Are you saying the other astronauts are in mortal danger?"

"Dr. Jane Holloway, I expect you to forestall the impending disaster."

"How? Tell me how. Tell me what to do. What's the danger?"

"Standby. Sending data now."

Jane staggered. The buzz inside her head magnified exponentially. Awareness converged inward with a new, unnerving acuity. She could feel the vibration on a heretofore unknown scale—the progress of each tiny bee, making connections, individual neurons firing far faster than they could possibly be meant to. She felt detached from herself, blandly observing, as the space between her ears expanded to accept....

She gasped. Three-dimensional maps of the interior of the Target, replete with what appeared to be itemized lists of each sector's function and contents, swamped her conscious mind. She fell to her hands and knees and struggled to comprehend the deluge. "Oh, God," she choked out.

"If you wish, I would be gratified to debate the existence of deitous life forms, but perhaps we should attend to the matter at hand? It would have been preferable to defer a bit longer before imprinting the command and control engram set. However, in this moment, it is expedient. Are you ready to commence?"

"No! Just...stop!" She writhed on the rough, dusty floor of the casita, her hands clutching her head. Tiny, blazing bees zoomed within, making connections, overwriting, leaving searing trails in their wake as they rendered data. "Make the bees stop! Please—it's too much!"

"Dr. Jane Holloway, you are overcome. I will assist."

She felt a lifting, a lightening, a shedding of pain. She opened her eyes to darkness, but felt no fear at the change, only simple curiosity. She felt embraced, warm and welcome. It was wonderful, but also worrisome. "What did you do to me?"

"I merely separated the cognitive layers. You are still there, and there, but also here. I dare not shield you for long. It could create cognitive dissonance. I have no idea how your species will react to such interventions."

She felt like she was wandering farther and farther from reality. "Where is here?"

"With me."

"Where are you? Physically?"

"I am here."

This individual was not the straightforward type. If it weren't such a dire situation, she'd laugh out loud. "What is this form of communication? How are we doing this?"

"I have tapped into a dormant area of your brain. Stimulating this area activates previously unexpressed genetic material, which, in turn, triggers ongoing structural refinements that facilitate this method of communication. In short, at my expert intervention, you are experiencing accelerated evolutionary changes."

She heard the words. She understood their meaning. She could not fathom them.

He continued without stopping, "It is a curiosity. You are conceptually aware of individuals on your world with this ability, yet it seems your culture resolutely denies the possibility of its existence. Blind-sight like this is a blight on the progress of your world. A failure of science, if not of imagination. Yet, on the whole, the six of you are educated in the standard methods of scientific inquiry. Your species is vexing, Dr. Jane Holloway."

She swallowed. "You're communicating with the others this way, too?"

"No. That is not possible."

"Why not?"

"I can skim the other's thoughts and memories, learn from them, in a limited fashion, but I cannot communicate with them. Perhaps, in time, it may be possible. They are not fluent in Mensententia. This prohibits communication."

She struggled to follow his train of thought. "Mensententia?"

"The common language."

"What? Look, you have to explain yourself. I don't understand what you're talking about."

"I would advise a patient attitude, Dr. Jane Holloway. I am not an educator. I have not received the instruction required."

Jane took a deep breath to still her mounting frustration, then continued, "Please, tell me what you know of Mensententia."

"I will be brief. The download is nearly complete. You must return. The common language was latent within you, a component of genetic memory, given to you by the Cunabula."

"Genetic memory?"

The voice made a sound like a sigh and went on, "Unmasked by most species during the epoch of pubescent change, it marks readiness to enter into discourse with those outside one's own kind. Your conversion was nearly spontaneous—quite unique and likely a product of your extensive linguistic experience. When I observed this awakening, I intensified my attempts at communication, leading ultimately to success. I must say, the Sectilius were intensely disappointed to learn that Mensententia was suppressed on your world, to discover that you had not been good stewards there, that your world was in such a state of disarray and on the verge of environmental collapse—"

Cunabula? Sectilius? She felt dizzy from the influx of information. "Wait," Jane interrupted. "You're saying that the symbols are...and we're communicating now, in Mensententia?"

"It is time, Dr. Jane Holloway. You will awaken with comprehension of this vessel fully integrated, and must act immediately. It shall be quite clear to you what must be done. We cannot yet converse while you are conscious, but if you listen, you will hear my communiqués. I will offer assistance wherever possible. Go now."

"Wait! Tell me your name!"

"I am the Gubernaviti. Ei'Brai."

"Aiyee-Brai?" She repeated it automatically, to be certain she'd heard every nuance of the name and would remember and pronounce it correctly, but there was no answer. Only agonizing pain.

Bergen stepped in first, triggering the lights to come on. A puff of air greeted him. It was another huge storage room. This one was filled with floor-to-ceiling, cylindrical storage tanks—all the same color as everything else in the ship.

"Somehow, I expected the interior of an alien spaceship to be a little more exciting," Walsh commented.

"Yeah." Bergen glanced at Walsh as they walked down the undulating aisle, getting a feel for just how far back it went. The aisles weren't in conventionally-structured, straight lines. "What do you think about what Jane said?"

"I'll wait to hear what Varma says on the subject." Walsh's tone let him know that was the end of that discussion. "Any idea what's in these tanks?"

Bergen yawned, then shrugged. "Same kinda stuff we've got in our tanks, probably. Water, compressed gases, fuel of some kind. It takes a helluva lot of gas to fill a ship of this size with air. I'm sure Jane'll figure it all out. She's fucking amazing." He shrugged again and suppressed the urge to giggle with a frown.

He glanced at Walsh to see if he'd noticed his expression or the comment about Jane. He hadn't. He was busy studying what appeared to be a valve on one of the tanks. He'd taken off his pack and harness and was bent over in an exaggerated, comical pose. He needed a really big magnifying glass to complete the picture. Bergen snorted at the idea.

"Speaking of air—it's really blowing around in here, don'cha think?" Walsh swayed a little bit and grinned. That was weird. Walsh never smiled. "Feels good after ten months of stale air crammed in that damn teapot."

Bergen spontaneously whooped with laughter. "I know, right? It's like the ventilation system's gone haywire."

Walsh clapped him on the shoulder, an uncharacteristically friendly gesture, dragging his pack and emergency breathing equipment behind him. "We'll tell the little green guys to fix it, if we ever find 'em."

"Yep. No, no. Jane'll tell 'em."

Walsh nodded solemnly. He was acting like he was drunk. That didn't seem normal. "Right. What was that about, yesterday, do you think?"

Bergen shook his head, trying to clear it. Things were a little fuzzy. "I just asked you that and you said you're gonna wait to hear what Ajaya says."

"Right. I said that. You're a total ass, you know that Berg?"

He gave Walsh a playful shove and Walsh went reeling across the room, laughing his ass off.

"Hey, hey, hey—careful! I think Gibbs bruised a couple of ribs yesterday when he fell on me." Walsh staggered to his feet and seemed confused, feeling around his torso with both hands. "That's funny—they don't really hurt much anymore."

Bergen approached Walsh slowly. "Did you tell Ajaya about that?"

Walsh heaved an exaggerated sigh. "It's nothing. Holloway was more important at the time." He looked around. They'd wandered down a narrow aisle between the tanks after he'd shoved Walsh. "A door," Walsh commented blandly. "Let's open it up and see what's next door. More of the same, I bet. Lots and lots of the same stuff. Gibbs was right—this is a really weird color. Why would they want every damn thing in this place the same color? Have we seen any other colors since we got here?" Walsh tapped the door control, strode through, and stood there blankly staring into the dark. That was strange. The lights had always come on automatically before, whenever they entered a new room. It gave him a feeling like maybe they weren't supposed to be there.

Walsh made a funny face, smacking his lips like a stretchy-faced comedian. "My lips are numb." Walsh's voice had taken on a deeper timbre.

Something was wrong.

Bergen turned around to look for some kind of motion sensor and recoiled. "Oh, fuck." His own voice came out sounding strange and deep, but they had bigger problems than that. He grabbed Walsh by the back of his flight suit and turned him around. "Look."

"Holy mother of God," Walsh said slowly. His voice sounded low, demonic. "What the hell?"

The only light came through the doorway from the other room. The wall around the door, as far as they could see, was studded with some kind of animal ranging in size from a cucumber to a large dog. In the dim light against the dark wall, it was hard to tell what color they were—maybe grey, maybe purple. They had a wet look to them, iridescent, slimy, and they were moving. Some of the bigger ones moved alarmingly fast. Even so, they didn't seem terribly threatening. Bergen decided to keep his distance nonetheless.

"Big-ass slugs," Bergen replied in a leaden bass, shaking his head and smiling with disbelief.

He and Walsh exchanged disconcerted expressions. Walsh giggled for a moment, but it sounded low-pitched and distorted. He stifled himself and looked disturbed. "Ok. Let's go back."

"Commander Walsh, this is Providence. Come in. Over." Both men jumped as Ajaya's voice blared over the radio.

Walsh drew himself up. "This is Walsh. Varma, report. Over."

"Jane is unconscious again. I cannot wake her. Over."

"What happened? Over."

"She started drifting and I realized she was unconscious. Her vitals are normal. Your voice sounds unusual, Commander. Are you all right? Over."

Walsh was squeezing his eyes closed, concentrating on listening. Why was it so hard to think? Bergen felt like he was falling asleep on his feet, numb and disconnected. They needed to get out of there.

He grabbed Walsh's arm and headed for the door. Walsh started, as though waking up, but then followed obediently. Bergen lost track of any thought except getting back to the door and through it.

There was a loud, piercing sound and both men stopped in their tracks. It took Bergen almost a minute to recognize the sound. It was Walsh's oxygen monitor. As soon as he made the connection, his own started alarming as well. The numbers were fluctuating wildly up and down the scale. No wonder he was feeling so lightheaded.

He slid the pack from his shoulder and then the compressed-air gear. He fumbled with the valve, but his fingers weren't working properly. They felt like blocks of wood and weren't cooperating with his brain.

Bergen looked over at Walsh, expecting to see him doing the same thing. He wasn't. He was watching the slugs. Bergen could see why. They were moving around a lot faster now. The alarm must be disturbing them.

Walsh seemed to be mesmerized by them. He was walking slowly toward a large one, his hand outstretched. Dammit—he was walking in the opposite direction of the door. Bergen shook his head vigorously to clear it and bounded after Walsh, pulling him back. "Don't be a goddamn Redshirt, Walsh!" Walsh didn't reply.

Their oxygen monitors were still alarming, which helped Bergen to remember what he was doing. He went back to fumbling with the compressed air. His hand closed over the valve, finally, and he pulled the mask toward his face. Then, the lights went out.

Walsh stumbled back into him and they both went down in the dark. It wasn't a soft landing; they both went flailing and cursing. Bergen dropped both his pack and the canister. He scrabbled around for it.

83

Walsh was grasping at him, alternating between speaking incoherently and laughing maniacally. Bergen fought down panic and froze in place for a moment, concentrating. His thoughts were disjointed…the deep voice. There was something…yesterday….

Why couldn't he think?

"Commander? Walsh? Bergen? Report. Over." Ajaya's voice again and still the monitors beeped.

Walsh's grasping movements slowed and he went limp, a dead weight, collapsed against Bergen's side. He was asphyxiating or something. Bergen knew he was next unless he could find that canister. He shoved Walsh's inert body to the floor and redoubled his efforts, blindly feeling all around them, searching for the canister, the pack, anything.

Walsh. Walsh has a canister too.

Bergen scrambled, adrenaline pumping, to turn Walsh over. *Dammit!* Walsh must have taken the harness off at some point; it wasn't on his back.

Bergen slumped. He and Walsh were going to die there, in the dark, on an alien spaceship—surrounded by ginormous, freaky, alien space-slugs.

He closed his eyes, giving in to the sleepiness. It was hard to sleep, though, with all the beeping. Someone should really turn that off.

His dozing was interrupted by the sound of Jane's voice and he roused himself half-heartedly to hear her. Her voice sounded urgent. "Walsh, Bergen—this is Jane. Can you hear me?"

"Jane?" *Oh. She's on the radio.* He grabbed at it, his fingers thick and unresponsive. The little red light came on. He could talk now. "Jane? S'Berg."

"Dr. Bergen? Are you...ok?"

He struggled to keep his eyes open. "Lost it. Both of 'em. S'dark, Jane."

"What—what's happened? What did you lose?"

"Dunno. Air, I think. So sleepy, Jane."

Beeping. Lots of beeping.

"Alan, listen to me. Stay awake. You—it—I think it's a gas. The room you're in is flooded with some kind of gas. You need to get out of that room!"

Well, he'd thought of that already. "Can't. Can't see a damn thing. Can't see the slugs." His voice sounded slurred. Was he drunk? How had that happened?

"Ok. Right. That's the problem, isn't it?"

"Yup."

Jane went quiet then.

The alarm still beeped, shrill in his ear. He started to nod off again.

"Alan? There are very tall storage tanks with access ladders nearby, right? Climb one of them. There'll be less of the gas, if you can get higher. I'm coming to help you, but you have to do some work too."

What was that beeping sound?

"Jane? What's going on?" Compton's voice. Now they were talking.

Bergen tuned them out and clung to what she'd just said. *A gas. Huh.* He pulled himself upright and stooped down to grab Walsh's arm. He stuck out his other arm, searching for one of the tanks, and took a step, clumsily dragging Walsh along.

There were going to be slugs on it. Icky, squishy slugs.

He staggered, dragging Walsh behind him. Something rattled, skittered across the floor nearby. What was that? It seemed important. He concentrated on the angle the sound had made and dropped to his hands and knees and felt around. Finally, his fingers brushed against something hard and cold and then closed around it.

Air. Oh, holy fuck, it was the air.

It seemed to take forever to get his fingers to close over the mask and bring it to his face, while he braced the tank against his chest and turned the valve with his other hand. He concentrated on inhaling deeply. After just a few moments, a comprehensible picture began to form.

Xenon gas. He'd detected unusual amounts of it in the air the day before. The storage tanks must contain xenon and apparently there was a leak. It was an odorless, tasteless gas. Who knew what the concentration was in there? They were lucky they hadn't suffocated.

The deep voice, the bizarre behavior, the disconnected thoughts. The effects of xenon were similar to nitrous oxide—laughing gas. He had to share the air with Walsh and he had to get them out of there. But the room was enormous and he had no way of knowing where another door would be.

Bergen took off the mask and pressed it to Walsh's face, slipping the band around Walsh's head. He put his hand on Walsh's chest. It seemed like it was rising and falling.

Bergen held his breath as long as he could, then breathed shallowly as he systematically searched again for the other canister, or either pack. He was already starting to feel woozy when he located one of the packs. He groped around inside until his hand closed over the shaft of a flashlight. He turned it on and passed the light over Walsh, who was coming around.

"Take deep breaths, Walsh!" he yelled. Then he started chuckling. What was so funny, again? *Oh, yeah.* The oxygen monitors were still going off, which helped him remember.

Walsh sat up.

"It's xenon gas!" Bergen shouted and then giggled helplessly as he waved the light around, looking for the other canister. He couldn't see it.

Walsh stood up. Good idea. Xenon was the heaviest, non-radioactive gaseous element. They needed to get farther from the floor. Bergen stood up too and swayed, blinking owlishly at Walsh.

"Where's the other canister?" Walsh demanded, taking off the mask and holding it over Bergen's face. Bergen took deep breaths, quickly purging the dense gas.

"I don't know." He shined the light around them carefully, but the second canister was nowhere to be seen. All it did was illuminate the number of slugs in the immediate area, which was far too many for Bergen's comfort.

They weren't just on the walls. They were covering the sides of the tanks all around them. In fact, one of the largest ones was currently covering the door controls that led back into the other room. That's why the light had gone out.

Their escape route had just been violated by a turgid, purple blob.

The radio crackled with Jane's voice. "Alan! Are you still awake?"

Jane. He remembered what she'd told him to do.

He passed the oxygen back to Walsh and approached the nearest ladder. "Still not dead, Jane. About to climb a ladder. We have one can of air between us." He motioned to Walsh. "Come on, we have to get higher. The air will be better and maybe we'll be able to see another door from up there."

Jane's voice came over the radio again, "Alan, don't touch the slugs—they secrete a substance that could give you chemical burns."

Bergen huffed and pulled himself up another rung. He couldn't spare a hand to answer her. The rungs were ridiculously far apart. He had to pause frequently to breathe.

The exertion of climbing made them both take in too much gas. Walsh wasn't doing so great. He wasn't saying anything and had to be reminded what they were doing frequently. Hell, he was having trouble remembering what they were doing.

The flashlight was hooked to Bergen's clothes, making visibility poor, but he needed both hands to climb and to pass the mask back and forth.

The slugs were all around him. He could see them glistening in the faint light.

Where was Jane? Goddammit, this needed to be over soon. How was she going to find them? How did she even know what was happening?

Life was about climbing an endless ladder and trying to keep Walsh alive. There was nothing else. Rung after rung in the near darkness. Breathe. Pass the mask.

Walsh grew less and less responsive.

The rungs were wide. Bergen hooked his elbow on a rung and slipped to the side, keeping his body carefully away from the tank and its gooey residents. He beckoned at Walsh to come up next to him, holding his breath to keep the oxygen inside as long as possible.

They would have to stay here, like this, until Jane could find them. To that end, he groped around until he had wrapped his body around Walsh's, hooking one foot painfully around the bar and over a rung, to keep himself securely in place. He wasn't about to let the bastard fall after all this.

After a long turn with the air, he risked trying the radio again. "Jane. Ok, look, this isn't funny anymore. What's taking so goddamn long?" His voice sounded a little closer to normal—a good sign.

"Are you safe now?" Jane asked.

"Not really. Walsh is in bad shape. I have no idea why. The compressed air isn't helping him much."

"I left Compton and Gibbs to keep trying at the door you went through. The door controls aren't responding. We couldn't get that door to open."

"If the slugs are dripping toxic juice—that's why. There's a slug the size of a small pony sitting on the door control on this side."

"I'm almost to another door that accesses the same room. It's going to take me longer to find you from there. Do you have a flashlight with a strobe?"

He took the mask back from Walsh and took a few puffs before answering. "I still have a pack. I'm clinging to a ladder, trying to keep this stupid fuck from falling off. I can turn on a strobe. Just tell me when."

He held back from saying what he really wanted to say to her: *Hurry Jane. I can't manage this much longer. Walsh is dead weight and he's going to pull us both down.*

Jane was afraid to believe Ei'Brai, afraid to trust him—
and she was afraid not to. She was in pain. There was an absurd amount of information unfurling inside her head. She
felt panicked and unsure, but she couldn't let any of that
show.

Walsh and Bergen were in desperate need—Ei'Brai
seemed to be quite correct about that—and, given the nature
of their predicament, it was extremely unlikely they were
capable of self-rescue.

Walsh and Bergen...*Alan*...they could be suffocating
even now.

That brought up so many uncomfortable thoughts and
memories. She wanted to suppress them, but the images kept
bubbling to the surface:

It had been a weekend day, with a bright blue sky and
rushing clouds. She chatted up the tourists, soaking up the
sun on the small boat, as Dad sought just the right spot.
Then she was watching their eyes light up with wonder as
she pointed out brightly colored fish and mesmerizing un-
derwater creatures to them. The storm was unexpected, blew
up quickly. The sea, suddenly turbulent, tossed them painfully into the coral. The day's vacationers were weak swim-

mers, were drifting too far away. She tried to help. She had helped. But it hadn't been enough.

No. Focus.

At least Ajaya had enough sense to observe Jane, rather than restrain or sedate her. Fortunately, Ajaya seemed to be sufficiently convinced by Jane's self-possession and certitude, as well as by Walsh and Bergen's strange behavior, to comply with her terse directions. That didn't stop her from asking a lot of questions, but Jane couldn't spare the time to explain. The best proof, for both herself and the others, was going to be a demonstration of this...collaboration—with a favorable outcome. There was no other option.

"Jane? What's this about slugs?" Ajaya gasped from behind her.

Jane was racing for the nearest entry point to the room where Bergen and Walsh were trapped. A large green canister of compressed air was slung on her back; the tubing that connected it to the face mask slapped against her neck and chest with each step.

She had to get there in time. In a dangerous situation, even a moment of indecision could cost a life. *Even a strong swimmer, they'd said.*

Too many minutes had been lost trying to get the other door open. She would have liked to have sent Gibbs and Compton to try yet another door, but it would have taken too long to explain how to get there.

She ignored Ajaya's question. Pulling off her mask briefly, she instead supplied a vital one of her own, "Ajaya, how many minutes of air are in the small canisters they took?"

"Typically, 40 minutes—"

"The same if they're sharing it?" She spared Ajaya a fearful glance over her shoulder. They had no idea how long they'd been sharing that canister. There might not be much time left.

"The rate of flow should be the same...." Ajaya trailed off. Even Ajaya wasn't sure.

One, two, three rows more, according to the layout that unfolded in her mind. She didn't slow down much, just slammed into the wall, her hand outstretched to the symbol. The door opened and she darted inside. It was dark. She fumbled in her pack for a flashlight. Had she taken too long? Would she find them, pale and blue, the way they'd found her father, trapped in the reef?

She pulled off the mask and grabbed for her radio. "Bergen, I'm here. Turn on the strobe so I can see where you are."

She replaced the mask and strained her eyes and ears to pick up any sign of him. He didn't answer. She could faintly hear the beeping of their oxygen monitors, but the sound was repeated in the cavernous room and was hard to pinpoint.

"Oh, my goodness. He wasn't kidding. Slugs, indeed," Ajaya panted.

Jane found herself saying, "They're a pest. Like rats on the sailing ships of the 18th century. They're commonly found on interstellar ships." She shut her mouth. That hadn't come 100 percent from her. The information Ei'Brai had put in her head was integrating with native thought and memory.

Ajaya just looked at her with a bewildered expression. Jane felt a light buzz as she turned to scan the room again. She wanted nothing more than to take off now. She had a general sense of where they must be, but running willy-nilly through the aisles wouldn't be efficient. Ei'Brai had promised to help and she had to concentrate to hear his whispers.

"Jane—" Ajaya began.

Jane shook her head to silence her and closed her eyes.

From this point, 17 units left, 43 direct, will take you to them....

She sprinted, staying mentally disciplined, counting each tank as she passed it. The beeping from the oxygen monitors was getting louder. As she drew close, she pulled the bulky mask down and called out, "Bergen? Alan? Can you hear me?"

"Jane? Jane! We're over here!" His voice sounded desperate. Finally, she could see him, probably 30 feet or more in the air, cradling Walsh in his arms. "Jane! Sorry, I couldn't manage the strobe. I dropped the flashlight trying to turn it on. Where are Compton and Gibbs? We're going to need help to get Walsh down!"

Jane hooked the flashlight to her flight suit, slung the two extra canisters over her shoulder, and started climbing. She pulled down her mask as she heaved her body up the next rung, the canisters and masks clanged together and slipped down her arm. Each canister, made from a lightweight fiberglass material, weighed less than ten pounds, but three of them were awkward to manage. She struggled to keep them from getting entangled with the ladder with each step. "Is he unconscious?"

"Yes! I can't hold him much longer—the pack is tearing. I'm sorry, Jane. Beautiful Jane."

"Do you have any air left?"

"Not much. Put yours back on, you nutcase!"

She did as she was told. She was already feeling dizzy. She didn't know how he could have kept his head so long.

When she reached him, he started babbling about everything he'd been through thus far. She passed him one of the canisters and helped while he laboriously slipped the harness over his shoulders and clipped it around his waist, then together they got the other one affixed to Walsh.

Once he had the mask over his face, Bergen went quiet, and Jane studied the situation. He had a pack slung over Walsh's shoulders, attached with a carabiner clip to a rung. That was supporting most of Walsh's weight and Bergen was keeping him in place. One of the shoulder straps was tearing away from the pack, though. She immediately moved to support his weight.

Walsh was passed out, but she could see he was still breathing and when she felt his pulse, it was strong. She relayed that information to Ajaya.

How were they going to get Walsh down? She considered a few different options, but they all sounded dangerous to her.

A thought occurred to her. She closed her eyes to concentrate on a single thought, *Please, if you can, turn off the gravity in this room.*

Nothing happened. It didn't work that way, apparently. Either he couldn't hear her thoughts or he couldn't—or wouldn't—do that for some reason. She let out a curse as she gave up on the idea.

She opened her eyes to find Alan watching her with narrowed eyes.

She pulled down her mask and pretended she hadn't just been trying to communicate telepathically with an alien. "Alan? Feeling any better?"

He nodded.

"How do we get him down? I have rope in my pack. Can we make a harness and lower him?"

His eyes lit up and he seemed to consider the possibilities.

Ajaya shined a couple of flashlights on them from below and called out, "Jane? Shall I climb up there too? Do you need another pair of hands?"

"No room. Get on the radio and give Compton and Gibbs directions to this location, ok?" Jane carefully wedged her pack between herself and Walsh. If it took insanely long periods of time to do something in microgravity, it took even longer to accomplish anything whilst clinging to a ladder trying to keep an unconscious person from falling in the dark. She pulled out a bundle of paracord and passed it to Bergen. "Do you have any idea how to make a sling?"

He slipped his mask aside and grinned roguishly. "I can do one better. I've done some rock climbing. I'll improvise a harness and then we'll use the carabiner as a simple, moveable pulley. That will nearly halve the amount of force we'll need to use to lower him."

Jane smiled at his enthusiasm and reached over to push his face mask back in place, because he was already busying himself with the paracord. He methodically looped the cording around Walsh's shoulders and legs, crisscrossing it around his back and groin.

As she watched him work, helping when she could, she noticed his hand was discolored, captured it in one of her own, and shone the flashlight directly on it. She gasped with dismay. "Alan—what happened to your hand?" It was red and splotchy, swollen, with some blistering in spots.

He pulled his hand from her grasp and kept working. "I'm feeling it now, but at least my hands are cooperating." He jerked his head toward the storage tank. He must have touched one of the creatures or the slime trails they left behind.

"What have you done to treat it? Anything?"

"I cut open my water pouch and stuck my hand inside for a good five minutes. It's fine. Ajaya will put some cream on it and I'll be good as new."

She knew it wasn't fine. He had to be in incredible pain.

He connected the carabiner to the newly fashioned harness and cut the paracord with a multitool he fished out of a pocket. He securely knotted one end of the remaining paracord to the ladder, slipped the other end through the carabiner, and made another knot to tether Walsh temporarily.

He pulled his mask down. "I'm guessing Walsh is about 170 or 180. By using a movable pulley, it'll feel like 90 to 100 pounds, roughly, ok? Between us, that should be a piece of cake. Let's get a good hold on him and I'll get him loose." He put his mask back into place and got to work moving Walsh into position.

Alan got the carabiner loose of the torn pack. Walsh jerked in their arms. Jane cried out involuntarily as she was wrenched against the ladder. Bergen muttered what she guessed were some choice words, smothered by the mask. He wrapped the slack around one arm and slowly untied the tether.

Jane steadied herself by letting Walsh's weight pull her forward into the rung that crossed her chest and reached out with her right hand to take the rope from Bergen.

His eyebrows drew together. His words were muffled by the mask, but she got the gist.

"Alan—your hand is badly injured. I can do this. You— you just back me up, ok? I can do it." She tried to sound firmer than she felt. She should be able to do it. She had to do it. With his right hand in such a state, she had to bear the brunt of the weight or he would injure himself further and Walsh might literally slip through their fingers.

He reluctantly nodded assent.

She let go of Walsh's makeshift harness and got a firm grip on the rope that would lower him by wrapping it around both fists. "Ok. You let him go and take the tail of the rope. Get ready, Ajaya! We're going to let Walsh down!"

Bergen's eyes were on her, not Walsh, as he slowly let go. The rope went taut and she grit her teeth. It wasn't too bad. She was holding him on her own. She felt beads of sweat break out on her scalp and upper lip as she was pressed painfully into the rungs of the ladder.

She was just getting used to the idea, when Bergen barked at her, "Jane—you have to let him down, hand over hand."

"Ok, ok. I know." She let loose of one hand. The rope bucked and Walsh banged into the ladder. She flinched. "Sorry, sorry, sorry, Walsh," she murmured as she took a hold of the slack to repeat the process, hopefully a little more gently this time.

"You're doing great, Jane," Bergen said in her ear. He was close against her, ready to grab the rope if necessary, she supposed.

Her biceps burned. All those workouts in the capsule were actually paying off. She'd mentally cursed through every session, but she was saying a prayer of gratitude for them now. Foot by foot, she lowered him. She didn't want to think of failing, but her arms trembled and the rope cut into her hands.

"Steady, Jane." Alan's muffled voice sounded in her ear.

Walsh slipped a few feet and bounced around. Jane yelped in dismay and pain. There were only a few feet left to go before he reached Ajaya, Compton and Gibbs' outstretched arms. She couldn't drop him now. Alan grabbed the rope between her two hands and slowed it down.

Finally, Ajaya was reaching up to take the weight. The rope went slack. Jane pressed her forehead to the ladder in relief. Her arms felt like rubber and all she wanted to do was go limp. She felt a hand on her shoulder.

Alan was smiling at her. "Bet you'll never look at those resistance bands the same way again, huh?"

She reached out and covered up that smug smile with his mask. "Keep your mask on. Let's go. We need to get Walsh out of here. You first."

He huffed in amusement but didn't argue. By the time they got to the bottom, Gibbs and Compton were getting Walsh into a carrying hold. There were a lot of looks being exchanged, but there seemed to be an unspoken consensus that the first order of business should be getting Walsh to safety. She took point, leading them out into the corridor and back toward the capsule.

They hadn't gotten far when she felt the unmistakable buzzing sensation again. She stumbled and could feel the others' eyes on her. She drug her feet a few steps, reluctant to fall unconscious under their direct scrutiny. She couldn't tell if this was another brief message or if he would call her away again and she wasn't sure she wanted either to happen. It continued, grew stronger, until she heaved a heavy sigh, stopped walking, and closed her eyes to concentrate— instinctively honing in on the feeling, to give him easier access to her thoughts. As soon as she did that, the rumbling ceased and she felt the lightest tendrils of thought easing into her mind.

The ship's air quality sensors indicate the corridor's atmosphere is safe for your occupancy, Dr. Jane Holloway. If the injuries your party has sustained are more severe than your resources can accommodate, Speroancora has a medical facility that is at your disposal. There are no air quality issues on any of the common routes or within those chambers.

The hum ceased and Jane straightened, pulling her mask over her head. It was time to face them, if not yet time to explain, perhaps. "It's safe to take off our masks now," she said, unclipping the harness, slipping the apparatus from her shoulders, and turning off the air flow. "How is Walsh, Aja-ya?"

Ajaya kept a leery eye on Jane as she drew her stethoscope and a small flashlight from her pack, then turned her attention to examining Walsh. Compton and Gibbs held Walsh with their arms linked in a chair hold. Walsh's head and torso sagged against Gibbs' shoulder.

Gibbs slipped his mask aside. "Jane, what's going on? How do you know it's safe now? How did you know all this stuff was happening?" He turned to Bergen. "Wasn't the radio signal getting through, before, when we split up?"

Bergen looked like he wasn't sure about any of it and slowly pulled down his own mask.

Ajaya redirected their attention. "Much as I would like to know the answers to these questions, my own questions are more pressing at the moment. How long has Walsh been out and what were you two breathing in there? Do you know?"

Bergen seemed to consider that. "He's been out a good twenty minutes or more. He had a much tougher time clearing the gas, even with the oxygen. I believe it's xenon gas."

Ajaya furrowed her brow. "I'm aware of the properties of xenon. It's occasionally used in pulmonology. That explains your symptoms."

Bergen frowned and nodded once.

Ajaya turned back to Walsh. "But why isn't he clearing the gas?"

Bergen rubbed his neck, thoughtfully. "He did say something about having bruised ribs from Gibbs falling on him yesterday. At the time, I thought he was joking."

That seemed to alarm Ajaya. "Oh, dear. That's a problem. He may have developed inflammation of the intercostal muscles and may not be capable of taking a deep breath, just now. The gas may have settled in his lungs and is simply sitting there. This has all sorts of implications. He may be at risk for pneumonia as well."

Bergen grabbed Walsh's dangling legs and shoved them over one shoulder. "Let's turn him upside down. If we change his position, that should displace it."

Ajaya was nodding. "Yes—good idea. That should work."

Gibbs and Compton slowly eased Walsh's head toward the floor. They suspended him like that until Walsh coughed and came around. They got him upright and Ajaya moved in to examine him again. "Commander, we have very strict guidelines for reporting injuries," she said primly.

Walsh looked confused. "What the…?"

"Welcome back, Commander. Take some deep breaths, please." Ajaya resumed her patient, clinical air as she unceremoniously unzipped the front of Walsh's flight suit and pulled up his t-shirt to palpate his ribs.

Walsh shook off the arms of the men holding him and slipped to his feet. He complied with Ajaya's instructions, but was unable to hide painful winces with each deep breath.

"What's the last thing you remember, Commander?"

Clearly discomfited, he glared at Bergen. "Climbing a ladder. Why aren't you all wearing masks?"

Gibbs said, "Jane says it's safe out here."

"Since when is Holloway an expert on air quality? What the hell is going on? Why isn't someone stationed in the capsule?"

They all turned to look at Jane. Her mouth opened, but nothing came out. She felt her face go hot. "I…we know we aren't alone here. There is one…person…on board. This ship is called the Speroancora and has a single occupant, aside from us. His name is Ei'Brai."

Compton touched her elbow lightly. "How can you know this, Jane?"

She lifted her chin. "I've been in contact with him. He told me what was happening, helped me find Walsh and Bergen. Without his help, we never would have found them before they both suffocated."

A single word, edged with disbelief and contempt, came from Walsh, "How?"

Jane shook her head. "I don't know, but he gets into my head somehow. He says he's been in all of our heads, that he's capable of seeing our thoughts and memories, but I'm the only one he can actually talk to…."

They openly stared at her—as though she were the alien.

Her hands balled up into fists. "I know it sounds insane. All this time I thought I'd be documenting the first alien language—but even if this mission becomes public knowledge, who's going to believe me when I say I communicated with an alien telepathically? Goddamn it!" Tears sprang to her eyes. She spun away from her colleagues and tipped her face up to blink the tears back before they spilled over.

Compton came around to face her, looking earnestly concerned. "When did this start?"

Her throat felt painfully thick. She choked out, "Yesterday. When I passed out. That's when he first made contact with me. Right after I deciphered the symbols in the hall-way."

Compton squeezed her arm and moved away. She could hear Walsh speaking in undertones. Gibbs and Bergen stayed silent, but Compton murmured words in support of Jane, encouraging Walsh to hear her out more fully.

She glanced back at them when Ajaya spoke up in a level voice, an incredulous look on her face, "For what it's worth, I'm inclined to believe her, Commander. Remember, I was with her the entire morning. She's been operating with an impossible amount of knowledge of your situation, your exact whereabouts, and the ship's layout. I could barely keep up with her. There were several instances where I honestly did wonder if she was communicating with someone silently, because I just couldn't explain her actions any other way."

"Is that your professional opinion, Varma?" Walsh said sarcastically.

"With all due respect, Commander, you weren't there." Ajaya replied.

"Then let's hear the details, Holloway. Start at the beginning."

Ajaya protested, "We need to prioritize. I need to treat your injury, Commander."

He waved her off dismissively and gestured at Jane. "It can wait. The details. Now, Holloway."

Jane solemnly came forward and carefully described the unusual sensations going on inside her head each time Ei'Brai had been trying to make contact the day before. She explained how the symbols in the hall had opened up to her, and how Ei'Brai had said that in that moment he knew that he'd be able to communicate with her. She recounted their conversation. Then she skipped to that morning, how it had happened again, and how events had unfolded. Ajaya added to Jane's narrative with observations and the timing from her point of view. When she finished, Walsh regarded her with a grim expression, but didn't say anything right away.

Ajaya glanced from Walsh to Jane and back again. "We need to begin treatment on your injury, Commander. Your condition could quickly become serious. The first rule of thoracic bruising is to control the pain so the patient can breathe properly, or secondary problems can develop. Believe me, you do not want to go there."

Jane felt uncomfortable under Walsh's intense scrutiny. She gestured toward Alan. "Dr. Bergen's hand is injured. It's a chemical burn."

Jane snuck a look at her own hands. The paracord had cut her palms raw, but the others' injuries were worse. She'd wait until they'd been tended to before pulling Ajaya aside.

Ajaya was already examining Bergen's hand. "You've got a nasty second-degree burn, Alan. I dearly wish I could stick this hand under running water for twenty minutes to make sure you're well-rid of the chemical that caused this."

That got Jane's attention. She probed clumsily at the newly implanted data in her mind, searching for particulars about the medical facility Ei'Brai had mentioned. "Can you treat them, Ajaya? Do you have what you need to treat Bergen and Walsh in the capsule?"

"I'll manage. I don't have all the comforts of home, obviously. I'd like to get some ice on Walsh's injury, but that's not possible, of course." Ajaya sent Jane an intrigued look. "Why?"

"This ship has a medical facility and it's not far. There's potable running water there. I might manage to find some ice too. There are medical scanning devices. We've been invited by our host to use all of it, as needed."

Walsh eyed her skeptically. "You're saying you could take us there? Where is it, from here?"

"It's three decks up via the deck-to-deck transport and 300 or 400 feet down a corridor." Jane slid a glance at Bergen. He was rubbing the back of his neck with his uninjured hand, watching Walsh with a serious expression on his face.

"No. We fall back to the capsule. It's a defensible position," Walsh said tersely.

Ajaya shook her head. "With all due respect, Commander, going back into microgravity right now would be a mistake—the fluid shift could be dangerous for you. In fact, I don't think it's wise for any of us to keep going back and forth for extended periods. The effects on electrolyte balance and blood pressure alone, well, there's no predicting the long-term effects of repeated rapid cycling through extreme environments like these. We're here to explore this ship. The ship has gravity. We need to make camp somewhere inside it. An infirmary is as good a place as any."

Walsh glowered at her. "We can make camp in the corridor outside the capsule then. Stay close to our supplies."

Gibbs ventured sheepishly, "With the kind of resources we're documenting here, the supply of water this ship is carrying has to be massive, meant for hundreds of people, maybe thousands. Do you think they have showers, Jane? I could really use a shower."

Jane smiled at him ruefully, "Yes, Ron. I believe there's a shower in the infirmary. I was thinking about that, too."

Walsh shot Gibbs a dirty look and then turned to Compton and Bergen. "Well?"

Bergen spoke up immediately, "I think it's a good idea to see something besides cargo. If Jane can deliver, we should investigate it."

Jane focused on Bergen sharply, but his expression was inscrutable.

"No surprise there. Compton?"

"I'm concerned about Jane. I want to know more about what happened to her."

Walsh sighed heavily and then grimaced at the pain that must have caused. "Noted. Agreed. Your opinion?"

"I agree with Ajaya. If we have to make camp here for medical reasons, that sounds like a good solution. I have doubts about our ability to use their equipment right away, but it's worth looking."

Walsh surveyed the group like they'd all completely taken leave of their senses. "Fine. Take Varma and Gibbs and get the supplies we'll need for twenty-four hours, then lock it up. We'll see what this is all about."

Jane slid down the wall and rummaged in her pack for a dose of ibuprofen. Her head ached and she felt utterly drained. She closed her eyes. Information was still unspooling inside her head. She caught glimpses of it now and then, filtering into her conscious mind when she wasn't distracted.

So much of it was technological in scope. It was the stuff NASA wanted—details of structure, anatomy of propulsion drives, ventilation regulation, star maps, and so much more. It should have gone to Bergen or Compton or Gibbs. They were engineers of various types. It would make sense to them. They'd be able to use it. In their hands, it would be an advantage. In hers, it was nothing short of mind numbing. How could she ever hope to convey all of it properly? It was incomprehensible.

She didn't want any of this. All she'd wanted was to learn the language. Now she had that and so much more. How had she ended up in this position?

As her mind wandered, she realized that the exterior of the ship, the way it was constructed, like a city skyline of jutting, geometric shapes, was for the purpose of hull integrity as much as for the optimal collection of solar radiation for the ship's most basic power functions. The many angles ensured that a portion of the ship was always collecting some amount of energy. The way the ship was oriented in its orbit maximized that.

But, why give her all of this? Why not give just the pertinent portions needed to get to Bergen and Walsh in time? At the edges of her mind she sensed there was far more that she hadn't quite grasped yet. It was an awareness of something intangible, but growing. Was that Ei'Brai?

Walsh kept in constant contact with Compton, micromanaging Compton's every move in the capsule, clearly compensating for his discomfort over what had happened. Compton set up a remote link so that Walsh could send a transmission to Houston. He glossed over the details of the morning and neglected to mention that Jane had made contact with the alien entity.

Bergen was pacing the corridor. He'd stop and examine the dressing Ajaya had wrapped around his injured hand or eye Jane and Walsh furtively, then resume his pacing. He looked as exhausted as she felt.

She gestured at him limply. "Dr. Bergen, it's been a rough morning. Why don't you just sit down for a minute and rest?"

He settled down against the wall about three feet from her, turned to her like he wanted to say something, then stopped himself and shook his head.

"What?" she asked wearily.

"Well, you…why are we back to Dr. Bergen? You called me Alan thirty minutes ago."

She peered into his face curiously. "I was trying to get through to you."

His lips twitched and he glanced away.

"I don't understand. I'm just trying to maintain a professional atmosphere."

"You call Ajaya, Ron, and Tom by their first names. Why not me?"

He actually seemed hurt. She frowned. "Why do you call me 'Doc?'"

He smirked—that looked more natural. "Because it irritates you."

She smiled back. "I'll call you Alan, if you call me Jane."

He bobbed his head and he leaned toward her, sticking out his good hand, his left. "You have a deal, Doc."

She took his hand and squeezed. "Smart-ass." She pulled up her legs and leaned her head on one knee. "Have you eaten anything today? I have some stuff in my pack."

"I could eat."

"Walsh? Hungry?"

Walsh had been maintaining some distance from them. He strode over now and slowly eased himself down, stifling a groan.

"Didn't Ajaya give you anything for the pain?" Jane asked, as she searched her pack for food.

He ignored her question and said, gruffly, "How'd you get me down from that ladder?"

Bergen was peering into his own pack. "Made a harness from paracord. It probably didn't help your situation much, but there weren't any good alternatives. I made the sling. Jane lowered you."

Jane shook her head, "I lowered you with some help." She couldn't stand to take all the credit when Walsh might have suffered a brain injury if she'd had to do it completely alone.

Walsh nodded slowly, his eyes narrowing on Jane. He clearly wasn't happy about being out of the loop on all the particulars. She passed him some jerky and mixed nuts. Walsh didn't like the energy bars. She opened one of those for Bergen and one for herself, then set a large plastic pouch of water between them to share. They chewed in silence for a while.

"Why'd you wait to talk, Holloway?" Walsh asked, with a sidelong glance.

"I thought I might be going nuts."

He grimaced and raised his eyebrows. "You sure you're not?"

She met his stare unflinchingly. "One-hundred percent? No. I did save both your butts, though. So, that's something."

Bergen smirked.

Walsh was unfazed. "Why's he hiding? Why not meet us face to face?"

"I don't know. I don't think he can. I don't know what he looks like. I'm not even sure he's a he. I just picked that pronoun because it fits his voice."

Bergen watched her with an intense expression. Walsh was grim.

She looked down at the sugary bar in her hand, connecting her disparate thoughts as she articulated them, "The structure of this new language is similar to languages with Proto-Indo-European roots—like Greek, Latin, and Sanskrit.

We know that there are common words that are very similar among many of our languages—'mama,' 'night,' 'star,' and 'no.' I can't help but wonder if this ancient language, stored genetically but never consciously examined, comes out of us in this beautiful, wonderful way. Most linguists over the last 50-60 years have rejected the idea of the monogenesis of a proto-human language. In fact, my own work would tend to discount such theories. Linguistic polygenesis is the current prevailing theory, but...." She trailed off, her enthusiasm deflating, as she became aware that this revelation probably meant very little to them.

Walsh leaned in slowly with a pained expression and took a sip of the water. "What's he like?"

Jane sat back, chastened, as she suspected he'd meant her to feel, and wiped her sticky fingers on her clothing. That's when she noticed small holes forming on the leg of her flight suit. She met Bergen's eyes and he tugged on his own suit, revealing holes of his own.

The others had been instructed to bring changes of clothing for all of them. Unless or until she started feeling unbearable pain, she'd keep the flight suit on. She'd rather be burned than strip down to her undergarments in front of Bergen and Walsh right now. She felt vulnerable enough as it was.

She continued, more solemnly, "He's pretty ambiguous most of the time. He doesn't like to answer direct questions. I thought for a while that he might actually be the ship's computer, but I don't think so now. He didn't want you two to die. A computer wouldn't react like that, would it?"

Bergen raised his brows. "It depends on programming. Could be an AI."

Jane frowned. "Oh. Artificial Intelligence? He sounded emotional. I...really?"

Bergen reached out and snagged the water pouch. "So it's just him, huh? No others in a ship of this size?"

"That's what he says. I got the feeling that they died a long time ago. I intend on asking a lot of questions next time."

"You do that." Walsh said a lot with those three words. He didn't believe any of it. She was surprised at how painful that was, given that was actually the reaction she expected from him.

She let her expression go blank and dropped her hands into her lap. She resisted the urge to try to make herself smaller, less conspicuous, or to close her eyes to escape his watchful glare. Walsh was efficient, critical, skeptical, but he was also fair. She would eventually convince him, but she wondered what that would take.

She couldn't be sure what Bergen was thinking. Given his personality, the fact that he wasn't openly disdainful was encouraging. But she suspected he might be humoring her because he was worried about her. She wasn't sure if she liked that. She suspected his forbearance toward her went back to their time in Houston. Either someone at NASA had assigned him the dubious honor of watching over her, or this was his way of expressing friendship.

The silence was thick and painful.

Walsh got back on the radio with Compton. It sounded like the others were about to return. They were wrapping up some details.

Bergen cleared his throat. He was reaching for her hand. "Jane, you're hurt too," he said softly, turning her hand palm up.

"It doesn't hurt much," she replied.

He held onto her hand. His hand felt strong and warm on hers. She let it linger, glancing curiously into his face. She liked this side of him and wished he would show it more often.

"This isn't how it's supposed to work, you know," he said, with a sly smile.

She resisted smiling back. "What?"

"You're supposed to be the damsel in distress. We're supposed to save you."

She snorted and pulled her hand away. "Times have changed."

"But what does that make us? Two dudes in distress? Pathetic."

"Two *colleagues* in distress. Gender doesn't matter," she replied and let a hint of a sad smile cross her face.

"Mm." He nodded and dug into his pack. "I have something for you. I've been saving it for a special occasion. Not-asphyxiating seems as good an occasion as any other." He pulled out a closed fist and held it out to her.

She put out an open hand and he plopped a small plastic pouch into it. She gasped with surprise and quickly closed her hand to obscure what was there. "Chocolate? Alan Bergen, I am going to tell your mother about this!" she hissed at him.

He chuckled. "She won't be surprised. Are you going to share?"

She glanced at Walsh again. "I shouldn't. But, I'm going to." She tore open the plastic wrapper. They were the kind of chocolates that usually came in heart-shaped boxes. The kind with flavored, creamy centers. She slipped Bergen one, popped one in her own mouth, and left the third in the plastic, secreting it in an intact pocket of her suit. She shook her head and threatened him with a menacing glare. She whispered, "You're terrible—blaming Ron and me for eating all the chocolate when you hid it somewhere. I'm going to tear that capsule apart until I find your stash!"

"Good luck. I have my own secret hiding places built in." He nodded smugly and popped the morsel in his mouth.

She beamed at him, shaking her head. She didn't doubt it was true. "Now, I'm complicit. You're going to have to pay me blood-chocolate for my silence."

He laughed, a loud, barking laugh. She couldn't help but giggle at him. He had a way of figuring out exactly what she needed sometimes. Just when she thought she had him figured out, he surprised her again.

Walsh shot them a censorious look.

Bergen slid closer and bumped her playfully in the shoulder. "I'm not passing any judgment here, but you two were going through that stuff awfully fast. Would it have killed you to choose peach cobbler now and then?"

She rolled her eyes, savoring the chocolate still melting in her mouth. The peach cobbler was a joke. She didn't know how it had escaped the excessive quality-control process NASA employed for every detail down to their underwear. Sometimes it rehydrated as a disgusting, soggy mass, sometimes it tasted like someone had used a heavy hand with some exotic spice, and sometimes it was perfect—well, as perfect as rehydrated food can be.

It was funny, but in a weird way, because they kept eating it anyway, because their choices were so limited. It became a joke. Which peach cobbler would it be this time? They'd complained to Houston about it, in a cheeky, teasing way. The brass in Houston got the director of the Space Food Systems Laboratory to send a reply, during which he admitted there'd been an intern in the lab on the day the peach cobbler had been prepared. He swore there'd be nothing amiss with the food waiting in the capsule on Mars for the trip home. The thought of the return capsule sobered her and she sighed.

"Hey." Bergen's arm snuck behind her and rubbed her lower back. He leaned in and asked softly, "You ok?"

"I'm fine," she answered automatically, stiffening under his sudden solicitousness.

"You sure?"

He was hovering so close, seemed so concerned, she could almost believe...but no, that was ridiculous. He was kind of a legend at NASA. Space geeks were surprisingly gossipy. He was the local boy who made good, on a regular basis, or so his wingmen bragged. She was definitely not his type. He was just being friendly and that felt awkward because he probably didn't have a lot of practice being friends with women.

117

"Yes." She stood up and pulled her ponytail loose, to cover her nervousness created by his sudden attention. With the band came a clump of damp, matted hair. She stared at it, uncomprehending, and then dropped it with a squeal. Her hand was glossy with slime.

Walsh and Bergen were on her in seconds. Before she could react, Bergen was sloshing her hand with water from the pouch until it was empty, but her hand was already becoming painfully red and sore. She fell to her knees and pulled a bag of wipes from her bag. She pulled out wipe after wipe, scrubbing at her hands, her face, in case she'd splashed herself, determined to not release the tears that were so close to the surface.

Walsh stood nearby, stoically observing.

Bergen knelt next to her and touched her shoulder, saying, "It's ok, Jane. It's just a couple of inches."

She flinched. "Stop it! Don't touch me. Stop looking at me. It's just hair!"

He backed away.

She turned her face up to keep the tears at bay. The tough nomex suit was holding up. She would take it off soon and get under running water.

She felt a light hum, almost tentatively, like a question, at the back of her skull. She tensed up even more. Was he watching them, through cameras hidden throughout the ship? Or was he dipping into their thoughts, listening to them like a telepathic peeping tom?

You need not endure such discomfort. The vermin's caustic exudate is a common affliction, easily treated. Please make haste to the medical facility where you may receive treatment without organic assistance—the Sectilius practice medicine quite differently.

Jane stood, her chest still heaving. She turned to see Tom, Ajaya and Ron striding toward them, laden with packs, bags, and equipment. Jane picked up her pack and set off down the corridor without a word.

9

Bergen, and the rest of the crew, trailed in Jane's wake. He brought up the rear, refusing to participate in the exchange of uneasy looks being passed around. He didn't want Jane to think he had anything but the utmost confidence in her.

She seemed to know exactly where she was going. She didn't hesitate at intersections in the corridors. She strode purposefully to a door and tapped the control to open it, revealing a small chamber. She entered, beckoning them to join her.

Bergen shuffled to a stop as those in front of him stalled.

Bergen hated the look on Jane's face, as she struggled not to betray whatever she was feeling.

"It's a deck to deck transporter. It's like an elevator," she ground out.

Still, they hung back. Walsh was staring Jane down with a pissed expression on his face. He was making this a lot harder on her than was necessary.

Bergen shoved himself roughly between Walsh and Gibbs, taking a place at the back of the transport chamber. Ajaya nodded and joined him, Gibbs following close behind.

Compton and Walsh lingered a moment longer, then followed suit.

Jane examined the eye-level controls briefly, then decisively selected a symbol. The door closed instantly, and reopened a moment later.

Jane stood motionless. If she was having qualms, he couldn't see her expression. Furtive glances were exchanged behind her back. They were probably all thinking the same thing he was: this hallway looked exactly like the one they'd just left. It hadn't felt like they'd gone anywhere.

Then she was out the door, charging down the hall again.

Bergen heard Walsh say something in a low voice to Gibbs. Gibbs pulled a piece of chalk out of his pack and tagged the wall with an orienting symbol of some kind.

Bergen huffed. *The fool should have thought of that before they got into the transport.*

Jane paused outside a door and waited for them all to catch up. "This is it," she said. "I'm not sure what to expect. The room inside is called the Assessment Chamber. From what I can gather, most of their medical interventions are carried out automatically. Most of the medical personnel that would be working here would be supportive staff, not like doctors as we know them."

"Interesting," Ajaya murmured.

Walsh was discontented. He motioned Jane back and drew his weapon, motioning for Gibbs and Compton to do the same. He tapped the door control and stepped inside.

It was an empty room with nothing more than a large disc-shaped platform in the center of it. The wall at the back of the room was curved, repeating the shape of the platform, and was replete with numerous doors.

A voice rang out, breaking the silence. Everyone, including Jane, jumped. It was a calm, even voice, non-threatening, slightly feminine. It was speaking in some foreign language. If he'd been asked to guess, he would have said Italian.

"Is that the voice you hear, Jane?" Compton asked her.

"No," she replied, obviously confused.

Walsh looked skeptical. "What did it say, Holloway?"

She stepped further into the room. She spoke slowly—sure, but full of wonder, "It said, 'Welcome, Undocumented Citizens.'"

The voice spoke again. Jane translated immediately, "Please step onto the diagnostic platform."

Bergen shot Walsh a pointed look. If Jane was making all this up, it was getting pretty damn detailed.

Walsh walked the perimeter, his weapon ready, with Gibbs and Compton following his lead.

Ajaya stepped close to the platform and examined it. There wasn't much to see. The platform itself was made from the same material and color as every other surface in the ship they'd seen. It was raised a good half meter from the floor, and the ceiling above it had a recess of the same dimension. When he stepped closer to look up into the vault, he could see it was inset with a dark, glassy screen.

Bergen sighed. "Ok, who's going first?"

Ajaya straightened. "Walsh's injuries are the most severe."

Walsh shook his head sternly. "No."

"Christ. I'll go first." Bergen made to step onto the platform.

Walsh held up a hand. "Hold on, let's investigate further, before we jump into anything. We don't know what this stuff does."

But even as Walsh spoke, Jane had already stepped onto the platform. Walsh's lips tightened. "Holloway, goddammit."

A blue-green beam of light emanated from the recessed area above, enveloping the platform from floor to ceiling in a tube of light, casting Jane's hair and skin in a ghastly, unearthly glow. She looked terrified, but she held her ground.

Walsh took a step toward her. "Holloway, get off—"

The voice, surely an automated computer of some kind, spoke again. Jane translated in a trembling voice, "Unidentified hominid species. Accessing files. Standby." The light undulated in bright waves up and down her body. The voice, then Jane, "Scanning."

Ajaya watched as if in awe. "Do you feel anything, Jane?"

Jane shook her head.

The voice spoke again. "*Genusis Terrano. Homo sapiens. Afirmeu opu neu.*"

Jane said, "Terran species. *Homo sapiens.* Confirm or deny."

Compton joined the crowd around the platform. "Terran?"

"That's the Latin term for Earth, is it not, Jane?" Ajaya asked.

Jane nodded, then said, "*Afirme,*" and seemed to brace herself.

Bergen swallowed hard, his heart slamming into his rib cage.

A full-sized, three-dimensional, transparent hologram appeared in front of Jane, mirroring her in every aspect, even down to her slightest movements. The voice spoke, then Jane, "Please state your full name for the record." She raised her chin and said clearly, "Jane Augusta Holloway."

All color flashed out of the hologram. What was left was a transparent outline of Jane's body. Then several areas on the hologram began to glow bright red—her hands, the area between her shoulder blades where her hair had touched, and her right leg in small patches. The voice spoke again, this time going on for a bit. Jane hung on every word.

When it finished, Ajaya prodded, "What, Jane?"

"It knows I'm burned with chemical as well as abrasion burns. It knows the chemical I've been exposed to and the species it comes from. The proper name of the creatures is *Coelusha limax*—literally 'space slug.' It says when I'm finished it will open a door to a chamber where I can take a medicated shower to neutralize the alkaline substance and then receive polarized light-based healing therapy and a medicated cream to recondition my skin."

Ajaya nodded slowly, her brow furrowed.

The hologram changed. Jane's skeletal structure glowed red as well as a few of her internal organs. When the voice finished, Jane said, "It says I have multiple, mild, nutrient deficiencies which can be corrected with either a prescription diet or an infusion regimen."

"Interesting," Ajaya murmured.

The hologram transformed again, highlighting a small, t-shaped object in Jane's abdomen. Jane went quiet and didn't translate anything. The light went out and she stepped off the platform. One of the doors opened, revealing another chamber. "Who's next?" she asked.

"What was that last bit about?" Walsh asked gruffly, then motioned for Compton and Gibbs to check out the room that had just opened up.

Ajaya stepped between them. "I know precisely what it was about. Jane and I will discuss it privately, later."

Walsh didn't like that answer and he didn't make any moves toward the platform, so Bergen hopped up next. It was obvious that Jane trusted this stuff. If she could trust it, he could too, because he trusted her.

The blue-green light lit up instantly around him. The voice asked a question. He thought he got the gist of it. He grinned at Jane. "It's asking if I'm human, right?"

She nodded.

"*Afirme*," he answered, mimicking her. She nodded again and produced a slight, tremulous smile.

The voice spoke again and he grimaced. Would he say his whole name, or edit himself? *Ah, shit. Jane did.* "Bartholomew Alan Bergen," he said, loud and clear. Jane's smile went a little wider. He fixed his gaze on her.

Then his hologram appeared. From there it went on pretty much the same as Jane's stint on the platform had. It highlighted his injuries and nutritional issues caused, he assumed, by the long microgravity flight. He stepped down.

So far, nothing was a surprise. Jane led them there and it checked out as advertised. Everyone turned to Walsh, waiting to see if he would step up there too. It was pretty obvious that he didn't like how things were unfolding.

Walsh turned to Ajaya. "Varma, recommendations. Do you think these treatments sound safe? How do they compare to what you would do?"

"I recommend they do only the burn treatments, for now. They sound benign and minimally invasive. Alan has a large second-degree burn on his dominant hand that will take weeks to heal—and, honestly, Commander, hand burns are very tricky. All I can do is put a soothing cream on it, control his pain, and hope for the best. This treatment protocol—well, I'd like the opportunity to observe its effects. This ship was built by people with greater technology than our own—on Earth, medical technologies develop on scale with other technologies. I cannot help but believe that Alan and Jane would be better served here than by my own hand. The nutrient infusion can wait until we know more."

"You want to make them human Guinea pigs?"

"With their consent, sir. I'd like Jane to ask the computer lots of questions about each treatment before it's begun."

Walsh's lips were pressed in a thin line. He sent Bergen and Jane hard, evaluating looks. "Are you volunteering for this?"

Jane nodded firmly and glanced at Bergen. He nodded too. At this point, he'd do anything just to get out of the flight suit.

Walsh turned back to Ajaya. "Fine. Go with them. Make sure they don't do anything stupid. We're going to secure the area."

"Commander—"

"That's an order, Varma." Walsh didn't wait for a reply. He made for the nearest door, opened it, and went inside, gesturing to Compton and Gibbs to follow. They disappeared, leaving Bergen, Jane and Ajaya looking at each other. Jane turned and strode through the door that had been opened for their treatment.

This second chamber was larger, but minimalist as well. Every wall and fixture was the same putrid green color that everything else in the ship seemed to be. There were several alcoves and the walls jutted with geometric protrusions in varying sizes. He wondered if it was for aesthetics or if it were some kind of storage system.

Jane moved around the room slowly.

"What's the first treatment?" Ajaya asked.

After a brief interchange with the computer, Jane replied, "A shower. Or, more precisely translated, a waterfall, in this recess." She gestured limply. "It says it's a slightly-acidic, lipid emulsion with a variety of salts, mineral oxides, and clays, all naturally and sustainably mined and harvested from unadulterated worlds."

Ajaya nodded. "That sounds like calamine lotion. I think it sounds harmless."

The voice spoke again. Waiting for the translations was getting really old. One of the first orders of business was going to be learning this language. Jane and the computer voice had an extended exchange. Bergen shrugged in his clothes. He wanted to get on with it. The stuff was eating through to his skin in patches and was starting to burn in new spots.

Jane was acting uncomfortable. "It expects us to shower together to conserve resources."

Ajaya raised her eyebrows at this. "Really, Jane? You can't talk it out of it?"

Was Jane blushing? He probably shouldn't be looking so hard, but it was a pretty awesome predicament from his point of view. Except for Varma hanging around, of course.

"No. It just keeps saying it's waiting for us to disrobe."

Her expression was completely forlorn. Geez. Was it really that terrible? It's not like they hadn't seen each other before. Sure, he knew he wasn't supposed to be peeking, but she wasn't innocent of that either. He'd caught her looking before. More than once.

He tried to look blasé. "Look, I'm sorry, Jane, but this shit hurts."

He turned his back to her to put her more at ease, and kicked off his boots while tugging down the zipper on his flight suit awkwardly with his left hand. He peeled off everything, including the wrappings on his hand, and stood there, covering up his junk with his hands to keep her from freaking out. Just getting the flight suit off was a relief.

He heard some rustling. Then Jane said, "*Paratiso.*"

There was a sound of rushing liquid coming from the alcove nearby.

He turned slightly to see Jane stepping under a running curtain of a milky white liquid that disappeared into a grate in the floor directly underneath. He followed, keeping himself turned away from her. It coated his body in a chalky film that was instantly soothing.

"How are you doing, Alan?" Ajaya called.

"Great. Feels great." Damn, it felt good to be in a shower, even if it was some weird alien fluid. It was warm. It felt fantastic.

The flow shut off. He was dripping from head to toe in what looked like milk of magnesia. *Now what?* He glanced at Jane. Her back was to him. Her hair was saturated with the stuff, grey and stringy. *She...damn, she has a nice ass.*

Ajaya was wandering around the room, testing various projections on the walls. A drawer slid out at her touch. "I've found something that resembles towels," she boasted.

Jane translated the newest set of instructions. "We're supposed to stand here for a few minutes and then we can rinse and wash before the next treatment." She peeked at him timidly, over her shoulder, her arms wrapped around herself.

"Jane, I'm not going to jump you."

"I know that!" she retorted.

Better change the subject. "So, ah, how can you be so fluent in this language, Jane? What's going on?"

"I don't know. I only know what he told me, which isn't much. It feels like I've always known it, somehow...."

She looked so vulnerable, standing there, hugging herself with her head bowed, her hair dripping, hiding her face. He wanted to reach out and touch her, reassure her, but that probably wouldn't be wise.

"Are you cold?" Ajaya asked.

"No," they replied, almost in unison. The floors were heated or something. He was pretty comfortable, for being covered in wet, chalky goo.

He gestured at her, though she wouldn't see it, "Maybe you have—always known it, I mean. On some level. If it's really some kind of genetic thing. Do you think we all have it? Or just you?"

"He made it sound like all humans have it, that it just has to be woken up."

The shower sprang back to life. It was a thin sheet of water, this time, rinsing most of the other stuff away. It was the perfect temperature. He forgot everything else for a minute, turning his face to the ceiling, letting the water flow over him.

"There's some kind of soap here, Alan. It doesn't suds up, though."

He turned. She was pointing at a boxy object, poking out of the wall. He strode over next to her, trying to keep his eyes to himself. "How does it work?"

"Put your hand under it."

Ajaya spoke up from behind them, "I'm going to track down Ronald. He's got your clean flight suits. Don't start the next treatment without me."

A layer of fine crystals sifted onto his hand. When they touched his damp skin, they swelled to form a dense mat. He rubbed it over himself experimentally. It was like a slippery, soapy glove that seemed to dissolve the residue left by the chalky substance. He wiped himself down then stuck out his injured hand, coating just his fingertips, and concentrated on his hair, which hadn't really been thoroughly washed for almost a year. He snuck a stealthy look at Jane. She was working the cleanser through her hair too. Her back was still coated in a fine sheen from the chalky shower and she seemed to be struggling with her hair, which had grown really long over the last year, despite the fact that she'd just lost a good chunk of it. He stepped back under the waterfall to rinse off.

"Ah, Jane?"

"What?"

"Need any help?"

"Definitely not." She sounded exasperated, maybe with a hint of amusement.

He grinned. "Oh, good. My back…a little help?" He thumbed at his own back.

He could hear her grumbling under her breath, but he couldn't make out what she was saying over the rush of the water. He clamped his own mouth shut.

"I'll scratch your back, if you scratch mine, eh?" she said sarcastically.

"Maybe," he said noncommittally.

She touched him then, tentatively at first, then with quick broad swipes. He immediately realized his mistake. Things were getting tumescent—way more than he wanted or could have anticipated. He cursed mentally and took a step forward. "Thanks," he said in a clipped tone and dived away from her back under the water. He hadn't felt that awkward since he was a teenaged boy. He contemplated asking her if she could make the water colder, but that would be too obvious. He'd better just get the hell out of there. Thank God Ajaya was still gone. She'd left a couple of fabric-looking things lying nearby, so he stepped out and grabbed one.

"Hey," Jane called playfully. "What about me?"

He held the soft cloth in front of himself as casually as he could. "Oh, you want me to—"

"Well, yeah. I'm sure my back looks just like yours did." She smiled shyly over her shoulder. *Oh, God. If she only knew how enticing she looks....*

She turned her attention back to her hair, tipping her head back under the water. She seemed to have miscalculated her angle as she stepped over the inclined floor under the flow of water. She was in profile now and that wasn't helping his problem in the slightest. She'd lost most of her Rubenesque roundness after the conditioning in Houston and the long flight, but what was left of it was still in all the right places. He couldn't help it. He was mentally filing the image away. It was just more fuel for the fantasies that filled his quiet moments.

His mind would wander and he'd find himself imagining Jane under him, moaning. Jane draped over him, satisfied. Jane pressed against a wall, her legs wrapped around him, kissing him as he.... He tore his eyes away and mentally cursed himself for being such a dick. She was going through some terrible thing and all he could think about was sex.

He tried to wrap the towel around himself, but that didn't actually conceal anything. The fabric was too thin. It was just comical. He looked around but couldn't see any other recourse. *Fuck.* He stood there another minute, trying not to look at her, trying to think through complex equations, baseball stats, conjuring images of dead puppies, anything that might make his problem go away.

"Anytime now, Alan."

Now? Now she decides to use my first name? Her back was to him again, so he stepped forward, dropping the towel, and loaded his uninjured hand with the crystals. He stayed well away from her and rubbed it over her back. She pulled her hair forward, out of his way, bowing her head. Her skin was unbelievably soft, smooth. He ran his hand over her shoulders and couldn't seem to stop himself from being thorough and getting it all, all the way down to her ass. He'd gone too far, surely, but she didn't complain, didn't move, just waited patiently.

He said in a strangled voice, "Your hair is, ah, still…."

She sighed and picked the tail of her hair off her shoulder, examining it. "I know. I can't get it clean. It was so dirty, I think it just soaked up that stuff."

He should turn around and walk away, but instead he offered, "I still have a lot of soap on my hand. I could—"

"Ok." She swung her hair back and it landed with a wet slap between her shoulder blades. Like him, she'd probably been a tow-head as a child, and couldn't give that up as she aged. The tips of her hair were still bright, golden blonde, the same color it had been when he'd met her, but as her hair had grown over the journey, it had grown in several shades darker.

He caught her hair in his hand and raked his fingers through it gently, trying to evenly distribute the cleanser.

This…this is a really bad idea.

"I haven't had long hair like this since I was a little girl. I'm not even sure how to take care of it properly."

"Really?" he squeaked. He was regressing, apparently. He cleared his throat. "I used to give my little sisters their baths sometimes. They hated washing their hair."

"That's sweet. How old were you?"

"I don't know. Probably ten or eleven." He reached up and smoothed his hand over the top of her head, still combing out the tangles with his fingers. He'd gotten closer somehow and could see the peaks of her breasts over her shoulder. He tried not to groan. If she so much as brushed up against him right now, he'd probably explode. Suddenly all the repressed need of the last year was crashing over him. It's not like there'd ever been an opportunity to take care of it himself. There were always five pairs of ears just inches away.

Oh, God this is torture.

What if I tell her I want her? Maybe she needs a little romp, too....

No. Don't be a moron. That would ruin everything.

"Maybe I should just dump a bunch of this stuff on my head and it'll come clean."

He barely registered that she'd spoken. Suddenly she was twisting, turning, reaching out to get more soap. He didn't have time to think, to react preemptively. She saw. Clearly she saw him in all his glory. She'd been less guarded, too, though, when she'd turned, showing herself fully to him as well.

He waited, stricken, to see what she would do.

She straightened and turned away very slowly. "Thank you. I think I can take it from here."

"Jane—"

Ajaya came bustling in. "How is it going in here?"

Oh, fuck. What next?

He moved back under the sluice of water. "Jane, the water's a little hot, can you adjust it?" he asked quietly.

"I...certainly." She reached out tentatively to touch a symbol. "How's that?"

The temperature changed instantly, but only by a few degrees. "More," he prompted. "A lot more."

"Ok." She tapped it several more times, glancing at him with a blank expression and hooded eyes.

"That's...good." He closed his eyes and stood there stiffly, letting the water do its work. He tried not to think about what had just happened, but wasn't terribly successful.

He'd always thought she secretly felt the same way, that the attraction was mutual. But now...her reaction...he wasn't sure. She was definitely straight-laced. She played by the rules. That would always be a factor. That's why he always knew he'd have to wait. The mission came first. He knew that logically, and yet, he'd always hoped that they might indulge themselves secretly at some point. He was too much of a hedonist to give up that hope, even now, faced with damn-near rejection.

They'd been lectured extensively in Houston about not giving in to what had been called "inevitable impulses," citing the potential impact on crew cohesion, performance, and mission success. Then there'd been the sessions where a cognitive behavioral therapist counseled the crew on strategies to cope with long-term abstinence. He tried to bring some of those strategies to mind now, but they hadn't been terribly memorable and he doubted they'd have been helpful in any case. He should have paid more attention at the time.

It didn't take long to cool off. He sauntered back to the discarded towel, dried off and cinched it around his waist, then occupied himself with poking around the room, which contained little of interest.

"I found these kimono-like garments that might do for the moment," Ajaya said, holding up a swath of khaki green fabric that could have been a bed sheet. "This is the smallest size I could find. These people must be quite tall and robust." Bergen slipped it on and wrapped it around himself. It was a thin, filmy material. The hem was below his knees and the sleeves were deep, to the waist. The tie was really long and slung very low. It was pretty ridiculous. He was completely over the whole process, ready to be done with it.

The computer's voice spoke again and Jane directed them back to the central room, then through a newly opened door. It was a fairly small room, dominated by another platform, this one squarish, waist-high, with just one large step in front of it. The platform itself appeared to be glass. At Ajaya's request, Jane queried the computer about the light therapy and said that it was commonly used for many types of skin afflictions. The wavelengths used were manipulated based on diagnosis. A drawer opened, revealing small oval pieces of greenish plastic that Jane said were eye protection.

"I'll just wait out here," Bergen said firmly, avoiding both of their gazes.

"It expects us to—"

"Well, I'll just skip it then. You have my clothes, Ajaya?"

Ajaya narrowed her eyes and stepped in front of him, picking up and examining his hand with a cool, professional air. "I think it would be a good idea to try the therapy, Alan. This burn is pretty severe. You could develop scarring that could impede the use of your hand."

"We don't know what kind of methodology they use. It could give us skin cancer for all we know," he countered.

Jane touched his arm lightly. "It's ok, Alan."

He sighed heavily. "Fine."

"Good. I'll wait out here and I expect a full report. This is quite exciting for me, you see. My graduate work was based on light therapy for psoriasis patients."

They stepped inside and the door closed behind them.

"Turn around," he said, more gruffly than he'd intended. She complied without comment and he untied the robe. "Are we supposed to stand up there or what?"

"We're supposed to lie on the glass. Another panel will lower from the ceiling to sandwich us between the lights."

"Great." He hopped up on the platform and stretched out on the surface. There was plenty of room for Jane and probably three other people. He draped the fabric of the robe over his privates, placed the slivers of plastic over his eyes, and said, "I'm ready."

Soon he sensed she was lying beside him. She said, "*Paratiso*," and there was a quiet whirring sound as the screen above them lowered. He lifted his hand, rapping his knuckles against it gently. It was hovering maybe a centimeter above his nose.

The glass warmed. Despite the eye protection, even with his eyes closed, he could see a faint magenta glow around the edges of his peripheral vision. He wondered how long this treatment would take, but he didn't feel like asking her any questions, so he stayed silent and spread the palm of his burned hand evenly over the glass.

"Alan?"

He sighed. "What?"

"You don't need to be embarrassed. It's a normal physiological response." She sounded crisp, rehearsed.

"I know that. We don't need to talk about this." This was why he never hung out with any individual girl for very long. He didn't like being drug through a bunch of emotional crap.

That didn't deter her. She continued, sounding less assured as she went on, "I know you saw the IUD. I just...I don't want you to get the wrong idea. I'm flattered. I am. But I'm not interested in casual sex. You...I just thought you should know that."

An IUD? Huh. He'd thought that was some kind of birth control, when he'd seen it. Her embarrassment seemed to confirm that. He wondered briefly if that had been her idea or NASA's. Then he realized that wasn't really the important part of what she was saying to him.

He needed to say something to her that struck some kind of balance between reassuring her and not shutting any doors. The minutes stretched out. What would sound like he was interested in having a real relationship with her, without sounding creepy after what just happened?

His voice came out a little harsher, a little more defensive, than he wanted. "You're reading way too much into this. I don't know anything about your female gadgets. I never made any assumptions about you. I don't see you that way, Jane."

"Oh—I didn't—I mean—you...."

He softened his tone. "Jane, you're a beautiful gi—" he caught himself, just in time, "—woman." He let out a breath from between tense lips. "Look, nothing I say right now is going to sound right. You know that, don't you? Can we just drop it, please?"

She snorted softly.

"You've got enough to worry about. You don't need to be thinking about...."

"I don't want to think about that either," she said quietly.

"I wouldn't either if some alien was mind-fucking me." He immediately regretted saying it. He was all riled up. He didn't know what he was saying anymore. He slid his left hand across the glass until he made contact with her...arm. Probably just her arm. He tapped it hesitantly with his fingertips, hoping she'd realize it was an apology.

"But he is doing it to you. I think he's doing it to all of us." She spoke softly, barely above a whisper, and her hand latched onto his suddenly, her grip almost painful.

He swallowed hard and squeezed back. "No, I'd know."

"Would you? How could he know everything that's going on? How could he know the trouble you and Walsh were in?"

"There must be sensors, cameras—"

"I thought so too, at first. But, he knew that when we went back into the capsule, I never said a word about what had happened to me to any of you."

A cold, uneasy feeling settled in his stomach. "Oh. Shit."

"Yeah."

He squeezed her hand again. "Well, so far he seems like a good guy. He's helping us, right? He helped you to get to us…in time."

He should probably tell her that it really had been barely in time—that he'd forgotten where he was and what he was doing a couple of times. He'd forgotten to share the air. He'd almost let go. But how could he tell her that—that seeing her face in that moment had been such a relief, that he owed her his life, that he'd do anything for her? He didn't know how to say that.

They went silent for a while. He let his hand go limp, but it remained in contact with hers. He wasn't sure what that meant to her. The light spectrum had changed at some point, he realized, was less intense, more red. He wanted to ask her to tell him everything, every detail that had happened to her from the first, but Walsh would eventually get to that and she shouldn't have to repeat everything three times. "Well, it's pretty effed up, but it's far better than what I expected to happen when we opened the hatch."

"What was that?"

"I was pretty sure there was going to be something really grotesque that was going to eat us. I thought they might play with us for a while, maybe, before they started tearing us limb from limb."

"You really thought that?"

"Yep."

"Then why did you want to go so bad?"

"Lifelong dream. Only opportunity and whatnot."

Her hand twitched. He imagined she was probably shaking her head, maybe even chuckling silently. "You must watch a lot of scary movies."

"Used to. Haven't seen a good flick in probably four or five years. Working too much. What was the last movie you saw?"

There was still laughter in her voice. "Hm. Can't remember. Probably some chick flick with my girlfriend, Sam. I didn't get out much."

"You weren't dating?"

"Since my divorce? No. I haven't dated since high school."

He hesitated, but he really wanted to know. "Why did you split up?"

"He's a lawyer. You probably knew that." She paused.

Maybe it was too personal. He shouldn't have asked.

But she continued, her voice sounding more melancholy. "One day I just realized he and I didn't envision the same future anymore. I began to feel like the time he spent with me was just another form of work. It felt like he was tallying in his head how many hours he was going to bill me for and I couldn't live like that anymore."

"He's an ass."

"He was involved with someone else within weeks. It had been over between us long before I came to that conclusion. I was holding him back."

"Jane—that's not true. He was being an idiot. You deserve better."

"We were kids when we got together. You can't know who you're going to turn into when you're seventeen. No, you—you've got the right idea. Perpetual bachelorhood. You get the best of all of it."

"Hardly."

"Oh, come on. Your place is a man-cave. You're quite a player. It must be fun."

He froze, clenching her hand involuntarily. "What? Who told you that?"

"Gene and Lisle when they came to visit from JPL."

Those bastards! He'd warned them to stay away from her. He sputtered uncontrollably, "They weren't there for a social call. They were there consulting, and I never left them alone with you!" *Crap.* Now he'd said too much. She had a way of bringing that out in him.

She chuckled, out loud this time. "No. You didn't. They joined me for lunch once when you were in an engineering meeting that they weren't required to attend. It was a very enlightening meal."

He had a new reason to make it through the mission alive. He had to get back to Earth so he could wring their geeky necks.

"They—they're not the most reliable witnesses," he said sourly.

Her voice was teasing again. It sounded delicious. "I could see that. They think you're a god."

"They do not. They both have girlfriends. Lisle is probably married by now. They don't know anything. They don't know what it's really like."

"What's it really like, Alan?" Her voice had turned husky. She was slowly stroking his middle finger with her thumb. His chest felt tight and his skin tingled—and not from the light. Why would she do that? *Dammit.* She was the queen of mixed messages. How could such a simple touch turn his brain to jelly? He could barely think.

"It's…I was thinking about getting a dog, but I work too much." What was this, some kind of confessional?

"Why not just settle down?"

He pulled on his arm a little and changed the position of his hand so she'd have to stop it. "I don't know how to…."

"Settle down? Just pick one and stick around for a while."

"That wasn't the problem. The problem was that I didn't know—I didn't know where to find the right one to do that with."

"Oh. That's not an easy one."

"No. I should have tried harder, I guess. It was too easy to just keep going the way I was going."

"Maybe when we get back, it'll be easier."

"That's the plan." He clutched her hand almost convulsively, hoping to transmit the message, hoping she was receiving it, interpreting it correctly.

She made a strange sound like a yelp and her hand yanked from his grasp.

"Jane? You ok?"

"Something's wrong. I think…."

"What?"

"I have to go. I'll be back soon."

"Jane, wait—tell me what's going on first!"

She didn't answer. He pulled on her arm, but she'd gone limp. "Jane?" He felt blindly for her shoulder, grazing—oh, crap—that was definitely a breast. "Sorry, Jane. Jane?" He pushed on her shoulder, but she wasn't responding. "Jane!"

His voice was drowned out by a blaring klaxon. He jerked, banging his forehead on the glass above them. He let out a string of curses. One of the eye pieces fell off and he realized that the lights had shut off and the screen was rising into the ceiling.

He sat up. The door opened and Ajaya peeked into the room.

"What the fuck's going on?" he demanded.

Ajaya looked bewildered. She shouted, "I've no idea. The lighting changed and then this alarm started."

He could see what she meant. The room beyond was cast in a reddish glow, making it seem darker, more sinister. He turned to look at Jane. She was slack-jawed.

"She's out again. I don't like this," he bellowed.

10

Jane relaxed her concentration and held back, before speaking. She'd expected to arrive in the casita but instead found herself in a cool place, obscured in shadow. She gradually became aware of limbs moving languidly in hushed, placid darkness.

Just as she registered this, Ei'Brai's voice rumbled in her head, startling her. "Dr. Jane Holloway, you seek my companionship. I am honored by your presence, gratified."

"How did I—"

"The mental connection—Anipraxia. It grows stronger. A portion of your consciousness and mine are converging on a single plane, a frequency, if you like. You learn quickly, navigate intuitively. This is auspicious."

"I was drawn here. I didn't...."

"Not so. You possess an inquisitive nature. You perceived a need and responded. You arrived here of your own volition."

She paused. He was right. *Oh, God, that's disconcerting.* "What...was that? I felt something."

"You sensed a minor hull breach. It has been contained. You are quite secure in your present location. There is no need for your attention to the matter. The squillae have been reordered, are containing the breach."

She would have to trust him on that point. She searched her mind for a translation of the unfamiliar word he'd just spoken. She frowned. The first word that came to mind couldn't be right. "Shrimp?"

A low, booming sound resonated in her mind and she smiled hesitantly. He…was he laughing?

Information poured into her consciousness. She couldn't discern if it was from the download he'd given her, as she made the mental connection with the unfamiliar word, or if it flowed directly from Ei'Brai. The boundary between her own mind and his seemed indistinct. Data streamed between them, she realized uneasily.

The veil of darkness lifted. A single, sedentary slug filled her vision. This was somewhere in the cargo hold. She could see it—not as she'd seen them from inside the room that morning—but, oddly, as though she were the wall itself that the slug was clinging to. Ei'Brai focused her viewpoint along a trajectory, zooming in ever closer on masses of swarming minute robots, working in concert. First, she became aware of one group forming a single microscopic layer between the slug and the void.

As each nanite was destroyed by the alkaline slime, another was already taking its place like soldiers on a front line, holding in the atmosphere and allowing the other machines to work unimpeded. Her point of view swung wide, to see others working to reconstruct the hull, micron by micron, protected from harm by the first group as they worked to effect repair. Ei'Brai commanded their movements. When the breach was detected, he removed them from other tasks, redirecting them to resolve the problem.

As she watched, some of the squillae emitted high-pitched sounds and the slug, disturbed, moved away, allowing them to work more efficiently. A thought occurred to her—why not command the squillae to attack the slugs directly and remove the problem outright, rather than repairing the damage they constantly wrought?

Ei'Brai answered, "Under Sectilius law, squillae are confined to inorganic repair except under rare, tightly controlled circumstances. Technology serves life. It does not destroy it. These lessons are rooted in the very foundations of Sectilius culture and law, without deviation, under threat of penalty of strictest nature. The slug population must be dealt with, but the squillae will not perform that duty."

Jane acknowledged this insight into Sectilius culture, still captivated by the movements of the minute machines.

"They're sacrificing themselves to keep us safe," Jane marveled.

"They are machines. Living beings do not make such sacrifices so readily."

She pulled her attention away from the squillae at work, sobered by the thoughts his comment evoked. "Sometimes they do."

"You contemplate your progenitor."

"My father, yes."

"A rarity among your kind," he said swiftly, as if he *knew*.

She felt anger quickening and quashed it down. She did not want him to speak of her father that way—casually, dismissively, but she had to remember her training. "What do you know of my kind? Why are you here?"

"You have many questions."

She was about to reply, to make demands, when she felt something cool flow over her in the darkness, like an eddy in a pool, sending her spinning. She was suddenly buoyant, lax, and free. She felt herself bob and lift to maintain her position. She'd lost her bearings. "What's happening?"

"Observe."

Lights flashed in the darkness—indistinct blobs, darting in the distance, sparking in cycles of magenta and cobalt. Then, she realized—she was seeing through someone else's eyes.

"My age-mates," Ei'Brai hummed. "Conveying danger in our most primitive form. Too weak, too small yet to communicate properly. We scattered, but it did not impede our capture."

She felt some kind of primordial panic, a pulsing squeeze, and frantic motion. She'd lost track of up and down and only knew the instinctive need to flee in random flails to evade whatever was in pursuit. She began to tire. Was she safe?

Her age-mates winked their fear.

She paused, confused, watching as they drew closer in an unnatural clutch, equidistantly spaced in orderly rows and columns. She inhaled with a great, fearful whoosh, preparing to take flight once again, when white light blinded her and she drifted, limp, uncaring, unknowing.

The world went dark again and Ei'Brai's voice buzzed gently. "I had never known confinement in my short existence. It was an affront. But, like you, I learned much, and quickly."

The light came on. Too bright. Jane wanted to squint, but her eyes couldn't do that. Instead, she darted back, trying without success to find some way to shield her sensitive eyes, and came up painfully against hard glass. Somehow she knew that this was like the day before and the one before that. She felt intense, primal loneliness, longing for home, freedom, and age-mates.

A creature came to look at her through the glass. It calmly watched her scrabble and dart, fruitlessly looking for refuge from the painful, artificial sun. It took up residence, like it always did, draping its angular body over the single structure in the blindingly-unnatural, white place.

It waited, like always. For what? What did it want from her? Again and again, day after day, it turned the soothing darkness into a searing blaze and waited. There was no end to the repetition of it.

Stupid, stupid being.

She hated it, hated its shrouded body, its way of moving, always upright, always in a single plane. She especially hated its steady gaze, interrupted periodically by the fleshy folds of skin covering over its tiny eyes.

Finally, she shouted at it—a single, negative bleat of rage. To her surprise, the creature rose. It moved out of her view for the first time and her world plunged into blessed, soothing darkness once again.

She timidly moved forward to peer through the glass. The creature slowly came back and faced her, inches away, but for the partition between them. The fleshy lips parted and she could see stony structures there.

She sensed its pleasure. She felt it, too. It was wonderful. She wanted more.

"That was the beginning," Ei'Brai murmured.

"That is...a man," Jane said incredulously. He could never blend in on Earth, yet he was startlingly familiar. He was tall, incredibly slight, with sharp, spare features. His proportions were distorted, every bone longer, thinner.

"Sectilius."

The man faded into black as they spoke.

"The people of this ship."

"Yes. A brilliant, prolific race with complex genetic variety. One of few borne of a rare planet-moon combination, both habitable."

Jane wrinkled her brow. "The Divided."

"Yes. The moon-race, adapted to the gravity of the low-mass moon, displays this phenotype. The planetary race's phenotype is far different. A world far larger than Terra gives rise to a shorter, denser form."

Images and snippets of data illustrating his point flashed through her mind. She was astonished at the diversity of body types that evolved after the peaceful civilizations on both worlds, having communicated for centuries via radio waves, finally developed the technology to routinely traverse the distance and interbreed.

"This man, he was teaching you—"

"To communicate with his kind before I'd learned to properly communicate with my own, yes. A great gift."

"The Sectilius speak to each other this way?"

"Only rarely. Masters of Anipraxia commit to many years of study. That was one such master—a high priest who devoted his lifespan to unlocking us, preparing us for service. My kind communicate over vast distances, over the span of my home world, effortlessly. I perceive your concerns, but you need not worry, Dr. Jane Holloway. You could not discern another's thoughts without my assistance."

He could sense that? Her worry, her fear that he was changing her into something that she didn't want to be?

"You were taken," Jane said. "Are you here against your will? Were you a slave?"

"I was taken, yes. Not as a slave. As an exalted guest. Had I evaded capture, inevitably I would have become a savage— a carnivore, consumed only with scrapping for food, grappling for a place within the hierarchy of my kind, struggling to maintain that position for a brief life expectancy. I would not trade my place for that feral existence. Not even now."

"But why did they do this to you?"

"Do you not take sentient creatures into service on your world? To perform tasks that exceed your own capabilities?"

She wasn't sure she fully understood what he was asking. She thought she knew what he meant, but cringed, uncomfortable with the answer she came up with. She felt like a school girl, put on the spot by a brilliant teacher that she was eager to please, struggling to think of a clever reply, but coming up short.

"The beast who pulls the cart? The dog who keeps watch over the flock? The cow, whose sole purpose is to manufacture surrogate mother's milk? Are they not utilized for a purpose, to fill a need?"

She agreed immediately, chagrinned that humans did not consider the animals he mentioned to be sentient. There seemed to be multiple layers of reality that humans were too self-involved to fully realize. It was mortifying. What else were they missing?

"As do I. I am the Gubernaviti." His voice rang with a smug note of narcissism.

"The governing navigator," she said hesitantly. "They need you to fly the ship."

"Just so."

"They can't do it without you?"

"Possibly. It is done, but rarely. No other race can perform to the same standard that the Kubodera have set."

"Kubodera?"

She sensed a physical swelling within him, growing as he spoke, literally puffing with pride. "The princes of the stars. We are harvested from a secluded world by a devout priesthood, tutored and enhanced, groomed from infancy to take our place at the heart of every ship-community. We are capable of multi-tasking at a level no hominid can match, interface easily with binary processors, and are capable of calculating with nearly the same efficiency and accuracy, should such systems fail. We are capable of making longer, more accurate jumps than any hominid species. Eons ago we proved ourselves to be far superior navigators to any other sentient species."

She felt awkward. What was she supposed to say to that? Did he expect some form of obsequience? Perhaps not, because he went on.

"For this we are adopted, embraced, and revered. In service and in leisure we extend Anipraxia to your kind. It is a great honor to be allowed to join Anipraxia with a Kubodera, to allow my mind to touch yours for our mutual benefit. The mating of minds goes far beyond any connection you have ever known, Dr. Jane Holloway. You sense this."

She did. She couldn't help but feel humbled, even as some aspect of her mind railed against his hubris.

And there was more. This encounter with Ei'Brai was very different. It was more than mere conversation. She was becoming more aware of his personality, getting glimpses of his world-view.

She sensed in him an emptiness that he wanted her to fill. There was no need to speak of it, because it was somehow glaringly obvious, pervasive in his every thought. She felt small and vulnerable in the face of it. What kind of commitment had she stumbled into? What did all of this mean?

"Allow me to demonstrate the wonder of it, Dr. Jane Holloway." His voice was somber, hushed. Could he perceive every fleeting thought? She felt a small measure of shame that she might be hurting him with her reluctance, with her fear.

The darkness burst into life. Stars. Unfathomable numbers of stars in gorgeous, nebulous heaps and clumps flooded the darkness with pricks of light. It was incredibly, undeniably vast.

She turned over and around, stunned by the views in every conceivable direction. "Is it the Milky Way?" she whispered.

"That is what you call it. And more. Far more."

Her throat ached. It was astoundingly beautiful.

"Choose one and we will go there."

"A star?"

He didn't answer. Instead, he revealed tantalizing promise in his mind.

A particularly bright star seemed to stand out to her.

"That is not one, but two stars—a binary system. Very intricate. Now take us there."

"I—"

"Do not contemplate what I ask, what it means, or how it is accomplished. Do not think at all. Merely do. Through me, it is possible. You shall see."

She mentally grabbed the star and tugged on it, in a way she somehow knew she could. She felt the change before she could see it. Her body shuddered with joy as she was stretched and pulled along. The nearest stars smudged and streaked, while those distant stuck like anchors, and together, she and Ei'Brai surged toward the twin stars. Space and time and breath parted and folded. They were sucked through a short straw and emerged in a haze of blinding dust. Jane wiped her eyes and coughed, laughing too, with delight.

The anchor stars receded. Her eye was drawn to the warmth, the light. Twin suns orbited each other, dancing and spinning and nearly kissing, their white light scorching hot. Their planets flirted with each other in long, lazy orbits, a mechanized waltz that had evolved over eons—over countless destructions and accretions until those that remained could each abide the presence of the others.

How could I know this?

"This system has no sentient life. It is unnamed. What will you call it?"

She couldn't tear herself from it. "I get to name it?" She felt deeply honored and searched her mind for something appropriate, reverent, reflective of herself and humanity. "Castor and Pollux. They were explorers, like me." How could she feel such pride in naming a thing that couldn't possibly be real, but was so utterly lovely that she throbbed with repressed sobs?

He let her linger, for how long, she had no way of knowing, observing from multiple points of view, to take it all in. There were barren rocks of planets. Gaseous planets, their atmospheres thick, nearly liquid, and whirling. Molten planets, endlessly remaking themselves under the friction of immense gravitational forces. Even a frozen planet—white and blue, looking from a distance not unlike Earth, but composed of ice and frozen methane, too far from the suns to feel their warmth.

Finally she turned away from it, sighing. "I cannot express how it feels to see this, Ei'Brai—"

"You need not. I am aware."

That disturbing reminder again. "Then you must also know that I'm aware that you're distracting me, deflecting me from what I really need to know."

The warmth on her back faded. She knew, without looking, that the twin stars were gone.

He was silent and she could sense little of him. He was guarding something.

"Why have you come here, Ei'Brai? What did the Sectilius want from Earth and what happened to them?"

157

His voice was pitched low, a guttural groan. He uttered four words, and fleetingly unleashed a tsunami of pain along with them, "I mourn them, still."

Jane recoiled under the onslaught, retreating from him instinctively to the furthest reaches of his mind, just to the tenuous point of disconnection. Regret followed hard on the heels of his misery, trailed by disjointed, chaotic images. Inside and outside of many minds, many viewpoints, she saw what had happened to the Sectilius.

In one moment, everything changed from organized, content symbiosis to some kind of hellish nightmare—as every man, woman, and child within the ship-community was suddenly and irrevocably changed by an unknown agent. Only Ei'Brai had been unaffected. He watched helplessly as his shipmates degenerated over the course of days.

Some became combative, at least at first. Most were simply mindless, unresponsive, until they ceased to function in any normal way and wasted away from thirst and starvation. He frantically assisted the scientists and medics, attempting to animate them with the sheer force of his will. Those individuals managed to hold out the longest, striving valiantly to determine what had happened in order to reverse it, but the discovery of the agent in their final moments hadn't been enough to save even a single life aboard the vessel.

Her heart wrenched painfully as she plumbed the depth of his agony. All of this had happened many years before. He'd drifted alone all this time, hoping for rescue, never knowing who had orchestrated the devastation. He replayed the events in his mind, looking for the point at which he had failed them, until he nearly went mad from it.

Empathy poured from her without hesitation. He gathered her thoughts and held them to himself like a child who'd just found a beloved lost doll. He seemed to be begging for forgiveness and she gave it freely, seeing no fault in his actions as they'd been displayed to her.

"But why did you stay?" she asked him softly. "Why didn't you go home? You're the pilot. Why stay here, alone?"

"It is not such a simple matter as that. I am not the pilot. I am the navigator. I, alone, cannot do what you suggest. The ship-community is a commonwealth. There are checks and balances, as there are in any democratic government. I do not have the authority to move this ship a single exiguumet without the presence of a Quasador Dux or a majority vote of documented citizens to give the order."

Quasador Dux? Loosely translated, the title meant admiral or general, but there was a distinct emphasis on a scientific component. Possibly, it meant some sort of chief investigator/scientist. The Sectilius leader? Ei'Brai indicated affirmation. "But, they didn't plan for every possible contingency?"

"There are measures. Elections, under normal conditions. A succession, if necessary, under martial law. Who could prepare for every Documented Citizen to be expunged in a single swipe? Who could foresee such a despicable act?"

"I don't know, Ei'Brai. I'm so sorry."

He sighed, an otherworldly, plaintive sound that conveyed his despair without words. "I fear for my brethren—that they may be stranded in isolated pockets of the universe, as I am. We shall all meet dusk before we may commune again, sharing the sight of the silhouette of Sectilia and Atielle against the radiance of their star."

Jane hesitated, knowing the answers to her questions must be negative, but needing to ask them nonetheless. "Why haven't they sent someone looking for this ship?"

"Either there is no one left to look, or they simply believe our mission took longer than anticipated." He was starting to sound less despondent, more in control again, as if she offered him some degree of hope. But what could she offer him besides companionship—and even that, only briefly?

"And there's no way to communicate?"

"The distance is vast. I will be long dead before any communication is received."

"The asteroid…do you know…?"

"In less than three orbital revolutions, it will make contact, obliterating this ship. Yes. I, alone, cannot prevent it."

The reality of that sank in. He was facing certain death, with little hope of reprieve.

She stayed quiet for some time, letting her presence offer comfort without demand, as she thought through all that he'd shared.

"You are not satisfied, Dr. Jane Holloway."

"Ei'Brai, we need to know why the Sectilius came here."

"The Sectilius are a pragmatic people. They value science, knowledge, truth, above all else. They have been searching for your world for a very long time. Many Sectilius have given their lives in the search for Terra."

Jane felt like she was perched on a precipice. She wasn't sure she wanted to know more. She could see bitter irony in Ei'Brai's mind. Still, she asked, "Why?"

"Ancient Cunabalistic writing indicates that the population of Terra could be the source of salvation."

11

Bergen was shoving his legs into the fresh flight suit Aja-ya had brought when Walsh and the others stormed in, their hair still dripping from their recent showers.

"What the hell is going on?" Walsh demanded.

"What makes you think I know the answer to that question?" Bergen countered irritably, as he slipped his arms into the armholes and zipped the suit up.

Walsh ignored that. "Where's Holloway?"

Bergen thumbed toward the small room where they'd had the light treatment. "She's out again. Ajaya's dressing her, I think."

Walsh's eyes narrowed on Bergen in suspicion. Bergen glared back openly.

Gibbs was oblivious to the subtext. "Did she say anything?"

Bergen shook his head. "Not really. She said something was wrong, that she'd be right back."

Gibbs looked worried. "How long ago was that?"

"I don't know. A few minutes? She said that and she was out. The alarm started seconds later." The alarm in question shut off mid-sentence and his last word rang out in the sudden quiet. They all glanced around nervously as the room's lighting changed back to its normal setting. All except Compton, Bergen noted. Compton looked unaffected, unconcerned, while the rest of them were clearly in freak-out mode again.

Ajaya emerged from the light treatment room, a grim expression on her face. "She's in the same state. I haven't been able to rouse her. I've tried everything I can think of—light, sound, even pain. Nothing I've tried has any effect."

Walsh rubbed his chin and lower lip with his hand and shook his head. "This thing—whatever it is—is playing some kind of game. It's picked out the weakest link and it's using her to control the rest of us."

Bergen bristled. "Weakest link? What the hell? She literally just saved our lives, you stupid fuck."

Walsh sneered in his face. "You think you're so fucking brilliant, don't you, Bergen? But you're so mesmerized by Holloway's sashay that you can't see it—she didn't save us. It engineered that whole scenario just to make her think she saved us—with its help. Get it? That's what's going on here. She's gullible enough to believe it—whereas the rest of us wouldn't have. That's why it chose her—not because she has some magical language power. This is a setup."

Bergen pitched his voice low. "I should've let you fall."

Walsh huffed and moved in closer. "Maybe you should have. You'd have done the little green guy a favor, because I'm the only one who can see what's happening here."

They were nose to nose. Bergen waited, his hands clenched at his sides, for Walsh to make a move, to say one more thing about Jane, anything, so he could smash that snide look off his face.

"All right, gentleman? That's enough." Ajaya pushed herself between them and Bergen allowed himself to be backed up, his eyes still locked with Walsh's. Gibbs was similarly moving Walsh out of range.

Ajaya positioned herself between them. "There is no doubt that we've found ourselves in an unusual situation. Fighting amongst ourselves will not resolve that. I don't know what's happening here. None of us do, for certain. We have options. We should explore them, plan a strategy based on what we know now."

Walsh grunted, leaning against a section of wall with few outcroppings, arms crossed. "That's easy. We go back to the capsule and fall back to Mars."

Gibbs and Varma exchanged shocked glances. Compton remained impassive.

Bergen shook his head, incredulous. "You can't be serious. We've been here for less than 24 hours. We haven't got what we came for."

"I disagree. We know what we're facing. We'll make our reports and leave the rest to the Bravo mission. They'll be prepared for this mind-game shit. This was never more than a scouting mission, Bergen," Walsh said.

Bergen forced himself to stay calm, to make measured arguments. "That's a helluva lot of time inside capsules for very little payback. We'll get back to Earth just weeks before they launch Bravo either way. Why rush it? The Mars window will be open for months. We can hunker down here, make some headway into the analysis of their technology. Come on, Compton, say something, here!"

Compton was unmoved. He had a stake in this. He was brought on board as a mechanical engineer. They'd worked together on the shuttle analysis team. He had to be as motivated as Bergen to stay. Was he formulating an argument? Or was he in on this with Walsh? He and Walsh went way back. They'd been on several missions together. Is that what his silence was about?

Gibbs spoke up, "Berg's got a point, Walsh. Why not give Jane a chance? Maybe this thing is testing us before it hands over the keys to the technology, or something."

"My objective was laid out clear—preserve human life. Don't risk everything for what could turn out to be a goddamn wrench."

Bergen threw his hands in the air. "A wrench? Seriously? They've got artificial gravity, Walsh. I think that's a little bigger than a wrench." He turned away from Walsh's condescending expression and banged his forehead lightly on one of the larger protuberances sticking out of the wall.

Ajaya extended a hand toward Walsh, appealing to him. "Commander, we've always known that Jane would likely be the only one who could communicate with anyone here. How is this truly different?"

"Oh, I don't know—maybe because she's unconscious? Because she's being manipulated? You all saw how scared she was. Whatever that thing is doing to her—she doesn't like it—but she's still going along with it. Doesn't that concern any of you?" He turned his attention to Bergen. "Do you really care what happens to her? Or is she just another piece of tail to you?"

Gibbs was ready, and pushed Bergen back. Bergen stood there, seething, with Ron's hands on his shoulders, physically keeping him from exploding.

Ajaya faced Walsh squarely. "Commander, I hardly think baiting Dr. Bergen makes for a convincing argument."

Walsh dismissed her with a wave of his hand and went on, "Do you seriously think we can trust anything she says or does now? Let the shrinks back home sort it all out. That's not our job. We were meant to find out what was here. That's it. We're done."

Bergen grit out, "If you're so sure we can't trust her, then why did we leave the vicinity of the capsule at all? And why didn't you report any of this with the last transmission to Houston?"

"That's simple. I don't intend on embarrassing Dr. Holloway any more than I have to. I had to humor her to determine if she'd actually made contact, or if she'd just lost it. Now, I can file my report. I don't know how I can make this any plainer—she's been compromised." Walsh took a few steps toward the door. "I'm going back to the capsule. I'm going to release the docking clamps and set a course for Mars. You can board that capsule, and be home in 17 months, or you can stay here and take your chances with Dr. Holloway's telepathic friend. The choice is yours."

"Now? Right now?" Bergen stormed through clenched teeth. "What's the rush?"

Walsh glared at him incredulously. "What do you think that alarm was about, Bergen? It's probably engineering another scenario for her to save us from, right now. It wants us running scared, dependent on Holloway. We've got to move before it can enact its plan. If you don't think these scenarios are going to escalate each time, you're crazy. That thing is going to ratchet up the stakes until one of us, maybe all of us, is dead."

Gibbs and Varma both seemed to be indecisive. Walsh was getting to them. Compton looked like he was falling asleep on his feet. What the hell was up with him? He normally contributed some kind of tidbit that everyone thought was the sage voice of experience.

Bergen said, "That's speculation. You can't know that. I can't believe that the brass in Houston don't expect us to put more time and effort into this. We've barely seen anything—just a bunch of tanks and crates and an infirmary. We need to give this more time."

"Your input is noted, Dr. Bergen. This is my call. Compton—go get Holloway. We'll take turns carrying her."

Compton blinked, but didn't move.

Walsh sidled up to Compton. "You got something you want to say, Tom?"

"Hm?" Compton roused himself and inhaled sharply. "You say something, Commander?"

Walsh took a step back like he'd been slapped, his eyes roving over Compton's face.

Ajaya moved in. "Thomas? Are you feeling well?"

Compton smiled, a slow, sloppy grin. "Sure. Whadaya need?"

She took a pen light out of her pocket and flashed it in Compton's eyes. "What were you thinking about, just now?"

His eyebrows crept up and his features contorted into a leer. "You sound like a girl I once knew."

Ajaya didn't hide her dismay.

Gibbs put his hand on Compton's shoulder. "Is the alien talking to you inside your head, Pops? Like it is with Jane?"

Compton made a face like that was absurd. "What? No."

Walsh motioned them away from Compton, who didn't notice or mind. "Do you see? It's already starting. We've got to get out of here before all hell breaks loose."

Gibbs and Varma nodded.

Bergen was so unnerved by Compton's unsettling behavior, he kept silent.

Walsh went out to check that the hallway was clear. Gibbs went for Jane while Varma coaxed Compton toward the door.

Bergen stood there, clenching and unclenching his fists. They didn't have the big picture, yet, he felt sure of that, but Walsh was right about one thing—it seemed pretty clear—all hell was about to break loose.

12

Salvation? Dread filled Jane, a cold, paralyzing feeling. "From what?"

"The Interspecies War. The Sentients from all corners of the known galaxies fight for dominance, for control of habitable worlds. Terra is untouched by this, due to its remote location. It was our hope to find you ready to answer the call." It was clear from his mood, his tone, that he deemed Earth exceedingly unready to answer this call.

Jane was reeling. "Are you serious? Earth will bring salvation from a war? But how? Why? I don't understand."

"Your species is such a curiosity. You thirst for knowledge of the origins of life, but fill in the unknown with imagination. It is peculiar that the Cunabula should withhold from your kind that which is commonplace among the rest of us. Perhaps they intended that hunger for knowledge to inspire you to reach out, to search."

"Tell me about them," she urged him.

"It is said they were a people without humor. Now that I have become acquainted with you and your colleagues, I am inclined to disagree." He rumbled with something akin to laughter. Waves of amusement washed over her.

She anchored herself, holding giggles at bay that were perilously close to breaking the surface. His moods affected her so easily when they shared this state. "Ei'Brai—you digress."

"A common accusation, you will find, in time. I have missed the company of others." He paused in reflection. "They are the oldest of the known races—arisen, it is said, from the farthest reaches of the universe, where the oldest stars are now burning out and dying—their light still illuminating from such distance, just as the Cunabula still bestow their influence, though they may be long gone. It is said they were bipedal, quad-limbed, yet not derived of apes, but some other species, lost to the ages. They were scientists, perhaps not unlike the Sectilius. They mastered the physical sciences primarily and began, thus, to explore the stars, seeking out life, much as you have wanted to do. They observed, made alliances, and catalogued all that they encountered."

"But what does this have to do with Earth?"

"It is said the Cunabula began to see disturbing trends, species arising with greater aggression, seeking dominance over all—to the point of precipitating extinctions of more peaceful, benign races. 'Evolution is inevitable, yet diversity shall be pinnacle, even to that.' That is a quote, as often taught to school children, from a text attributed to them. They worked tirelessly to forestall the aggressors. The histories say that, to that end, they set their sights on mastering the biological sciences.

"The earliest forms of genetic transmission at that time were more primitive, confined primarily to three types, found throughout the cosmos. What you now call DNA,

RNA and mitochondrial DNA once existed each to its own realm. They combined these three elegant systems, creating a more robust form of life, fit for their own purposes, in order to disseminate it as far as their reach would allow.

"They seeded barren planets with this genetic information, programmed by their deft handiwork to explode into lush worlds, like your own—where the genetic information could subdivide and increase at will, filling every niche with extraordinary, diverse life.

"You see, we—all of us—are alike at our core. From the lowest microorganism to the highest form of Sentient, we share the most basic aspects of all living things from protein folds to cellular organization. The secrets lie within the dual nature of intron and exon—expression and suppression and recombination of these—allowing life to seek infinite forms.

"It is within this duality, and the two strands of DNA, that are the source—and an Ark to usher that duality safely into worlds devoid of life—two of each?—two *strands* for each kind. Your kind misunderstands the literal nature of it, obscured in the unknowing, in the infancy of your science, in your violent, primitive history. But it resides there, within the collective psyche, despite the fact that you cannot name it.

"The Cunabula continued thus, through the eons. Growing wiser, depending on their legacy as a defense against the growing giants, always grasping for more space, never satisfied. The Cunabula turned the tide with their cleverness, with sheer numbers.

"It is said they favored the ape-derived hominids as being most like themselves, though their many gifts extended to so

173

many races that hardly seems likely—my own race being a perfect example of this. Regardless, it is your form they must have felt would be the one that would hold the line in the final fight. Some say Terra was nothing more than a social experiment. Others give it rich religious significance. Only the Cunabula know the truth of it and they are not here to tell us."

"A social experiment? I don't understand."

"History suggests the Unified Sentient Races of that time had suffered a terrible setback. They longed for peace, but the hungry evil would never allow it. The Cunabula revisited their young, seeded worlds, seeking the fittest, the strongest. They found, on Terra, several races of ape-hominids developing into species with much potential. Terra was remote, distant from any busy nexus or hub. It is said they took the most promising ape-races from several worlds—nine in total, the texts tell us—and put them in competition for the resources of your world. They adjusted their genetics, amplifying aggression, entitlement, the drive to expand to all borders, making the need to lay claim to land as urgent as the need to reproduce—all attributes rampant among the enemy, but only mildly expressed among the majority of the Sentients of the time. These races competed, interbred, struggled for dominance. It was perhaps unexpected that you would not be prodigies to the stars—turning instead to subjugate your own kind and to war amongst yourselves. An oversight? Perhaps you required more guidance. Left to your own devices, you disappoint."

"Oh, my God." There was a truth to this story that reso-nated. It felt more true than any Sunday sermon she'd ever been forced to attend by her pious grandparents.

"Many believed Terra was a myth—that the Cunabula in-tended us to search for you, in order to expand our bounda-ries and search for alliances, rather than be complacent or accept the inevitable. There have been Sectilius searching for you for all of recorded time. Now we have found you and still we have failed."

"But what did the Sectilius intend to do?"

"Bring you into the Alliance."

"But how? Are there Sectilius on Earth now?"

"Alas, no. We were implementing the early stages—learning about your culture, gathering specimens—"

"What kind of specimens?"

"Humans, of course. A necessary step. It was decided that a group of Sectilius would be surgically altered to pass among you, to infiltrate your governmental-militaristic-industrial complexes, to gain trust before revealing their ori-gins and goals. Specimens were needed to study certain fea-tures of human anatomy and physiology. We did not harm them. They were returned." He sounded affronted in the face of her revulsion.

"The universe is insane. The shuttle—the crashed shuttle in New Mexico—that was Sectilius too?"

"Indeed. The inhabitants were en route to Terra when...."

"Oh. I see."

"Yes. It led you here, however. Perhaps all will be well, Dr. Jane Holloway." Hope surged in him again.

Jane felt dazed. She struggled to make sense of everything she'd just been told. "We were meant to be this way. Not to fight the worst aspects of our nature, but to embrace them."

"Just so. To exploit your inherent qualities, in the service of others. It is the belief of many that they hoped to create a warrior class that would turn the tide, yet leave their brethren to live in peace. To respect the diversity and protect it."

"But they abandoned us. They didn't follow through."

"A mystery, true."

"It's too much to ask. They poisoned us. We're not...happy."

"Many suffer. Many exceed these limitations. Be grateful it is the Sectilius that found your world first. Not the Swarm."

Jane gasped. She inhabited the memory of a young Sectilius woman, fighting to squeeze herself and her children into an escape vessel. A fearful mob crushed them, bruising skin, cracking bones, in the desperate struggle to survive. Shielding one child in her arms, another clinging to her waist, she could smell the coppery scent of blood. She could hear the clamor of the anguished, the plaintive. And over that, a deafening, ominous roar.

The sky darkened and lowered, pressing down, a blanket of flashing, metallic bodies streaming over every living thing like locusts. The hatch closed, severing limbs, and the vessel was away, sluggish, overburdened by a mass of frail, living mankind. Children cried. Men and women keened. She watched through the small portal in the hatch as her world disappeared forever under the gnashing jaws of the Swarm.

"No!" she cried out, involuntarily—an outraged denial—and she wasn't sure whom it came from—the woman who had lost too much—or from herself. She could not unsee the violence she had witnessed. She could not unknow the pain or terror.

She curled into herself, ineffectually trying to protect herself from the horror.

"Dr. Jane Holloway," Ei'Brai purred, buoying her into a warm embrace, tendrils of soothing thoughts flowing over her and through her mind. She began to breathe again, in strangled, gasping sobs as the tightness in her chest slowly subsided.

She choked out, "Why would you show that to me?"

"I could not allow you to trivialize the need. This is what we face."

Images continued to trickle through the connection with Ei'Brai, gentler now, more like a documentary than first-hand experience. They seemed less immediately threatening. Her pulse slowed.

Immense insectile creatures sunned themselves on a hillside. The scale was astonishing. The group of arthropods, all the size of elephants, roused themselves, lifting armored carapaces and unfolding monstrous leathery wings. They took flight, hunting a herd of a deer-like mammal. The deer didn't stand a chance. It was over in moments.

"The Swarm is a formidable foe. They developed first as you see here, large-scale, flying insects, dominating their home world, carnivorous and ruthless, with little to keep them in check. Their population reached unsustainable, peak levels, their food supply over-hunted to extinction. It might have meant the end of their species, or merely a chance for another species to rise to dominance. Then a single individual was born with a mutation that allowed it to seek prey under the surface of water."

A graphic formed behind her eyes—a 3-D, transparent depiction of the insect's anatomy, highlighting some kind of swim-bladder. "That individual survived to procreate, to create a new lineage that was more versatile. They ravaged their home world eon upon eon, populations rising and falling, multiple adaptations allowing them to consume more and more of their world, until the day came that that world could no longer sustain them."

There was a large group of them diving in concert, scooping up sea-life, then basking on a sandy shore. The sequence changed smoothly from image to image showing the gradual changes in the insect's evolving morphology. Words like 'hydrolysis,' 'storage organ,' and 'organic fission reaction' were highlighted along with various parts of the arthropodal anatomy, now very much changed from its original form.

Ei'Brai showed her a sandy ocean floor. A school of large fish swam into view. The sea-floor lifted as one. As far as the eye could see, streamlined aquatic insects rose from under the sand to devour every fish in sight.

"They move in concert, like hive insects," Jane murmured.

"Indeed."

The insects rose to the surface in formation and soared into the sky, higher and higher into the clouds, leaving thin, white jet-trails behind them. As they gained altitude, their numbers became fewer as those who could not sustain the velocity needed to escape gravity dropped off. Only a few broke free of the atmosphere. The viewpoint zoomed in to reveal one of them was female with a fully mature egg-sack attached.

They drifted through space, homing in on another blue-green sphere, the moon of another planet in the habitable zone of that solar system, also rife with life. One individual survived the heat and stress of reentry. A male. He found the dead female, fertilized her eggs, then began to hunt.

"A new species was born, their unique adaptations allowing them to eventually move between stars—to consume a world's resources and lay eggs for the next generation of devastation to begin. They do not give themselves a name, do not communicate with their prey, never acknowledge sentience in another species. It is unknown if they have language or culture. The Sentients have given them the name, the Swarm."

Jane shuddered.

"Your kind considers outsiders to be alien. The Swarm is truly alien, without conscience or soul. There is no other consideration for them, beyond sating hunger."

The lesson was over. The shadowy darkness returned.

"You knew that woman? The one in the memory?" Even as she spoke, she knew the answer.

"She was the Quasador Dux of this vessel. She gave her life to find your world."

"After surviving that...she.... I don't know what to do with this. What am I supposed to do now?"

"Bring her voice to your people. Make ready."

"I don't know how I could ever make them understand this. It's not like I can show them the things you've shown me. All I can do is describe it. How can that ever be enough? They won't see it the same way. They'll want to protect themselves. They'll want to stay in hiding, here, where we're safe."

"You will convince them. There is no other way. Safety is an illusion. You know this to be true."

"I…do."

"You must go. Your companions have need of you. Tell them of this, Dr. Jane Holloway."

"Ei'Brai—I—you should call me Jane."

"Without your earned title? I will not be so disrespectful as this. Shall I call you Dr. Jane?"

"No. It's a gesture of—"

"Ah. Friendship. I see. Quaint. You will understand if I insist on using my own title?"

She let out a single, baffled laugh at this.

Indignation rolled off of him in waves. She could see plainly in his mind that the prefix Ei' indicated his high status and rank, earned over many years of faithful service. "Of course. It's short and to the point."

"Indeed."

She withdrew slowly, tentatively, feeling her way back, and gradually became aware of jostling movement and discomfort. There was something hard jammed into her midsection. Was she upside down?

"Aughpf," she wheezed, trying to orient herself. A hand tightened…on her ass? "What the—?"

"Sh," someone hissed in the dark.

Apparently she was being carried, bodily, over someone's shoulder. That person stopped moving and stooped. She slid down slowly, becoming aware, as she did, of a familiar, masculine scent. Her eyes adjusted to the dim light, but she already knew she was face to face with, pressed tightly up against, Alan.

His bearded cheek slid over hers, his breath warm against her ear. *Good grief, he feels good.* She hadn't been held like that for far too long.

"Are you ok? You were out for hours," he whispered. He sounded worried.

She answered in kind, a million questions tumbling over themselves inside her head. Why was he carrying her in the dark? Why was he embracing her so ardently? Why did everything change every time she turned around? Where the hell were they? That one, at least, she thought she might be able to answer. "Yes, yes, I'm fine. What's going on? Why were you carrying me?"

"It's Walsh. I fell behind, but he'll notice soon. He's flipping out, Jane. He wants to retreat to Mars already. He's trying to get us back to the capsule, but, well, I think you know you're the only one who can do that. We're lost. He's tried several times to use the deck-to-deck transport, but he has no idea how to select the right deck. He—"

"Keep up Bergen!" Walsh's voice rang out sharply. The light from a flashlight blinded her momentarily. She heard some quiet cursing and heavy boot steps, heading their way.

Alan squeezed her tightly and murmured in her ear before releasing her, "Careful, Jane. Walsh doesn't trust you."

"What? Why?" But there was no time for him to answer.

"So, Holloway, what do you have to say for yourself, now?"

She drew herself up straight and turned away from Alan, shielding her eyes with a hand against the glare of the flashlight that Walsh had aimed directly at her face. She had a quick insight into why this hallway was dark—Ei'Brai did not approve of this excursion. "Why does that sound like an accusation, Dr. Walsh?"

"What have you been doing all this time?"

She took a step toward Walsh. He tensed, his posture defensive. She slowly reached out and pushed down on the flashlight, aiming its bright focal point a little lower, so she could see. "I was doing the job I was recruited to do—communicating with our host. What about you? I thought we agreed we were going to make camp in the medical facility?"

"Things have changed."

Jane darted cautious looks at the others. They all looked uneasy. Walsh was adroitly using his military background—they were more comfortable with his leadership style. Technically, she was supposed to have taken command under any scenario where the Target was inhabited, but all that changed with the new orders from Houston and he was capitalizing on the lack of a clear chain of command. Nothing had gone according to any of the plans they'd laid out at Johnson. Nothing.

"I didn't know you were such an impatient man."

"Not impatient. Practical."

"Is that why we're eleven decks away from the capsule?"

Walsh's eyes narrowed. Jane studied the others' reactions. Was there hope they'd hear her? Alan stood behind her. He'd warned her; she could count on his support. Gibbs looked conflicted. Ajaya was watchful, frankly assessing the situation. Tom seemed strange, blank.

Walsh spoke, distracting her from Tom. "Am I supposed to believe you know exactly where we are? Just like that?"

"I know precisely where we are. This level is primarily crew quarters." Jane gestured at a nearby door. "Through that door is a cafeteria."

Walsh nodded at Gibbs, who then cautiously opened the door, then stepped inside. The lights came on, illuminating a vast room full of an eclectic mix of tables and chairs of various shapes and sizes, in the same murky green as everything else in the ship.

Jane took a step toward Walsh. "Is this exploration or escape?"

Walsh's lips tightened. No one said anything.

"Escape, then. From what, exactly? There've been no threats from the alien—quite the opposite."

"I disagree."

"What are you basing that opinion on?"

"This is pointless. I have no way of knowing if I'm even talking to Jane Holloway."

"What are you talking about? That's ridiculous."

"Is it? You said yourself he's inside your head. Even if you're you, there's no way you can be objective."

"That's simply not true. Look, you haven't given me a chance to explain anything. There's a lot as stake here. This is bigger than all of us. Bigger, even, than Earth."

"I'm sure it is. I'm sure he's told you how he's a victim of circumstance. How he needs your help to survive."

"He—I...." Jane took a step back, nonplussed, and glanced at Alan. He had a thunderous expression on his face.

Walsh pressed his advantage, "He's told you you're special, you're the only one who can make a difference, you have to convince everyone what he says is true. He hurts you and then he makes it better? Right?"

"You don't know what he's said to me," she retorted hotly, trying to mask her confusion while she figured out what was actually happening.

"It's classic Stockholm conditioning, Holloway. I can see it all over your face. Everything I've just said is true."

"You're twisting everything before I've even said a word. NASA—"

Walsh spoke over her, cutting her off. "I'm trying to protect you. I'm trying to protect all of us. I don't know what that thing wants. None of us do—least of all you."

"It's not like that, dammit! I'm not going to allow you to discredit me this way. Is this going according to plan? No. I can understand how that would make you uneasy. You aren't in the loop. You don't know what's going on. That's scary. I get that. But, we can't run away from this. We can learn so much from him. This is an opportunity of a lifetime—"

"It's going to be a very brief lifetime, if we stay here," Walsh cut in acidly.

Bergen surged forward. "Quit bullying her. Let her talk."

Jane grabbed him by the arm and pushed him behind her before things escalated out of control. She filled her voice with conviction. "Listen to me—this ship has been vacant for decades. There's been no one here to perform routine maintenance, so some things have gotten out of control. We can work around that. We can perform the maintenance, if necessary. We can still do what we came here for—we can learn about the technology. You're all capable of meeting this challenge. You're experts at the top of your fields— electronics, computers, engineering. I think that if we worked together, diligently, we could learn to fly this ship. We could take it home, with his help. We don't need to shut ourselves up in the Providence for another year and a half. We don't need to run. We can do this. This is why we're here."

Ajaya spoke up for the first time. "Is this what he's telling you, Jane? Is this what he wants?"

Walsh was shaking his head derisively, but stayed silent.

She raised her chin, refusing to back down or try to deceive them. "Not directly, no. He's not like us. He doesn't speak plainly about anything. But, yes, I think that's what he wants."

Gibbs asked, "Why isn't he doing the maintenance?"

"He can't. He's not...he's integrated into the ship somehow, stuck in one location. He can't move around the ship."

Ajaya said, "But, what purpose does he serve here, then?"

"He's the ship's navigator. Look—you all have to learn the language and then you can ask him all the questions you want. You can talk to him like I do. There's a language lab on this deck. It's meant for adolescents, but there's no reason why I can't use it to teach you. We can use these crew quarters. We don't even have to go back to the capsule for supplies—there's plenty of food here. We could thrive here—do work that will go down in history. Just give me the chance to show you. Trust me. I want us to succeed."

Walsh glared at her. "If you're so sure it's safe here, tell me, Holloway—why is he the only one left?"

Jane breathed deeply and squared her shoulders. "I won't gloss over this. He trusted me with the truth and I'll share it. The universe is a dangerous place. We—Earth is completely unprepared. If we don't get up to speed, our home and everything and everyone we love could become food for another species. The people that came here inside this ship were peaceful scientists. They were looking for allies against these kinds of predators. They intended to help us prepare to fight. They all died trying to bring us this knowledge. Someone didn't want them to find us first. Someone engineered some kind of disease that wiped them out, all at once, before they could make contact with us."

Ajaya was instantly concerned. "A disease? What kind of disease?"

"I don't know. They all just stopped functioning—all at the same time, all brain activity blocked, and they died of starvation within days…. What?"

They all looked alarmed, every last one of them. And they all turned to look at Tom Compton, who was standing there, staring off into space, drooling.

13

"Tom?"

Bergen watched as Jane approached Compton slowly and touched his arm. Tom didn't respond to her.

She turned, stricken. "What happened?"

"It sounds like you know more about it than we do," Walsh uttered with slow, menacing calm.

She opened her mouth to speak, and shut it again, pivoting back to Compton. "Tom?" she said, shaking him gently. She touched his sagging face. Nothing happened. He didn't make eye contact with her. "Oh my God. What do we do now?"

Ajaya said urgently, "Jane—how is this disease transmitted? Are we all exposed?"

Jane turned, her eyes glittering with unshed tears. "I don't know any of the specifics. I'm just a linguist. I'm so sorry."

"Holloway," Walsh boomed. "This is why we have to get out of here. Before something worse happens. Can you get us back to the capsule?"

Jane was slowly shaking her head. "Yes, but...."

Ajaya cut in, "Commander, if this is contagious, we can't risk returning to Earth and exposing the population there."

"They'll put us in quarantine," Walsh countered, irritably.

Ajaya scowled and snapped, "We don't know what the vector is. Just getting through the atmosphere may be enough to transmit it to Earth. We don't have the right to risk that. It sounds like we'll be dead long before we get there, anyway.."

"Ei'Brai said they found the agent just before they…. It wasn't enough to save them, but it could save us. We—he—he'll help us. We'll figure this out." Her voice trembled as she spoke.

"No!" Walsh grated at her. "Don't you see? That's what he wants. He's pulling the puppet strings, through you. I can't stop you from going back there. I'm asking you—no, I'm ordering you—do not go back there, Holloway. I don't believe any of this is real. This is a mind game. He's amused by us. We're like zoo animals to him. We're going back to the capsule and then we're going home, goddamn it."

"I don't know, I don't know…." she murmured.

Walsh grabbed her arm roughly. "Pull yourself together, Holloway! You're the only one who can read the symbols. We need you to get us back."

Jane looked shattered.

Bergen couldn't hold back anymore. He shoved Walsh away from Jane. "That's enough! She heard you. Lay off her." Walsh took a swing at him that almost made contact, but Bergen's reflexes were faster. He ducked and barreled into Walsh, shoulder down, knocking Walsh stumbling back into the wall. Bergen took a step back and waited. Walsh was staggering to his feet and coming back for more when Gibbs and Ajaya pulled them apart.

"Come on, man, this isn't helping anything," Gibbs chided.

Ajaya shot him a censorious glare. Walsh was shrugging her off, pushing away any attempts at checking him over.

"Where's Holloway?" Walsh snarled.

Bergen's heart stopped. She wasn't in the immediate area anymore.

Gibbs shone his light up and down the corridor. Jane was curled up some distance away, back against the wall, knees drawn up to her chin, head on folded arms.

"By God, if she's gone there again," Walsh spat.

Ajaya turned him away, murmuring in placating tones.

"Jesus, Berg. I think you better go talk to her," Gibbs said, tilting his head toward Jane.

Bergen nodded agreement and sauntered over to her. She didn't react. He settled down next to her, mimicking her pose. She didn't stir.

Was she there?

Her hair was spilling over her face. Normally smooth and neat, it had dried in long, lanky waves. He reached out a hand to pull it back so he could see her expression. Her grey eyes gazed back at him with a bleak expression.

"It's a symptom," she said softly. Her eyes shut tight, wrinkling with strong emotion. She sat up. "I…didn't realize at first, because you two bicker so much,"

"What?"

"Some of the Sectilius became aggressive before they succumbed to the illness. They were peaceful people, yet in those moments, some of them came to blows over nothing. They knew they were fighting something, they just didn't know what. It manifested like this. Ei'Brai showed me."

He shook his head. He'd been hoping for an opportunity to throttle Walsh for months. "Jane—"

She shook her head and looked anguished. "I don't believe that he's bad or evil. Am I crazy? Am I a fool?"

"No," he said firmly.

She pressed her lips together in a tight line. "Ajaya's right. We can't go home like this."

He stretched his legs out and tried to relax. He'd been carrying Jane for over an hour. This was a welcome break. "I know."

Gibbs withdrew the light as they spoke, leaving him and Jane in near darkness. The others were breaking for a meal. Ajaya must have convinced Walsh to give Jane some space. She was occupied with trying to feed Compton. They were huddling around the glow emanating from the open doorway.

Bergen huffed. Why didn't the idiots just go inside and leave him alone with Jane?

Jane said, "We do have to go back to the capsule—but not to leave. We have send a transmission to Mission Control, as soon as possible. I have to tell them everything Ei'Brai told me, everything we know, in case we don't make it back. The future of Earth may depend on this information. They'll be ready, then, when they send the Bravo mission. They'll be able to protect themselves. We have to give them a fighting chance."

He nodded slowly, agreeing with her. "Ok. How do you want to handle that?"

"I think...oh, God, this is awful." She had her hands clasped together and she ran the knuckles of her thumbs up and down her forehead from the bridge of her nose to her hairline, rhythmically. "I thought Walsh understood, that he could see the value, the potential. But everything's changed. Now I can see that won't work. Walsh—I suspect, from the moment I first lost consciousness—has decided I'm unfit."

She met his eyes, seeking confirmation. He gave it. She was right.

She took a deep breath and let it out slowly. "I'll pretend to go along with Walsh's wishes. It'll be easier that way. Aja-ya will be with us. She knows what's at stake. We just have to figure out where Ron's loyalties lie, without tipping Walsh off. We have to know if he'll fight us, or help us with Walsh. If we have to, we'll use a weapon." She swallowed and looked panicked for a moment, but quickly concealed that. "Then we'll find a laboratory. We have to try to solve this. I want to go home."

"Me too."

He was painfully aware that this moment might be the only chance they would ever have to be together in any sense whatsoever, now. He snuck his arm behind her and she leaned against him, the top of her head against his cheek. He swallowed thickly. He still didn't have any idea if she felt the same way. It seemed like maybe she did. Or was this just friendship to her?

"Are you...do you feel normal?" she murmured.

"I feel fine." He did. He couldn't sense anything out of the ordinary happening. If the disease was doing anything to him, he was blissfully unaware of it.

"I do too. Walsh and Ajaya seem a little different to me, though. Ajaya doesn't lose her temper. Ever. She just yelled at Walsh. And Walsh…."

"Yeah. I noticed."

"I'm sorry, Alan. You seem different too." Her voice broke.

He squeezed her tighter. She thought he was doing this because of some germ? "No. I'm fine. I'm telling you, I'm thinking clearly. I'm ok."

She moved slightly, glancing at him then back down. "Ok. I just…Alan, it's not like you, it doesn't seem like it's in your personality to believe the kind of things I've been saying. I just, I would expect you to be more skeptical. It's scaring me a little bit."

"You've presented plenty of evidence, Jane. It's fucked up. It's weird. But, I believe you're communicating with him."

"I know, but it seems to me that you would be more likely to side with Walsh in this."

"No. I trust you. I trust your instincts."

"But why? Walsh has more experience—he's done tours in Afghanistan and Iraq. He's been in tight spots before. He's a good leader. He's a hero. I'm not anything like him."

"He was following orders. He had military training to rely on. But you didn't have any kind of backup when you were tromping through the jungle, trying to survive. You didn't have anything or anyone to depend on except your wits and your gut. That's what got NASA's attention, Jane. It's why they wanted you to lead this mission. It's why I'll follow you to hell if I have to."

He was thinking specifically about an essay Jane had written about her experience in the Amazon, in which she'd described how she'd been searching for water, in a febrile state, unaware, that after uncounted days of wandering, encountering one bizarre, dangerous situation after another, she and her companions had wandered fairly near a paved road. She encountered a woman washing clothes beside a stream.

The woman was mistrustful, had never seen a person with blonde hair before. Bergen was pretty sure most people in such a dire situation would have just prostrated themselves, begging, when they finally found another human being that wasn't immediately hostile. Somehow Jane knew that would just scare her away. Instead she'd calmly sat down some distance from her, quietly asking questions to determine if they shared a language in common. When they settled on some kind of pidgin version of Portuguese, she didn't ask for help or food; she complimented the woman's infant and offered to help her with her chore.

When the woman left, Jane laid down next to the stream to gather strength before returning to her companions with the hopeful news that they were near a village that might be sympathetic to their plight. She awoke surrounded by native men, who, after a few confusing hours of propositions, bitter cups of local tea, and the first food she'd eaten in days, led her to the road and salvation.

Jane sat up, searching his face in the dim light. He reached out to stroke his thumb slowly over her cheek, and leaned in to kiss her. She stiffened. Her lips were lifeless under his.

He was taken aback, suddenly insecure about his instincts. He'd felt certain, in that moment, that he'd felt something from her, some kind of encouragement.

He pulled back, mumbling an awkward apology, when he felt her fingertips on his face, in his hair, and suddenly she was kissing him back, fervently. His stomach tightened in response and his pulse raced. He turned her, slightly, so that he was hunched over her, shielding her. If the others glanced at them, they might wonder, but it wouldn't be obvious, he didn't think.

He touched his tongue to her lips, a question. She opened to him, deepening the kiss, their tongues smoothly flowing around each other. He wanted it to escalate. He ached for more of her. He wanted to pretend they were alone, safe, that they had all the time they could want. He imagined his hand moving to her zipper, slipping inside her flight suit....

But she ended it far before he was ready. She pressed her forehead to his, exhaling raggedly.

"Distracting ourselves like this could be dangerous," she whispered.

"I don't care. I want you, Jane." His voice sounded hoarse. His hand was tangled in the hair at the nape of her neck, keeping pressure on her, keeping her close.

A choked laugh escaped from her. "I'm beginning to comprehend that."

"Do you—"

She laid a hand over his pounding heart. Her voice was resolute. "We can't do this now."

He was surprised by how much that hurt. He'd never done this before—confessed, tried to make something real happen. But this wasn't a rejection, exactly. It was more like a deferral.

So, that's how it would be. Survival would be a prerequisite. Well, then they were damn well going to survive this.

"The old carrot, huh?" he said ruefully.

"Did you mean it when you said you would follow me to hell?" She was pulling on his arm, forcing him to release his grip on her. He lowered his hand reluctantly and she put some distance between them.

She gave him a small concession. She wrapped her fingers gently around his and squeezed. His hand still hurt, but he didn't care.

"Yes."

"Good. This isn't going to be easy, especially with Compton the way he is and Walsh…." She trailed off and her expression glazed over.

He panicked and clutched at her arm, but she snapped out of it. "Jane? What just happened?"

"I don't know if I can explain it, adequately. There's a place, inside my mind, that's plugged into him. Each hour that goes by, I'm closer to him, and, by extension, the ship. The download he gave me was part of that. It fits like puzzle pieces in my mind. It's a kind of awareness—like knowing that someone you care about is there next to you, without having to look or speak. It's getting easier and easier to hear him. I'm vaguely aware of his thoughts, some of them, any-

195

way, in real time. It's scary. But…." Her breath hitched. She stopped looking at him, staring instead at her hand, twined with his, in her lap.

"What?" he prompted her.

"I like it."

He didn't know what to say to her. This thing was changing her and he was powerless to stop it.

"I wish I could share it with you. You will, won't you? You'll learn the language and come here, with me?"

"Yes," he answered, huskily.

"The Sectilius formed a mental community revolving around him, each member of the network abstractly aware of the others, building a dynamic experience. The synergy, the creative possibilities—artists and engineers, community leaders and philosophers, scientists and entertainers—the entire city feeding off this mental energy, generating novel associations and ideas. The Sectilius initially created these connections with the Kubodera to keep them happy, to keep them challenged, because they take them from everything they've ever known to fly these ships. They're starved for experience. They thrive under this kind of mental stimulation. It's necessary to keep them from going mad. But the Sectilius quickly learned that Anipraxia was a richly rewarding symbiotic relationship for everyone involved. It's incredible."

Her eyes were shining in the dark. He reached out and brushed back a stand of her hair that had fallen forward over her face.

"He knows about Tom. He's very upset about it and he wants to help us. He's letting me decide for myself how to handle it. He's not telling me what to do—I want you to know that. He's not influencing me, ok?"

"Ok. What's he doing now?"

"Right now he's very busy managing the, um...I think you would call them nanites. That's taking most of his attention at the moment."

He mentally shifted gears. Nanotechnology on Earth was in its infancy—little more than research and development—an engineer's dream. "Nanites?"

"Yes. The whole ship is swarming with them. They repair things at a microscopic level. They were never meant to be the only defense against the slug population, but without a crew, there's no other way to maintain the ship. Ei'Brai kept life support levels at absolute minimum all those years to keep the slug growth rate as low as possible, but when he turned the life support back on for us, the population exploded and the nanites are barely keeping the damage under control. Do you see? This isn't his fault. He's doing his best to protect us. There are things that are beyond his ability to control."

He stared at her, trying to understand. This alien guy was using nanites as damage control? It was plausible, he supposed, to a certain degree. He'd kill to know how that was done. Yet, with the number of slugs he'd seen in that one room alone...that seemed like it was verging on impossible. He started to feel skeptical, but tried not to let it show. "But why didn't he warn us from the start, Jane?"

"He's very proud. He feels like the ship's an extension of himself. These mishaps feel like failures. It's mortifying to him. He wanted so badly for this to go well. He knows we're his only hope to survive. He knows about the asteroid, Alan."

Didn't that give her pause? Bergen frowned. Jane got to her feet and extended a hand to him. He knew he should say something, but everything he thought of sounded like something Walsh might say and he didn't want to risk putting distance between them.

14

As Jane rose, Walsh and the others immediately gathered their things. She stood apart from Bergen, her chin lifted, her expression stern. No one else needed to know that inside she was roiling with conflicted thoughts. A good leader acted the part no matter what they felt.

She didn't allow her gaze to linger on Alan as he labored to his feet. Alan's confession was heartening. He believed in her. She hoped his faith wasn't misplaced.

But there was the nagging doubt, that he was affected by the agent that felled the Sectilius. She'd had hints from him all along that he was attracted to her. That had always seemed sort of tantalizing and thrilling, but she'd never believed he really meant any of it. She'd concluded that it was just part of his nature to be flirtatious in a razor sharp way, that he couldn't help but be enigmatically charming to stoke his own tremendous ego.

Now he seemed to be saying it was more than that and the timing couldn't be worse. She was already scattered enough, dealing with a constant influx of revelations, insights, foreign concepts—all creating a tumult inside her head. She didn't have the luxury of time to consider what his proposition might mean…about him, to her, the mission…any of it.

She wondered, if he'd done something similar just a month before, would she have responded in the same way? There'd been that moment in the capsule, the day she'd succumbed to childish grief, reeling from the news that her closest confidant had just given birth to a healthy child. Suddenly she'd found herself unable to contain her feelings, which ran a gamut of extremes—joy, sadness at missing the event, jealousy, loneliness, disconnectedness, and shame.

He'd embraced her tenderly, throwing her concept of his character into complete disarray. It was a bewildering moment because it didn't change anything between them. Things continued on just as they'd been before, as though she'd just imagined it. It left her watching him curiously for other signs of depth or gestures of goodwill. When nothing else surfaced, she decided it meant nothing to him and did her best not to think about it. Though if she was being completely honest with herself, that had been hard.

At the time, she found herself behaving like a young girl, suddenly self-conscious about her appearance, finding reasons to engage him in conversation, asking for his assistance when she didn't really need it, surreptitiously watching him work, eat, exercise…dress.

She tricked herself into thinking he was playing along, that he felt the same, that they were both feeling their way in that bizarre environment, knowing that such thoughts were prohibited, should be ignored, or extinguished. Then he'd do something callous or say something that was so off-color that she was sure she was fabricating the whole scenario as a mental defense against boredom.

She shouldn't have kissed him. In that moment, it felt like clinging to life as it shattered around her. She couldn't deny her attraction to him. He felt solid and real when her grasp on reality felt like it was slipping. But it also gave him a hold over her, every bit as strong as the hold Ei'Brai was wielding. She was being pulled in too many directions. If she wasn't careful she'd be drawn and quartered before she could achieve her goals.

Time was a trap. After all the months of confinement—to be confronted with a ticking clock, after only a single day aboard the ship, was cruel. If she waited to send a message to Houston, concentrated on understanding this enigmatic disease, she might wait too long and doom the Bravo mission as well. But every minute spent getting to the capsule, arguing with Walsh, and then getting back again might be letting life trickle through her fingers.

If only Walsh had trusted her, then everything would be different now. They could split into two teams, send a couple of people to the capsule to transmit a message home while the rest of them worked on a solution. But it wasn't like that. She wondered where along the line she'd lost his trust, or if she'd ever really had it to begin with. Maybe he didn't think she was a worthy leader. Deep inside, she was afraid he was right.

She didn't have any business leading others. She'd lost people in the Amazon. No one had ever faulted her for that, except for herself. The circumstances had been horrible. But she always felt that if she'd been a little better prepared, a little more vigilant, a little more proactive, she should have been able to save them.

And now it was happening again. Tom was clearly sick, possibly irreparably. Walsh, and maybe Ajaya, too.

Ei'Brai felt there was hope and she clung to that like a lifeboat adrift on a stormy sea. He believed she could solve it. That seemed frankly absurd. She wasn't a scientist. How could she hope to understand an alien disease that struck so suddenly, dragging down the faculties needed to stop it? Like Alan, she didn't feel affected, but knew that might be self-deception. She'd let her guard down with him, let herself get caught up in a self-indulgent moment. When so much was resting on her shoulders, so much was at stake, that in itself might be a sign that something was already going wrong.

She led the way down the hall, the lights in the floor lighting up in front of her, a demonstration of support from Ei'Brai. She didn't have to look back to know that the lights coming on that way were pissing Walsh off.

Ei'Brai, on top of everything else, was feeding her the at-mospheric mood of the rest of the group. She caught flashes of images, thoughts, emotional states—all on a level verging on subconscious. She was aware of perceiving it, even when she wasn't giving it her full attention. She wanted to tell Ei'Brai to stop, to quit pushing her, that she couldn't take any more of it, but that wouldn't be true. It was unnerving how fast she was adapting to it.

The others filed into the deck transport behind her. Jane didn't like the way they were all looking and feeling so un-certain about her. Walsh seemed more pacified since things were going the way he wanted, but still grim and angry.

Gibbs gently urged Compton to keep up, caught Compton's arm when he tottered. Compton was shuffling along, completely withdrawn. He seemed to have aged at least 20 years since the last time Jane had seen him. Once a lively junior/senior pair of colleagues, a gulf of age seemed to have opened up between them. Gibbs fell naturally into the role of youth, caring for revered elder.

Jane pressed the symbol for the deck where the Providence was docked. A beat later, the door lifted midway, paused, then shut again. Everyone watched her expectantly. She frowned, reaching for the control, but before she could make contact, the door slid up, this time completely opening.

A large grey mass, slightly larger than a football, hit the floor with a sickening, wet thud and wobbled to a stop. Thin, webby tendrils stretched from the object to the top of the open doorway. A fetid odor, redolent of rotting garbage, hit them like a wave. The hallway was dark.

"What the hell?" Bergen grimaced, pulled a flashlight out of his pack, and shone it on the mass at their feet.

Walsh's face was red with choler. "Holloway—what are you playing at? Is this the right deck?"

"Of course it is," she replied, trying to hide her own bewilderment.

Ei'Brai surged in her head, a disorienting, buzzing flood, and she reached out a hand to steady herself against it. He was filling her head to overflowing with urgent warnings.

Ajaya was pulling on latex gloves. She took a pen out of her pocket and scraped it over the top of the door, effectively lifting off the gooey strings connecting the object with the door, and stepped out to inspect the object itself.

"It's not safe here anymore," Jane murmured out loud to the others.

"What's that supposed to mean?" Walsh eyed her suspiciously.

"We need to go. Come back inside, Ajaya." Jane took a step forward, reaching for the door control.

Walsh blocked her. He towered over her, manner threatening. "Stay put, Varma. Nobody's going anywhere until we have some answers. What is that thing?"

Jane stood her ground, resisting the urge to back away from him.

She could sense Alan's protective ire rising one second and Walsh's seething anger the next. It was coloring her own state of mind, making her feel like lashing out, losing control.

She forced herself to stay calm. "I don't know what it's called. It's the next stage in the life cycle of the slugs. Whatever is going to hatch out of there—we don't want any part of it. We need to go."

"More delay tactics," Walsh growled.

"It's a pupa," Ajaya murmured and they all turned to look at her. She was using the pen to move the mass from side to side. The tip of the pen disintegrated under the gentle pressure she exerted at the point, leaving blue plastic blobs dotting the thing.

Then the mass moved, swelling under the surface on one side. Ajaya gasped and scrambled back.

"That's enough. Let's go," Walsh barked. The others stared at him, unmoving.

"Wait. Hold on. I'm not saying we don't go back to the capsule. I'm saying we protect ourselves better first. I can take us to—"

Walsh bellowed over her, silencing her, "I said, enough! Move out."

Gibbs looked back and forth between Jane and Walsh and then put an arm around Compton, urging him forward around the mass at their feet. Gibbs' eyes darted around nervously, his weapon still clutched in his hand.

Jane reached out to touch Walsh's arm. "No! This is too dangerous. You have to listen to me."

"Like hell I do." Walsh leveled his gun at her chest and swung wide, ready for an attack from Alan.

Alan's fists were clenched. His nostrils flared. He was on the verge of doing something reckless. Ei'Brai was silent in her head—he was as appalled and unnerved as she was.

Chagrin left her feeling cold. Hadn't she just been contemplating using the same tactic against Walsh, if necessary? How could she possibly change the balance of power now?

Jane slowly raised a placating hand. "Ok, ok, Commander. You're in control. Let's go, Alan."

She moved cautiously toward Alan and turned him bodily, forcing him through the doorway, just as Gibbs had done with Compton.

Walsh ordered, "You two take point."

Jane glanced over her shoulder. Ajaya and Gibbs looked uncomfortable, but weren't saying anything. Alan shone his flashlight down the hall in the direction of the capsule and started moving. Jane stayed at his side. She didn't have a flashlight or her pack. They must have been left behind.

There was some murmuring behind them, then Ajaya quietly handed Jane an air canister/harness and an oxygen monitor. Jane slipped the harness over her shoulders and glanced at the monitor as she fixed it to her flight suit. The levels were normal.

Inside her head, Ei'Brai was perturbed, exasperated. Jane struggled to keep her own thoughts moored. He informed her he was working diligently on getting lights back on for her. He said there was damage to certain neural-electric pathways, the conduits that carried his commands all over the ship. He reassured her that air quality sensors and controls were fully operational, but regretted to tell her he was barely keeping gravity under control. There was a 57% chance of losing gravity in the immediate future. She considered sharing this information, but Walsh's current mood was not receptive to input from her, so she stayed silent.

As they walked, there were more pupa in various sizes clinging to the walls and ceiling, sometimes singly, sometimes in clusters, oozing thick, stringy slime. After seeing what that slime had done to Ajaya's pen, Jane stayed alert to avoid walking into any of it.

Ei'Brai was desperately searching the ship's data banks for scraps of information about this species. Apparently, it was virtually unheard of for it to ever reach this life stage. In fact, it was prohibited by law to allow it to happen. There were many, many safety protocols in place to prevent such an occurrence. Unfortunately there'd been no one on board to carry out those protocols for decades.

The slugs were regarded as problematic enough. Capable of spawning in the larval-stage, they reached maturity swiftly under optimal environmental conditions, even when minute in size. Both the larvae and their eggs were also capable of near indefinite dormancy, making them a prolific and tenacious foe. Every shipyard and dock was infested despite constant vigilance. They developed resistance to every chemical agent used against them, thwarted every method intended to retard their growth. Constant vigilance and mechanical removal were the most effective means of control. They were essentially monster cockroaches in space.

Ajaya mused, "So many, so quickly. We've only been gone for a few hours. How can this be?"

Jane walked steadily on, experiencing two disparate states of mind simultaneously. On one level, she was alert to her surroundings—tense, adrenaline pumping through her. Yet, on another level, she carefully monitored Ei'Brai's intake of information, noting each important detail he uncovered, knowing it could be critical to their survival. This mind-sharing—it allowed her to think in new ways she couldn't have conceived of before. It gave new meaning to the concept of multi-tasking.

She came to an abrupt halt, heedless of the others, as she centered all her attention to a razor sharp point. Ei'Brai had just uncovered something of monumental importance—and in his surprise and dismay, revealed information that he did not intend to.

These slug creatures were originally native to Sectilia's moon, Atielle. After the two cultures integrated, some of the creatures were inadvertently transferred to the planet. The population exploded—like rabbits in the Australian Out-back. Without a natural predator, they multiplied out of control. A highly adaptable species, they filled many new niches and interbred with similar terrestrial fauna until their genetics were quite different from the original, moon-based creature.

When this newly hybridized creature was reintroduced to its native habitat, new characteristics were unmasked. Atielle, as one of several moons orbiting such a large planet, was extremely geologically active. The annual cycles of tectonic and tidal activity influenced by Sectilia's gravitational fields resulted in a localized volcanic emission of xenon gas. The gas, normally present in Atielle's atmosphere in low percentages, became quite concentrated, triggering a transformation. The formerly benign species became a dangerous predator: the nepatrox.

All of this was new information to Ei'Brai. Normally, the slug population was not his concern. He didn't bother himself with trivialities that had no effect on him. Perhaps this was common knowledge among the Sectilius who inhabited the ship—so common, it wasn't necessary to discuss it.

It was the leak...the xenon gas...that had set this in motion. The despicable part was that it hadn't been accidental. There had been a leak of xenon gas, but it'd been minor. Ei'Brai augmented it, purposefully, for effect—to create a scenario that would push her to be dependent on his help so that he could demonstrate his power and ultimately gain her trust.

He'd tried to hide that from her. It had been but a momentary lapse in his control of the information she received from him. But she'd seen it. And it changed everything.

A painful, tingly sensation rioted from her core outwards. Her face felt hot. Her ears burned. Why did he think he needed to force anything by manufacturing a situation? Why couldn't he just have given her the time she needed to adjust to communicating with him?

He'd wanted her to learn to trust him. But he hadn't trusted or respected her at all, had he? He could have killed Alan or Walsh, or both, with that gas. She could never have forgiven that. And what he'd started wasn't over yet. There were still plenty of opportunities to die from the reckless choice Ei'Brai had made. Jane stood there, stunned. *Walsh was right all along.*

Ei'Brai inundated her thoughts with apologies, contrition. He begged her to see his desperate need, reminded her of the bigger picture—the Sectilius goal, the Cunabula and the hope humanity could provide to the uncounted centillions of species in the universe. It was a torrent of ingratiation and regret. She wanted none of it.

"Neu!" she cried aloud.

She came to herself abruptly with the others gathering around her. She closed her eyes and stood stock still, raging silently, *Get out of my head, goddamn you!*

All at once, he withdrew. She rocked on her heels as she felt him slip away. She was completely alone inside her head for the first time since they docked with the ship. The hum had gone silent. Not even a tingle at the back of her mind was left. She felt surprisingly empty. Now, in his absence, she could see that he'd infiltrated her mind so completely, she'd begun to feel normal with him there.

It was a relief. And it was lonely. That was disconcerting.

Walsh nudged her roughly. "Quit stalling, Holloway. Keep moving."

Alan pulled her away from Walsh, propelling her forward again. Before he could query her about what just happened, she whispered, "Do you still have a weapon?"

He nodded slowly, looking confused and uncomfortable. "In my pack. Jane, I did fine at the shooting range, but I'm no match for Walsh."

She put a hand on his arm, squeezing, and darted a look back. "I...no, no. Walsh is right—I think we should go. I'm just worried we aren't going to make—"

She froze. Something had moved in her peripheral vision.

15

A preternatural feeling of dread washed over Jane. She felt a strong urge to run, but logic told her that was a bad choice. She turned slowly, peering into the shadows around them, instinctively looking for a place to hide.

They'd covered several hundred feet since they left the deck-to-deck transport, but there were no doors in the immediate vicinity. They'd passed one just a minute or two before, but in the dark, without the connection to Ei'Brai guiding her through the mental maps of the ship, it was difficult to guess how far away that had been or how close another one might be.

Oh, God, turn on the lights, Ei'Brai, she thought, but he was no longer listening. Banishing Ei'Brai from her thoughts no longer seemed like the most sensible decision.

"Holloway—"

"Sh!" Jane sent Walsh a quelling look.

Something scuttled in the dark nearby.

"What...was that?" Ajaya whispered, her eyes gone wide.

Jane put her hand over Alan's, steering the flashlight to one side. A creature the size of a house cat stood there watching them. It was hard to tell what it was, exactly. It didn't precisely fit into any category Jane knew. The nepatrox had a maroon, segmented shell like a lobster or scorpion, but its head grew from its trunk more like a fish. It whipped an ominous-looking barbed tail around, as though agitated.

It crouched and opened its mouth. A hinge on each side unfolded, revealing fuchsia and coral-colored flaps as well as rows of jagged teeth. It hissed defiantly and took a few steps forward.

"Holy fuck, what next?" Bergen muttered.

"Where the hell did that come from?" Walsh grit out.

Ajaya spoke softly, "It hatched, didn't it Jane? From the pupa."

Jane nodded gravely. "Yes."

Gibbs' voice sounded mildly disturbed. "That little dude looks pissed."

Ajaya said, "It looks like an arthropod of some sort. It appears to be territorial. Will it attack if we go further, I wonder?"

"I think it will," Jane said. "This is what I was trying to warn you about. We should go back. The deck above this one stores Sectilius battle armor. We need to protect ourselves."

"From that little thing?" Walsh said dismissively.

Ajaya frowned. "Some of the pupa are quite large, Commander."

"Then let's get going before they hatch. Move," Walsh barked.

No one budged.

Gibbs spoke up, "Maybe Jane's got the right idea. There might be a lot more of these things. They're going to be hungry, don't you think? What are they going to eat?"

The nepatrox advanced, hissing and slashing at the air in spirals with its tail. It was closest to Jane. She backed up involuntarily, bumping into Alan. He put a hand on her shoulder and tried to push her behind him. She resisted his gentle shove and stayed put, noting that motion of any kind seemed to enflame the creature's temper. But even that subtle movement antagonized it. It lunged forward, hissing, clacking its teeth together rhythmically, flaring and pulsing the bizarre, hinged flaps that framed its mouth.

"What else do you know about these creatures, Jane?" Ajaya asked.

Jane felt Alan's hand on her shoulder, tensing as the nepatrox crept closer.

"They're extremely aggressive. The stinger contains a paralytic. They prefer to eat their food while it's still alive."

Walsh glared at them with disdain. "I've seen rats bigger than that thing." He shrugged off his breathing harness and gripped the strap at the top of the tank, moving deliberately toward the creature.

It held its ground, front claws prancing like an excited dog. The rhythmic gnashing and flapping escalated. It charged.

Walsh was ready. He swung the tank of compressed air like a golf club, striking the animal with a solid whump, sending it flying. It hit the wall and slid to the floor, lifeless.

Jane's stomach turned over.

"Well, there's a strategy for you," Alan said dryly.

Walsh turned and glowered at them. "All right? Move out."

"Ah, Walsh, you've got another little friend," Gibbs said nervously, gesturing down the hall with his flashlight, revealing another creature emerging from the darkness.

Walsh's eyebrows came down into a thunderous expression and he pivoted. Alan lifted his light a little higher, to join Gibbs'. Jane gasped. There were actually several creatures approaching Walsh's location.

One of them was the size of a full-grown labrador retriever. It opened it's hinged jaw, flaring the winged flaps to a span of three to four feet, then turned and scooped up one of the smaller creatures, choking it down before the thing could even struggle. It flared and pulsed its mouth flaps, letting out a shrieking cry.

The call was taken up by those around it. The chilling sound echoed and was answered again and again from farther and farther back down the hall.

The blood drained from Jane's head. She felt lightheaded and cold. Her heart thudded and her muscles tensed to run.

The largest nepatrox regarded Walsh intently, its dark eyes gleaming with hunger, its tail swinging in long lazy arcs. It hissed.

"Walsh!" Jane called out. She wasn't sure if she was warning him or pleading with him at that point. She felt helpless, rooted to the spot where she stood.

Time slowed to a trickle. She felt, rather than saw, Alan behind her rummaging inside his pack for his nine millimeter. Ajaya and Gibbs took up defensive stances, shoulder to shoulder, guns pointed at the end of trembling arms.

The lights came on with a bright flash. Jane flinched and blinked.

The creatures stopped advancing for a second and in that second Walsh fired a deafening shot into the largest animal's open mouth. Its head exploded into a four-foot radius of gore, the hollow-tipped bullet designed for maximum destruction upon impact. The beast dropped instantly.

The other creatures sprang back at the sound, but quickly recovered, sniffing and hissing around their felled neighbor. Within seconds they'd ripped its carapace apart and were feasting on it.

Bile rose in Jane's throat and she coughed reflexively. She was glad she hadn't consumed anything for a few hours. She didn't have anything to bring up.

Walsh stood there watching them, weapon at his side.

"Walsh!" Jane screamed, "Defensive formation!"

He came to himself with a start. He looked at his weapon, then back at them as though confused.

The others started yelling too, calling for him to come back to the group.

"Jane—get Compton's gun out of his pack," Alan urged in her ear.

She grabbed Tom and shoved him behind Ajaya and Gibbs, sliding the pack from his shoulders. She fumbled in the pockets until her fingers closed over the textured grip of Tom's Beretta. There was a clip already loaded. She scooped up three additional cartridges and slid them into the side pocket of her flight suit. She pulled back the slide, and let it spring back into place, effectively loading the first round, then brushed her thumb over the safety, just like she'd been taught.

"You got it, Jane?" Alan's eyes were wide and dilated. He jerked his head back toward the way they'd come. "Take Compton back to the deck transport, where he'll be safe. We'll never make it to the capsule."

She started to protest, but weapons fire cut off any sound she might make. It was overwhelmingly loud in such an enclosed space. She looked up. Walsh had returned to them with more creatures in pursuit.

As a group, they retreated. The four of them fired into a growing mass of hungry animals, trying to keep them at bay. There seemed to be more arriving every second.

Jane glanced back. The hall behind them was clear.

"I'm not getting much penetration here!" Gibbs yelled.

"Aim for an open mouth!" Walsh barked. "It's their weakest point! When you empty that cartridge, load armor piercing rounds!"

Alan shouted, "For the record, I'm very uncomfortable firing ballistics inside a space ship!"

Jane grabbed a hold of Tom's arm and pulled. He took a single staggering step and stopped.

She pulled again. He resisted, swaying.

Gibbs backed into Tom and there was a precarious moment when it seemed like Tom might go down. Jane wrapped her arms around him, supporting his weight so he wouldn't pitch forward and tried to ease him into movement.

But his legs just crumpled under him. He fell to his knees and Jane buckled too, under his weight. She struggled for a long, desperate moment, trying ineffectually to lift him back to his feet. He was dead weight against her.

"Jane!" Alan's face was contorted in a tortured expression. "We'll have to leave him."

Gibbs and Ajaya kept looking back at her, desperation plain on their faces. They needed to move. The nepatrox were relentlessly pressing them back.

She shook her head in denial and eased Tom to the floor. She slipped the weapon in a pocket, grasped Tom's arm, and pulled with everything she had, dragging him across the floor, back the way they'd come.

She pulled with a strength she didn't know she had, Tom's inert frame trailing behind her, ducking and swerving to avoid the slimy tendrils dropping from the ceiling. She glanced back, her breath coming in ragged gasps. She'd managed at least 100 feet back toward the deck transport. She'd hoped the others would be right behind her, but there was still a lot of distance between them.

She heard Ajaya declare, "Cover me—reloading."

Seconds later, Alan yelled, "I'm out of ammo."

Jane stopped in her tracks and turned, her hand going to her pocket and the clips there, but Gibbs had already passed Alan another clip. He was reloading.

"Make every round count!" Walsh roared.

Those few moments gave the creatures an opening. They surged forward, a few of them circling around Alan to attack from behind.

"Alan! Behind you!"

He and Ajaya were already aware, moving into a diamond-shaped defensive formation, backs to Walsh and

Gibbs, as the animals gained more ground, slowly surrounding them.

She dropped Tom's arm. She hated herself for doing it, but it couldn't be helped. She slipped the breathing gear off her back and grasped it with her left hand, just as Walsh had done. Then she palmed the cold steel of the Beretta in her right and flicked off the safety with her thumb.

She couldn't let them get cut off from her. She refused to lose all of them to this madness.

Her body vibrated with tension, itching for movement. She blinked in slow motion, a hyper-awareness sharpening her senses. She took off at a run. Nothing would get by her. She couldn't allow it. Every pounding heartbeat brought her closer. They came to meet her with a greedy glint in every eye.

She swung her left arm like a metronome. Each sweep cleared the path between her and the others. She glanced back. One of the larger ones was smart enough to see she was distracted by the smaller ones and snuck by, heading for Tom.

She raised the weapon and braced herself. Without a second of hesitation, she fired. The recoil painfully compressed every joint in her wrist, elbow and shoulder. The scent of hot metal and burnt carbon stung her nostrils, but she'd hit it. It went down, possibly only stunned, but it was down for the moment, anyway.

"Jane—try to get away!" Alan shouted.

She didn't reply. Resolution pushed her forward, inch by inch. She ignored the ache in her left arm and kept swinging. If she missed a shot the first time, she hit it the second. As she drew closer to the rest of the crew, the monsters came on her harder, faster.

Some of them got too close. She kicked at them viciously, hoping the military-issued boots were tough enough to protect her from the flailing stingers.

She curled her lip in contempt. The nepatrox would just as soon have a bite out of each other as they would out of the humans. The mass of them hissed and spat and sniped at each other as they advanced. There was but five feet left between her and the rest of the group. It might as well have been 100, because it was swarming with nepatrox.

The others were trying to use their tanks in a similar manner but they were tightly grouped and fighting both sides at once. They were being overwhelmed. They weren't going to make it unless they tried something else. They needed some kind of strategy. She cast around, taking in the immediate environment.

Now that the lights were on, she could see there was a door, a few feet back and to her left. If that room were empty—if they could get inside—they would have the time to hatch a proper plan to get to the capsule and escape. That was as far as she could think, for now. They couldn't keep going on this way. There were too many and more kept coming. They were all getting tired.

At worst, it would be just a break. Maybe they could pick off the larger ones, one at a time, through a crack in the door. At best, there might be something inside that room they could use. Tom was the only hitch in the plan.

She darted back to the door and tapped the door control. The door slid up. She smashed a few more animals then slipped inside. The lights came on, but nothing came to greet her. It appeared to be empty. Not even a slug. It was full of crates, like the first room they'd entered on the ship.

This room, like many in the storage hold, was vast. There was another door that opened into the room about 40 feet on the other side of Tom, closer to the deck transport. She wanted to kick herself. If only she'd dragged him that 40 feet farther or noticed the door sooner.

Old doubts prickled at her. She forced herself to ignore them and pounded back up to the group. "I've got a plan!"

"Oh, yeah?" Walsh called. "Let's hear it!"

She looked down. A creature lashed its tail at her, way too close for comfort. She jumped back just in time, then bludgeoned the animal. Unless she got the angle just right, brute clubbing was far more effective at taking a nepatrox out than the pistol was.

"We're going through this door. Ajaya, you'll get there first, so you'll have your hand on the door control and shut that door the second the last man is through. That's your job."

Ajaya nodded crisply. "Affirmative."

"Ron, you're the fastest runner. Once you're through, I need you to head straight for the other door that opens to the corridor." She gestured behind her with the pistol, toward Tom and the deck transport beyond him. "Don't look back. Just get there and open it. I want you to lay down cover fire from there."

Gibbs met her eyes and bobbed his head. "Understood."

"Walsh, Alan, your task is to kill anything that gets through that door before it closes."

"And what is your part in this plan, Holloway?" Walsh hollered.

"I'm going for Tom."

Alan was shaking his head. "Jane—"

She cut him off with an order, "Spread out. You're too bunched up. Give yourself room to move. Start moving toward the door."

She clubbed a small one, then grit her teeth and fired at one that was getting too close to Alan. Her aim was true. It fell over on its side.

Alan jumped. "Jesus Christ, Jane."

She ignored him and fired at one scuttling down the corridor, but all she got was a hollow clicking noise. She made an angry, frustrated sound. "I'm reloading! Someone shoot the one that's going for Tom!" She fumbled with the release until the spent cartridge clattered to the floor.

There was hissing and magenta and orange flapping at her knee. *Dammit!* She hopped back and raised the canister a fraction of a second too late. The creature's tail was quicker. It slashed at her leg. She grunted in disbelief before smashing the animal to bits.

"Jane, are you hit?"

"No! Stop looking at me and concentrate on what you're doing!" She leveled a few more nepatrox before she could get a glimpse at her leg. She felt a small amount of pain in that leg that seemed to be growing. The fabric of her pants' leg was torn, but she couldn't see skin.

She stomped her foot as she moved a step closer to the group. She felt that. That was reassuring. She pushed down fear and ignored the pain. She'd be safe soon enough.

Over the din, Ajaya enunciated, "On a count of three, step back, Jane, and reload. I'm going to try something."

Jane sent her a terse nod. Ajaya counted. Jane readied herself to slip the harness over her arm, go for a clip, and back out of range—in a single, time-saving motion.

Ajaya called out, "Three!"

Jane leapt back. As she slipped the new magazine into place, she looked up to see Ajaya executing some kind of ninja-worthy move.

With her tank of compressed air held neatly before her, Ajaya went low to the floor and spun in a swift, forceful arc, sweeping the animals out of the way, effectively clearing a swath before her. Then, in a sprightly leap, she was one foot closer to the open door and safety.

"Move!" Jane yelled. The men were reacting sluggishly to the sudden advancement. "Do that again, Ajaya!"

Jane put two bullets down the throat of a large animal that was under the mistaken impression that it was about to face off with her and smiled as the image of Indiana Jones shooting the swordsman in Cairo spontaneously came to mind for a split second. She vaulted back at Ajaya's three-count, attempting a similar move as she went, shoving them sideways and back. The creatures were flung in their wake, sliding into each other, disorienting the general mass of them for just a moment.

They were almost there. It was working. She couldn't keep the grim smile from her lips as she kicked one in the side of the head and put another one down with a round into its yawning mouth, spattering its brains in every direction.

"Again—then inside! Everyone get ready. No mistakes. Do your part!"

She counted aloud with Ajaya, humming with excitement, primed to run. She knew they would succeed. She wouldn't look back.

On three, she turned. She pumped her legs like pistons. She sprinted for Tom.

Then, the gravity went out.

16

Bergen was sweating profusely. It was stinging his eyes.

It was happening so fast. *Too fast, damn it.* He shouldn't have listened to her. He should have gone with her. Why hadn't he done that?

The next few seconds would be crucial and he'd be cut off from her. He was letting her down. What was he doing?

Jane. He was having a hard time tearing his eyes from her. He'd never seen her like that. She was turning those animals into carcasses like a blonde Lara Croft. The woman looked invincible...like a fucking fantasy.

Where was the prissy librarian now? Goddammit, she was hot.

She should have come inside with them. Maybe the animals would have stuck around, trying to get through the door. Maybe they wouldn't even have noticed Tom. Maybe there was no hope for Tom, anyway. He hated the thought of her risking everything if Tom was beyond help.

They were almost through the door. Jane's plan was working. With difficulty, Alan concentrated on his assigned task as she streaked down the corridor toward Tom. He could hear Gibbs' boot steps pounding for the other door.

He used his tank to block an attack, took another step back, then lunged forward, swinging the tank with vicious, deadly accuracy. All he had to do was keep these little piss-ants from getting through the door.

Unfortunately, the animals had revved things up, scrambling over each other, launching themselves at them. Perhaps they sensed they were about to be cut off from their prey. The sudden retreat probably stimulated their prey drive.

The battle armor Jane had mentioned would have been damn useful at this point. Walsh was such an ass. That little miscalculation was going to go in his next report to Houston. If there was another report to Houston.

His eyes drifted to Jane. There were a bunch of the little bastards hot on her heels.

Walsh was counting down. There wasn't much time left.

Alan stood stock still, forgetting anything but Jane's need. He fired, picking off as many of the creatures following her as he could. He felt a slash into his leg. It burned like a mother-fucker. He ignored it.

There was shouting. He ignored that too, completely focused on Jane. Finally, someone grabbed him, pulling him forcefully through the door. It shut in his face even as he lunged forward to take another shot.

He turned to take off sprinting for the other door, but something was wrong. He blinked rapidly.

At first he thought it might be the creature's venom, that maybe he was hallucinating. It felt like his feet had lifted out from under him. His stomach lurched into his throat and his chest felt full.

He was drifting away from the door, pivoting at a strange angle. He shook his head to clear it. Quickly, the mental processes he'd developed to cope with microgravity kicked in.

"The gravity is malfunctioning," Ajaya yelled. She was already some distance away, floating at a point midway to the other door. She must have taken off at a dead run as soon as she'd hit the door control, just as he'd planned to do. Gibbs was nearly to the other door.

Bergen suddenly realized that in a room this large, he'd have to anchor himself before he drifted too far from anything he could grab. He pulled up his knees and rotated.

Walsh was wedged into the doorframe with his back against the door and held out a hand. Alan met Walsh's eyes. They were grim.

Alan snapped to alert with a start. "Oh, fuck. Jane!"

"We'll do what we can for her," Walsh said as he pulled Bergen back to the door.

There was nothing to hold on to. This ship was never meant to be a microgravity environment.

"Let's assess the situation," Walsh continued tersely. "Open the door, Berg."

Alan glanced over his shoulder at Ajaya. She was swimming in the air, trying to make progress toward the other door. He huffed. It'd take years to get there that way, but if anyone could, it'd be Ajaya.

He covered the door control with his hand, using as little pressure as possible so he wouldn't be propelled back into the room.

The door slid up. There was a lot of hissing going on out there, but very little other sound. Walsh swung his tank carefully, deliberately. He was just using enough force to knock the creatures back but not with so much momentum that he would hurl himself into their midst. Alan grabbed the back of Walsh's flight suit, to keep him anchored.

"Holloway," Walsh yelled. "Stop flailing around—you're wasting energy."

Bergen pulled himself into the doorway. The creatures were floating around in clumps—corpses and live, pissed-off things—spinning, drifting in every direction, caroming into each other in comical slow-motion.

Jane appeared to be ok. She was whirling, arms outstretched, momentum still carrying her down the hall toward Tom. There were creatures all around her, but it didn't look like anything was too close. She sounded bewildered as she met his eyes briefly before rotating again. "I'm stuck in the middle—I can't—there's nothing to push off of—"

He ventured out a little farther, clinging to the doorframe. "You can use your weapon, Jane. Do you have any rounds left?"

She looked at the gun in her hand like she was mystified. "I think so."

"Try to make yourself aerodynamic—you'll go farther if you reduce drag—and fire in the opposite direction you want to go. Kill a few of those things for good measure, while you're at it, too."

She beamed at him. "That I can do."

She flopped around, orienting herself. She'd never completely adapted to zero-g, probably never would. He tried not to let his amusement show, not that she was looking.

Bergen glanced over his shoulder. Gibbs had made it to the other door and was tying a length of paracord around a crate. He narrowed his eyes. The crates weren't floating—they were anchored somehow.

She got herself oriented, roughly parallel with the floor, arms outstretched in front of herself, and fired. She was propelled quite a distance. "That," she said with a laugh as she started to slow, "was awesome."

Gibbs was bracing himself in the other doorway, ready to thrust himself toward Tom.

Then she fell out of the air. They all did.

17

Jane slammed into the floor with a nauseating crunch. All the air whoofed out of her with a groan. Her vision narrowed to a spiraling tunnel of light. The pain was a shock. She'd never felt anything like it. She struggled to draw breath, to cling to consciousness, as white-hot agony tore at her throat.

She had a fleeting thought, that she should try not to scream. It might draw the creatures. Was it too late? Had she already done that? She wasn't sure.

Blood throbbed in her ears. Her vision swam. She pushed herself up on her elbows to assess her situation. She saw her leg at once, curled at an unnatural angle under her. She collapsed back down, pressing her face to the cold, plastic surface of the floor, gathering strength, as hot bile stung the back of her throat.

It could be worse. She wasn't dead yet.

The gun. Where was the gun? Her hands were empty.

"Jane!" Alan yelled. It was a hoarse, desperate warning.

She should try to reassure him, somehow, but that seemed ludicrous.

Brilliant colors filled her field of vision—like a perfect sunset, in pastel hues of tangerine and magenta. She stared at them in wonder until she realized what she was looking at. A creature. A nepatrox. It was tottering toward her, teeth exposed, regarding her warily.

A calming presence blanketed the flood of panic, before she could even react. It was Ei'Brai. *The weapon is within reach of your dominant extremity,* he soothed.

She couldn't take her eyes off the animal. It acted almost drunk, still trying to adjust to its constantly changing circumstances. But there was no doubt it was hungry. It was just a matter of time.

She slid her right hand over the floor, Ei'Brai guiding it to the pistol. She clutched it gratefully, then clamped down hard on her jaw and rolled, with considerable effort, onto her side. Why had that been so hard? She paid no heed to the racking pain in her leg and fired point blank into the thing's head. It exploded, raining blood and disgusting chunks over her.

She coughed, swiped at her face with her sleeve, and tried to sit up. That was a mistake. She came close to passing out again.

She laid back down, panting, and considered her options. Her compressed-air tank was a few feet away. She should go for it. Maybe she could crawl there before the nepatrox were completely recovered and alert. She could buy herself some time that way, so that someone could come get her.

With a grunt, she rolled back onto her stomach. She tried to raise herself up on her uninjured knee. It wouldn't cooperate. She squeezed her eyes shut and fought down despondency. One leg badly broken—that was clear—but the other was…what? Paralyzed? She searched her memory for a clue. The venom. She had felt a burning sensation earlier, but she hadn't had time to really think about it.

Hate seethed inside her, a bright, glowing thing that eclipsed everything else. She braced herself on one elbow and fired at anything that moved within a few feet of her until the clip was spent. She dropped the clip, awkwardly hurled it at one of the animals, and shoved her last clip home.

Ei'Brai's voice rumbled inside her head, *All will be well. My arrival is imminent.*

She heaved with incredulous giggles, certain she'd completely lost touch with reality. How preposterous. That wasn't even possible. He couldn't come for her. She had to be hallucinating his voice. Oh, she was really in a pickle now.

Ei'Brai, she mused. He'd said something once about debating the existence of deities and she wished she'd had the chance to do that with him. She needed a deity now. Her grandparent's fire and brimstone God seemed as good as any other at the moment. *Oh, God, help me survive this.*

Dimly she registered that people were yelling. Weapons were firing.

Blood. Some of it was hers. The floor was slick with blood and brains and other nepatrox gore. She drug herself through it. The horror of that made her throat close up.

"Jane! Can you hear me?" It was Gibbs, coming from the direction of the closest door. "I'm going to set off a flash-bang. Cover your ears and close your eyes!"

She heard him. She knew what he was going to do, but it seemed so impossible that it could make a difference. The animals were hissing, closing in. There were too many of them. Doggedly, she maneuvered on her elbows toward the canister, retching and spitting when she wrenched her leg.

Boots thudded heavily on the floor at her ear. She looked up, expecting to see Alan, Ajaya, Walsh or Gibbs, thinking, *but, he hasn't used the stun grenade yet, has he?*

She was pretty sure she would have noticed that. They were supposed to be really loud, blindingly bright, weren't they?

It was Tom.

His expression was spiritless and unblinking. There was no life behind his eyes.

The flashbang went off, and with it came a concussive force that knocked her jaw painfully into the floor.

She hadn't been ready for it. At least she'd been looking in the opposite direction, so the searing of her retinas was short-lived. But she couldn't hear a thing now. That would last a few seconds, she remembered.

Anticipate discomfort, vibrated pleasantly inside her brain.

She gaped at Tom, and rolled over. "Tom? Wha—?" She couldn't even hear herself.

Tom bent mechanically, at the hinge of his knee, and rested stolidly on his heels. His arms slid under her. He scooped her to him in a single, efficient motion and stood. She blacked out as the movement jarred her leg and came around to find him marching down the hall at an unhurried pace. Each jostling step sent pain shooting up her thigh. A few of the hardier nepatrox surged around them, lashing at his legs and chomping their jaws in frustration.

She touched Tom's face. He didn't respond. Not even a flinch. He didn't turn his head to look at her, just plodded on. "Tom?" she questioned softly.

It is not your Dr. Thomas Compton that secures your health and safety, Dr. Jane Holloway.

She stared at Tom's face in confusion. She felt so light-headed. She must have lost a lot of blood. "Ei'Brai?"

Tell your shipmates—it is imperative that they go into the chamber.

She continued to speak aloud to Tom's blank face, "Why?"

It is only a matter of time before this individual's structure malfunctions. Tell them now. I cannot protect them without your assistance.

She could sense then, that this undertaking was tasking him to the reaches of his capability. He let her see his determination, his assurance, that he was going to make amends. He was almost to the deck transport.

She wrapped her arms around Tom's neck and lifted herself to look over his shoulder. The others were fighting fruitlessly. Alan was yelling her name, over and over.

She called to them, "Go inside and shut the door!"

"Jane! Are you ok?" His voice was so full of anguish.

She blinked hard. Her vision was blurry. She didn't know how to respond to that. Everything was swirling out of control. She wanted to trust Ei'Brai, knew she didn't have a choice and...they didn't either. "Yes! I'm ok! I'll be ok!"

That was all she could muster. She leaned her cheek on Tom's shoulder, fighting her eyes closing, and watched dully as Gibbs and Ajaya went through the closest door and shut it.

Seconds later, she saw Walsh haul Alan through the farther door by the scruff of his flight suit. That door shut. A moment later, Tom strode into the deck transport. Another door shut between them.

A few nepatrox followed them inside. Jane couldn't maintain consciousness as Tom's body, forced like an automaton by Ei'Brai's mind, kicked them into death or submission.

She roused again as Tom staggered through the outer chamber of the medical facility. He stumbled past the diagnostic platform and through one of the many doors there.

His breathing was labored. Something was terribly wrong. The calming force that had tethered her, kept her from shrieking in pain, was gone. Her vision was fuzzy around the edges. She grit her teeth and clung to him.

All will be well, he thundered clumsily in her mind. *Do not fear.*

His loss of control did not engender trust. She couldn't comply.

This room harbored a sea of large, molded tubs, each filled with a sparkling-clear, gel-like substance. Tom lurched to the nearest tub and unceremoniously dumped her in without a word of explanation.

Her head went under and she thrashed at the shock of it, arms blindly seeking purchase. Ei'Brai gushed reassurance as she broke the surface, gasping. Tom's body was collapsed against the side of the tank, clearly no longer inhabited. There was no time to contemplate what that meant.

Calmly, now. This is critical care. You are unaware of the damage you have sustained.

There was some kind of activity taking place, she realized faintly, within the goo. Bright blue lights gleamed under the surface, beautiful and surreal, highlighting the swirls and disturbances she'd made in the crystalline-clear gel. She watched numbly as a purple blob seemed to bloom from her leg. A tiny tube emerged from the side of the tank to suction it away.

Her horror grew as she became aware that the tank was alive with nearly invisible mechanical devices. She squirmed, grasping for a handhold to pull herself out. Ei'Brai clamped down on her, mentally forcing a semblance of calm. She could no longer move.

She peered through the gel in a confused stupor as thread-like filaments swarmed over her body. Some of them brandished small tools at their tips. Others snaked over her skin, effectively binding her. Still more painlessly pierced her skin, slipping inside to deliver some form of treatment, she supposed, with dismayed detachment.

The royal blue pants' legs of her jumpsuit were swiftly snipped to ribbons and swept away, revealing a jagged, white bone protruding from the torn flesh of her thigh. She closed her eyes. Even through the distortion of the gel, it was too much to see.

Warmth flooded her body and she felt her skin flush, sweat prickling her hairline. Pain dissipated to nothing but a numb, hollow feeling. Some combination of drugs seeped into her, promoting pain relief and relaxation. She felt her taut muscles yielding, even as a network of filamentous webs

237

encased her and tugged her lower into the gel. Her arms grew heavy and sank into the gel of their own volition. Or had they been pulled there?

She sensed movement and opened her eyes to see Tom rise and shuffle to the next tank, then awkwardly dump himself in, head-first. She couldn't even react beyond a mewling sound of concern. His booted feet stuck out. As she watched, they twisted and were sucked down, disappearing from view.

She felt drowsy. Something tugged at her leg, manipulating the injured appendage. She felt pulling, a brief grinding, then a sensation of blessed relief. She looked down with heavy-lidded curiosity, but could no longer see anything amid the swath of fibrous filaments that enveloped her.

The gel lapped at her lips. It tasted acrid, bitter. She tried to shake her head, to sit up, to raise her chin, but she was so sleepy and the tug was strong.

You will not suffocate, Dr. Jane Holloway. The device will supply your organs directly with all that is needed. Trust.

She railed against the word. She wanted to hurl it back at him. But she couldn't. She didn't have the energy. She couldn't stay above the surface much longer. She could feel the slender tentacles brushing against her face, like a lover's gentle caress. Whisper soft, they infiltrated her nose, her mouth. She couldn't deny them entrance.

She felt her breath and pulse slow.

Her last conscious thoughts were of Alan. Was he hurt? Was he safe? Ei'Brai had promised he would be.

If he wasn't…when she got out of this…whatever this was…there would be hell to pay.

She went under.

18

It was womb-like and quiet. No sound disturbed her drifting slumber. She bobbed in and out of twilight, opening her eyes for brief moments of clarity, gazing into the gloom through the glowing, colored-glaze of the gel, long enough to register that she was there and whole and mending somehow, before something like sleep swept her under again, to wander through unknown landscapes, to touch foreign stars, amidst the scores of remembrances Ei'Brai had gathered from the individuals his mind had touched.

Only the broken leg was completely immobile now. Her other limbs floated within the slackened web-matrix that anchored her, the mechanicals of the device still swarming over her like busy insects. In the hushed stillness, she was aware on some level of the filaments piercing her skin, threading her veins, flushing her body with various medicaments that made her want to move restlessly or slip back into the quiet recesses of Ei'Brai's mind.

Her hands were limp things. She brushed them against herself absently. She felt numb and unquiet. She noted with faint surprise that her garments had been completely removed, giving the filaments greater access to her.

Ei'Brai was always there when she woke, but he was reticent. He occupied himself diligently with the incessant needs of the ship, rarely resting himself for more than moments. He was a soft reminder of life beyond the gloaming.

She dreamt of Alan...of urgent, open-mouthed kisses and swirling tongues...of heavy-lidded eyes and feverishly hot skin...of inhaling musk and tasting salt...of arms and legs restlessly twining...throbbing...aching...rolling...opening to him...her hands sliding over his broad back...kneading his flesh...rocking...her legs wrapped around him...panting for more...pulling him deeper....

She aroused to find her hips bucking against the ribbons of confinement, acquisitive fingers wending their way to seek release.

She felt dizzy.

Her body was tensed with anticipation, poised at the tipping point. With only a light touch, she was riding unending waves of bliss. It multiplied and compounded in her sleep-soaked, foggy mind, her body arching, contracting....

And choking.

Even as the last twitches of the aftershocks trembled, she fought for breath that wasn't there. Her heart exploded in her chest. Her heels drummed against the floor of the tank. She gagged, tried to cough, tried to pull in nonexistent air, writhing against the bindings.

It was only seconds before the apparatus compensated, filling the alveoli of her lungs with a greater supply of oxygen in counterpoint to the pounding of her heart. But she'd had enough.

She thrashed—arms, head, feet—against the sides of the tank in a blind rage, desperate to get to the surface.

Ei'Brai leapt to her mind to calm her, to console her, to assure her it was not much longer now.

She didn't care. She pushed him away, forcefully. It'd been too long. She needed to see the rest of the crew, to know they were ok.

She felt cool sedatives flow into her veins and grappled with the strands, trying to pull them out, to free herself. But even with the new strength of the additional air and a surplus of adrenaline, she couldn't stop the flow of the drugs, couldn't remove the latticework of strands tethering her to the device.

Her struggles gradually slowed along with the rhythm of her heart. Her muscles went lax and the fibers ceased to contract against her exertions. She could feel them resume their minute ministrations. A wracking sob rose to her throat that she was powerless to express. She closed her eyes on tears of frustration and drifted away, again.

She opened her eyes to semi-darkness. The glowing lights had been extinguished. She blinked. The drag against her eyelashes, the pressure against her corneas was gone. She inhaled sharply, and let the breath back out as a surprised laugh. She was out of the gel. How had that happened?

She heard movement and froze, every sense acutely attuned to the sound. She couldn't tell where she was or how she'd gotten there. She felt for Ei'Brai, but he was silent, disconnected. She tried to still her frantic breathing and search for a clue to what was happening.

"Jane?" a groggy voice uttered. "Are you awake?"

"Alan?" Her voice sounded thin, child-like, and choked from disuse. She coughed a little to make it sound stronger. "Where are we?"

She could hear rustling movement, the soft, padding steps of bare feet, and the dry sound of a hand brushing the wall. Then Alan was looming uncertainly above her, shifting from foot to foot, an intense expression on his face. He was wearing some kind of oversized tunic, which frankly was a bit ridiculous. He seemed self-conscious and worried.

"You ok?"

She realized she was lying flat on her back on a bed. She sat up. "Yeah. I think so."

Alan's lips twitched into a secretive-looking smile before he averted his eyes and turned toward the door.

"What happened?" she asked him.

"I'm, ah…I'm going to get Ajaya. She told me to get her right away when you woke up."

"Wait a minute," she called after him. But he was already gone. She looked down and cursed. Why the hell was she always waking up naked? She pulled the filmy sheet up and wrapped it around herself, then eased herself to the edge of the platform bed. The sheet worked its way up onto her lap as she scooted, revealing her leg. It was unmarked, pristine. There was no evidence that it had ever been broken and torn. She was still puzzling over that when Ajaya strode into the room, exuding brisk efficiency. The lights came up to full-strength.

"Jane. It's so good to see you awake. How are you feeling?" Ajaya was already taking vitals, testing reflexes. She was wearing a tunic similar to the one Alan had been wearing. It was Sectilius, Jane realized with a start.

Alan did not reenter the room. It was just the two of them.

She searched for an answer to Ajaya's question. *Disoriented? Overwhelmed? Unnerved?* "I'm not sure what happened. What's going on?"

Ajaya met her eyes, briefly, and nodded. "Understandable. May I?" Ajaya gestured at the uncovered leg.

Jane nodded and mentally braced herself for pain as Ajaya ran her hands over her leg, pressing and feeling the long bones under her skin.

"Feel any pain when I touch here?" Ajaya asked, peering at her quizzically.

"No."

"How about here?"

"No. Nothing. It feels normal."

"Good." Ajaya held out a hand to Jane. "Let's try putting some weight on it, shall we?"

Something was wrong. Why wasn't anyone explaining anything?

She slid down from the bed and stood, slowly, carefully, clinging to Ajaya's firm, warm grip. She expected the blood to rush to her feet, to feel weak or sick or incredible pain, but nothing happened. She just stood up.

Ajaya tilted her head to the side. "How does that leg feel now?"

"It feels completely normal. Like nothing happened."

Ajaya nodded, looking thoughtful and pleased.

"What *did* happen Ajaya? Are we safe now? You have to tell me something!"

Ajaya smiled indulgently. "We are safe. Things are progressing quite well. We've accomplished a great deal. We still have plenty of concerns, issues, but things are falling into place. You need not worry, Jane."

That was a paltry explanation. "Why is that all you're saying?"

Ajaya sighed and settled on the edge of the bed, primly, assuming her most patient air. "Jane, I hesitate to say too much, because I have no idea what you experienced, what you know. I think it might be best if you tell me what you remember. Then I can fill in the blanks for you."

She felt a surge of anger. Ajaya's answer was infuriatingly pat. "I'm not a mental patient, Ajaya!"

Ajaya raised her brows and spoke slowly. "Of course you're not."

Ajaya's methods were always cautious and considered. Jane knew that. She swallowed her anger. She was not a petulant child. "I'm sorry. I'm feeling overwhelmed."

Ajaya nodded and waited for her to begin.

"I was heading for Tom. I…the gravity went out, then came back on. When I fell, my leg was broken—"

"Did you see your leg? How did you know?" Ajaya interjected.

Jane ran her fingers through her hair, pushing it back in a practiced, unconscious gesture and wished she had something to tie it back with. It felt clean and silky. That was unexpected and she filed that fact away with some confusion as she continued, "I'd never felt pain like that before. It looked wrong—really, really wrong."

"Yes, that's what Walsh and Alan said. It was the angle."

Jane nodded, slowly—the mental picture coming quickly to mind: that horrible, disgusting angle—and then the bone, the ragged, bleeding tissues through the gel. "Yes. Then Tom came and rescued me. Except it wasn't Tom."

Ajaya's eyes narrowed, but she betrayed no other sign of emotion.

Jane hesitated, not sure Ajaya would believe her. "It was Ei'Brai."

Ajaya nodded curtly. "That would explain it."

Jane stared at Ajaya hard. She'd expected disbelief. Blithe acceptance felt wrong. Warning bells were going off in her brain, but she couldn't figure out for sure what they meant.

"He carried me and put me in some kind of medical device. He put Tom in one too."

"Yes. That's where we found you. Thomas is still submerged."

"Oh. He—is he ok?"

"I believe so. Every indication is yes. Of course, my methods of measurement are primitive by comparison. The device is still working on him. I have the impression he'll be in there a long time. We've submerged Walsh as well."

Jane took an involuntary step back and put her hand out to the wall to steady herself, the other still clutching the sheet to her chest. *What the hell is going on here?* She looked up and noticed Alan was standing in the doorway, holding a ship-colored, plastic object in his hand, listening intently to their conversation. How long had he been there?

"Walsh? You put him in a tank? Why?"

Ajaya stood and moved briskly to a large protuberance on the wall. She touched it lightly and it slid open. She pulled out a voluminous article of clothing—greenish, just like theirs—and extended it to Jane. "We had no choice. He became catatonic, just like Tom. The rest of us appear to be fine—for now, anyway. We're working on it, Jane. We're going to find a solution. I'm confident of that."

Jane looked from Ajaya to Alan, bewildered.

He surged forward. "Are you hungry, Jane? The food we've managed to make has a weird texture, but some of it doesn't taste too bad. We're still analyzing the parameters of the printer's output. The technology is pretty fucking amazing. It's fun to tinker with."

Ajaya rolled her eyes. "Yes, Alan and Ronald have spent a lot of quality time with the food machine. Do you want to get dressed first or nibble on something?"

Jane swallowed hard. "How long have I been out?"

Ajaya grimaced before answering, "Seventeen days, Jane."

She sat on the bed heavily and let all of her disbelief show on her face. It had felt like a long time, but not *that* long. "How—when—did you find me in the gel? Did you pull me out?"

Alan ducked his head. "I tried to cut you out with a knife. The tank didn't like that. It sort of…fought back."

Ajaya patted Alan's arm. "We decided it might be wise to leave you alone and just observe you for a while."

"It healed my leg."

"So it would seem," Ajaya agreed. "I'd like to get back to work, if you don't mind? I think Alan can take it from here?" Her voice was light, breezy, but she sent Alan a meaningful look as she left the room.

Jane watched her go, completely nonplussed.

Alan perched himself casually on the edge of the bed a couple of feet away.

"Back to work? What is she doing? How did you all get past the nepatrox? Food machine? What the hell, Alan? Start talking!"

"A lot's happened, Jane. Sure you don't want to eat?"

"Do you want me to drink the Kool-Aid, too? No, Alan— tell me what's going on!"

He smirked and rubbed the back of his neck. "Well, the most valuable thing that's happened is we've had some very primitive communications with your alien friend."

"What? Ei'Brai? How? I thought he couldn't communicate with us unless we could speak Mensententia?"

"Oh, he's not speaking to us, at least not anything we can understand. He sends us mental images. It's like playing a game of telepathic charades. We have to figure out what he's trying to tell us to do. When we do, he, ah…." He seemed embarrassed. It was a new look for him.

"What?"

"He stimulates the part of the brain that registers pleasure."

She raised her eyebrows.

"He does that to you too, Jane?"

She looked down and clutched the sheet a little tighter. The memory of the erotic dream in which Alan had played a starring role came vividly to the front of her mind. Her cheeks felt hot. She hoped she wasn't blushing.

He huffed. "I'll take that as a yes."

She searched for something to say that would obviate their mutual embarrassment. "What does that mean? What has he told you?"

"He convinced us to stay in the storage room for a while. That was the first thing. That…I didn't…that was…." He was clenching and unclenching his fists. His eyes were hard and hot on her.

"Why?" she whispered. Her voice sounded husky to her own ears.

"We think he released a gas in the hallway. We heard a lot of noise. It sounded like they were climbing the walls and killing the shit out of each other. Then it got quiet and the doors opened. When we walked out there, they were mostly dead or dying. That's not to say more haven't hatched by now, I'm sure, the stinky little bastards. One of 'em got me in the leg. I couldn't walk on it for two days. We're going to have to deal with that shit eventually."

"How did he convince you to stay there?"

His jaw worked. "I told you. He showed us images of stuff. We talked about it. Ajaya put it all together." He didn't seem to want to say any more about it, so she decided to drop it for now.

"He told you where I was?"

"Yes. And how to find you." His lips tightened. "We didn't know what was going on. I thought—I thought you were dead at first. It took us a while to figure out what was happening to you, and to Compton. We decided, eventually, to put Walsh in there too. That decision wasn't made easily. Ultimately, we let Ajaya make the call." He took a deep breath and blew it out slowly.

He was so intense. More so than usual. His eyes would probe hers, then travel down hungrily before he would twitch them away self-consciously. She felt a thrilling feeling growing inside her, settling low, and throbbing. It seemed they were safe now. She wanted to trust that, but she needed to hear more.

"What have you been doing all this time?" she asked him.

"Learning." He smiled, his eyes lit up with enthusiasm. "Ajaya and Gibbs have been learning the language—they go down to a language lab on level 15 and spend a large part of every day there. Ajaya knows some Latin, but we're all just limping along. It's not coming as easily to us as it did to you, Jane. Ajaya says she can almost get the gist of what the alien dude is saying to us now."

"But you haven't been studying the language? What have you been doing, Alan?"

"I've been studying it some. But I go down to Engineering. He shows me stuff, amazing stuff. How it all works. This ship is so much more than we ever could have imagined, Jane. This is going to change everything."

She smiled at his expression. This was the side of him that she could understand. Their interests weren't the same, but they shared the same kind of enthusiasm for them, nonetheless. She wanted to reach out to him, to touch him, but she didn't know how to uproot herself and get closer to him, without feeling silly and forced.

"You mentioned a printer, earlier—what did you mean by that? Some kind of food machine?"

"Oh, yeah." He picked up the green container from the bed and held it out to her. Inside was a small mound of speckled, tan cubes. "The closest thing we have to this back home is 3-D printing technology. You pour in the raw material—the stuff we found the first day in those tubs—and it spits out these things."

She wrinkled her nose. "The stuff that looked like cat litter?"

"Oh, yeah. Yep. That's exactly what it looks like." He laughed his raucous laugh. She liked the way he laughed. Unfettered. It was so true to his personality, to the way he lived his life.

She tittered and took the container from him, slowly, intentionally letting her fingers brush his. He scooted closer, clearly interpreting the gesture as an invitation.

She felt flushed.

"Yeah. You pour it in and make selections and it configures the crystals to taste different ways. We've been experimenting with it. Some of it's pretty weird tasting. Most of it's palatable."

"What does it taste like?" she asked hesitantly.

His smile turned mischievous. "I'm not saying. You'll have to see for yourself."

She looked down into the bowl, sure she was grinning like a loon. "Are they all the same? They look the same."

"I didn't know what you'd like. Each one is different. You tell me what you like."

Somehow he'd gotten closer when she wasn't looking. She felt pleasantly unfocused. He was so near, she could feel his warmth on her bare arm.

She selected one at random and nibbled at a corner of it. It was moist and dense. Her first thought was that it was bland, barely palatable, but as she chewed, flavor burst from tiny granules imbedded in it. There were fruity elements— no single fruit came to mind, though. It was pleasantly acidic and slightly sweet and there were floral notes that made it seem really refined and lovely. It was somehow the essence, the very best of fruit.

"Which one is that?" he asked, light dancing in his eyes as he watched her chew.

"I think it's some kind of fruit. I like it."

"Yeah, that one's ok. Try another one." He seemed to come to himself with a start. "Oh, sorry. You probably want something to wash it down with. Here." He pulled a limp object from a concealed pocket on the loose tunic he wore. It was a tube, made from a soft version of the ubiquitous greenish plastic. It was warm, from being close to his skin. "It's a water pouch. Works pretty much just like ours. Just stick that thing in your mouth and slurp." He leaned in close to point at the outlet of the pouch and his other hand snuck behind her to rest on her back. It felt like a hot brand. It was all she could think about.

"So, we haven't talked about the fact that you're wearing a dress," she said with a soft snort. She felt giddy. She sipped the water, eyeing him slantwise, like a teenage girl.

He seemed to like that. He leaned closer, amused. "It was this or the bathrobe." His hand slid up to cup her bare shoulder and pull her closer. "I like what you're wearing, though," he murmured in her ear.

Oh, God. He was good at this.

This was probably a really stupid idea. It would surely end badly. But she didn't want it to stop.

She couldn't say anything to him. What could she say? She couldn't think.

She just sat there, head bowed, waiting for him to make his move. Her chest heaved and fell. The sheet was slipping and she wanted it to.

He wanted her. Her—frumpy Jane Holloway. This gorgeous, genius of a man wanted her.

So, his nose was too big. So, he needed a shave. So, he laughed too loud. So, what?

He smelled divine. Musky, masculine. A hint of sweat. The good kind. He'd been exercising or something.

"Aren't you hungry, Jane?" His breath was hot on her ear and his hand was already taking the dish and pouch away.

She managed a tremulous smile. She was going to let this happen. It would be ok. He might hurt her later, when they finally got back to Earth. He might find someone younger, prettier. But she wouldn't worry about that now. That would take all the fun out of this.

This. This moment was all that mattered, right now.

He was hovering so close, just a breath away from kissing her. He was teasing her, drawing it out. The anticipation was delicious.

He was panting softly too. His hands roamed over her back, bare now; the sheet had slipped down.

She looked into his eyes. They were boring into hers, hungry and questioning. He was waiting for her to say this was ok.

She leaned into him, just the slightest movement, her hands finding their way to touch him, his bearded face, his shoulder. He reacted instantly, pulling her hard against him, covering her mouth with his.

Kissing wasn't nearly enough. She clutched at him, trying to get closer. The angle was all wrong. Sitting perched on the edge of the high mattress was awkward.

His hand slid up to her bare breast and she gasped against his mouth. Gently, reverently, he kneaded and squeezed and lightly brushed his thumb over her nipple.

She pulled ineffectually at the filmy tunic that was keeping his skin from her.

He broke off the kiss and stood, pulling the tunic over his head. He dropped it to the floor, and came back to her, pushing her back and scooping her legs up onto the bed in a swift, practiced motion.

He rested his hip on the bed, his hand skimming her skin. His eyes roved over her body. They seemed to devour her. It was a heady feeling.

The evidence of his desire pressed firmly against her thigh.

She experienced a moment of disquiet. The only man she'd ever been with had been Brian and that was a long time gone now. Alan was athletic. His body was firm. She was out of practice, out of shape, and accustomed to a mindless succession of uneventful missionary. She wondered if she could be the kind of lover he wanted.

He dispelled her fears instantly. He touched his nose to hers playfully and kissed her hard and deep, his tongue swirling around hers, while he slowly ran his hand up her thigh, pushed her leg aside, and cupped her. His touch wasn't greedy or callous, but reverent with an aching sweetness that seemed counter to his nature.

She arched against his hand and let out a whimper. His caress was gentle, insistent and, precisely targeted for maximum impact. Leave it to the engineer to know how things worked.

Was this an indication of the kind of care and sensitivity she could expect from him? If so, she'd underestimated him utterly. She was so overwhelmed that she was unable to do much more than cling to him, as his fingers and lips played over her, until she was at the very edge of it, trembling and gasping with it.

She opened her eyes to find him contemplating her unguarded expression with a hint of a smug smile on his lips. A giggle bubbled up out of her, unbidden. She ran her hands over his back, restlessly, putting pressure on him, trying to pull him into position.

He resisted, his fingers sliding in her slippery wetness, his tongue rasping over a nipple. She put her hand over his, stilling its movement and the incipient waves that were imminent. She captured his mouth in a kiss and took him in her hand to increase his sense of urgency. "I'm so close," she moaned against his lips. "Please, Alan, come with me."

He moaned against her neck, a guttural sound that made her pulse race even faster, then complied without further prodding. It was just the two of them. There was nothing else.

His eyes locked with hers as he slipped inside. It felt entirely new, more intensely gratifying than ever before. He held his body high and, glancing between them, slowly moved, the length of him dragging over her sex.

Her legs trembled. She arched, crying out, heedless to who might hear, as she shuddered with potent, chaotic spasms.

She gasped for breath. Still, he watched, nostrils flaring, jaw set, sharp eyes penetrating. He picked up the pace.

She rocked to meet each thrust, every sensation heightened, building already, again, to the next peak.

He buried his face in the hollow of her shoulder, clasping her closer, grunting, pumping, tracking her ascent, until he drove them both over the edge, together.

He stayed in place, his weight pleasantly pressing on her, and kissed her fervently. He rested his forehead against hers and choked out, "We thought...I thought. Oh, fuck, Jane. I thought I'd lost you before I could ever even have you."

Anguish? From Alan Bergen? Over her?

He smoothed her hair. She searched his bloodshot, watery eyes and saw truth staring back at her.

She didn't know what to say.

"Alan, I'm ok. Everything's going to work out. We just have to trust him. It's the only way."

His lips tightened and he slid to her side, one hand left possessively at her waist. "Yes. I see that. At what cost, Jane? What does he want from you?"

"I—I'm not sure what you mean. He's trying to protect us, keep us alive."

His expression turned fierce. "He wants more than that and you know it! What's he telling you, right now? Did he just…?" His expression shuttered down and he sank heavily onto the bed, one hand capturing one of hers, squeezing hard.

She closed her eyes so she wouldn't have to see his angst. It didn't look right, didn't settle right over his features. She didn't like seeing him so uncertain. She wanted to see him smirking, confident, strong.

"He's not here right now," she murmured, shrugging self-consciously. Why did she feel guilty? Ashamed?

"Tell him to take us home, Jane." There was a plaintive note in his voice that didn't belong there, not when he seemed so sure of himself half an hour before.

"He can't. It's not possible. Can't you and Gibbs figure out how to fly it?"

"I wish. I'm in fucking alien-preschool, Jane. That's not happening. Some of this shit's organic or something. We could die of old age before I figure this shit out. We brought a fucking lot of computing power, but I don't have a clue where to begin to interface it."

So much cursing. That meant he felt supremely frustrated. If the situation weren't so awful, she'd be smiling at the sound of it.

She rolled to her side and slid her hand reassuringly over his shoulder. "We'll figure it out."

His blue eyes roved over her face. "Will we? Before we turn into zombies? Before Bravo shows up and nukes us? Do you have a plan, Jane?"

A plan? A chill swept through her, clammy and uncomfortable. Her heart thudded, heavy and dull. She resisted the urge to press herself against him, to cling to him for warmth and security. Their roles were decidedly non-traditional at the moment and tipping the balance back in that direction now was not the right thing to do.

He was asking her to lead them. Command had never been her goal. Duty, honor, altruism, self-sacrifice. Those were qualities she knew she possessed. But good leadership required something intangible that she couldn't define.

NASA believed her capable before they'd even met her. They'd construed her reservations as humility. Perhaps they thought her personality was a good counterpoint to Bergen's raging hubris.

Had she deceived them somehow? That had never been her intent. She'd just...*dammit*...she'd just wanted to go on an adventure.

And, her conscience told her, she could see now that the draw would never have been as strong if they hadn't sent Alan to persuade her. During those early days in Houston, she'd vacillated wildly as she strove to make her decision. She had moments, certain she was going to walk away, hop a plane home, and dismiss the notion as a ridiculous whim. Then they'd escort her through some building and she'd spy

Alan working, his massive intellect broadcasting like a beacon. He'd intrigued her almost as much as the mission.

"Jane?" His voice was husky, hoarse, and he didn't meet her gaze. He was looking down, watching his own fingers trailing languidly over her skin. She'd always longed for someone to touch her that way—possessively, adoringly. It was intoxicating. He could do that forever.

"Yes?"

"I love you." It was just a whisper.

Blood rushed in her ears. A thrilling sensation washed over her even as cold dread settled in her stomach. She pulled away to scrutinize his expression.

It wasn't right.

Something wasn't right.

No.

This wasn't real.

19

It hit her with a certainty she couldn't deny.

She scrambled up and away from him, grabbing the discarded sheet and covering herself. She glared at Alan, reeling with panic and revulsion. She felt physically ill.

He wasn't surprised. He just stared at her blankly, unmoving.

"This scenario displeases you, Dr. Jane Holloway?" rumbled in her head. "Shall I choose another? Perhaps a milieu of a less intimate nature? A memory? Mayhap Sectilius? To further familiarize you with cultural convention and conduct?"

"Ei'Brai—you bastard!" she spat at him.

"Contextualize this comment, if you please. You experience anger. Explain."

She coughed against the back of her hand. "You just violated me!"

Shock and indignation met her outrage. "None of my appendages were involved in this tableau."

She shook her head. "What?"

And yet, as she took a ragged breath, she could sense his confusion was real. She struggled to rein in the feeling that some kind of atrocity had just been committed against her—

evaluate dispassionately what had actually just happened. They'd been reminded countless times that their cultural references meant absolutely nothing, hadn't they?

She was human. He was not. That was a certainty. Did he have any idea what he'd just done?

His tone, his manner, said no.

A sense of astonished inquisitiveness suffused his mental touch. Tendrils of thought were moving in gingerly to investigate and analyze her reaction.

She tried to sound calmer. "Ei'Brai—you just manipulated me in a vile, disgusting manner!"

"Mating requires privacy among your kind. It is also a reprehensible act? This I did not perceive." She got a brief flash of insight into his species' mating rituals and her eyes went wide at the deadly savagery of it.

"You—it—I—oh, this is ridiculous." She slumped on the bed, covering her face in her hands. This went so far beyond mere mortification. It was too much to process.

"This act was coveted by the pair of you, as individuals. It is much on Dr. Alan Bergen's mind—the sequence you enjoyed was lifted almost seamlessly from his habitual musings on the topic of copulation. It is clear he greatly desires to engage in these behaviors with you. You also cogitate on the possibility of coition with him, frequently. It seemed a natural departure point, given your subconscious maundering."

She clenched her fists tight, nails digging into her palms, the resultant pain fueling her fury. "I don't want you rooting around in my subconscious maundering!"

A consternated, probing purr was his reply.

She concentrated all her mental energy to push him back through the mental layers to the surface of her thoughts. She registered nothing but startled surprise from him as she forced him back.

"Where am I—really? I'm still in the tank, aren't I?"

His voice came back haughty, hurt. "Convalescence is nearly complete."

"I want out. *Now*."

"Unacceptable. Premature egress could result in permanent infirmity."

"I don't care. Let me out."

"That is not rational."

"It most certainly is. You're toying with me. I'm not going to play along anymore."

"On the contrary, I—"

"I see plainly what you *think* you were doing. You thought you were distracting me, but the scenario you chose crossed a line, Ei'Brai. Again."

"It is to be expected. The Sectilius tolerate my shortcomings when it comes to cultural sensitivity. You are not as forbearing. The contrast is noted. I shall employ more caution going forward. Enlighten me, if you will. Is this an example of human cultural mores? Or more properly assigned to your own personal construct? How may we resolve this concern?"

His voice had taken a patronizing tone, precisely the kind of tone Brian took with her frequently—disdainful, like she wasn't sophisticated enough to understand. It rankled, especially staring into Bergen's blank expression.

"Turn off this fantasy—now!"

She sensed a begrudging reluctance as her surroundings dissolved. The reality of the tank crashed over her—the dark room, the light bathing her in a magenta glow. The complex network of filaments—now, seemingly doubled—restricted her movement even further.

She closed her eyes against it, wishing that other world had been real, that Alan had been real and safe and in love with her. She didn't want to face this reality, trapped, where Alan might actually be dead.

But it didn't do any good to wish. That didn't solve anything. Nothing happened without action. It was time to stop *letting* things happen and start *making* them happen.

She painstakingly wove her fingers through the mesh toward her leg.

Ei'Brai emanated something akin to a mental glower. She ignored him. Her leg was numb and foreign-feeling, bristling with strands over every square inch. The fibers rustled under the brush of her hand like some kind of amorphous, invertebrate sea creature.

She lifted her head to look, but the gel distorted her vision and the threads formed a tight matrix that bound her, nearly mummified, in place. Frustration throbbed in her. The impulse to thrash and yank on the filaments was strong.

Ei'Brai manifested a thought, hidden from her before she could fully glimpse its purpose. Instinctively, she extended herself to follow it. It led her down pathways she had only glimpsed before, had never tried to explore. She sped down them, heedless, gleaning information along the way. Data flowed through her mind at a seemingly impossible pace. She marveled at how much of it made sense.

The atmosphere changed subtly from organic to digital as the thought she traced transitioned, bridging the gap between Ei'Brai and the ship's neural-electric pathways. The sensation was wholly bizarre, but not troublesome. This was a command pathway, she realized, it was how he maintained control over the ship's functions.

Abruptly, she became aware of his intent. Without hesitation, Jane countermanded Ei'Brai's order for the device to deliver greater sedation and yet more restraint. Stunningly, the device accepted her command. Ei'Brai contracted, nonplussed at her sudden involvement.

She flexed within the system, feeling for other controls that she knew must be there. She couldn't let the moment slip by. The layout was intuitively designed. The imprint in her mind seemed to include a blueprint of this framework, permitting unconscious ease of navigation.

Ei'Brai's state of mind reflected some form of breathless anticipation as she explored the root command controls for the tank. Within seconds, she had it. Ei'Brai didn't try to stop her as she executed the command. He merely watched as she directed the device to withdraw all medications, release and retract the mechanical filaments, and drain the gel.

Red warnings flashed into her consciousness. She ignored them. Circumventing safety protocols, consenting releases…she exhilarated, relishing the power of it. She felt a sense of accomplishment and realized with surprise that the same sentiment resonated in Ei'Brai's mind.

A wave of nausea swept the gratification aside. Her body was regaining sensation. She gagged, trembling with a sudden chill, as she worked to accomplish her goals before she was dragged back to her own immediate, visceral needs. She didn't have the control Ei'Brai had. She was incapable of segmentation, unable to multitask away pain or discomfort.

"Such mastery is within your reach, Dr. Jane Holloway," he rumbled reassuringly. "I will instruct you. In time."

She noted his smug satisfaction as he watched her struggle. He'd wanted this.

There was no time to contemplate that. Numb for so long, it was an incomprehensible flood.

The filaments retracted—all at the same time, tenting her skin, slithering over and through her. Her lips curled and she coughed as the strands drug over her lips, exiting her throat *en masse*.

She hit the bottom of the tank with a thunk, sending a painful jolt through her leg. Ei'Brai was right. It wasn't healed yet. Well, he hadn't lied about that. That was something.

She shuddered with a bone-deep chill. Slowly, she reached up and wiped the gel from her eyes. That helped. Sight was definitely helpful.

She sat up slowly, expecting weakness after the long, inactive submersion. But weakness wasn't the problem. Her teeth chattered and slimy, chilled strands of her hair slapped her face, dripping with gel.

She gripped the side of the tank and hauled herself up on the good leg. Her right leg ached and burned. The slightest movement sent pain slicing through her. She was going to have to use it. There was no other way. The violent shivering was only making it worse.

She tested the edge of the tank by leaning against it, then put all her weight on it and swung both legs over the rim and slid down, faster than she intended. The residual gel was slippery. Her feet slid out from under her. Her head struck the side of the tank, narrowing her vision to a tunnel of light. After a few moments, she came back to her senses, leg throbbing from the impact. She grunted, regained her footing, then half walked, half hopped to the wall.

Her fingers touched a protruding module. It eased out. She grabbed the silky material inside, wrapping a length around her hair, using another to dry herself. The fabric was incredibly thirsty and efficient for its weight. She felt better almost immediately.

She opened various drawers and shook out the garments inside until she found a tunic and a pair of drawstring pants. The pants and sleeves were far too long, but she tight-rolled them at wrists and ankles and left her feet bare. The gauzy fabric instantly warmed her, allowing the chilled tremors to subside. She tugged at her turbaned hair and found it slightly damp, lanky, and matted. She ran fingers through the tangles for a moment, then gave up. There was no time for that now.

Ei'Brai tried to convince her to do a scan, to hear the computer's assessment of her condition, provide some kind of mechanical support—at the very least get some kind of an injection to control the pain. But she wouldn't let him slow her down or distract her again. She'd make do.

She hobbled out of the infirmary and down the corridor to the deck transport. Just a few floors away was the protection she needed—Sectilius battle armor. It would keep the nepatrox off her, give her defensive weapons. Since it was mechanical, used minimal effort to operate, it would take some of the stress off her leg.

By the time she got there, she knew Ei'Brai had been right. Healing was far from complete—she could be doing permanent damage. Her breath hissed through clenched teeth with every jolting, painful step.

She leaned against the wall and slapped her palm on the door control. The door slid open to reveal undulating rows of gleaming obsidian armor. Jane wrinkled her brow. These things were designed to protect, to kill, and yet the sight of a sea of them in graceful, inverted U-shapes was compellingly beautiful, moving.

Each suit was designed to conform to fit the entire spectrum of Sectilius body types. Meant to be stepped into, the legs stood short and squat, open at the waist, compressed like an accordion. The torso was split down the center and arched back, the compacted arms terminating in gauntlets that gently rested against the floor, like the advanced yoga pose upward bow, *urdhava dhanu*, that she'd never successfully managed.

She took a tentative step inside. The nearest suit twitched. She staggered a step back to grip the doorframe, until she realized it had just turned itself on in response to her presence and intent.

She stared at it, bemused. There was no good way to get into the thing. She'd have to put all of her weight on the bad leg at some point. She was afraid she might fall in the process. There was nothing to hold onto.

Ei'Brai's voice flitted gently against her mind, a recommendation.

She frowned, but followed his thought toward a simple command and watched with awe as the suit picked up one foot and then the other, moving toward her in odd, shuffling, mechanical steps. She hopped back, pressing herself into the wall as the suit positioned itself precisely before her and the contents of the entire room shifted in a roar of clinks and thuds to fill in the empty space the suit had left behind.

She laughed out loud. She almost expected it to wag a tail.

This was going to be a far different experience from the EMU.

The smile remained plastered to her lips as she eased the warm clothing back off. The suit was meant to be worn naked, which was simply absurd, but utterly Sectilius. Their attitudes about the physical body and sexuality were completely different. They were Pragmatists by culture and inclination, innately.

That thought gave her a moment's pause. How did she know this with such certainty? She mentally raised a brow at Ei'Brai. She could feel him now—smugly swelling. He didn't have to say a word. He'd used her time in the tank wisely, indoctrinating her mind with Sectilius experience and knowledge.

She cursed at him viciously in Mensententia and felt his vibrating, answering chuckle. She was bound to this lunatic now, for better or for worse.

She turned and braced herself against the wall, put all her weight on the good leg, and lifted the injured leg with a hand, guiding it up, back and into the corresponding leg of the suit.

She inhaled sharply as the boot constricted around her foot and lower leg, locking into place.

She gripped the doorframe, easing her weight onto the injured leg, partially supported now, and slipped the good leg in, quickly. She managed to stay upright, knuckles white, inhaling in a strangled gasp from the pain. She leaned down and gripped the handholds inset into the waistband in a practiced manner, almost like she'd done this before, and lifted up. Her every muscle tensed as the suit took over with a whirring boost, adapting to the contours of her lower body and molding over her injury. There was a brief squeeze as the internal computers tested her anatomy and then settled the suit into a semi-comfortable position. It'd do better once the entire suit was donned, she knew.

To that end, she had only to lean slightly to the side and slip her arm down into the gauntlet. It stretched and constricted against her shape. She expected it to be heavy, but the gear moved proactively, reducing the load for her. The other arm was waiting, exactly where it needed to be, for ease. She bit her lip and shoved her fingers down the tube.

A dizzying flurry of mechanized movement made her pulse throb. Her right arm was enveloped. The suit closed and locked over her chest. The helmet closed up and over her head. She winced as the plumbing engaged with an uncomfortable rasp to her private parts, surprisingly sensitive from her recent mental diversion.

She was protected now—from the vacuum of space, from the elements, from chemical or biological warfare, and all but the most potent weapons. The suit was designed for combat with the Swarm. It would easily handle the nepatrox.

She stood there for a moment, dazed, adjusting to the new sensory input. A huge red symbol hung before her eyes, its three-dimensions telescoping in and out of focus.

"Delay action momentarily," it said.

She wasn't done with the filamentous medical devices. The suit utilized the same technology to medically assess and deliver rudimentary care under combat conditions. Without the gel buffering the sensation, they pinched as they drove under her skin at strategic points all over her body.

The suit triaged her. She realized with a start that it had threaded her brain and was delivering a digital assessment of her medical state in a real-time HUD behind her eyes. The suit's right leg adjusted its configuration slightly, to support the healing skeletal structure and minimize further damage.

A shunt was established at the site of the nerve root of her right leg, which already felt blessedly numb. New pathways of control for the movement of that leg were routed. A software patch was installed and coupled with the primary motor cortex on the left side of the prefrontal lobe of her brain, to ease the transition.

Behind her eyes, a dazzling symbol prompted, "Practice?"

She felt the suit moving nearly effortlessly, in servomotor creaks and whirs, as she unconsciously nodded her head. She let out a soft laugh. She felt like a comic-book hero. Which one was it? She couldn't remember the name. Alan would know.

The suit wanted to optimize the customization of the suit for her personally. In her mind's eye she could see that it was requesting that she perform a series of maneuvers, first like calisthenics, then increasingly more complex movements like some kind of martial art.

She had to find him—all of them. Ei'Brai claimed he didn't know where they were, or what had happened to them. She didn't know what she was going to find, but she had to go now.

Her primary concern at that moment was simply to master walking in that getup. She turned carefully toward the door, intending to make headway as she worked it out.

Her gait was clumsy at first. The right leg pounded into the floor, jarring her all the way up to her teeth. The suit's adaptive software adjusted the code-patch with each step, until walking became less drunken crashing and more slightly-disjointed stomping. Perhaps that was the best she could do.

The suit prompted her to continue the practical exercises to perfect the hardware/software integration. She forcefully disregarded the request. She didn't need to move like a ninja. She just needed to get there. She set off for the deck transport, picking up speed as she went.

So fucking tired.

Alan's eyes drifted shut. He let them, forcing his mind to stay active, alert, while he caught a little rest. Just a few minutes. As long as he was quiet, he'd be relatively safe. Just...no sleeping. If he slept, he might snore. Snoring was a bad idea.

He was in the fucked up state he was in because he'd fallen asleep some time ago—no idea how long ago that was now. He'd lost his watch—as if he could keep track of anything like time in this nightmare, anyway. He hadn't eaten in what felt like days. He wasn't even hungry anymore.

Waking up with a startled snort to find some creature feasting on his own leg? That was fucked up. The fact that he hadn't felt it or that he was still alive? More fucked up. He should be dead by now.

He lifted one eyelid slightly to look down at his leg. The flight suit was shredded from the knee down, exposing a calf that resembled chopped steak. It hadn't bled much, which was weird. Damn things must have some kind of coagulant in their saliva—to keep their meat alive and fresh. He coughed a little, then twitched and came to full alert, remembering he wasn't supposed to make a sound.

He was lucky that there'd been some kind of epic battle going on in the hallway that drowned out the sound of him killing that little son of a bitch. Sound drew them.

Above all, he had to stay as quiet as possible. It was the only way. So, no sleeping, no groaning, no whining. No anything. Just hanging on.

The urge to scream profanity was strong, but he held back, barely. Something inside him kinda wanted it all to just be over. If he couldn't go out fighting, at least maybe he could go out raging like a lunatic.

Goddamn mother-fuckers. He was not an all-you-can-eat sushi bar.

He felt kind of feverish and light-headed. There was no telling what kind of germs those bastards had left on him and no way to clean the wound. He had nothing left. He'd lost everything except his gun and even that had precious few bullets left.

How many? One? Two?

He was too tired to check. He was loath to use it anyway. The noise created more problems than it solved.

His head sunk to his chest. He jerked himself awake and blinked owlishly, trying to remember the last thread of thought he'd been meandering down before he'd drifted off.

He'd given up hope that Walsh and the others would come back for him. They'd already pushed off. They'd spend months drifting toward Mars and if they weren't all zombies by the time they got there, they'd touch down, connect the two capsules and hunker down to wait for the launch window to open to head for home. They'd have a year to explain to Houston via radio what had happened. Houston, without a doubt, was going to send Bravo to blow this shit up. And good riddance.

He was just hanging out in this tomb, waiting to kick it. The only thing keeping him from cracking up completely was the hope that maybe…maybe Jane was still alive.

Walsh released the back of his flight suit and Alan spun around angrily, getting in Walsh's face. "We have to go after her."

Walsh eyed him steadily. "How do you propose we do that?"

"We—we—fuck! What the fuck just happened?" Alan swung around, hand raising to the back of his neck, gripping hard, thoughts racing through every possibility. "Fuck, fuck, fuck!"

Gibbs and Ajaya approached them slowly. The animals were clawing and scrabbling and hissing on the other side of the door.

Ajaya spoke up, "We should explore the room, see if there's anything here we can use."

Walsh nodded solemnly. "Agreed. Spread out—but maintain visual contact."

Gibbs' gaze darted from person to person. "We're not going to talk about what just happened? That wasn't Tom Compton…."

Ajaya's eyes were glassy. "Clearly not."

Gibbs went on, his expression stricken, "I mean, it was his body, I know…but…." He trailed off and turned a pleading gaze on Ajaya. "Do you have any theories as to what or how?"

Ajaya looked pained. "I've no idea. This is so beyond the realm of human medical science, Ronald."

She wouldn't say what they were all thinking—that the alien had wanted Jane for something from the start. Now it had her and Compton, both.

Walsh ground out, "At this point, it doesn't matter how, or even why. It's getting its rocks off watching us spin our wheels. We just have to get the hell out of here."

The sounds from the hall amplified suddenly. There was a cacophony of thuds, unearthly screams, and strident hisses. They all turned toward the door. Alan half expected it to open—or for something to break through it.

Ajaya crossed quickly to put her hand over the door control, ready to shut it again if one of the animals got lucky and tapped the right spot outside.

Something large slammed against the other side of the door, shaking it. Ajaya flinched. Walsh stepped between her and the door, pistol ready in one hand, tank in the other. Alan and Gibbs joined him. They stood, shoulder to shoulder, waiting.

The enraged and agonized shrieks from the other side of the door reached a deafening zenith. Alan glanced at the others, psyching himself up for the next onslaught that he knew was likely to be the end.

Then, the sounds died off. It went silent.

Minutes went by without a sound. No hissing, no screams, not even the scratch of claws against the door.

Cold sweat ran down the side of Alan's face. He shrugged it away with his shoulder. He was intensely thirsty, chilled from the evaporation of sweat, and his muscles ached from the exertion and tension of the last hour. The fiery sensation in his leg was waning, quickly replaced by an unnerving stiff, wooden feeling.

They remained ready, but Alan felt silly about it.

"What just happened?" Gibbs asked nervously, adjusting his stance and aim.

Alan rolled his eyes. "Is that a rhetorical question? What makes you think we have more information than you do, Gibbs?"

Walsh shot him a dirty look and lowered his weapon. "Stand down."

They broke apart and stood motionless, listening. Ajaya went to the door and put her ear to it. Walsh sidled up to her and she moved out of his way, shaking her head. He listened for long minutes.

Walsh stepped back and motioned Ajaya to the door control, then gestured for Alan and Gibbs to flank him. "Cover me," he said gruffly. Once they were in place, he nodded at Ajaya. She tapped the control and took up a defensive stance.

The door slid up. A pile of animals that had been leaning against the door fell toward them. Walsh stepped back, cursing, but didn't fire into the carnage.

They were all dead. As far as Alan could see, the floor was littered with contorted corpses. Many had a painful, twisted look to them—eyes bulging, hinged-maw yawning, winged mouth-flaps extended, scaled-tongues stiffly erect. In death, they were even more grotesque than in life. No small feat, that.

"What the hell?" Walsh muttered.

Ajaya moved forward and stooped, turning one of the specimens over with the business end of her weapon.

"Any theories, Varma?" Walsh grunted.

She replied, "If I had to guess, I'd say asphyxiation."

Walsh huffed and poked one with the toe of his boot.

Gibbs' actively avoided looking at the animals. "That's insane. How could that happen?"

No one knew. No one answered him.

Walsh eased through the door, stepping over and around the corpses. He scanned up and down the hallway, looking unsettled.

Alan could see the wheels turning. Without conscious thought, he followed Walsh into the hallway, bellowing, "We're going for Jane, you bastard!"

Walsh inhaled slowly, raising his head a fraction. He turned a questioning gaze on Ajaya.

Ajaya squared her shoulders and nodded. "We should, yes." She turned to Gibbs.

Gibbs couldn't seem to find a comfortable place to rest his eyes; he closed them. "Johnson's got no idea what's going on here. We owe it to them—at the very least—to get a message back home. I think that should be our priority."

"Jane just saved our fucking lives, Gibbs!" Alan blurted out in disbelief.

Gibbs screwed up his mouth and leveled his gaze on Alan. "Yeah. But how can we possibly find her in here? We have to be realistic, Berg."

Walsh said, "It's split. Fifty-fifty."

Alan's hands clenched at his sides. "No, it's not. Jane's the deciding vote. She wants to be found, goddamn you."

Walsh cleared his throat. "How long can she survive with an injury like that?"

Ajaya's expression was thoughtful. "It was a compound fracture. That's very serious. She'll have lost a lot of blood. I can't imagine her lasting more than three days. Even without taking blood loss into consideration, she wasn't carrying water, and sepsis is inevitable with an injury such as that. It's dire."

Walsh nodded slowly. "Can you treat that injury with the supplies in the Providence?"

Ajaya's chin came up. "Affirmative, Commander."

A bit of bravado, then, from Ajaya. If that worked on Walsh, it was all to the good.

Alan watched Walsh, willing him to make the right call. Regardless of Walsh's decision, he'd already chosen for himself. He wasn't leaving this ship without her. Whatever that meant—he'd do it.

Walsh scratched absently at his beard, then jerked his head toward the deck transport. "Let's go, then."

But it wasn't that simple.

They threaded through the carnage, weapons at the ready. Alan kept to the rear so the others wouldn't feel compelled to comment on the growing difficulty he was having with his leg.

When they picked their way over the spot where Jane had fallen, Alan swallowed hard. She'd lost a lot of blood. There was a large, dark pool, a smaller one nearby, with a long smear between them, from when she'd dragged herself, trying to save herself.

He'd failed her. They all had.

Ajaya stopped to survey the area before stepping around it. Her voice remained clinical. "It always looks worse than it is. Liquids…volume looks like more when it's spread out, Alan."

He nodded and turned away. He couldn't bear her sympathetic expression.

The contrast, once they'd cleared that area, was sobering. The hallway near the deck transport was virtually untouched, like a life or death struggle on a monstrous scale hadn't just taken place a few meters away. If he didn't turn around, he could almost believe it'd been a terrible dream.

The slimy pupa on the floor in front of the deck transport lay limp and broken open, its contents unleashed at some point since they'd last seen it. Inside the chamber were the remains of several creatures, smashed to shell and jelly by Compton, apparently.

They stepped inside. Bergen leaned against the wall, grateful for a break from dragging a stiff, tingling foot at the end of a leg that was starting to resist moving at all.

Walsh radiated disgruntlement. "Where do we start?"

"Let's assume a best case scenario." Ajaya reached out and touched the symbol for the level with the infirmary. Nothing happened. She pressed it again. The door didn't close. They went nowhere.

Alan edged her out of the way, pressing the button himself, then trying various other keys. Pressing all the keys. Pounding the keys with his fists.

They were locked out.

The three of them silently watched him gimp-marching up and down the hall, swearing, until he finally fell on his ass. No one said a thing. They just sat down in a defensive cluster around him to share a meager meal and some water.

Ajaya didn't say a word, but efficiently slit his pant leg to the knee, examined the wound, smeared an ointment on it, and bandaged it. He knew he should thank her, but all he could manage was a nod. He immediately started theorizing about where the nearest deck transport might be, from an engineering standpoint.

Walsh kept his eyes on his food. His voice was flat. "It's locked us out, Berg. I think you'd better come to terms with that. It doesn't want us going after her."

"The deck transport could be malfunctioning," Bergen said quietly, every muscle in his body tensing.

"That would be some coincidence, don't you think?"

"Not if weapons had been discharged inside."

"We saw no evidence of that."

Alan stood, hopping on one foot, hands clenching at his sides. "She's one of us."

Ajaya rose too and laid a hand on his arm, subtly supporting him. "We have to talk this through, Alan. You must remain calm."

Walsh stayed put. "This isn't the movies, Berg. We lose people. It's a fact of life. Every one of us knew that when we signed up. We all knew we probably wouldn't be going home."

"You're giving up on her too fast. There have to be service ladders in here somewhere. I'll find them."

Walsh leaned back and grimaced. "That could take days to find. She hasn't got long."

Ajaya's hand tightened on his arm.

Alan's voice came out as a low growl, "You don't know that for sure. I could get lucky."

Walsh raised his eyebrows, gesturing limply. "We're running out of ammo. What if there are more of those things?"

"What if I kick the living shit out of you?" Nevermind that he couldn't actually manage that.

Ajaya gripped his arm forcibly and led him some distance away. He leaned against the wall, chuffing like a locomotive through flaring nostrils, barely keeping from exploding.

Ajaya waited patiently, until he turned to her, throwing up a hand. "I'm not leaving unless I know she's…. You guys go, if you have to. I won't leave her here to…I won't leave her here alone."

Ajaya nodded slowly. "Do you trust me to fairly arbitrate this issue, Alan?"

Ajaya? Fair?

"Yes," he said through clenched teeth.

He had no idea how long ago that conversation had taken place. Time seemed interminable without any way to mark it. They'd agreed to wait for him for three days while he searched for a way off this deck. Those three days were long-past being up.

Once the paralytic in his leg wore off, he'd found other deck transports. None of them worked. He never found a service ladder leading to another deck. He'd been returning to the capsule before the others took off, to ask for more time, to get more supplies and a cutting tool. He hoped to cut into the wall around the deck transport controls and manually trigger it to work again. It was a pretty desperate approach, but then, he was feeling pretty desperate.

That's when it became clear a new brood of the creatures had hatched. Once they'd caught his trail, they hunted him. He was an easy target until he realized all the noise he was making was the problem. He never made it back to Providence.

There'd been a few tight moments. He'd backed into a room and barricaded himself into a small area by stacking storage crates around himself, like circling the wagons. The bigger animals couldn't get to him unless they could knock down the stacks of crates, but the smallest ones could slip between them—smaller, but no less vicious. Just one had taken him by surprise. And now he was in a bad, bad way.

There was something going on out in the hall again. He listened for a few moments, to determine how close it was. Damn things were at it again. Some kind of war was being waged out there. They were fighting for dominance, for food.

Damn cannibals. He guessed if there was some other kind of food available, they'd want to eat that. He wasn't about to broadcast his location and advertise that he was a willing smorgasbord. Not yet.

He thought about Jane to pass the time, as he often did. He closed his eyes and contemplated the day, early in the journey, when she'd spent hours washing her hair for the first time in microgravity.

She was self-conscious about it, trying to be as inconspic-uous as possible. He'd watched her, surreptitiously, as she went through the many steps of her ablutions, her hair float-ing like a cloud around her face as she worked on it pains-takingly, section by section. Afterwards, she let it air-dry, combing through it occasionally. He'd observed her pulling a lock forward, twitching it under her nose and rubbing it between her fingers, like she couldn't decide if it was actually clean unless it smelled a certain way.

He chuckled to himself silently. She'd have been morti-fied if she'd realized he'd seen that. She kept her dignity wrapped around her like a mantle, always steady, always calm, always reasonable. She helped him feel more…stable? Sane? Happy? He wanted to please her, so he tried harder. He wouldn't do that for just anyone. She was special.

He imagined holding her again, one more time. The way he'd held her that day in the capsule, his chin resting on her glossy, silky hair. She'd smelled heavenly when the rest of them stank like baboons. She was earthy, woodsy, almost floral. She was warm and soft. She fit against him perfectly, no awkwardness at all. She was a gift.

He blinked back wetness and looked up at the ceiling, rubbing at his face and beard. A silent laugh escaped his lips as he remembered her reaction to his beard when he'd first started to grow it. He was the first of the men to give up on shaving with dull razors—without running water it was just a pain in the ass and the vacuum-assisted shaver they'd built into the capsule was worthless. So, he'd just grown a beard. It was the easiest thing to do.

First, she'd teased him about his hipster stubble. When it really grew in thick, she'd joked about his swarthy pirate-beard. Then she'd presented him with an eye-patch, painstakingly fashioned out of used food packaging, beaming as she handed it over. He patted the pocket on this thigh and felt the plastic crackle under his fingertips. Still there.

She was the glue that had held them all together. Without her, they probably wouldn't have made it to the Target alive. He and Walsh probably would have killed each other a few months in.

His throat constricted painfully from emotion. It was just as well they would never get a chance to be together. He'd never get it right. He'd do something stupid, hurt her somehow. This way, their relationship stayed pristine. They'd have those few meaningful moments. He'd never make love to her, but he'd also never have the opportunity to fuck it all up.

He woke, hyperventilating, flinging his arms out to ward off the predator he was certain he was going to find there. He caught his breath, taking stock, cursing himself for having fallen asleep again.

He felt hot. He was drenched in sweat. His vision swam. But there was nothing there.

Oh, fuck. Do not look at the leg.

What woke him? He blinked rapidly, forcing his eyes to stay open instead of drifting shut again. The creatures were making a ruckus nearby, again. They were close. Really close.

This was it. They'd tracked him down. They'd bring down the walls of his makeshift barricade, overwhelm him with sheer numbers any minute. He could barely bring himself to care. Surely it wouldn't hurt. Much.

Still…. He fumbled for the pistol. It was so damn heavy. It was enough to have it in his hand, for now. There were still some bullets in there, right? Weird how that burn on his hand still hurt more than the leg that was just a pustulant lump of meat.

The sounds the creatures were making out there were weird. Curiosity made him ease forward to peer through the crack between two storage crates. A larger creature that lurked out there, the one that had kept him from getting to the door and closing it, immediately filled his limited view, hissing and lashing its tail around. He called that one Barnabas. They were old pals.

Bergen rolled his eyes and scooted to the next crack. There was a stomping and smashing sound coming from out there that he hadn't heard before. Was there a third stage in this disgusting creature's life cycle? Could this actually get worse?

The scent of sizzling meat reached his nose and he wrinkled it in consternation. Was he so hungry he was hallucinating a barbecue? That was just sick.

He caught a glimpse of something black and shiny in the hall. His eyes widened and he forgot everything else. Something large and heavy lurched into the room and crashed to the floor, pushed over and overrun by the creatures. He couldn't get a good look at it. He smashed his eyes closed and shook his head to clear it, then turned back to the crack, squinting with one eye to see better.

Whatever it was, it was strong. It was flinging the animals off itself ferociously, clanking heavily against the floor and wall as the animals swarmed over it, trying to keep it pinned down as they lashed and nipped at it.

A creature slammed into the crates that sheltered him. They rocked into each other, unsteadily. He thought for a moment they might topple over on top of him, but they settled back into place.

What was that thing?

Wait, was that an arm?

Oh, shit.

It was an arm. An arm equipped with some kind of weapon. The air seemed to bend around the arm's outstretched fist and a silent, concussive force emanated from it—sending the creatures flying in all directions and smashing them to bits.

Bergen swallowed hard as more of the black beast was revealed, as the animals splattered and rained in every direction and the air filled with the sickening smell of rot and cooked meat.

It was human in shape. And it was damn scary looking.

So. The alien bastard was finally showing its face.

He watched with fascination as the thing floundered like a bug caught on its back, trying to get itself upright. If he weren't so freaked out, it might have been comical.

Finally it flipped itself over and got up on all fours, then raised itself up on its knees and blasted a few more of the creatures. That was something, at least.

He raised the pistol and braced it on a crate. He was probably only going to get one good shot before this was all over. He couldn't miss. He'd aim at the head and hope that was a vulnerable place.

The thing was struggling to get to its feet. That seemed odd, but it was the perfect opportunity.

He fired.

21

Bergen held his breath. He'd hit his target, dead on. The alien's head snapped back. It staggered, crashing back into the wall, seemed to be stunned. Maybe he'd injured it. It seemed to be slow to recover. Maybe....

It straightened. Its head whipped around, zeroing in on his location.

"Oh, fuck," he muttered. He tried to send another round into it, but the chamber was empty. He heard nothing but hollow clicks. Awesome. Great time to run out of ammo. Fucking perfect.

He couldn't tear his eyes off the thing. He was frozen, couldn't move. It stomped a few steps toward him and cocked its head to the side. It swiveled at the waist gracefully, in an almost feminine way, neatly dispatching the few creatures that remained.

It was menacing and beautiful. Now that the animals had been silenced, he could hear that it made mechanical sounds. Holy shit. That wasn't the alien. The alien must be inside it.

The analytical side of him couldn't help but admire the elegance in the design of the thing. It looked and sounded heavy, but moved nimbly. Some part of him lusted for it. He wanted to take it apart, figure out how it worked. Just that single, complex device in front of him represented an exhilarating lifetime of insights and discoveries. But that was looking like a pretty unlikely scenario at the moment.

Bergen heaved himself back with an energy he hadn't known in days when the thing reached out, grabbed the nearest stack of crates, and flung them aside like they were tinker toys. He wasn't about to die lying on floor, broken and beaten, damn it. He staggered to his feet, swaying and wheezing, close to passing out, and clung to the nearest stack of crates to keep from falling over.

The black behemoth stepped inside the enclosure and stood there, facing him. Long minutes passed. The fucker was taking its time, savoring the goddamn moment.

Bergen couldn't take it another minute.

He flung expletives at the thing—raged like a rabid animal, spittle flying. He felt his face turn scarlet, the tension in his neck building as his blood pressure went up. He cursed the alien, its race, its ship, its home planet, its goddamn suit and its lack of proper ship hygiene—letting the equivalent of space rats infest the vessel, which was a fucking affront to cleanliness and decency everywhere. Just everywhere, goddamn it!

As he ran out of scathing words, he began to notice the thing had raised its arms, almost defensively…or what? Was it confused? What the hell was going on?

He lost his balance and slid back down to the floor as an ear-splitting voice boomed into the silence. He covered his ears. It was so loud he thought his ears might be bleeding.

"—just tell me how to turn on some kind of speaker so he can hear me! He can't hear me! Oh. I—now he can." It lowered its arms and took another step toward him. "Alan?"

Berg's eyes widened. That thing knew his name. Then it all clicked into place. It'd been inside Jane's head. It could know anything about him.

It crouched down in front of him, held out a hand. It was no less threatening in that position, he told himself.

"Alan—it's ok. It's me."

He shook his head, hands still over his ears. Goddamn it. That fucker loved its mind games, didn't it? What the fuck did it want now? It had Jane and Compton—now it wanted him too? It waited until you were a crippled, crushed shell, incapable of any kind of defense, and then it took you—for what? What deviant shit was this thing going to do to him? Torture? Anal probing? Live dissection?

He cleared his throat, gathered what saliva he could, to spit at that fucker's blank, shiny, expressionless face.

At that exact moment, the voice thundered, "Retract the helmet."

Even as it gave the command, the helmet split at the chin, tilted up at a forty-five degree angle, and began to lift, rotating on an axis, level with the point where ears would naturally be.

He'd already let the spittle fly...when he saw her face.

Saw Jane.

It struck her on the cheek. She blinked. "Really, Alan? Is this how you treat all the girls?" She lifted a hand, like she would wipe it away, but frowned at the black, gauntletted hand ruefully. The obsidian shoulders shrugged with a soft, mechanical whir as she dropped her hand again. She sighed and turned to scan their surroundings.

He stared at her hard and sank down farther, thoughts racing. He had to be hallucinating.

This wasn't real. Couldn't be. It was a trap. The alien was inside his mind, could make him think anything, do anything, if he let it.

Her voice was soft. So alluring. So tempting to believe. "It's not safe here. You're hurt. Where are the others?"

"Safe. You'll never get them." His voice came out a groveling whisper. He hated himself for it.

She seemed confused, worried. "I'm glad they're safe, Alan. You know it's me, Jane, don't you?" She crab-walked forward a small measure. "This is Sectilius battle armor. I told you about it, remember? I had to protect myself before I came down here. There's no way I could have gotten to you otherwise."

Jane went in and out of focus. The adrenaline was wearing off. He just couldn't be scared of Jane, no matter what she wore, no matter who was pretending to be her. Not enough to stay alert, anyway. He shook his head and whumped it against the crate behind him. That didn't help.

"Alan?" She stood. Her face was a mask of concern. She turned and clomped away.

His eyes fluttered closed, but he still heard the juicy crack as she blew away another creature that had wandered in. It was nice of her to do that. He wanted a good look at that weapon. For sure.

She came back, stooped right next to him this time, and slowly reached out a hand to touch his knee with just a single, black fingertip. It felt heavy and cold through the fabric of his flight suit. He didn't like it. "Can you walk, Alan?"

He huffed. "I'm not going anywhere with you." It came out more as a moan than actual words, though. So humiliating.

"I guess I'll have to carry you. I can barely control this thing, honestly. I'm afraid I might hurt you. It seems like I could probably crack you in two without even trying." She flashed a quick, tentative smile. Her eyes darted over him and he could have sworn that they were filling up with tears. Determination was in her voice, then. "I'm not going to, though. I'm going to make it work the way I want. Everything's going to be ok. I promise."

He tried to fight, but his limbs just flailed a little bit, like limp noodles. Jane was going to have her way with him, alien or not.

22

Jane took her time, willing her ham-handed movements to obey her intentions. She gathered Alan up as she would a fragile child, in her mind's eye remembering the moment Ei'Brai had lifted her using Compton's arms. His touch had felt mechanical, just as hers must now feel to Alan. That was where the similarity stopped.

Alan drifted in and out of consciousness, murmuring at her. There was no more room for mistakes. A sob escaped her lips and tears slid down her cheeks as she tramped away from his rank pit of survival to someplace safe where he could mend. She ignored the angry tears, the overwhelming surge of protective feelings, and barraged Ei'Brai with demands for information about the others.

She no longer believed that he didn't know where they were.

She feared they were all dead. She couldn't forgive that, if it were true.

"Alan says they're safe. I need to know. You can sense them. I know you can. Where are they? Do they have enough food, water?"

It took everything she had to just walk in that getup. She couldn't break her concentration and force him to answer.

She wasn't sure how she would do that, actually. But that wouldn't stop her from trying as soon as she got the chance, should he refuse to give a satisfying reply.

She detected a brisk sensation swirling around Ei'Brai as he replied. "You have done well. I could not ask for more."

She grit her teeth. "I've had enough of your Machiavellian crapola. Tell me. Now."

Something akin to a smirk flitted from his mind to hers. "They withdrew to their vessel as you commenced the recuperative process. Dr. Alan Bergen searched for you, solitarily."

Her brow wrinkled. She didn't like that answer, but felt it was probably true. "Okay. And?" There was more. She knew it.

"Presently they reside outside the periphery of my awareness. They have detached. They travel on a trajectory toward the nearest planetary body."

"They left us here?" *Damn it.* Why did that hurt so much?

He didn't answer.

She arrived at the Assessment Chamber. The computer immediately greeted them in bland, unruffled tones. "Welcome, Documented Citizens: Jane Augusta Holloway, Bartholomew Alan Bergen. Please step onto the diagnostic platform."

She visualized herself settling a sleeping child upon a bed and willed the servo-motors to comply with that level of control. It mostly went well. She didn't think she'd hurt him further, though his head hit the surface of the platform harder than she would have liked. The blue-green tube of light enveloped Alan and his holographic twin appeared, mirroring his supine form.

"Recording data. Machinutorus Bartholomew Alan Bergen presents in an unconscious, non-ambulatory state, demonstrating disruptions of multiple metabolic processes. Catabolysis. Hypohydration. Thirty-seven neurotoxic and hemotoxic metabolites detected in the lymphatic and cardiovascular systems. Is enumeration necessary?"

Jane's brows drew together. "No. Continue."

"Gross lacerations and trauma to lower left quadrant. Prognosis, with 95% confidence interval: level seven. Damage has reached near irreversible levels. Prosthesis may become necessary. Recommendation: immediate Sanalabreus immersion for extensive detoxification, regeneration, nutritional supplementation."

That was disappointing news. She'd hoped.... She indulged in a moment of hesitation, then moved forward to recollect him.

"Alan? Alan, wake up. I need to tell you something." She cradled him against her. It flashed through her mind how ridiculous it was for a woman of her size to be holding someone who measured eight inches taller and outweighed her by at least 50 pounds, probably a lot more. But there she was.

Alan's eyes opened to slits as she moved toward the Sanalabreus Chamber. He gazed into her face, his mouth turning up on one side. "Is this it, Jane?"

She smiled a tremulous smile. "Nope. There's hope for you, yet. But you're not going to like what comes next."

"Really?" he whispered. "I'm not really very enthusiastic about much these days."

She wished she could get out of the suit, ruffle his hair, coddle him, soothe him with her hands.

He cleared his throat and sounded marginally stronger. "Lay it on me."

She lowered him up to the suit's elbows in gel.

His eyes went wide. He grasped at her weakly, finding little to cling to on the suit's slippery surface.

She kept her voice calm, reassuring. "I've just come out of one of these, Alan. It healed my leg. It's unpleasant, but it's your best chance. Don't—don't fight it, okay? Just rest and sleep. I promise you'll be safe. I'll be watching over you."

He relaxed a bit and nodded wearily. He managed to push a bit of snark into his voice as he muttered, "If you say so."

"I do."

He made a face like he was vexed.

"What? Alan, it's ok—"

He stiffened a bit, but didn't open his eyes. "I know it's ok. I'm just fucking tired of playing Princess Buttercup to your Wesley. Next time, I'm rescuing you, goddamn it."

She couldn't help but smile. After all the months of listening to the crew bicker about movies, she finally got a reference.

She could see the filaments weaving their way around him. It made her skin crawl, but he didn't seem to notice. She lowered him farther, up to his chin. She kept a firm hold on him. The device didn't have control yet. "You're going to go under the surface of the gel. It's ok. You'll be able to breathe."

He opened his eyes. The filaments slid purposefully up his neck, pausing at his lips and nose, waiting to time entry perfectly. "Let go, Jane. I trust you. I feel better already."

She located a command to force her arms to stay steady, to compensate as she lowered her face to his. She kissed his bushy brow. "I'll see you soon. Be good."

"Shut up and give me something good," he grumbled.

She chuckled and bussed his lips.

He rolled his eyes, then closed them. "You can do better than that."

Her chest felt tight, remembering how much she'd done, when she thought she'd been alone with him. "Later," she choked out.

"There better be a later, or I'm going to be pissed."

He sank under and she stood there watching for a long while. A few small bubbles escaped his lips, remaining suspended in the gel above his face. She caught glimpses of the filaments as they moved over him, began their work. He didn't struggle. His eyes were closed. He looked peaceful.

Ei'Brai broke into her reverie. "He is in hand. All is well. You must conclude the attendance upon your own injuries, Dr. Jane Holloway."

She straightened and squared her shoulders. "No. I'm not done yet."

"The remaining nepatrox will wait. Your brethren are safe."

Jane blinked slowly and pushed him back to the periphery of her mind, holding him there, so he couldn't see her intention.

She turned away from Alan's tank. She marched.

23

This part of the ship was distinctly different from the rest. For one thing, the climate control was set far lower—it was downright chilly. When Jane shivered, the suit's internal systems engaged and she felt waves of dry warmth radiating from the dense walls of the suit.

Little puffs of warmed air blew around her face, tickling tendrils of loose hair around her ears. She'd left the helmet open because it didn't seem necessary to close it and she felt more...human this way. Still, her nose was cold and occasionally she could see her breath frosting up in front of her.

She was heading toward the heart of the ship.

The lighting was also different here—more blue-green and not nearly as bright. In fact, as she strode deeper and deeper, the light dropped off substantially until she was walking in twilight, just on the cusp of absolute darkness.

Ei'Brai's presence in her mind was calm, expectant. He knew by now what she was about. He wouldn't try to stop her. It was time.

She could no longer see the walls as she walked. They'd long since receded into darkness. There was a light integrated into her suit that she could turn on with nothing but a thought, but she held that in reserve, letting her eyes adjust to the gloom.

The blueprint inside her head told her she'd reached the point where all the ship's corridors converged like spokes to a central point. She slowed down, every sense on alert.

A wall of cool air slapped her in the face. She'd just walked into a vast, open space.

Her eyes drifted to a small pool of reflected light. It rippled.

She froze. She'd been here before. Except she'd been on the other side of the glass, looking out, from inside Ei'Brai's mind.

She squared her feet with her shoulders and stepped out onto the railed gantry that led to Ei'Brai's domain. She leaned out and darted looks up and down over the side of the railing. Every deck had its own service-gantry leading to hundreds of gangways circumnavigating the core habitat, identical to the one she occupied. They seemed to go on for miles in each direction.

She strode up to the glass, reached out a hand to touch it, and lifted her chin. She cleared her throat, though she wasn't speaking aloud. "Show yourself to me."

He didn't answer. But she felt him inhaling, burgeoning to the fullest point, limbs languidly drawing together to a tight star as he exhaled in an enormous whoosh, sending himself shooting like a torpedo down many deck levels toward where she stood, peering through the glass.

He stopped his rapid descent by throwing his arms out, the membranous webs between them billowing, creating friction. He constricted the flow of the squeeze to a trickle and came to a full stop opposite her, while at the same moment a pair of soft lights came on, illuminating his environs so that she could see him, fully.

She flinched and berated herself for it. She knew he'd make a dramatic appearance.

She'd had some inkling, of course, that he was an aquatic creature before now, but nothing could have prepared her for the fact that each of his eyes was larger than her head, or that his longest limbs appeared to be five times the length of her body or more.

His many arms twined around him as they regarded each other, just a few inches of air, glass, water between them. Each of his eight arms was studded along its length with pale, semi-transparent suction cups, a large portion of which brandished a prominent, barbed hook curling over the top, clearly meant to shred prey as it was dragged relentlessly toward his mouth, currently hidden from her.

In the murky light he was creamy white, shimmering with a metallic sheen, alternately silvery and golden. Every languorous, sinuous movement drew her eye to the light reflecting off his gilded, iridescent skin. He was mesmerizing.

Tears pricked the backs of her eyes. She hadn't expected him to be beautiful.

Though she tried to remain guarded, he picked up on her mental state. Proximity seemed to be a factor. She felt an even greater sense of the multiple layers of his racing thoughts. She could almost see, as well as sense, the multiple brains beneath his translucent skin.

His mantle swelled in an almost child-like expression of pride. He bobbed in place. "My appearance pleases you?"

One of two tentacles extended toward her, far longer and thinner than his arms and terminating in a leaf-shaped club. Suction cups, with serrations, like teeth, flattened against the glass where her own hand rested. His words reverberated in a hushed timbre, full of surprise. "Unexpected. Your kind is indeed dissimilar from the Sectilius."

As he spoke, his skin flashed crimson and glowed with an inner luminescence. Simultaneously, he fed her the meaning behind the primitive communication. It was a cordial greeting, meant for an age-mate. It implied that he felt connected to her, that he was grateful for her presence. He called her friend.

She nodded slowly, unable to take her eyes off him, but ready to broach the subject she was there to tackle.

But he distracted her again. This time forcing a flash of insight into how he perceived her, both visually and mentally. Through his eyes, she could see herself in almost microscopic detail. Small, by comparison to him, he divulged that her body was also small by Sectilius standards. More fleshy, soft, rounded, than a typical Sectilius female, though, he'd decided that he preferred her appearance to their more angular, muscular structure, for no other reason than it was more like his own, if only in an abstract way.

He saw her as upright, tightly controlled. Her jaw was set with determination and her eyes were expressive, burning with an inner fire—a fire he knew to be rare and valuable— juxtaposed against the hair, flowing wild around her head, similar to the way he perceived her internal landscape—disorganized, fluid, organic.

He saw her decisiveness, her duty, her compassion, her sense of responsibility as most desirable traits. He presumed her to be the very pinnacle of humanity, the ideal specimen. Perfect.

She leveled her gaze on the eye closest to her. He was unblinking. That was a little unnerving. She pushed that feeling down as irrelevant and put steel in her internal voice. "Perfect for what purpose, Ei'Brai?"

He pivoted slightly, his arms curling around himself. He was calculating the reorganization of the micro-robotic squillae to prevent a minor hull breach. But she knew those were calculations he could literally do in his sleep. He was not truly preoccupied by them. That was a misdirection.

"Quit pretending to be distracted. Quit putting me off. What do you want from me?"

"You know. You've always known."

She wanted to scream with frustration. She wracked her brain for any kind of hint of what he might be referring to, but came up blank.

He waited for her to reply, his limbs drifting around him on a silent current. His only intentional movement was the slow undulation of the fins on either side of the conical mantle above his eyes.

Her muscles tensed to such a degree that the suit's internal sensors brought up a prompt, asking her if she was experiencing a muscle spasm. "I know that you're doomed, that you've decided to try to bring all of us down with you. You've managed to keep Alan, Tom, and myself here while the others escaped. But for what? To keep you company, until the moment the asteroid hits? You would sacrifice us, too—so that you won't be lonely in your final hours?"

"None of us are doomed."

It was a flat statement of fact—she could see he was completely convinced of its truth.

"What?" Was he mad? There'd been moments she'd suspected....

"Dr. Jane Holloway, you are the key that will unlock all of our futures. Terra's future as well. We can still fulfill the primary mission."

He didn't *sound* crazy. He sounded calm, certain. That was so damn infuriating.

"We? You—"

It struck her, suddenly, what he must mean. He'd been obliquely feeding her clues all along. One of the first things he said to her was that he wanted something from her—not *them*—her. He'd told her, "You are home," which she'd dismissed as a cultural reference, a welcoming gesture, a throwaway. But there was the moment he described the command hierarchy of the ship...the journey to Castor and Pollux...the download...his satisfaction when she'd gotten herself out of the gel...the computer's greeting in the infirmary only an hour before....

It snapped into place.

"You can't seriously want me to—?"

"I have already appointed you—you have already utilized your proto-command when you extricated yourself from the Sanalabreum. Under martial law, an expeditious vote of the Quorum is all that is necessary. I am the only surviving

Quorum member. It is merely a formality now. You have only to accept."

She staggered back from the glass, blood pounding audibly in her ears.

"What then?" she mumbled aloud.

"I am your servant." Another fact. Another truth, from his point of view.

"Oh, give me a break!" She raised a hand to pinch the bridge of her nose, but caught sight of the gauntlet just in time and threw her arm away. They really should retract like the helmet, for goodness' sake. "So, we just…we move the ship."

"Obviously. We complete the mission and return."

She stared at him, aghast, her lips formed in a moue of disbelief. "To Sectilius? You're joking!"

"I do not dissemble. It is your duty to complete the mission begun by your predecessor. It is not in your nature to shirk duty, especially to those to whom you believe yourself responsible. I am now your ward. That responsibility extends to me."

"That—I—that's ridiculous! I don't know anything about—"

She paused. But she did know, dammit. She knew everything about it, if she just searched in the right corner of her mind. The sneaky bastard had put everything into place at the very beginning with that insane download.

She half-expected to see some kind of maniacal grin on his face, which wasn't there, of course—only an innocent, wide-eyed look, that bespoke nothing of the devious nature of the mind beneath the white flesh, still rhythmically flashing a crimson "friend" signal at her.

She turned and walked a few feet away, grateful for the support of the suit. Her legs felt wobbly and weak within its generous support and her injured leg ached. "This is nonsense. We'll go to Earth and let the bureaucrats there work it all out. They'll appoint someone suitable for this task. It's not me you want."

"It is you, Dr. Jane Holloway. There can be no other."

She stopped, began to form a retort.

He interrupted her thought. "This is what you will give me over to them for?"

He pushed a memory at her. She meant to resist, but when she saw familiar faces, curiosity got the better of her. It was a small conference room, somewhere on Earth.

In the memory, she stood stiffly, with folded arms, and made eye contact with the Deputy Administrator of Johnson Space Center.

What was his name again? Dr. Marshall?

Marshall nodded brusquely, indicating that she should dim the lights. As she turned, she glanced into the faces of three others that occupied the room—Ajaya Varma, Tom Compton and Ronald Gibbs stood at ease nearby, dressed in fatigues. She was feeling grim. She moved forward, picked up a remote, and looked up. She could see her reflection in the television screen before it came to life. She was Walsh. This was his memory.

As she watched, ancient black and white film footage played on the screen, hastily shot, documenting some long ago event that the military had been brought in to deal with.

Walsh had seen this before, but he still squinted to see the grainy images, interspersed with snow and flashing jumps. It was dark. There was smoke, lots of smoke. There were floodlights in a perimeter, flooding a large object with harsh light, making the camera white out from time to time.

Then she recognized the ship that the soldiers were swarming over—a Speroancora shuttle—and she realized this had to be the 1947 New Mexican crash site. There were Sectilius inside that small ship. The cameraman drew closer and asked questions of men working on and around the ship in a disgustingly jaunty manner, belying the seriousness of the moment.

Ei'Brai watched and listened, silently absorbed in her reaction. She perceived him and the video on different levels as information streamed between them. He did not understand the language spoken, only the emotions conveyed. She was surprised at how accurate his interpretations actually were.

Several soldiers put their backs into some large tools to pry open a hatch, which suddenly gave way with a hiss. Someone barked an order at the cameraman and he moved in closer. The camera shook, making the footage difficult to watch. He didn't sound so jolly anymore. Soldiers moved in with weapons drawn. The camera followed.

There were four Sectilius inside—three men and one woman. One of the men was obviously dead, impaled by a twisted component of the control console. The other two were stunned and moving lethargically—they would have been affected by the same mysterious illness as Compton at some point during their journey to Earth.

The female Sectilius was in the process of donning an armored suit, exactly like the one Jane was wearing. The woman was exceedingly thin, tall, lithe, sharply featured—to Walsh's eyes, alien and suspicious.

She was ordered to stop what she was doing. She answered calmly, matter of fact, in Mensententia that she meant no harm, that she intended to protect herself from the violence of this bizarre, chaotic world. These men couldn't comprehend her, nor Walsh, but Jane could and the following sequence made her blood run cold.

Two soldiers advanced on her while other soldiers crowded the unresisting, catatonic Sectilius men, slumped at the controls of the vehicle. The soldiers ordered the woman to stop again as she slipped one arm down into the suit. She narrowed her eyes and slowly continued, no expression of any kind on her face. They tried to stop her physically. She pushed them away with a force that clearly surprised them.

There were angry words, cursing. A shot rang out. The Sectilius woman looked down at her torso, registered that she'd been wounded, and shouldered the suit, which instantly enveloped her. She returned fire, obliterating the man who'd just shot her with a single concussive blast from her wrist. The camera rocked violently and it was hard to tell what was happening for a few moments. When it righted itself, bullets were pinging off the Sectilius woman as she staggered forward, arm raised, sending out a few more pressure waves before she collapsed.

The screen went blank for a moment then lit up again in a new location. This scene was very different—the contrast was stark. Bright light flooded the room from above. It was a surgical suite filled with gowned, masked men crowded around the center of the room. It was very quiet. The men spoke in low murmurs as they worked over someone.

Then she heard an agonized moan.

Jane involuntarily put the back of her hand to her mouth and tasted blood as the mechanical hand smashed her tender lips.

One man smoked a cigarette nearby, watching the proceedings with intense absorption.

The camera moved in. Men with oiled hair and horn-rimmed glasses glanced up and stepped aside. One of the Sectilius was naked on an operating table. It was the short, stocky male—his body corded with dense musculature.

The camera moved in closer, revealing that his body was flayed and cut wide open from neck to groin. They were dissecting him. He was alive and awake and in agony.

Jane could sense Walsh's unarticulated emotions. It was very clear. He approved of this.

Jane fell to her knees against the glass and wretched. Ei'Brai stopped the flood of the memory and she thanked him for that kindness while she recovered her composure.

If Ei'Brai saw this in Walsh's mind—from the beginning? That explained a few things.

When she was able to stand again, she choked out, "I will not let them do that to you!"

"How will you prevent it? They will be curious about the similarities and dissimilarities between my kind and homologous creatures on your world. I have seen in your mind, my form is not unfamiliar to you, yet my intellect, my abilities, are singular—you have encountered nothing that compares in your cumulative experience as a species. The precedent has been set. Surely you must see that this is the natural conclusion to any alien introduction to your culture. They will not be able to help themselves." All his concentration was fixed on her every move, every thought. "You, however, are different. You know me as they cannot."

She shook her head slowly, perplexed. "Ei'Brai, I won't let that happen."

"I'm gratified that your intent is unadulterated, but I'm less certain that this pledge is truly within your dominion. A brief appearance in your skies, messages to your many governments with all the necessary information is in order—in your own words, with your reassurances—that will more than fulfill that portion of the mission.

"Eventually another diplomatic ambassador will be dispatched from the Unified Sentient Races to your world, assuming the coalition still exists—that will permit a more equal footing, less risk to any single individual, such as myself. Certainly you can see that logic dictates we must proceed immediately to Sectilius for a full investigation into the genocide of the Speroancora Community, to discover the extent to which the fleet has been affected, Sectilius itself, or if this was an isolated event. Now that the ship's binary systems recognize the presence of a Quasador Dux, there is nothing to keep us here. The time has come. We are much delayed."

"Nothing to keep us here?" she asked, incredulous. "What about the illness that killed your crew? Are Walsh and the others going to infect Earth with it? What about

Compton? Is he contagious? I'm not just going to sit back and ignore all of that and let you zoom off into space!"

"It is improbable they are infected. Far less likely that it will be capable of replication in any meaningful way. Contagion is highly unlikely."

"Improbable? Meaningful? Highly unlikely? You mean you don't know? I can't gamble with their lives that way. I will *not* gamble with Earth that way!"

"Commander Mark Walsh chose not to step onto the diagnostic platform. That was his election and does not affect you. You have not been infected. Nor has Dr. Alan Bergen."

Again, certainty.

Jane stood resolute before him. "I've trusted you. Now you must trust me. We should go back to Earth, bring our best scientists onboard. I'll teach them Mensententia and we'll deal with this thing, whatever it is. Then, we'll talk about Sectilius. Decades have passed since the attack—a few more months will hardly matter in the greater scheme of things. I'm certain there will be volunteers for that kind of mission—people far better suited to the role of Quasador Dux than myself! I'll be careful. I'll be adamant with my government. I'll be strong. I won't let them bring anyone on board that I don't trust."

"This is not a negotiation." His voice had suddenly taken a different tone, resonated on a different frequency.

She felt small stirrings of unease in her belly. "What's that supposed to mean?"

"I possess the power of eternal night—the balance between dusk and dawn for your Dr. Alan Bergen."

Her heart fluttered in her chest. She felt weak.

His finger was on the trigger. If she didn't agree to his terms, he would end Alan's life.

Jane backed up a step and shook her head. Panic rioted through her. "You can't be serious! Why would you resort to that? You're insane!"

He was extremely agitated. The sensation of barely leashed power that she'd felt from him early on pervaded her perception of him again now. His arms were whipping and swirling around him. He inhaled through his mantle, exhaled through his funnel more rapidly than seemed to be necessary, and this required tense countermeasures to maintain his place in the water opposite her. His mental touch was shielded, though. She had a hunch he might be bluffing, but she couldn't be sure.

He sounded contemptuous, his voice vibrating louder inside her head than it ever had before. "I am rational. You are allowing yourself to be motivated by fleeting emotional states, instead of by reason. Elimination of this individual would free you. I am needed elsewhere, immediately. You and I are bound to this mission. This supersedes your paltry desires for intimacy."

She stared at him, open-mouthed, outraged that he was so dismissive of Alan's life. Her voice cut like a knife through the air, so angry that she had to speak out loud. "He is more to me than that and you know it."

Ei'Brai growled, "I have not waited this many solar cycles to find my end, desiccating and bleeding in your primitive surgeon's theatre. I am far too valuable an individual to meet dusk in such a manner."

Her voice also dropped to a lower register. "Alan is equally valuable to me, to the people of my world. Be careful where you tread, Ei'Brai, or I may just let the asteroid give you this dusk you speak of."

But he was going on as if he hadn't heard her, "In fact, one session with a Sectilius mind-master would relieve you of these insecurities, allow you to embrace your inner desires, fully transmute you into the commanding individual you are meant to be."

She was afraid to force his hand. "I'm fine how I am. Stop this charade. You're bluffing."

"Am I?" Ei'Brai sputtered. Then a wall came down and a crashing torrent of experience broke through—she was gasping and choking inside the gel—except it wasn't her. It was Alan.

She fled to the controls that had freed her just hours before, looking for the command that would give Alan the air he needed, but Ei'Brai was concealing them from her, masking everything so it seemed like gibberish.

She refused to give in to panic.

Withdrawing from him in a rush, she came back fully back into herself and severed the link between them. She turned on a dime and strode back down the gantry, ordering the helmet closed as she went. Eleven swift paces to the left, she stopped at a precise point and raised her arm. The blast cannon would discharge with a mere flicker of thought.

Her teeth ground together in defiance. She turned the helmet to face him with a servo-motor whir.

"Your life support lies behind this wall, Ei'Brai. If you *dare* to hurt Alan, I will destroy that equipment and you will suffocate—not as quickly as Alan, but you will suffocate, nonetheless—while I watch."

"You may injure yourself in the process. You will be stranded here," he said warily.

"I don't care," she uttered with deadly certainty. She wasn't bluffing. She'd do it. She'd kill him if he murdered Alan.

She sensed an easing of Alan's distress and allowed herself to take a long, relieved breath.

She felt the need to press her advantage, to challenge him. He wanted her to lead, but then gave her ultimatums to force the issue? It sounded like an antagonistic maelstrom in the making, not a peaceful working relationship at all.

Was she actually considering taking him up on his offer? Did she really have a choice?

"Ask yourself, Ei'Brai—am I your enemy or your ally? Do you trust me as your Quasador Dux—or is this mutiny? Confirmed mutineers on this ship receive the death penalty, under Sectilius law."

She wasn't precisely sure how she knew that, but she did know it and it was damn useful information.

Ei'Brai's gaze was unwavering. His limbs slowed. His voice was solemn. "Does this mean you accept the appointment to the rank of Quasador Dux, Dr. Jane Holloway?"

There was gravitas in this moment. She knew it.

Instinct told her that her life had been spent barreling toward this moment. Every decision she'd ever regretted, she'd agonized over. There was no time for that now. She had to take the upper hand somehow. She had to trust her gut. She barely hesitated. "I do."

As soon as those two words transmitted to him via thought, she realized what he'd been doing. In that moment a new channel opened between them and she experienced Ei'Brai on an entirely new level. The ship hummed through him—now through her as well. She could be aware of any part of it that she pleased at any given moment, through this connection with him. There were no walls between them anymore. She could see any part of his inner dialogue or memory that she might want. She could monitor any system or any individual.

In that moment, all Ei'Brai felt was raw relief. His bravado was instantly supplanted by a release of anxiety and a flood of reassurance and calm. So much so that it affected even her. That was a small comfort as she quickly uncovered the series of machinations he'd used to bring her to this point. His deceptions, which he deemed a series of necessary tests, were laid at her feet. He begged her forgiveness for them.

She looked over at him. His limbs were drawn together to a point and he had maneuvered his body so that he faced slightly away from her, more laterally than vertically at the moment. It was a form of submission.

She lowered her hand and intuitively used her new access to check on Alan. He slept peacefully. He hadn't just gone through any kind of trauma. That had been a ruse.

She shook her head, utterly baffled. "You tricked me!"

"A regrettable and heinous act of subterfuge. It will not happen again—is not even possible now, as I'm certain you have ascertained. I am completely open to you, at your service."

She staggered back a step as he revealed that the xenon gas…the transformation of the nepatrox…these were all carefully concocted tests to see how she would handle herself under pressure, to see where her loyalties would lie, to evaluate her sense of fairness, her self-control—all to see if she would measure up to his exacting standards. He wouldn't serve just anyone, it seemed.

"Calculated risks," he hummed deferentially.

That included the interlude with Alan—testing her ability to accept cultural differences and not put her own ego first when feeling affronted.

"I need to sit down." She backed into the wall and slid down to the floor with a heavy clunk. Drawing her knees to her chest, she opened the helmet to rest her forehead on crossed arms.

"You put people's lives at risk." It was an accusation. That was the part that rankled the most.

He did not sound the least bit defensive. Instead, he resumed his patient, instructive air. "Normally, every potential leader among the Sectilius, myself included, is assessed in an academic setting under naturalistic, simulated conditions by accomplished proctors. This was not possible in your case. Therefore, I created a real-world scenario and endeavored to minimize risk, while keeping the overall goal of assessment within similar parameters, always with the goal to preserve life when possible. There is much at stake."

After a moment, she raised her head. He was still respectfully floating horizontally, eyes averted from her.

"Stop that," she said crossly.

"As you wish." He came to vertical and relaxed his limbs. He exuded tranquility. It was infuriating.

"But why put anyone in danger at all? You're certainly capable of creating any scenario you like, making it feel as real as...reality. Why do all of this?"

"I regret I do not posses the imaginative traits needed to endeavor to plot such a scenario. I am but a practical individual. I utilized what I had to hand, so to speak. It was imperative that your experience be heuristic in nature. I believe I accomplished that admirably, did I not?"

She drew her brows together. "But Compton really is infected then...."

"With the latent squillae that infected the Speroancora Community, yes. I had presumed them all uncovered and eliminated by now, but—"

"Clearly a few hid from your efforts," she said dryly.

She could see in his mind that over the decades he had ordered his own cadres of squillae to comb the ship, seeking and destroying the rogue squillae that had lain dormant, unnoticed under their noses, biding their time until something triggered them, infecting everyone on board simultaneously. Only Ei'Brai was spared, because his environment was encapsulated, kept separate from the rest of the ship, impervious to infiltration.

"Agreed. They were programmed by a sophisticated and resourceful individual."

"Who?"

"I regret I cannot say, but I am eager to take revenge in whatever manner you see fit, should we discover the perpetrator's identity and whereabouts."

317

She exhaled slowly, determined to come to terms with her new role as the Quasador Dux of the Speroancora. "Is there any hope for Compton?"

"Unknown. The Sanalabreum has declared him clear several times, but then another is found replicating elsewhere within his anatomy."

"I see. They're tenacious and not easy to detect. So, there *is* risk to Alan and myself and to Earth—if Walsh, Ajaya or Gibbs are infected with even one of them."

"Regrettably, yes."

"How do we get rid of them, once and for all?"

"That, Qua'dux Jane Holloway, I do not know."

Bergen was paddling his ass off toward shore, building speed. He glanced back and could see the swell rising over his shoulder. He'd missed the last one. It broke sooner than he'd anticipated, but this one was his.

Today, the wave trains weren't tremendous, but a good solid five feet, shoulder high, and perfect glass. He was starting to tire; he'd been at it for a while, and he should be heading back into the lab to get started on his day, but it was hard to say no to just one more wave.

Surfing was like a drug.

He huffed at that thought and paddled harder. Almost there.

Nope. Not a drug—it was like sex. You spend a lot of time working up to doing it, it's mind-blowingly awesome for a few moments, then it's over and you want to do it again. And again. Always good. Even if it wasn't perfect. Still good.

He felt the wave catch his board and fought the urge to rush to his feet. He let the board match the momentum of the cresting wave, and pushed up slowly, keeping the board well-balanced as he got his feet under him and corrected his course.

Such a fucking rush. Nothing else like it. He knew intellectually that the energy pushing his board had been transmitted from wind to water, that the water molecules rotated in that energy, passing it on from molecule to molecule, forming the waves, moving relentlessly for thousands of miles before reaching shore, the energy slowly dissipating as it went.

A different kind of energy surged in him. Everything was right and good in this moment: the warm sun, the fine spray of the water on his exposed skin, the sounds of breaking waves and the raucous calls of gulls—the amazing feeling of disbelief that he was actually doing it—flying, skimming the sea, walking on water.

This was a pretty popular beach. Normally by now he'd be annoyed with the other people in the surf and on the beach, getting in his way when he'd caught the perfect wave, truncating the experience, spoiling it with buffoonery or ignorance. But today he was alone. It struck him as a rare pleasure. He didn't dwell on his luck. He just savored it.

He scanned ahead. The wave was starting to break up. Something moved in his peripheral vision and he turned slightly to see what it was. It was probably just a gull, but something told him it was larger.

There it was again.

The thrust from the wave destabilized. He lost his balance and plunged into the water. Just before he went under, he got a decent look at it. It was long and thin, like an arm or a tentacle. An octopus this close to shore would be unusual on this beach and he was pretty sure the local octopi were supposed to be small and reddish.

He stayed under for a moment, orienting himself to catch a glimpse of the creature from beneath the surface. He bobbed as the sea churned around him, the tether from his forgotten board tugging on his leg. That leg ached, and for a moment he felt *deja vu* or like he needed to remember something important.

He forgot all that when he finally caught sight of it. *Oh, fuck.* It was way bigger and way closer than he'd realized. He'd heard news stories of Humboldt squid attacking divers near San Diego—plucking at masks, ripping hoses, tearing skin—but those were supposed to be around five feet long and confined to deeper waters. This thing was easily ten times that size. And it...*holy shit*...it was watching him. One of its tentacles snaked out and came within inches of his arm.

He reacted instinctively, lungs burning for air, kicking like hell for the surface and his board, every bit of the zen he'd gained during the last hour of surfing obliterated. He gasped for air and didn't bother to look around. He knew he was alone. There was no help for him out here if this freaky, misplaced kraken decided it wanted to have him for break-fast. His only recourse was to get to shore as fast as possible.

He busted his ass to get there, just aiming for sand, half expecting to be pulled under any second. His thoughts raced with the legends he'd heard of ships being destroyed by sea monsters—legends he'd once thought were embellished, but now he wasn't so sure.

As soon as he could get his feet under him, he trotted on-to the sand, dropped his board, and collapsed. He sat there, panting, and scanned for signs of the creature in the surf. He was so absorbed that when he heard someone softly clearing their throat beside him, he leapt to his feet, whirling.

It was Jane.

She smiled sheepishly and gestured at the sea. "I'm sorry, Alan. I should have told him not to do that. He's thrilled to finally meet you and when he saw you were dreaming of the ocean, well, that only fueled his excitement. He didn't realize how his greeting might affect you. It's a cultural thing. The Sectilius are not as easily ruffled when they encounter something out of the ordinary."

He looked from her to the pounding surf, confused. "What?" He reached out a hand to her arm. "Jane, what are you doing here? What's going on?"

"You're dreaming. You're in a Regeneration Basin, recovering. You remember the ship, the slugs, the nepatrox?"

He took a step back, letting his hand fall away from her. He couldn't stop himself from looking down at his leg. Suddenly he felt very silly and very unsure.

He nodded slowly. "I'm dreaming. Of course, of course. That makes sense. Gotta pass the time somehow."

He turned back to her. All her attention was on him. He liked that. He felt his lips turn up into a libidinous smile. She looked stunning. Her hair glowed in the early-morning sun, whipping around her face in the breeze coming off the water. She wore some kind of long tunic that was pressed against her body by the wind, revealing every wayward curve.

This was going to be a dream to remember.

She held up a hand, her lips twitching. "That's not where this is going, Alan."

Damn it. His subconscious mind was a real bastard. Why would he fuck with himself this way?

"Hey," he said out loud to himself as much as to Jane as he wrapped his arms around her, "This is my goddamn dream. It'll go wherever the hell I please." Her face was turned down. He reached into her hair, tugging gently and lowered his lips to her temple, her cheek, hungrily seeking her mouth.

"Um, no. It's not as simple as that." Her hand came up to cover his lips. "Listen to me, Alan. You were dreaming. But you aren't precisely dreaming anymore. I'm actually here. We are here." She removed her hand from his mouth and put some space between them, gesturing at the sea again. A tentacle raised out of the water again and made a limp gesture.

"What the fuck...is going on here?" He felt queasy and tense.

She led him to the waters edge. "Dr. Alan Bergen, meet Ei'Brai, Gubernaviti of the Speroancora."

"Greetings. It is an unbearable pleasure to finally interact with you, Dr. Alan Bergen."

The voice was deep. And it was inside his head.

Water lapped at his ankles. The white tentacle remained visible on the surface, rolling with each heave and swell of the sea.

He felt nothing but disbelief. His thoughts spun in place, stuck in the wrong gear. "I...ah...."

The voice continued, "We approach now, Dr. Alan Bergen, because Qua'dux Jane Holloway insists upon your input. It strikes me as a futile effort, however I am bound to comply with every caprice of the Quasador Dux."

Bergen turned back to Jane, blinking.

She had an intense look on her face, gazing out to sea. "What we need are ideas and you don't have any, Ei'Brai." The tentacle withdrew from the surface with a splash and he could faintly hear some kind of disgruntled, crackling grumbling deep in his ear.

Jane's eyes narrowed and she turned back to him. "Alan, you have some knowledge of nanotechnology, don't you?"

He shook his head. "Wait a minute. What did he just call you?"

Her lips drew together in a thin line. "That's not important right now. I want to show you some things, see if you can make sense of them."

"No. I think it is important. What did you do, Jane? Are you in danger?" He grabbed her arm, harder than he should have.

She shrugged him off. "I'm fine. He called me the Quasador Dux because I've taken control of this ship. I'm in command now. He works for me."

The deep voice rumbled again, inside his head. "I do, indeed. I could not have envisaged a more propitious commanding officer. It is my honor to serve the honorable Qua'dux Jane Holloway. We are here to consult. Are you prepared to begin?"

He ignored the gnarly beast for the moment. "You command this ship? What? How?"

"It's complicated, Alan. I will explain, I promise. But right now we have a more pressing issue. This ship is swarming with nanites—I've already told you that—they perform many repair functions throughout the ship. They were programed by the Sectilius to perform those functions, coordinated through Ei'Brai. What the Sectilius didn't know is that a portion of those nanites were hijacked and re-programed to attack the central nervous system of every living thing on board in a synchronized strike."

Bergen's eyebrows drew together. "That's what happened to the crew of this ship?"

"Yes. And it's what's happening to Compton, right now. He's fighting for his life in the tank next to you. It could be happening to Walsh, Ajaya, and Gibbs too, out there in the capsule. We need to find a way to turn these things off or reprogram them. I have no way of knowing if the damage is irreparable. I hope not. But there's no way to know for sure."

Bergen opened his hand and gestured toward the sea. "Shouldn't your buddy out there be the expert on this shit? Why do you need me?"

Disgruntlement rumbled in his head again. He ignored it.

"He's been trying to solve it since 1947, Alan."

Alan put a hand to the back of his neck. "Okay. What makes you think I'll succeed where Cthulhu has failed?"

She smiled. "You're not him. You don't think like he does."

Jane felt out of sorts, like she should be doing something important, though she had no idea what that might be. She'd eaten and found herself wandering the corridors of the ship. Her trajectory seemed aimless, yet she was compelled to continue. She was giving herself a tour of her new domain, layering her own concrete experience on top of the mental map in her mind's eye.

The ship seemed different to her now, since her immersion in the Sanalabreum. It seemed shockingly silent, lonely, perhaps even haunted. She half expected to see Sectilius purposefully bustling by as she rounded every corner.

Alan and Ei'Brai wouldn't need her for a few hours. She should have slept, but she felt restless. She'd been sleeping in the spartan crew quarters within the medical center to stay near Alan. Those were adequate, but they weren't intended to be permanent quarters for any crew member, just a place to nap during a long, uneventful shift. They didn't feel…right. She spent as little time there as possible.

Neither Alan nor Ei'Brai could be convinced to rest much either. The two of them were inexhaustible when faced with an intellectual puzzle. They went round and round for hours on end, arguing about how to deal with the rogue squillae.

Alan had come up with a solution straightaway, but Ei'Brai rejected it just as quickly, insisting Alan's plan was fraught with pitfalls that neither of them could adequately anticipate. So the endless research, analysis and translation began. It was draining and frustrating for Jane, because she was forced into the role of translator within a sphere that she knew nothing about.

Alan was picking up Mensententia quickly, but even a genius immersed in a language wouldn't be immediately proficient in the complex vocabulary of engineering. Jane had to pull from deep within and all of them had to exercise extreme patience as they learned how to communicate in this complex way.

Ei'Brai made the link possible and Alan adapted to Anipraxia quickly. He seemed to like it, though he wasn't about to admit that, because he harbored intense levels of mistrust toward Ei'Brai and his motives. He'd heard the whole story, all the justifications for it, and he didn't like any of it. He made it very clear that he thought Ei'Brai should have been upfront from the beginning.

Jane did her best to keep the squabbling between them to a minimum. Since she was the intermediary for nearly every conversation between them, that was a constant role she was forced to play.

It didn't help that Alan was stuck in the Sanalabreum. He seemed to despise being interred there every bit as much as Jane had. He was a restless type, needed to keep moving, keep busy.

At the moment, Alan was occupied with picking apart lines of computer code and he'd be immersed in it for hours.

They'd recovered a single example of the miscreant squillae from Compton's Sanalabreum and immobilized it for study. Jane downloaded its code under Ei'Brai's instruction. Alan was studying that code, line by line.

He'd picked up on the structure and rules of the alien code quickly, drawing parallels to his extensive knowledge of code on Earth.

He'd riffed, "It's all just ones and zeros no matter where you go in the universe, Jane."

She hadn't gotten the joke, but she didn't think he expected her to. Before she could ask what he meant exactly, he was back in it again.

She'd been walking for some time and he was still at it. She came back to herself and realized she was standing in a deck transport. She selected the deck that contained the public and private rooms of the ship's governing body. Soon she was standing outside the door of the rooms of the Quasador Dux. This corridor was the same dull green as any other on the ship. It could have been any door on the ship.

She reached out her hand purposefully to the door control. She knew the woman who had occupied this room in an unsettling and unearthly way. Jane had seen many of her memories. No, not just seen them. She had, in fact, inhabited them.

Jane knew what it was like to be Qua'dux Rageth Elia Hator. Jane knew her favorite places in the ship, knew who her lovers were, knew what her favorite foods tasted like. Jane had seen her ferocity in battle, had seen her coping stoically with adversity. Jane knew her—knew that she'd been intelligent, determined, secure in her own abilities and those of her crew. She was respected and revered by the majority of the Sectilius onboard. She'd been an intrepid woman. Her loss was a tragedy. These were deep boots to fill.

The door slid into the ceiling with a near-silent whisper. Jane gasped with surprise and stepped inside the large, sparsely furnished room, mouth still agape.

Color. A riot of color.

Each wall had been painted in great blocks of swirling color. The wall opposite the door was particularly stirring. She moved forward to examine the work up close.

It was painted with wide smears of pigment so thick there were peaks and ridges within the medium itself. At the top third of the wall, the colors blended from amethyst to azure, thin streaks of vivid, contrasting colors commingling so well that they could only be distinguished at close range.

There was a break in the painting where the dull green of the wall was exposed, much like a Rothko, and the lower portion of the wall was a study in blues and greens, lighter near the top, gaining depth and mystery as the heavy strokes of darker pigments blended toward the bottom of the wall.

It was a depiction of dawn over a vast sea. She knew it intuitively, as if she'd been there, as if the experience was personal. She fingered the textured surface with the lightest of touches, thinking. Maybe she had, indirectly. Her own memory was a mixed-up jumble now.

It seemed like the break between the two paintings wasn't meant to separate them entirely, only to highlight the contrast. They co-existed. They depicted the same location. They were different realms within the same world, a watery world. Ei'Brai's home world, she realized suddenly, stepping back and taking it all in again. Water and air.

Qua'dux Rageth Elia Hator had felt so strongly connected to Ei'Brai that she felt compelled to create art from the memories he shared with her.

Jane flashed on a memory of standing in this room, holding a wide, shallow bowl containing a traditional mixture of mineral clay slurry thickened with a bright blue pigment. There were many more bowls on tables nearby, filled with similar shades as well as contrasting colors that she had painstakingly mixed. Some of them had strong, chemical odors. Others were earthy and pleasant.

She reached into the bowl, scooping the cool paste into the spoon-shape she made with her fingers. Then, with a practiced hand, twisted and twined her fingers to release the thick pigment on the wall with special attention to how the paint flowed from each long finger. With a new color, she went back to that same spot, arching, extending her willowy body to reach, creating highlights, ridges and valleys, building up texture and color with each stroke.

She'd been at it for some time. Her fingers were stained, cold, and stiff. The muscles of her arms burned and her back ached, but she took little notice. This was her space and she would fill it with something lovely. She felt content and highly motivated to complete this section before someone interrupted her.

Her form was still very good, she thought, as she paused, scrutinizing her progress. She frowned when she realized she'd brushed her hand against her brow, smearing her forehead with dark cyan pigment.

Painting was imbedded in her. She'd practiced this technique since she was a child, had been good enough for formal schooling, but the stars had beckoned to her. She wasn't fanciful about it. She was thoroughly practical. She could have had a good life as an artist. A safe life. But she knew she was made for more.

As the wisps of the memory faded, Jane imagined what might have happened, had circumstances been different, had the squillae not destroyed this incredible women, so that Jane might have met her, on Earth, as Rageth had intended.

Jane sighed and turned, realizing the adjacent wall wasn't just a depiction of geometric shapes as she'd originally presumed. It, too, was an impression of a place that meant something to Rageth. This painting was more detailed.

From this angle, she could see it was a view of Sectilia from her moon, Atielle, where Rageth had been born. Sectilia hung large and low on the horizon, a misty, blue-green sphere, dominating the painting. Dawn encircled the planet with a brilliant halo of color—violet and coral and tangerine on a sky that was a slightly different cast of blue than Earth's sky. It was so lovely, this moon with another world looming in the heavens.

There were other rooms adjoining this one, including a bedroom, but Jane didn't have the desire to explore them yet. This room was appointed with plenty of sturdy-looking, simple seating. It was a room meant for social events. Jane approached a piece of furniture that resembled a streamlined, low, modern couch and sat down opposite one of the paintings, still absorbing its details.

"You have many attributes in common with her," rumbled softly in her head.

"That's very kind of you to say," Jane replied with a wry smile.

"I do not contrive the assessment to inflate your sense of self. I observe. I do not embellish."

"Thank you, then."

"Do not compare yourself to her. You exceed the necessary criteria required to perform."

Jane looked down at her hands in her lap. "I know you believe that's true, but entire worlds full of innocent people are depending on me to get these next steps right. It's such a heavy weight. I don't want to fail."

He acknowledged that, silently. He felt a similar responsibility. They communed in that. It helped, somehow.

After a moment, he rumbled, "Those other worlds beckon to you."

She frowned. "They terrify me."

"No. This is not who you are."

She saw a face in her mind's eye and wrinkled her brow. Ei'Brai was summoning a memory that'd been buried deep. She hadn't thought of Mowan for decades. He was a Nawagi boy she'd met when bushwalking with her parents in Queensland in the months before they started their new venture on the coast. The two of them had spent more than a week romping in the scrub before it was time to move on. One day, he'd arrived at their campsite and said he wanted to take her to a special place.

He'd held her pale hand in his warm, dark one and led her across the plain to a rocky outcropping and an ochre pit.

He said the adults in his tribe ground the brightly colored, soft stones with fat to make a paste that they used to paint the body for secret dancing ceremonies that sometimes lasted for days.

He picked up a bright orange stone and rubbed it against a flat rock jutting out of the dry landscape, quickly creating a small mound of orange, chalky powder. Smiling, he pressed his finger into it and drew his finger from her hairline at the center of her forehead, down her nose, over her lips and chin. Jane chose a small, yellow lump of ochre and ground it against another stone nearby. She smoothed the powder in stripes over his cheeks.

They took turns daubing each other with the mineral dust—faces, neck, arms—giddy with the results. They transformed each other into otherworldly-looking creatures. His lips twitched when he said his mother had painted his sister's chest to make her breasts grow. Jane laughed and told him she didn't need breasts yet.

The sun grew hot overhead and they tired of smearing each other with the colorful rock dust, so they crossed the dry grassland until they came to a greener place with a rushing stream. They splashed the pigment away with cool water and laughter, then went off to explore some other delightful thing.

As the memory faded, Jane eased back into the stiff furniture. Ei'Brai had uncovered a long-forgotten memory of Australia that was untainted by the aftermath of her father's death. He made his point eloquently. She'd arrived in Australia, a child eager for experience—curious and open. The months and years that followed had changed her.

It was more than just coming of age, slipping into an adult skin. She'd always thought her proclivities toward adventurism, risk-taking, exploration, hedonism had simply been tempered by time. They hadn't. They'd been crushed by fear—her own and her grandparents—who feared losing Jane the same way they'd lost their daughter to the wildest corners of the world. They questioned her every inclination, brandished the potential worst-case result of every action, relentlessly reminding her of her father's death, until she began to doubt all but the most mundane desires for herself.

She'd learned never to trust herself.

Yet somehow she'd still ended up here. What was keeping her from reveling in this adventure now?

Some worry was normal. Paralysis was not.

Ei'Brai was right. Just look at the child she'd been. She owed everything to that child—her language ability, her curiosity, her passion. How could she have ever buried her so deep?

Jane slipped off her boots and pulled her feet up onto the low couch. She hadn't slept properly for so long. The meal she'd just consumed was making her feel drowsy.

She could hear Alan now, the murmuring of his mind as he worked. She could tune him out if she wanted, but she didn't need to. It was comforting. She curled on her side and tucked her hands under her cheek, adrift on the sound of his mental voice.

Jane woke to Bergen cursing.

"Fuck! Oh, shit! Jane! Fuck-fuck-fuck!"

Jane sat up, wiping moisture from the corner of her mouth, struggling to shake off grogginess.

"What is it, Alan?" she asked, scrubbing at her face.

"We've got a problem. A big fucking problem."

Ei'Brai broke in without preamble, "Indeed. Counter-measures are already implemented."

Alan continued, urgently, "These nanites are pro-grammed to destroy the goddamn ship if they're discovered, Jane. The only reason we aren't dead yet is because there are so few of them left."

Ei'Brai cut in irritably, "There is no need for explication. I am presenting Qua'dux Jane Holloway with the particulars now."

She barely heard that, immersed as she already was in the memory stream of Alan's thought process just moments pri-or. Ei'Brai had been monitoring Alan's progress as he worked through the code, when Alan discovered that there was an additional layer artfully hidden in plain sight within the squillae's most basic command code. Ei'Brai indicated that this was a section of code the average Sectilius scientist would ignore or only look at cursorily, since it would vary little within the spectrum of types of squillae.

But it was all new to Alan. He wouldn't ignore any part of it. She felt Alan's flash of insight as several seemingly dispar-ate pieces of information flitted through his mind and he connected the dots between them. Jane could see the pattern form just as clearly—as Ei'Brai interpreted what it meant in real time.

If even a single squillae were discovered, scrutinized with this level of intensity, it was programmed to send out a signal, organizing all the rest of them to abandon whatever they were doing and congregate in groups along the major hubs within the network of the ship's neural-electric pathways, where they would work together to build structures intended to create a series of feedback loops simultaneously.

In other words, a self-destruct—a massive, redundant, instantaneous overload. And it was probably already underway. It wouldn't take many squillae to make an explosion happen. With fewer individuals to do the work, it would take longer to accomplish, but they could still blow a very large hole in the ship. There was no way to estimate just how many of them there were, how long it might take for an explosion to happen, or where the explosions would take place.

The ship was absolutely teeming with squillae and they were impossible to sort. Only at the microscopic level could one squillae potentially detect the difference between itself and an individual that was different. If a squillae worked hard at keeping to itself, which these clearly did, it could avoid detection altogether.

Jane stood, fully awake now, blood pumping at an alarming rate, and left the room, heading for the nearest deck transport, ready to go wherever she was needed. As she strode down the hall, Ei'Brai showed her how he'd already begun to organize the squillae in every sector of the ship to police the neural-electric pathways in search and destroy mode.

Alan interjected, "That's not enough, Jane. They've already missed a few of these before—and these things are capable of rapid replication, using whatever materials are at hand. They will miss them again. Eventually we're going to go boom—unless we get rid of all of them at the same time. It's the only way, Jane."

She'd heard this argument before.

As well as Ei'Brai's rebuttal, which he began anew, "Unnecessary and imprudent. Entire sectors of the Speroancora would experience explosive decompression from the *Coelusha limax* infestation, alone. Every system on board would be affected—repair and maintenance would be impossible. That course of action would have far-reaching consequences."

"More far reaching than blowing all this shit up? Really? Come on! This would only be short term," Alan insisted. "We can make more nanites."

"You underestimate the amount of time it would take to repopulate the ship. You would leave us in a vulnerable state for, at minimum, a complete revolution around this star," Ei'Brai protested.

Jane hesitated in the deck transport, not sure where she was going.

Alan countered, "Jane—listen to me. I've only scratched the surface on this code and let me tell you, it was written by some devious bastards who did not want to be identified under any circumstances. We now know there were at least two different ways they intended to kill everyone onboard this ship. Who's to say there aren't three more ways to die programmed into these things? Every second we delay, we're gambling. What if these damned things are already working on life support or the engines or something I can't even think of yet? Jane—"

Jane held up a hand as she came to a firm decision. It was time to exercise her new role. "Ok. I've heard enough. We'll do it. Begin the preparation for an ionic burst, Ei'Brai."

His voice was acquiescent, "Acknowledged."

Jane felt a small measure of relief followed up by trepidation. This really was up to her.

Ei'Brai continued, quietly, "All Speroancora binary processors are locally shielded to varying degrees. However, most of the vessel relies on the escutcheon—external hull shielding. With your permission I will work to augment local shielding while simultaneously disabling the escutcheon. Such a precaution will take some small amount of time, but will greatly augment future probability of survival as we go forward."

Jane saw that he was troubled about deactivating the escutcheon. It was a risk, but that couldn't be helped. "Yes, of course. We should protect the computers and anything else that could be affected. You did say the ionic burst will be harmless for living things, though, right? We're not going to be exposed to radiation or anything are we?"

"We shouldn't," Alan cut in testily. "Tell him to show me what he's going to do."

Jane smiled and bit her lip at the mental glower Ei'Brai emanated, as he illustrated how he would modify the ship's engines to create a burst of positively charged ions and send it on a magnetic wave coursing through every corner of the ship. The minute circuitry of every single squillae aboard would be overwhelmed and rendered inert, useless, effectively dead.

"Ironically, it is the squillae that will perform this preventive work. Pay close attention to the details, Dr. Alan Bergen. You may be required to reverse these changes manually, without squillae to perform such functions," Ei'Brai commented reproachfully.

Alan responded without antipathy, completely enthralled with the images and concepts Ei'Brai presented. "Understood," he replied eagerly.

Jane watched with amusement as their interaction changed from antagonistic to one of esteemed teacher and earnest student.

She hated to interrupt them. Her stomach churned with nerves, but she put an authoritative note in her mental voice. "There's just one more thing we have to do, before the ionic burst."

Jane perched herself upon the front edge of the oversized command chair and scooted back with a distinct lack of grace. It reminded her of being a child in an adult's chair and she was glad there were no other eyes on her. She'd have to work out a more dignified way to manage the seat eventually. It had some mechanism of adjustment, but she was too nervous to mess with it at the moment.

The bridge of the ship felt absurdly large with only Jane's solitary presence. She plucked and tugged at the complex latch to strap herself into the seat and noted there were four rows of glittering consoles and their corresponding empty seats in front of her as well as a large screen broadcasting the image of some asteroids and a distant grey ball she assumed was Jupiter. Ei'Brai had told her she didn't need to physically be on the bridge, but it seemed like that was where she needed to be.

Her muscles ached with tension, but she was ready. If this went poorly, she had her seat belt on at least, she thought, shaking her head. Ei'Brai was waiting for her to begin, a palpable sense of excitement permeating his communiques.

She gave the command.

The bridge receded instantaneously. Her thoughts plummeted to the bowels of the ship with a sickening lurch. Time slowed to what felt like minutes between heartbeats.

She felt the engines flare to life—a white-out that temporarily blinded her. The ship rumbled around her, through her. The heat made her vision hazy. Something was spinning, momentum was building…microseconds ticked by…the energy actively transmuted to force and then to motion.

They were underway.

She could sense the movement herself, through him.

A triumphant laugh bubbled up out of her. She trembled, gripping the command console with white knuckles. *I am doing it!*

She felt a release of tension from Ei'Brai. He, too, reveled in the sensation of movement. Waves of approval flowed over her.

And from the third party within the Anipraxic circle, she heard wordless cheering. Warmth and pride gushed from Alan. She heard him utter, the whispered words caroming around inside her head but not really taking hold, "That's my girl!"

Ei'Brai fed her the complex equations needed to move through three-dimensional space. Jane comprised the personification of the physical relay that was necessary between Ei'Brai and the ship's computer to execute them.

She breathed deeply, striving to juggle this new level of control while staying in touch with herself and her surroundings. The distance closed quickly. The capsule came into view on the large screen in front of her. It was time to add another level of complexity to the mix.

"Please reestablish communications with Providence, Ei'Brai." she commanded crisply.

"Hailing, Qua'dux Jane Holloway."

Jane straightened in her seat, concentrating on the image of Providence. Ei'Brai sifted through data coming from arrays of sensors that converged on the capsule.

She was beginning to see the advantage of the Anipraxic link. It was pure genius, really. It reduced the amount of information that had to be articulated out loud—it was all right there—information streaming in real time. If Ei'Brai noted anything of importance, she knew it immediately. When every second counted, that could save lives.

"I can't tell, Ei'Brai. Are they still moving?"

"Only under momentum. There is very little electrical output onboard. Channel is now open. You may speak."

If the thrusters were no longer burning, that was a good sign, she hoped. Jane cleared her throat because she hadn't spoken aloud for at least a day. "This is Jane Holloway. Providence? Are you there?"

Worry sat like lead in her stomach. Would they ignore her this time? Had Walsh been so angry after their last communication that he'd decided not to respond when she called back?

He'd been curt last time, dismissive, and barely able to make coherent arguments. It seemed clear that he was infected. This could be a rough encounter. He was opposed to coming back aboard. She was hoping that in the intervening hours Ajaya had softened him up.

Jane tapped her fingers on the console impatiently. Was it too late? Had there been some kind of catastrophic failure onboard? "I repeat: Providence, come in. This is Jane Holloway. I'm ready and able to provide assistance."

Nothing.

She leaned forward, the straps adjusting, moving with her. "Over?"

Silence.

They'd already conceived of several ways to deal with an unresponsive Providence. None of them were good choices. If the capsule was still traveling at a high velocity, that made everything very complicated for her and very dangerous for the people inside that vessel.

Why weren't they answering? Could Walsh have gone nuts? Had they all gone catatonic shut up in such a small space together? Had someone made a fatal mistake? *Oh, God—I should have done something sooner.*

"Do you sense them, Ei'Brai?" she asked him silently.

He responded coolly. "I perceive three individuals. There appears to be a fracas in progress."

Jane knit her brow. "So they heard my transmission?"

"I believe so, Qua'dux Jane Holloway."

"And the channel is still open?"

"Affirmative."

Jane sat up straighter, never taking her eyes from the capsule on the screen. Some kind of drama was playing out over there and she was powerless to help. "Providence. Jane Holloway. I want you to know that Dr. Bergen has devised a permanent solution to the nanite problem. Here, on the Speroancora, we will eliminate all of them at once with a tightly controlled EMP. If you can't or won't dock with us in a timely fashion, I'll be forced to use another method to bring you aboard. I won't allow you to transmit the nanites to Earth. Please respond."

Again, minutes rolled by.

Alan's mental voice exclaimed, "Jane, we don't have time for this shit. The clock is ticking on teeny-tiny nanite bombs with big booms."

Ei'Brai silently grumbled, neither agreeing nor disagreeing with any clear articulation.

Jane frowned. "I know, I know."

Alan sounded impatient, "Just scoop them up, like we talked about."

She sighed. "Alan, I don't have the finesse you seem to think I have."

"Jane, let me out of this damned thing!" His frustration was immense. Then he softened. "I want to help you."

"There's nothing you can do out here. I have to make these decisions. I have to do this."

She shut her eyes, concentrating on the distance between the capsule and the ship, turning many miles into feet, until it loomed large on the view screen in front of her. She wished she could see inside.

Then she remembered. She slipped her consciousness closer to Ei'Brai. It was like a mouse sidling up to an elephant. She knew it. But it didn't matter, because this mouse was master over that beast. "I want you to show me what's going on in there," she told him.

"Inadvisable," he responded instantly.

"Why?" Jane narrowed her eyes, but he was an open book. He may recommend she not go there, but he wouldn't stop her, if that was her decision.

"You are emotionally attached to your colleagues. At best, the experience could have a negative impact on you psychologically. At worst, it could be injurious to your nascent experience of Anipraxia. There is no need for such risk. There is significant evidence that they are not as they were. In my estimation, they are incapable of performing as you'd hoped."

She nodded, centering herself more fully inside herself. It was disappointing, but she was mentally prepared for this scenario. "All right. We'll match their speed, like we discussed."

Alan's voice tickled in the back of her head, a whisper, "I know you can do this, Jane."

Her mouth pursed in concentration, she put all her mental energy into channeling the commands correctly. The Speroancora eased forward to match the speed of the Providence.

She told the ship's computer, "Open the external service hatch on Deck 37, chamber 2-4-6, and terminate synthetic gravity to that chamber."

She sensed it opening, slowly, a giant garage door in space. Ei'Brai confirmed the gravity was cut.

As each second passed, Ei'Brai labored over extensive calculations. They flowed past her. She waited patiently for him to calculate the best formula as they adjusted course.

"Trajectory and velocity are currently optimal, Qua'dux. You may proceed with lateral thrust."

This was it. If Ei'Brai's calculations were wrong, or if Jane didn't execute them correctly, all would be lost. Even at these low speeds, the capsule wasn't that robust. It was not made to endure impacts at that kind of magnitude. It would crumple like aluminum foil. Pressurization would fail. The three of them would be dead almost instantly in the vacuum of space.

"Yes," Ei'Brai conceded. "Yet no other option exists. They've met dusk already if we do not act. You give them hope."

Jane lifted her chin. "Right. Engage lateral thrust."

The nose of the ship maintained course and speed alongside the Providence, acting as the fulcrum, while the tail of the ship swung around laterally toward the capsule.

Jane held her breath.

Ei'Brai switched the source of her view screen feed to a camera inside chamber 246. Providence grew in size at an alarming rate. Her heart pounded a tattoo.

"Prepare to terminate lateral thrust," Ei'Brai reminded her gently.

"Yes, yes—terminate lateral thrust on my mark," she told the computer.

Speroancora pivoted inexorably.

Jane bucked against the straps. "It's not going to fit!"

"Steady. My calculations are impeccable. Standby, Qua'dux."

There couldn't be more than inches of clearance.

Her hand went to her mouth, physically keeping herself from screaming, "Abort!"

Her eyes widened as the Providence scuttled across the floor of chamber 246.

"Qua—"

"Mark! Mark!"

The Providence bumped against the far wall of chamber 246 and bounced around, but Jane and Ei'Brai, joint in thought, didn't think it was enough to cause much damage. It settled into place near the open door. It hovered there, slightly cocked at an angle, just a few inches from the floor as the forward momentum of both vessels equalized.

Jane exhaled in a whoosh. "Close the external service hatch on chamber 246, repressurize the chamber, and reinstitute synthetic gravity. Execute ionic pulse."

Jane unlatched herself and headed for the door.

Ei'Brai's voice rumbled in her head, "Ionic pulse has been successfully effectuated, Qua'dux. Squillae transmission has gone full-silent. The pulse was successful."

"We've got them. We should be out of the woods, so let's find a safe place to park," Alan said.

Ei'Brai's mental voice sounded flat, resigned. "This location will serve, Qua'dux, if that is your wish."

Jane shrugged as she tapped a key in the nearest deck transport. They hadn't even discussed what they needed to do next. The priority had been the ionic pulse and the rescue, that wasn't even complete yet.

It suddenly occurred to her that back on Earth, the maneuver she'd just performed would have been recorded. They also may have received some unsettling transmissions from Providence over the last few days. The folks in Houston and Washington were probably beside themselves with worry and apprehension. She'd need to send them a reassuring message ASAP. But that would have to wait a few more minutes.

"Ok. Let's just stay here for a while, then," she said abstractedly.

"Full stop, Qua'dux?"

Jane sighed. "Yes, full stop."

"It would be advisable to don protective gear before approaching the vessel."

"Ei'Brai—"

"Your colleagues are not themselves; their actions, unpredictable. I urge prudence, Qua'dux." His voice vibrated with insistence.

Jane turned a corner and stopped short. A single suit of armor squatted in the middle of the hallway. Ei'Brai had sent it there to wait for her.

Jane shook her head, remembering Alan's response to the armor. "I don't want to frighten them."

"That hardly matters," Ei'Brai countered disdainfully. "A single ballistic missile could bring dusk upon you. Prevention is preferable to remorse."

His reasoning was selfish, but he was right, she conceded. She'd harbored a childish hope that the ionic burst alone would instantly cure them. That wasn't realistic. If she really was to save them, she had to protect herself from them. She stripped down, wadded up her clothing, and shoved it into an armored compartment, then stepped into the suit.

The suit conformed to and integrated with the brace she wore on her right leg. It enveloped her, squeezing her lightly, like a warm hug. The HUD came up. She silenced its prompts with a thought.

Ei'Brai's voice vibrated in an effusive manner that she hadn't heard before. "This endeavor has proceeded more than satisfactorily, Qua'dux Jane Holloway. We work proficiently together, despite our nascent alliance. As I predicted, we comprise a union far superior to the sum of its components. An illustrious future awaits us. There will be elaborate tales woven into great tapestries of narrative about this exalted day. The female Terran, Quasador Dux Jane Holloway and the sislix Kubodera, Ei'Brai."

Jane didn't reply. She wasn't in it for fame and glory on some remote planet. He knew that.

He wasn't really either—well, not much anyway. It was just easier for him to say these kinds of things than to express gratitude for her companionship, for accepting the role he knew she didn't really want. But she knew how he felt. It was an undercurrent in every conversation. She wasn't ready to acknowledge it yet. It was too fresh.

She stretched and flexed within the suit, retrieving the muscle memory she needed to operate it smoothly, and turned to resume her course toward chamber 246.

The capsule was locked from the inside. No one responded to her attempts at communication. Standing outside, she could hear muffled voices. From time to time the capsule vibrated.

Finally, Jane activated a cutting tool embedded in the armor and carefully circumscribed the outline of the hatch.

There was a loud hiss as the pressure between the two environments equalized. Jane grasped the hatch and lifted it outward with exceeding slowness, so as not to alarm anyone inside.

Even with Ei'Brai's preparation, she was shocked. Walsh was slumped in a corner, his eyes vacant and glazed over. Ajaya was perched on top of Gibbs, hammering a fist into his face, repeatedly. Gibbs pulled his knees to his chest and used them to push Ajaya off him. Ajaya picked up a piece of analytical equipment and raised it over her head when she caught sight of Jane.

Jane backed up a step. "Ajaya? It's me, Jane, inside this suit."

Ajaya growled. Her eyes had gone feral. She launched herself at the opening in the hatch, clambered through, and knocked Jane to the floor.

The HUD flashed several options. One of them was an anti-combatant sedative injection. That sounded like a fantastic idea. The suit calculated Ajaya's mass and prepared the dose.

Ajaya raged on top of Jane, spittle flying, hair whipping around her face.

Jane stayed limp and rocked in the suit until the dose was ready so she wouldn't inadvertently hurt Ajaya.

A sound came from the capsule. It was Gibbs climbing out of the hatch. His face was bloody, contorted and swollen. Ajaya ceased beating Jane's armored head against the floor and turned, eyes wild.

It was the perfect opportunity. Jane injected her in the stomach.

Ajaya bucked and screamed, but fell limp on top of Jane a second later.

Jane eased Ajaya to the floor and rolled to her feet. She held out a hand. "It's me, Ron. It's Jane."

He shook his head slowly. He circled her in a crouch. He was like a coiled cat, ready to pounce, but warily exploring his options before deciding his next move.

Jane realized he might slip out the door into the hallway. She didn't relish the idea of chasing him around the ship. Ei'Brai shut that door before Jane could even formulate a question.

That seemed to make the decision for Gibbs. He barreled into Jane, knocking her back into the capsule with a crash. She was ready with the sedative. It was over a second later.

Jane slipped Gibbs to the floor and staggered back to survey the scene. She felt a little weak from the emotional turmoil of the day. What would she have done if the decades-old sedative hadn't worked? She didn't want to contemplate that.

Ei'Brai was silent. The nanites had not been his fault. She couldn't blame him for this. They'd taken a million different risks when they stepped aboard the Speroancora and a million more when they'd gone in without protective suits. The nanites were programed to seek out and attach themselves to humanoids. It was a small miracle that she and Alan had remained clear.

The tight quarters of the capsule must have allowed the nanites to infect all three of them and replicate rapidly. Ei'Brai had been correct when he'd dissuaded her—she wouldn't want to be in any of their heads right now. All three of them needed some quality time in the Sanalabreum. She just hoped it would be able to reverse the damage done to them.

She slipped back into the hallway for the stretcher she'd left there and piled all three of their bodies onto it. It was undignified, but they'd never know as long as she got them all to the medical chambers as soon as possible.

She retracted the helmet as she pushed off for the nearest deck transport. The worst of this business was over. It was time to tie up the remaining loose ends from her past and look ahead.

The future seemed inscrutable, formidable, frightening, but...exciting.

She couldn't wait.

27

The Squid said Jane was in the captain's quarters—the Qua'dux's quarters. Whatever. She'd taken up residence there, called it home, apparently, and that's where she was. Bergen was pacing the corridor just outside her door, attempting to minimize his limp, and rehearsing what he hoped to say to her...if he could just get it to come out right.

Where are we?

Where do we stand, Jane?

Or....

Where do I stand, in your life?

Do we have a future?

Do you want one?

What do you want?

Is it...my leg?

Ugh. No. He looked down at the leg, disguised inside a fresh flight suit. *Don't say anything about the goddamn leg. Just relax. Smile. Be charming as all fuck and it should be fine.*

Everything was going great until the damn Squid messed everything up. Alan wasn't aware of all the details, since he'd been on an extended stay in Jello-land, but the squid got what he wanted from Jane, it seemed, and she hadn't been the same since.

He shook his head. They'd survived. He guessed that's all that really mattered. All six of them would make it back alive, if not completely intact. A normal life was within their grasp, for most of them, anyway. He still wasn't sure about Walsh.

Bergen wondered if Varma had included in her mission report the incident that happened a few days prior when they'd attempted to take Walsh out of the tank prematurely in preparation for the upcoming meeting today. Walsh had been disoriented, narcoleptic, then suffered a grand mal seizure, so they'd hurriedly plopped him back in to marinate a while longer.

It hadn't been pretty. The reprobate nanites clearly inflicted some pretty extensive damage to Walsh's central nervous system. However, Compton had been infected the longest and he was fine now, so theoretically Walsh should be the same eventually. While things hadn't turned out as Walsh predicted, the irony of him possibly being the only one left with a serious deficiency wasn't lost on Berg.

They were so close to home, now. Jane could have them home in a matter of hours. He could almost taste the french fries. They were going to be heroes when they got back. Not only that, they'd be bringing home the most exciting piece of technology man had ever known. He was going to savor every moment of dismantling this ship and learning its every nook and cranny. He was already picking out teams of engineers in his head, along with their initial assignments.

He turned on his heel and decided he'd gimped back and forth long enough. If he didn't get on with it, the Squid might tell her he was out there, assuming he hadn't already.

Alan had decided to exclude the Squid from his thoughts as much as possible, as soon as he got out of the tank. It was too disorienting to have all that extra shit going on all the time. It was advantageous for problem solving in a crisis, but a nuisance otherwise. It was simply another form of communication and vocal speech worked just fine, thank you very much.

He knew he could get used to it eventually, but he just didn't feel like it. It was a bit of false advertising. It hadn't brought him any closer to Jane at all. Quite the opposite, it seemed.

Maybe he was being petty or childish or stupid. He probably was. He didn't fucking care.

It was actually fun, there for a while—studying the alien tech, solving the puzzle, proposing a solution—being right. That was the kind of stuff he lived for. Then, while he healed and the cybernetic leg was being installed, there'd been the long conversations with Ei'Brai about technology, theoretical physics, astronomy—all the stuff that just geeked him the fuck out. That probably kept him from going nuts in there.

The concept of anipraxia, alone, blew his mind. It wasn't some paranormal mumbo jumbo. It wasn't magic. It was fucking quantum entanglement!

On a quantum scale, particles inside organelles located in Ei'Brai's brain reached a singlet state with particles of comparable organelles within the mind of whomever he was anipraxing with—allowing communication far more instantaneous and comprehensive than speech. It shouldn't be possible, but the Squid said the human grasp on quantum mechanics was in its infancy. And there were realms beyond that humans hadn't even glimpsed yet.

But the guy's arrogance...his possessive attitude about Jane...his smug surety about everything was too much to take. Bergen knew damn well they had a lot in common. Maybe that's what it was all about. Jane didn't need him anymore because she had the Squid. He felt useless. Completely emasculated.

Fuck.

Alan opened the hand that was about to knock on her door and splayed it out across the door's surface. His forehead joined it there and he closed his eyes.

Jane. He hardly knew her. All the softness had gone out of her. There was a stern set to her mouth now that never went away and she rarely smiled these days.

But they were going home. They could have their happily ever after. As long as he didn't screw it up.

Jane was playing close to the vest. He'd tried over the last few weeks to get closer to her, to rekindle something between them, but she was cool and preoccupied, so he'd reluctantly left her alone.

She was busy. She methodically went through all the decks swarming with critters and blasted all that shit to oblivion. Then she began repairs—not how you might expect, though. She collected freshly made nanites and distributed them by hand to critical places all over the ship—the engine room, life support, and all the last known locations that were critically damaged by the slimy monsters. It was time-consuming and she worked around the clock. He tried to help, once he got out of the damn Jello-bath, but he just felt like he was in the way.

She didn't need him wielding a wrench. That stung. He tried not to dwell on it. He wasn't a damn whiner.

It was a lot. He knew that. He wasn't stupid. He just didn't think she needed to go through it all alone. It wouldn't be weak to lean on him, just a little, when no one was looking. He hated that the only person she was leaning on was a goddamn telepathic space-squid.

If he could just break through whatever barrier was between them. If he could just get things back to the way they were—the playful banter, the warm looks, the smiles that made her eyes glow and his loins throb.

He banged his forehead against the door then panicked when he realized he'd just knocked and covered it by pounding on the door loudly and taking a few steps back.

She came to the door looking confused. "Alan? It's almost time for the teleconference. Are you ready?"

He glanced at his watch and blanched internally. He'd just procrastinated away all his time. He'd meant to come sooner, have a long heart-to-heart with her.

He'd fucked up. Again.

He faked a smile and a relaxed posture. "Yeah. Yeah. I was just hoping to have a word with you before it begins."

Her eyebrows drew together. "A new batch of squillae was just manufactured. I was about to walk down there and dump them into the electrical system before heading to the bridge. Walk with me?"

He smiled genuinely this time. It was cool to watch those shimmering, swarming masses of nanites spread out and disappear before their eyes, off to do their invisible work. But a knot had formed in his belly. This was not going how he'd imagined. "Sure. Of course."

He gave her an appreciative, sidelong appraisal. She'd scrounged up some exotic-looking, alien uniform made of thick, creamy fabric. The asymmetrical, tunic-length jacket had a high, stiff collar that wound around her throat and seemed to force her chin up and out into an almost defensive position. One of the overlapping fronts of the jacket was heavily embroidered with a non-contrasting thread. It was cut into three uneven sections that each split off to wrap around her torso in a different way.

One section went over her chest and up around her neck. Another wound under her breasts. The third swathed her hips. The embroidery continued down long, narrow ties that wrapped around her body, culminating in ornate knots on the opposite-front side. Rather than being loose like a robe, it hugged her body, accentuating her feminine curves. It was an impressive and commanding outfit—if he didn't think too much about its resemblance to a straight jacket.

They walked in silence for a bit, the soft whirring and clacking of his leg the only sound audible in the empty hallway. As usual, she was tight-lipped. He longed to reach for her hand, but was afraid to. Suddenly he blurted out, "Did I do something that pissed you off?"

Shit. That's not what I meant to ask.

She stopped walking, a quizzical expression on her face.

Bergen could almost feel the Squid's tentacles insinuating themselves inside his brain. He concentrated on keeping him locked out, but it might have been too late.

Her face had gone pale. Was she feeling guilty? "Alan? I haven't meant to hurt you—"

His teeth clenched. He made his lips form words. They sounded angry to his ears and he didn't know why. "You haven't hurt me! Goddamn it!"

"It's not that I don't want…there's a lot on my plate. This transition has been difficult. I thought you understood that. I'm trying to adjust. I'm trying to make important decisions. This isn't just about us."

He stared at her, trying to process her words, her tone, but he was seething with feelings.

"You're shutting me out." He flinched. Why did that just sound like an accusation?

She shook her head. Her tone turned plaintive. "No. Never. You shut me out and you know it."

He took a step back from her, his heart hammering painfully against his ribcage. "I shut the Squid out. Isn't there a difference, Jane?"

She looked hurt and he regretted the words instantly.

Her expression hardened. "I don't have the energy for this, right now. Your timing couldn't be worse—"

Was it his imagination? Had she just swallowed down the words, "as usual?" Or had the squid jumped in and subtly fed the suggestion of them to him to start shit? Did it matter?

His heart screamed, *Grab her! Kiss her! Tell her—we can have it all!*

He nodded and worked his jaw. "Right. Never mind."

"Alan, please try to understand. Now…just might not be…our time."

He stared at her pained expression a moment longer, then turned and walked away, alone.

Jane glanced at the bridge's view screen as it flickered to life. Displaying primarily a dark field without stars, only a slender crescent of light shimmered on one side. She'd put the ship in a holding pattern, hovering on the far side of the moon.

It seemed sensible to keep considerable distance between the Speroancora and Earth for the time being. It was unlikely that anyone was aware of their current location besides the U.S. government. Others might have satellite data, but wouldn't be able to render that data into anything meaningful for weeks or months. By then, she'd be long gone.

She was acutely aware of Bergen leaning against the wall at the back of the room, arms folded, exuding indifference and disdain. She felt a pang of regret. She hated putting him off again, but there were so many reasons she felt like she'd done the right thing.

When he'd come to her door, looking twitchy and shy, she'd wanted nothing more than to melt into his arms. But now was not a good time to be distracted by a new relationship. She couldn't possibly give him the attention he deserved. His interactions with Ei'Brai bordered on hostile. He was needed on Earth. It was all so complicated.

Above all else...she wanted him to be able to choose freely, not get pulled into something he didn't really want. That thought lingered uncomfortably until she forced herself to stay rooted in the here and now.

The others were milling around, talking in low tones, their thoughts full of images of home and family, their excitement contagious. The entire Providence crew was present, except Walsh, who was still in the sanalabreum, recovering. He'd be out soon.

Compton had been the first of them to emerge. Shortly after the ionic burst, the tank drained spontaneously, leaving a naked, bewildered Thomas Compton blinking up at her from the bottom. She'd just slipped Ajaya into her own tank when she felt the alert and turned to peer down at him. He looked a full ten years younger and said he never felt better. The joy she'd felt in that moment was incomparable. It was a lightening and lifting moment.

Now Compton was clapping Gibbs on the back as they bickered about what they should have as their first meal when they got back to Earth. It was refreshingly normal.

Gibbs guffawed. "Come on Pops, let's grab a steak! Or at least something good, like sushi. Why you wanna eat your old-man food, first thing?"

Compton rolled his eyes and chuckled. "You've never had Mia's pot roast and mashed potatoes or you wouldn't talk like that."

"Korean barbecue? Work with me here!" Gibbs exclaimed.

Jane stifled a smile and silenced them with a look. It was time. They came to attention and a view of Mission Control came up on the screen. A quick scan told her all of the leadership was present and accounted for.

She had transmitted detailed mission reports from each crew member to Earth a few days before. This was to be a Q and A session to go over those reports and to flesh out what was going to happen next.

Gordon Bonham, NASA Administrator and two-star general, stepped forward and nodded gravely, his eyes shrewdly flicking over a monitor off-screen. "Providence crew, it's good to see you looking so well. I don't see Commander Walsh among you."

Jane lifted her chin. "Commander Walsh is still under treatment for the illness discussed in my report, General Bonham. This—" She paused, closing her eyes briefly to instruct Ei'Brai to change the video feed. "—is an image of the chamber he occupies currently. He cannot respond to you, but you can see he is alive and well."

Bonham appeared to be unfazed, but many of the others surrounding him did not have the same level of self-control. There were a few gasps, some looks of dismay, and knit brows among most of the remainder.

Bonham turned back to the camera with a skeptical look. "It's my understanding that every one of you has been inside one of these devices within the last month. Dr. Varma, you described the experience very thoroughly in your report. Do you have anything you'd like to add?"

Ajaya still stood at attention. "No, sir. My report stands as written."

Bonham pursed his lips and picked up a piece of paper. "Your FGF code, Dr. Varma?"

It was a code, unique to each one of them, that they'd been ordered to memorize and not share with another soul. Bonham was trying to determine if it was really Ajaya he was talking to.

Compton's change in appearance must be evident, even to them.

Ajaya rattled off the 20 digit alpha-numeric code without hesitation. A few beads of sweat pricked at Jane's hairline. It'd been a year since she'd last thought through her own code.

Bonham's eyes followed along on the sheet of paper as Ajaya recited the code. When she finished, he nodded briefly and set the paper aside. He folded his arms and tilted his head to one side. "Can you come any closer to the camera, Dr. Varma?"

Ajaya strode forward several feet.

Bonham nodded again, his eyes smoldering with intensity. "Dr. Varma, is Dr. Holloway sound in mind and body?"

Jane stared straight ahead.

Ajaya responded immediately. "Sir, Dr. Holloway has been nothing short of honorable and brave."

Bonham's eyes narrowed. That wasn't the answer he wanted. "She's capable of flying that ship, without any training or experience—with just her thoughts? Do I have that right?"

Jane cut in, "Not precisely, no."

Bonham folded his arms and nodded Ajaya's dismissal. "Edify me, Dr. Holloway."

Jane did not allow her expression to change. "It's all in the document I transmitted to you. The knowledge needed to do these things was freely given to me. And I'm not doing it alone. I have the assistance of the Kubodera, Ei'Brai. We spoke often of the Clarke quote in Houston, if you remember."

"Any sufficiently advanced technology is indistinguishable from magic."

Jane simply nodded at Bonham and waited.

Bonham exhaled loudly. "That was some fancy maneuver you pulled a few days ago. How much of that was you? How much the Kubodera?"

"It was a joint effort. Dr. Bergen collaborated as well. This ship cannot be flown without the Kubodera. He is integral."

"Yes. You made much of that in your report."

"That's because it's true. I won't allow you to injure him in any way."

Bonham's expression was incredulous. "I assure you I have no intention of harming him, Dr. Holloway. We just want all of you home safe."

The conversation hit a lull. Bonham and Jane watched each other warily.

Bonham motioned to someone off screen who rolled a monitor into view.

"To that end, we've set up a landing site for you at Area 51. We want to assist you however we can. We'd like to set up a beacon of some kind for you. Do you have any idea what might be most useful to you? Radio transmission? Infra-red?"

An aerial photograph of Area 51 came up on the monitor with an 'X' marked out on the ground next to a large hanger.

Jane could feel agitation in Ei'Brai's mental touch. "That won't be necessary. I have no plans to land the ship."

"It seems to me, based on what we've seen you do so far, that landing the ship should be a rather simple affair."

"Not simple, but possible. Nevertheless, I won't be doing that."

Bonham took a step closer to his video camera. His face filled the screen. She could see every pore on his craggy, lined face. "Need I remind you, Dr. Holloway, that your mission was to bring that vehicle home if it was at all possible?"

"I don't need reminding, General Bonham. *My* mission was to make contact, be an ambassador, be a voice of welcome from our world. I was to use my skills of translation to assist in bringing this vessel back to Earth—only if there was no one aboard."

"Your reports say the ship is all but empty. There's no one aboard."

"There were no *humans* aboard. I don't believe we expected there to be humans aboard, though, did we, sir?"

"We couldn't have anticipated this turn of events. I would have expected to see Commander Walsh standing before me right now, telling me when and where he would bring that bird home."

Jane slowly blinked. "Walsh commands the Providence. I command the Speroancora. Therein lies the difference."

That comment seemed to stun Bonham. He turned and conferred quietly with Deputy Administrator Marshall and a few of their aids.

Jane's jaw was set tight. She forced it into motion. "General Bonham, have you prepared the teleconference with the multiple national heads of state that I requested?"

Bonham whirled, looking angry for the first time. "I'm not feeling particularly moved by a spirit of cooperation at present, Dr. Holloway." He turned back, distractedly, to Marshall.

"That communication is vital. I've explained all of this in my reports. This is not an American issue, it's a planetary issue. You do understand the gravity of our situation?"

"I understand that you think it is, Dr. Holloway—but I don't think you understand. It doesn't matter what I think. I don't have the authority to make something like that happen. Your reports—and these proceedings—are being recorded and transmitted to the White House. It's up to the President and his staff how that information will be disseminated."

Bonham's tone was verging on patronizing.

"I see," Jane said coolly.

The Providence crew was feeling uncomfortable about the mood shift. They hadn't expected things to get so antagonistic. They were frowning and stealing furtive looks at each other.

Jane flicked hooded eyes at Alan. He glowered at the screen, shrugging like he was uncomfortable, his hand at the back of his neck.

Bonham and the President would be getting a rude awakening in a day or two if they didn't follow through with her request, but she wasn't about to make demands or issue ultimatums. She didn't need them to make that communication happen.

It would be far better if the government would set it up with heads of state, but Ei'Brai was perfectly capable of hacking into the communication satellites that encircled the globe and broadcasting a message she'd already prepared in dozens of languages.

Jane's voice rang out, strong and sure, "I've just told you what I will *not* do. Would you like to hear what I am willing to do?"

Now she had Bonham's attention. He swung back to the camera, his features pinched. "Let's hear it."

"As you know, the Providence was affected by a massive EMP, but Dr. Gibbs assures me that most of the information gathered in flight should still be salvageable. The capsule is no longer capable of return to Earth under its own power, however."

Bonham's nostrils flared and he inhaled sharply. He appeared to be about to unleash some military wrath.

Jane held up a hand. "I know what you want. I'm sorry. I can't give it to you. But I can give you something of great value."

She paused. Tension on the bridge was running high. She was about to make it worse. "I'll put the Providence crew in a Speroancora shuttle and program the autopilot to land anywhere you designate. You'll have an intact specimen, exactly like the one from 1947. You'll finally be able to unlock all of its secrets, General Bonham—including a database I will download to its computer core that will contain information vital to the survival of the human race. And you'll have the capsule too, which is certainly valuable. I'll deposit it in the Pacific for you, off the coast of California. You'll have all of this as soon as Commander Walsh is well enough for travel."

She felt the shock of her companions. Fleeting impressions of their feelings percolated through her mind. Ajaya was torn. She was considering asking to stay aboard. Compton and Gibbs were both relieved, ready to go home. She knew Walsh would feel the same.

Alan was pissed. He outright rejected the concept of getting on that shuttle and leaving her behind. That set off a small flutter of hope in her heart.

Bonham sat back against a desk and frowned. "What on Earth are you planning to do, Dr. Holloway?"

Jane's lips twitched involuntarily. "I'm going on an adventure."

Mission Control went completely silent. Everyone on the bridge froze.

Bonham looked shocked. He asked, "By yourself?"

Jane lifted her chin a fraction more. "Yes."

The Providence crew converged on Jane with an outcry of objections. Mission Control erupted into chaos as well.

Bergen rounded on her, pushing Compton out of the way. He grabbed her arm so hard it hurt. "Jane? What the fuck? No way are you going out there, alone. Where the hell do you think you're going?"

Jane raised her voice above the din, speaking to those back on Earth as well as those around her. "I'm going to take Ei'Brai home, to Sectilius."

Despite the noise, Bonham honed in on Jane. "Is this a one-way trip?"

She blinked rapidly and smiled slowly. "I don't believe it will be, no. Who knows where it'll take me."

Jennifer Foehner Wells admits to being a bit of a hermit, but happily tolerates two boisterous boys, a supportive husband, a filthy Labrador retriever, and three pet rats as housemates at their home in Indiana. Having studied biology at Monmouth College in Illinois, she's possessed with a keen interest in science and technology. Jen is pure, unadulterated geek and celebrates that. You can find her on Twitter, extolling science and scifi fandoms, as @Jenthulhu. Find out more about Jen at: JenniferFoehnerWells.com

If you enjoyed this book, please consider leaving a review on your favorite online site. That's the best way to help other readers find it and support the authors that you want to see more from.

Made in the USA
San Bernardino, CA
10 August 2014